ACROSS AMERICA,
PEOPLE ARE SINGING
THE PRAISES OF

THE PASSING BELLS

"PANORAMIC." *—Los Angeles Times*

"A HUMDINGER OF A BOOK . . . BLENDS THE BEAUTY OF ROMANCE AND THE HORRORS OF WAR SO WELL THAT THE BOOK FAIRLY BREATHES WITH THE DRAMA OF LIFE." *—Columbus Dispatch*

"A NON-STOP READING VENTURE."
—United Press Syndicate

"A MAJOR SUCCESS . . . NOT SINCE THE DELDERFIELD SAGA HAS A NOVEL SO BEAUTIFULLY CAPTURED THE PASSING OF A WAY OF LIFE IN ENGLAND."
—The Chattanooga Times

"VIVID AND CONVINCING . . . DEEPLY EMOTIONAL, IRONICALLY DEVELOPED, CAREFULLY RESEARCHED . . . YOU CAN-NOT HELP BELIEVING IN ALL THESE CHARACTERS AND, MORE IMPORTANT, CARING ABOUT THEM."
—The Cleveland Plain Dealer

"WELL-WRITTEN, EXCITING . . . ECHOES OF HEMINGWAY, GRAVES AND *UPSTAIRS, DOWNSTAIRS.*" *—Library Journal*

P9-CAL-850

"VIVID AND ENTHRALLING."
—*The Philadelphia Inquirer*

"EVERY TWENTY-FIVE YEARS OR SO, WE ARE BLESSED WITH A WAR NOVEL, OUT-STANDING IN THAT IT DEPICTS NOT ONLY THE HISTORY OF A TIME, BUT ALSO ITS SOUL."
—*West Coast Review of Books*

"A POIGNANT TALE . . .
A SPECTACULAR JOB." —*San Diego Union*

"ONE OF THE FINEST EFFORTS TO CAP-TURE THE TREMENDOUS UPHEAVAL ENGLAND ENDURED DURING AND AF-TER WORLD WAR I. . . . THIS BOOK IS A WINNER." —*The Peekskill Star*

"SPELLBINDING." —*Publishers Weekly*

"A TIMELESS TALE . . . A DELIGHT TO READ." —*The Cleveland Press*

THE
PASSING
BELLS

Phillip Rock

A DELL BOOK

Published by
Dell Publishing Co., Inc.
1 Dag Hammarskjold Plaza
New York, New York 10017

Grateful acknowledgment is made to the publishers
of the following for permission to quote
from material in copyright:

Excerpt from "I Have a Rendezvous With Death" by Alan
Seeger, reprinted from *I Have a Rendezvous With Death* by
Alan Seeger with the permission of Charles Scribner's Sons,
copyright 1916, Charles Scribner's Sons. Five lines from "Sons
of the Widow" by Rudyard Kipling from *Barrack Room
Ballads* with the permission of A. P. Watt Ltd., London, and
the National Trust.
From the last stanza of "The Send-Off" from *The Collected
Poems of Wilfred Owen*: Edited by C. Day Lewis, copyright
1946, 1963 by Chatto & Windus Ltd. Reprinted by permission
of New Directions Publishing Corporation. Acknowledgment is
also made to the Owen Estate and Chatto & Windus Ltd.
Excerpts from "The Dead" and "Peace" by Rupert Brooke
from *The Collected Poems of Rupert Brooke*, copyright 1915,
by Dodd, Mead & Company.

Copyright © 1978 Phillip Rock

All rights reserved. No part of this book may be reproduced,
stored in a retrieval system, or transmitted in any form by an
electronic, mechanical, photocopying, recording means or otherwise, without prior written permission of the author. For information address Seaview Books, New York, New York.

Dell ® TM 681510, Dell Publishing Co., Inc.

ISBN: 0-440-16837-6

Reprinted by arrangement with Seaview Books.

Printed in the United States of America

First Dell printing—February 1980

*Let there be rung the passing bells
to call the living, to mourn the dead.*

For Bettye Cooper Rock
from Kingston-upon-Thames—
with all my love.

AUTHOR'S NOTE

All the characters in this book, with the obvious exception of historical personages, are imaginary. The Royal Windsor Fusiliers will not appear on any list of regiments of the British Army, past or present, but all other regiments are real and fought in the actions mentioned.

I have tried to be faithful in the description of events, but this is not a work of history and if I have erred in places or taken license, may the historians forgive me.

No novel set against the background of the Great War could be accomplished without help from the works of other writers. I am especially grateful to the following: *Gallipoli* by John Masefield (New York: The Macmillan Company, 1918), for details of the landings from the *River Clyde* and the battalions involved; *The Age of Illusion: England in the Twenties and Thirties* by Ronald Blythe (London: Hamish Hamilton, 1963), for Mr. Blythe's chapter on the Unknown Warrior; *The Great War and Modern Memory* by Paul Fussell (New York: Oxford University Press, 1975), for countless details; Siegfried Sassoon's *Memoirs of a Fox-hunting Man* (New York: Coward, McCann, 1929) and *Memoirs of an Infantry Officer* (New York: Coward, McCann, 1930); *Good-bye to All That* by Robert Graves (New York: Doubleday Anchor Books, 1957), a tattered paperback bought long ago which inspired the writing of this book in the first place; and to Martin Middlebrook of Boston, Lincolnshire, for the superlative historical craftsmanship of his *First Day on the Somme* (W. W. Norton & Company, 1972).

And a special debt from the heart to all the poets who died too soon.

BOOK ONE

Summer, 1914

*Blow, bugles, blow! They brought us,
    for our dearth,
Holiness, lacked so long, and Love,
    and Pain.
Honour has come back, as a king, to earth,
And paid his subjects with a royal wage;
And Nobleness walks in our ways again;
And we have come into our heritage.*
          —RUPERT BROOKE (1887–1915)

I

The dawn came early, tinting a cloudless sky the palest shade of green. Cocks had been crowing before first light, heralding the June day the length and breadth of the shire. On Burgate Hill, woodcutters paused to rest after the steep climb to the top, lit their pipes, and watched the sun rise. It was another clear, dry day and the men could see Sussex and the South Downs far off across the Weald. The Vale of Abingdon lay below them, still dark with shadows, but by the time they had finished their smokes—tapping the ashes carefully onto bare ground—the sun had reached the spire of Abingdon church and the brick chimneys of the great house, Abingdon Pryory, three miles to the west, the house itself shrouded from view by the dense foliage of oak and birch woods. Beyond the vale, the men could see a thin plume of smoke rise from the gentle hollows of the heath—the 5:10 from Tipley's Green bearing the rich harvests of Surrey to the London markets.

Anthony Greville, 9th earl of Stanmore, heard the distant hoot of the train as it approached the crossing at Leith Common. He lay drowsily in bed, following in his mind's eye the passage of the goods train as it meandered across the county before joining the main line at Godalming. It was the same train—larger and more sophisticated, of course—that he had known as a boy, although in those days it had not crossed the heath but had come from Tipley's Green by way of Bigham through five miles of his father's land. When would that have been exactly? he wondered. Eighteen seventy?

Seventy-two? About then, he imagined. The early seventies because the land had been sold off later in the decade and parceled into farms. A new railroad line had been built to skirt Abingdon proper, a much more efficient line, he remembered the farmers saying, but he had missed the ancient train with its tall, bulbous smokestack and gleaming brass.

He turned his head on the pillow and glanced at the bedside clock, a ship's chronometer set in a rosewood case. Five twenty-three. The great house was coming alive, and he stretched his long, leanly muscled body under the comforter and listened to the muted sounds— the murmur of pipes as the scullery maids drew water for the cooks, the faraway ring of shovels as coal buckets were filled, the faint whistling of a stableboy washing up at the courtyard pump. Soon there would be scurrying footsteps in the halls as the upstairs maids brought hot water for shaving and pots of tea for the early risers. There were forty servants in the house, counting stableboys and grooms, and they could make a fair amount of noise as they began the day. They were sounds that Lord Stanmore found as comforting as memory.

He shaved himself, standing before the mirror in his stocking feet while his valet stood near him holding towels and a bottle of bay rum. His valet's name was Fisher, and he had been the earl's man for over ten years.

"And what does your lordship have in mind for today?"

He studied his face in the glass. "What do you think, Fisher? Is the mustache getting a bit too military?"

"It is rather fierce, if you'll permit me to say so."

"And aging?"

"I'd hardly go that far, m'lord. Martial, yes."

"We shall trim it later, Fisher. Blunt the ends."

"Very good, sir. And as for your needs?"

The earl made one final stroke along the chin line and then dropped his razor in the shaving bowl.

"Morning clothes after my ride . . . and there will be guests for dinner. Black tie."

"Very good, m'lord."

The morning ride was the earl's unfailing ritual, in the heat of summer or the dark frosty mornings of winter. He dressed for it in old whipcord breeches and a Norfolk jacket, with a sweater beneath it if the air was chill. There were thirty pair of riding boots in the dressing room closet, but his choice was habit-set for the morning ride, a pair of Irish hunting boots, the tan leather cracked into fine lines like the face of an ancient weatherbeaten man. The boots were as supple as gloves and fitted his long legs like a second skin. He was getting into them with Fisher's help when there came a discreet tap at the door and Coatsworth entered the room, followed by one of the maids, bearing a large, silver tray, on which stood a teapot, a jug of hot water, milk, sugar, a basket of scones, a pot of marmalade, and a dish of butter. The elderly butler walked slowly, his dark trousers almost obscuring his slippered feet.

"Good morning, m'lord."

"Morning to you, Coatsworth. How's the gout this morning?"

"Better, sir, I do believe. Soaked my feet in hot vinegar last night at Mr. Banks' suggestion."

"Hot vinegar indeed."

"Works wonders, Mr. Banks says."

"Been damn effective on the hunters, I'll say that."

Mr. Coatsworth cleared a table next to the chair in which his master was seated and motioned for the maid to set the tray down. She was a young girl, slender and dark haired, with high cheekbones and a thin uptilted nose. A very pretty girl, the earl thought as he smiled at her.

"Thank you, Mary."

"Ivy, sir," the girl whispered.

"Of course, Ivy." One of the new ones. Mary was the plump ginger-haired girl with buck teeth.

"Shall I pour, sir?" the butler asked.

"Yes, please."

"You may go, lass," Coatsworth murmured. She was lingering, looking about the room. It took a while to train them properly. This one seemed more intelligent than most. She gave a proper curtsy before leaving. He poured tea into a cup and added a teaspoonful of sugar and a dash of milk. He then split a hot scone and buttered it. "I think you will find the scones to be quite delicious this morning, sir. Cook changed the recipe. A higher proportion of rye flour than usual."

"You don't say so."

"Ross says they remind him of the scones his mother used to bake when he was a lad in Aberdeen."

"Gets about a bit, doesn't he? Told me he came from Perth."

The butler chuckled as he spread marmalade on the scone. "I'd say Glasgow or the East End was nearer the truth."

"Perhaps. Still, a good man with a motorcar."

"As you say, m'lord," Coatsworth said through pursed lips before turning to leave.

A bit of resentment there and the earl knew it. Jaimie Ross was a brash young man of indeterminate geographic origin, but a first-rate chauffeur and mechanic. He was badly needed now that the number of motorcars in the family had increased from one to four. The previous chauffeur had been a man of Coatsworth's age, an ex-coachman who had known little about cars other than how to put one in gear and steer it in a reasonably straight line. He and the butler had been close friends and had spent their off hours together at the Crown and Anchor in Abingdon, where dart playing was an almost holy rite. Young Ross, on the other hand, preferred female company to darts and spent his half days off dashing about the countryside on his motorbike, impressing maids and shopgirls from Guildford to Crawley.

Lord Stanmore did not linger over his first breakfast of the day, but drank his tea and munched his scones, a

man in a hurry to be someplace else. He could feel the
tug of field and wood, hedgerow and thicket. There
wasn't a part of the vale that wasn't a challenge to a
horseman, not a yard of the land that didn't provide a
sense of exhilaration and triumph. There was no better
way on earth to start the day than by riding full tilt
across that blessed landscape. His only regret at the moment was that he would be riding alone on this bright
and glorious morning. William wouldn't be down from
Eton for another day or two and Charles had lost his
zest for riding. The thought of his eldest son cast a momentary pall over his mood. He couldn't fathom the
lad. All Charles had done since coming down from
Cambridge had been to moon about, listless and apa-
thetic. His scholastic record at King's had been most
gratifying, but when the earl had tried to discuss his
son's future with him, he had drawn a total blank. The
lad's direction seemed clear enough to Greville. He was,
after all, the eldest, which would mean the eventual
inheritance of the title. He should apply himself dili-
gently to understanding the complex structure of the
family holdings—not merely Abingdon Pryory with its
score of tenant farms, but the land in Wiltshire, Kent,
Northumberland, and the West Riding, as well as the
various parcels of London commercial properties. A job
enough for any man. Of course, if Charles had expressed a desire to remain a scholar and wished to return to Cambridge, he wouldn't stand in his way, but
any discussion of the future had been met with what
was fast becoming unendurable, aggravating, exasperating, bloody *ennui*! He drained his cup as though it contained a dram of whiskey.

"I'm off," he said, getting abruptly to his feet. The
valet hurried from the dressing room carrying a jacket,
tweed cap, and a riding crop with a polished bamboo
handle. Properly attired, the earl strode across the room
to the door which connected his suite with his wife's. It
was a source of inner satisfaction to him that never in
the course of twenty-five years of married life had that

door ever been locked, a symbol of love that effectively quelled the dark predictions of his friends, who had said that the marriage could not possibly last, "American women being what they are." He had not understood the meaning of that remark then, nor did he now.

The contrast between the two suites symbolized the difference between men and women, as the earl saw it. His rooms were paneled with dark oak, Spartanly furnished, and devoid of frivolous ornamentation. A large, untidy bookcase contained books on country life and hunting, a novel or two by Hardy, Shakespeare's plays in five volumes, and a Bible given to him by the local vicar on the day he had left home for the first time to go to school at Winchester. Between the slim stacks of books stood hunting cups and other trophies of horsemanship. The sword that his grandfather had carried, but never used, at Waterloo rested in its scabbard above the brick fireplace, and a large telescope, the gift of an admiral uncle, was fixed to a tripod in front of one of the mullioned windows. Study, bedroom, and dressing room had survived intact his transition from young manhood to middle age.

The rooms of Hanna Rilke Greville, Countess Stanmore, had been decorated by a man who had been under the spell of the Belle Epoque: rooms of deep-pile carpets, embossed wallpapers in shades of lemon and milky green, gilt-framed paintings, mirrors, and rococo furniture. Silk drapes diffused the light, bathing the room with a softly feminine glow. The rooms of a warm and sensuous woman. In all the years of their lovemaking, she had never come to his rooms, only he to hers.

She was still asleep, her long blonde hair tied in two thick coils that lay across the pillow like strands of spun gold. The earl did not intrude on his wife's slumber. It was his ritual to simply stand for a moment at one end of the large bedroom and look at her. He then closed the door quietly and retreated into his own room, slapped his boot top with the crop, and strode briskly toward the hall.

"Good morning, your lordship." Four of the upstairs maids stood on the landing and whispered their greeting in unison. They curtsied as they did so, their heavily starched uniforms making a pleasant rustling sound.

"Good morning . . . good morning," Lord Stanmore said, barely glancing at them as he descended the broad staircase.

He left the house through the glass-domed conservatory, with its riot of potted palms and hanging baskets of ferns, and then went out across the shadowed west terrace, where two gardener's helpers were sweeping the flagstones with brooms made of twigs. The men paused in their work long enough to touch their caps in respect, and he acknowledged their gesture by a slight nod of his head. Steps of weathered granite curved down to the Italian garden, where four men were busily trimming the topiary work. An ornamental iron gate purchased long ago from the estate of the duke of Fiori in Urbino led into the rose garden, with its central fountain of Carrara marble tumbling green water over carvings of Neptune and Europa. Beyond the brick wall that enclosed the rose garden, several long, low greenhouses marked the edge of the vast kitchen gardens and their neat rows of vegetables and well-spaded earth. A tree-shaded gravel path wound past the gardeners' cottages, the compost pits, and the storage sheds to the stable area, separated from the domain of the gardeners by a high stone wall. There was a scattering of musket and pistol balls embedded in the chinks between the stone blocks, mementos of a brisk fight between Prince Rupert's horse and a company of Roundhead infantry in 1642. As a child, the earl had dug for them with a pocketknife, but had recovered nothing but rusty flakes of iron and thin clurlings of lead. A solid wood gate painted a dark green pierced the wall and gave access to the paddock and stables beyond.

This was his world, and the earl was intensely proud of it. The new wood buildings with their slate roofs were painted in his colors—buff with accents of dull orange. They were the finest stables in England, and the twenty-five hunters and jumpers housed in them were the best horses that could be bought, bartered, or begged. His favorite of them all, a seven-year-old chestnut gelding, was being walked in the paddock by a groom while a stocky, bandy-legged man wearing tweeds and brown leather gaiters eyed the horse with a critical and practiced eye.

"Good morning, Banks," Lord Stanmore called out cheerily. "Have a saddle on him, I see."

George Banks, trainer and vet, jocularly referred to as Master of the Earl's Horse, removed a knobby briar pipe from between his teeth and tapped out the ash against his palm.

"Fit as a fiddle, sir, and strainin' at the bit as you can see. I'd venture to say that old Jupiter's as good as new."

The earl peered intently at the horse's left front leg as the groom walked it toward him.

"Not favoring the leg at all."

"No, sir," said Banks. "It's the hot packs what done the job good and proper."

"Let's just hope he won't be jump-shy after this."

"Well, sir, we'll never know that till the old boy takes a fence, but he's had his knocks before this."

"Quite so, Banks, though not as severely." The earl patted the horse fondly on the neck and then ran his hand along its smoothly curried withers. "Good Jupiter. Good old boy."

"Full of mustard."

"Quite so."

"He watched Tinker go and they're proper stablemates. I reckon he's eager to be catching up with him."

"Tinker? Who on earth . . . ?"

"Why, the captain, sir," Banks said, refilling his pipe from a yellow oilskin pouch. "Captain Wood-Lacy. Came down from London last night, sir. Got in a bit late and didn't want to disturb the household, so he bunked in with me. He was up with the lark and eager for a ride."

The earl swung up into Jupiter's saddle.

"Damn. Wish I'd known. Which direction did he take?"

"Toward Burgate and Swan Copse," the groom said. "But he weren't spurrin', m'lord. Just ridin' easy."

"Thank you, Smithy. Perhaps I can catch up with him."

He tapped the big gelding with his heels, and the horse responded eagerly, breaking into a canter down the hard-packed sandy path. He had to hold him from bursting into a flat-out gallop as they swept past the stables and the feed barns. The path curved to the right toward the Abingdon road and was bordered on the left by a five-foot fence.

"Take it, Jupiter." He tugged the left rein, and the horse veered sharply off the path and soared over the fence with feet to spare. He could hear Banks and the groom give a cheer, but he did not glance back.

Captain Fenton Wood-Lacy, Coldstream Guards, rode slowly and morosely through the dappled shadows of a beech wood. He was a tall square-shouldered man of twenty-five with dark deep-set eyes, a prominent high-bridged nose, and thin lips. It was a face with a look of studied arrogance about it and a hint of cruelty, like the face of a falcon. It was a face that, when angered, could reduce incompetent subalterns to twitching terror. But that was his parade-ground face, acquired with his commission. With friends, women, small children, and the meek and humble of the earth, the face underwent an almost magical transformation. The hard line of the mouth softened, and the eyes lost their beady coldness and became warm with humor and compassion. At the moment, the eyes were leaden and the face troubled. A passing stranger seeing this man seated on a magnificent bay, dressed in fine London-cut riding clothes, and wearing a bowler of impeccable fit and

style would have taken him for a rich squire. In actual-
ity, he carried in his pocket a letter from Cox's Bank
informing him in a respectful but terse manner that his
account was seriously overdrawn. The matter of his un-
paid bills at the Marlborough Club had been brought to
his attention the day before by the club secretary.

"I should not enjoy mentioning this matter to your
colonel, but you are so deeply in arrears that unless . . ."

"Oh, go to the devil," he muttered without passion.

A ring-necked pheasant broke cover and whirled
away toward the open fields beyond the wood. Fenton
raised his riding crop and traced the bird's erratic flight
with the tip, leading it just the proper distance to have
assured a clean kill with a shotgun.

"Pity," he murmured. The pheasant went to ground,
and he lowered the crop and slapped it in a desultory
fashion against his leg. The beauty of the morning, with
the sun filtering through the leafy beech trees and the
golden haze lying over the hedgerowed fields, mocked
his mood. Something had to be done, but he couldn't
for the life of him figure out what it could be. A
hundred pounds would clear his present debts—and he
could probably borrow that amount easily enough from
Lord Anthony, as he had done in the past—but a
hundred quid wouldn't solve the mathematical inevita-
bility of his problems, merely delay it for a few months.
His share of his late father's estate came to an inflexible
six hundred pounds a year. That and his captain's pay
were not enough to maintain himself in the Coldstream,
a regiment—like others in the Foot Guards—that
prided itself on the tone of its officers. All Guards officers must join the Guards' Club, but it was almost man-
datory that, as a captain, he join the Marlborough as
well. An unmarried officer in a less socially eminent
regiment might live in quarters at the barracks, but an
officer in the Guards was expected to maintain, at his
own expense naturally, suitable lodgings in Knights-
bridge or Belgravia—the higher the rank the better the

address. His promotion to captain had merely hastened his ruin. And on top of all the other expenditures, there was the matter of clothing. Only mufti could be worn when off duty, except for certain social functions, and mufti of the most stylish and expensive cut. His tailor's bill had been outrageous, and only a lucky spell at cards had permitted him to pay it. That luck had not continued long enough for him to settle matters with Cox's Bank and the Marlborough Club.

"Dash it to hell," he whispered to the trees. He gave his mount a gentle tap, and the graceful animal trotted briskly on, threading its way through the wood and out into a meadow thick with cornflower and buttercup. There Fenton reined in and sat stolidly in the saddle, gazing ahead. Far off across the rolling meadows, partially obscured by the willows of Swan Copse, rose the Gothic façade of Burgate House. There was a permanent solution to his monetary problems in that place, but at a cost that he had so far been reluctant to accept. He was still reluctant, but he couldn't see that he had much choice. Archie Foxe lived in Burgate House with his daughter, Lydia. Archie Foxe of the bluff and hearty East End manner and the dropped aitches. The Foxe of Foxe's Fancy Tinned Goods and the ubiquitous White Manor Tea Shops. Archie's offer of a place in the firm was genuine and of long standing. One thousand pounds a year to start. Not a trifling sum, that. He slipped a silver cigarette case out of his jacket and lit a cork-tipped Woodbine. It would mean chucking in his commission, but there wasn't much of a future in the army anyway. His promotion to a captaincy at twenty-five had been the blindest of luck, one of those once-in-every-century reorganizations of a battalion. It would be ten to fifteen years before they raised him to major.

He blew a thin stream of smoke to the wind and watched the distant house through narrowed eyes, like a scout surveying the movements of the enemy. It was a hideous building, built by a duke in Queen Anne's time. The duke's only son had been killed, and the man had instructed his architects to alter the design of the place so as to create a monument to the boy's memory. They had outdone themselves by erecting a structure that looked more like a cathedral than a house. No one had ever been happy living there, except Archie. Archie Foxe loved the place. "Like livin' in Westminster Abbey," Archie said.

"Oh, damn," the captain sighed. His personal Rubicon lay in front of him. A thousand quid a year. And Lydia? The answer to that little question eluded him the way a will-o'-the-wisp eludes a man's grasp. Lydia Foxe would make up her own mind about that. She was beautiful, twenty-one years of age, and the daughter of the world's most indulgent father. There were no restrictions placed upon her. She could flit over to Paris for a month or dash up to London for a weekend without fear of censure from Archie. It had been her suggestion in the first place that he turn in his commission and join "Daddy's shop," as she so quaintly understated the firm of Foxe, Ltd. That idea had been given to him when she had helped pick out the proper furnishings for his flat on Lower Belgrave Street, her taste far exceeding his budget. "You're a man who should live among beautiful things," she had said. "You're quite wasted in the army." Well, he could have told her the same thing, but then didn't Archie see his role in the firm as a sort of military one? The stalwart ex-Guardsman, Archie's adjutant, reviewing battalions of apple-cheeked, nubile White Manor Tea Shop girls in their sky-blue dresses, starched white aprons, and perky white caps? Of course he did. "Fenton," he had said, "Fenton, lad, Lydia tells me you might be chuckin' the army. Blimey, I could use your sort. 'Ow does a thousand quid per annum strike you?"

Very well indeed, thank you very much. And yet . . . and yet . . .

"Oh, damn," he whispered fervently, tossing his cigarette into a weed-choked drainage ditch. It just wasn't as simple as that. Six years with the colors. D Company's captain, First Battalion. A man's regiment became something a little sacred, whether one wanted to be seduced by the tradition or not. It was like a marriage . . . for better or worse . . . till death do us part. There were times when he despised the uselessness of his profession in an age when war was a virtual impossibility. And yet when the regimental band struck up the march from *Figaro* and the long scarlet-and-blue-clad column swung up Birdcage Walk from Wellington Barracks, with the wind whipping the King's colors and the fifes shrilling, he felt an almost indescribable sense of pride. That was merely being boyish and he knew it. Echoes from childhood when he had sat spellbound in front of Uncle Julian, back home after fighting the Pathans on the Northwest Frontier or the cruel dervishes in the Sudan, Uncle Julian of the 24th Foot, the Warwickshires, with his VC pinned to his tunic, spinning his stories of bravery and battle and stalwart men.

Fife and drum and the colors streaming. The Guards marching shoulder to shoulder over the icy mountains to Corunna, Sir John Moore watching them with tears in his eyes and knowing by the very sight of those ordered, unbroken ranks that Napoleon was doomed. Boyhood dreamings. Uncle Julian's tales . . . Fortescue's history of the British army . . . entwined inextricably with the social aspects of the game, for game it was, this playing at soldiering in London town. St. James's, Buckingham Palace, the Tower . . . an officer in the Coldstream Guards, the King's thin red line . . . a *Guards officer* and thus set apart in his own exclusive, distinctive class. To give that up, to be merely "Mr." Fenton Wood-Lacy of Foxe, Ltd., purveyors of meat pies and sixpenny teas, cheap foods in tins, tea shops strategically placed on busy corners in major towns and cities—Brighton, Plymouth, Margate, Manchester, Leeds, Birmingham, Liverpool, and the Greater London area—was to reduce himself to the level of the general herd. And if that be snobbery, make the most of it!

He leaned sideways in the saddle and saber-cut a milkweed with his riding crop—a vicious, backhanded slash that reduced the tall, slender plant to stubble. On straightening up, he heard a distant hallooing and glanced idly over his left shoulder to see Lord Stanmore several fields back coming on at the gallop, the chestnut gliding over hedges and blackberry thickets with the grace of a swallow.

The Earl of Stanmore in his proper element, Fenton mused. Coming on like the wind, horse and rider as smoothly integrated as a fine watch. It had been his initial view of the man when first visiting Abingdon Pryory at the age of nine with his younger brother Roger. The sight had impressed him then as it impressed him now. He rode just as smoothly himself, he supposed. And so he should, for it had been Lord Stanmore who had taught him the proper way to sit a horse, and how to take a jump without flinching. The summer of 1898, he reflected, the year his father had begun on the plans for the restoration of the great house. Abingdon Pryory had become a second home for the Wood-Lacy family, and his education as a horseman and huntsman had begun. A bond had been created between himself and the earl in that long-ago summer, and it had grown stronger with time. He watched the man galloping toward him and his spirits lifted, the gloom that had been so crushingly pervasive beginning to fade.

"Dash it all, Fenton," the earl cried out as he drew alongside, the two horses whinnying, rubbing necks, "you could have waited for me."

"Sorry, sir. Didn't think you'd be up that early."

"Not up? What the deuce do you mean, *not up?* You know my habits as well as anybody."

The captain smiled and proffered the open cigarette case. The earl took one.

"My apologies."

"Accepted." He leaned toward Fenton for a light. "Well, now, caught up with you at last. Did you see how we took that last hedge?"

"Yes, sir, I did. Like a champion."

"You wouldn't think the old boy'd been laid up for two weeks, would you? I'll be taking him to Colchester next month for the point-to-point. By the way, did Hargreaves speak to you about the Tetbury hunt?"

"We discussed it over lunch at the Savoy. His treat."

"You said yes, of course."

"I did."

"Fine. You shan't regret it. You can have your pick of mounts—except for Jupiter, of course."

"That's very kind of you, sir."

"Nonsense, my dear chap, nonsense." Lord Stanmore patted his horse on the neck the way another man might pat a well-loved dog. "Let me rest him for a bit and then I'll race you to Hadwell Green. We'll knock up the publican at the Swan and have a pint and a wedge of cheese." He puffed on the cigarette, not inhaling. "Damn, but it's a fine morning. That crowd at the house don't know what they're missing, lying abed to all hours. Anyway, at least you're here. How long can you stay?"

"A lengthy weekend. I have palace guard on Wednesday."

"I suppose you know your brother's here."

"I assumed he would be. Roger wrote me that he and Charles had plans for the summer—in celebration of graduating."

"Dashed if I can understand the lads. In my day, chaps came down from Cambridge with a sense of purpose and a damn clear idea of where they were going in life. Neither Roger nor my son has the foggiest."

"It's just a phase."

"Damned if I can see why your blessed mother had to sacrifice so much to keep Roger up there. Now you take what occurred during snooker last night. Roger and Charles were in some sort of conversation about prosody, and Roger said that in his opinion the Georgians were on the proper track . . . so I put in my oar after sinking the five ball with a perfect bank shot and agreed that *Childe Harold* was still a damn fine bit of poetry even if its author *was* a self-confessed bugger. 'Oh,' Roger said, 'not those Georgians, sir, the *New* Georgians, Rupert Brooke et al.' Rupert Brooke! Have you ever heard such nonsense in your life? The chap walks around with his hair down to his shoulders and no shoes on his feet. Well, later, after a glass or two of vintage, I asked Roger what he intended doing, and he said, 'Oh, edit a poetry magazine in London starting in September.' 'Editor,' I say. 'Good for you. How much they paying you?' And *he* says, 'Pay? Oh, there's no pay, one can't expect to make money out of poetry.' Now I ask you . . . !" His voice ended on a note of heartfelt exasperation. Four jackdaws rose from the top branches of a solitary oak and flew, cawing lustily, toward the granite towers of Burgate House. "Well, enough of that. Let's spur off."

"Can you lend me another hundred pounds?" Fenton said, gazing stolidly ahead.

Lord Stanmore tugged at his muctache. "Can I what?"

"Lend me a hundred pounds. I know that I still owe you—"

"Nonsense! No talk of that, my dear fellow. Of course, I'll lend it to you—if you need it badly enough."

Fenton's smile was faint. "I suppose I shall always need it badly enough. I'm in a rather awkward position."

"I quite understand. You're in the worst possible regiment for a man of your means. I would like to make a suggestion, Fenton, and I hope you won't take offense."

"I'm sure that I won't."

"Well, then . . ." He took a final puff on his cigarette and then crushed it out against the handle of his crop. "It's quite simple, really. So simple that I'm rather surprised you haven't done it before this. The season is upon us again. London is simply overflowing with the marriageable daughters of substantial men, as well you know."

"Marry money," Fenton said flatly.

"Yes, and where's the harm in it? By God, you're a fine-looking fellow—positively gorgeous, I might add, when you're wearing your scarlet jacket at one of those Mayfair balls. Be honest, lad, is it such a crime to rescue a Manchester mill owner's daughter from marrying some pasty-faced solicitor?"

The captain laughed for the first time in weeks. "I suppose it isn't, not when you put it that way."

"Only way to look at it, old boy. As Archie Foxe might put it, you're a marketable commodity."

"Like tinned beef."

"Precisely. Look, we'll be opening the Park Lane house next week, and Hanna has half a dozen parties and balls in the works to get Alexandra launched. We could kill two birds with one stone: find my daughter the right husband and you the proper wife. Will you cooperate to the fullest?"

"I have little choice."

"Why, dammit, man, you might enjoy it. Lord knows what pretty butterflies we may entangle in our net." He pointed his crop toward Burgate House, where the jackdaws wheeled and cawed above the spires. "By Harry, there's a pretty one in that place I'd like to see taken off the market—for reasons I shan't go into, but I'm sure you understand."

"I believe so, yes," Fenton said quietly.

The ninth earl of Stanmore frowned and looked away from the great monstrosity of a house that, to his way of thinking, only a millionaire cockney with no sense of taste would consider grand.

"Dash it, Fenton, I've been more than accommodating over the years, permitted Charles his puppy love attraction to the girl when he was sixteen, but by God he's twenty-three now, time he got over it and faced reality. Then again, she may see the futility herself and give him the— What's that slang word?"

"Gate?"

"Right, the gate—and opt for a more suitable mate.

. . . The quicker the better." He dug his heels into his horse's flanks. "Let's ride!"

More suitable to *him*, Fenton was thinking as he kicked his own mount into a gallop and trailed the chestnut across the field, meaning, of course, that an earl's son didn't marry the daughter of a Shadwell greengrocer, even if that greengrocer could buy and sell most of the peers in England, Lord Stanmore included. Archie Foxe's daughter, despite her Paris clothes and Benz runabout motorcar, was still Archie Foxe's daughter. A friend of the family since her childhood, to be sure, but no more than that—ever. Lydia Foxe was fated by her class to wed in her class. Not the son of a greengrocer—Archie's millions obviated that—but someone a good step below the peerage. The soldier son of an architect perhaps, and a knighted architect at that? The late, lamented Sir Harold Wood-Lacy, refurbisher of old buildings, a master of his craft and the delight of such clients as Queen Victoria, for his work at Balmoral and Sandringham House, and the present earl of Stanmore, for his painstaking restoration of Abingdon Pryory, work which Anthony had paid for with part of his wife's dowry, the million dollars or more that Adolph Sebastian Rilke had gladly handed over to see his daughter wed to a nobleman, dollars that had been earned in Chicago and Milwaukee, USA, by the brewing of beer. No loss of social status in *that* union. Money was the American peerage: beer barons, steel barons, coal barons, robber barons of Wall Street, an occasional prince of industry tossed in for good measure. An American heiress ranked with a Hapsburg. And even if someone *had* sneered at the idea of a Greville, an Earl of Stanmore, marrying the daughter of a brewer, it could be pointed out that the Rilkes of Milwaukee, Chicago, and St. Louis were simply a branch of the von Rilkes of Mechlenburg-Schwerin, and that Hanna Rilke had met the bachelor earl at a London garden party tossed in her honor by her fourth cousin, Princess Mary of Teck. Yes, one could so easily understand the difference between the Rilkes and the Foxes, even if one found the hypocrisy of it all slightly amusing.

"Come on! Come on!" the earl shouted over his shoulder. "Catch me if you can!"

"I'll give it a try, sir," Fenton yelled, spurring his horse, but keeping a politic half-length behind.

II

"Mr. Coatsworth informed me how satisfied he was with the way you conducted yourself this morning, Ivy. But you must remember what I told you about dawdling and staring."

"Yes, ma'am," Ivy Thaxton whispered.

"You may go have your breakfast now and then give Mrs. Dalrymple a hand with the linens."

"Yes, ma'am . . . thank you, ma'am."

Mrs. Broome, for all her formidable size and regal bearing, was not unkind nor overly demanding. She prided herself on her ability to so train the household staff that reprimands were rare. There were some housekeepers who were veritable ogres and martinets, constantly bullying and punishing the help. She had only contempt for such creatures. She looked approvingly at the slender dark-haired girl and then reached out and touched her gently on the mouth.

"Let's see a little smile now and then, Ivy. You'll soon get used to it here."

"I'm sure I will, ma'am."

"That's the spirit, child. Now run off with you and have your breakfast."

"Thank you, ma'am," Ivy said, curtsying respectfully before hurrying down the passage toward the servants' hall. Ivy Thaxton was seventeen years old, and this was her first week away from home, her first week of service. She found it all very bewildering, but not unpleasant. She was not unhappy, as the housekeeper thought, not like that Mary Grogan from Belfast, who cried all the time. It was just that there was so much to remember and so much to see. The huge rambling house fascinated her. There were so many corridors and passageways, so many stairs and rooms, that sometimes she got lost when instructed to go to the "Blenheim room in the east wing," or the "blue suite in the south passage." She had grown up in a comfortable but crowded house in Norwich, the eldest child, with two brothers and two sisters and another child on the way. It had been the baby in her mother's womb that had necessitated her departure from the house. The older birds must make room for the fledglings, her father had said.

There were a dozen or more servants seated at the long table having their breakfast, but Ivy couldn't see anyone she knew. Valets, footmen, and the kitchen help, mostly. The kitchens were just beyond the servants' hall, and she went in there to get served: a plate heaped with bacon rashes, eggs, and a thick piece of bread, fried golden crisp in bacon grease. Urns of tea and pots of marmalade and jam were on the table in the hall. The amount and quality of the food that they were given still astonished her. There had always been enough food on the table at home—Mum had seen to that only God knew how—but it had been plain fare, heavy on boiled greens, carrots, and thick barley soup with a few bits of meat in it.

She found a place at the end of the table and ate her breakfast with a single-minded purpose that verged on gluttony. When she had finished and was mopping up the last trace of egg yolk with a piece of fried bread, she became conscious of someone staring at her from across the table. She glanced up into the amused face of a freckled young man with sandy hair who was nursing a mug of tea and smoking a cigarette. He was dressed in livery of some sort—a tight black jacket with pearl gray buttons, the jacket unbuttoned, revealing a starched dickey.

"God," the young man said, "but you don't 'alf put

your grub away. Where does it go? You can't weigh more'n a half-starved cat."

"It's rude to stare," she said, looking down at her empty plate. Her face was burning.

"Sorry, lass, but I couldn't help it. I mean, I *am* sittin' here and you *are* sittin' there, you see. It was either look at you or look at one of them ugly mugs up the table. I'd rather glim a comely lass any old day in the week. Jaimie Ross is my name, what's yours?"

"Ivy," she said, almost inaudibly. "Ivy Thaxton." She stood up, but the young man reached across the table and took hold of her wrist.

"Don't go for a minute. You didn't finish your tea. If I gave you a start, I'm sorry. I'm the sort of chap who says what he's thinkin'. It don't half get me into trouble sometimes, I can tell you."

She sat down again, and he let go of her wrist and smiled warmly at her. It was an infectious smile and she smiled back.

"That's more like it," he said. "You've only been here a week, haven't you?"

"Yes . . . that's right . . . a week since Thursday."

"You from London?"

"Norfolk. Are you from London?"

He tilted his head and blew a perfect smoke ring toward the high vaulted ceiling.

"I'm from everywhere if you want to know the truth. Glasgow . . . Liverpool . . . Bradford . . . Leeds . . . London, too. I get about a bit in my tea half-hour an' that's a fact. Like to keep on the go. That's why I took up chauffeuring."

"Is that what you do?"

He stared at her in disbelief. "Can't you tell? Can't you see the uniform I'm wearing? Of course I'm a chauffeur. I'm his lordship's and the countess's driver. The poor dears couldn't go anywhere without me."

One of the valets, a large, portly man, glanced down the table. "Oh, put a cork in it, Ross."

The chauffeur dropped his cigarette in the dregs of his tea, leaned across the table, and spoke in a harsh stage whisper.

"They're all jealous of me, see. 'Cause I've a proper trade and they don't know nothin' but how to polish a bloody pair of boots."

"I find you quite impossible," the valet said huffily. "I shall have to change my mealtimes."

Ross ignored him. "I can do anything with a motor. I can pull it apart and scatter the pieces and then blindfold myself and put it back together again."

"I should like to see *that*," the valet said with scorn.

"Put up a quid and I'll give you the pleasure," he snapped.

"Can you really do it?" Ivy asked.

"Of course I can . . . an' make it run better than it did before. I'm somewhat of an inventor, see. I think up all sorts of things."

"Think up a muzzle for your mouth," the valet said. There was a wave of laughter from others at the table, and the man looked pleased with himself.

"Haw haw," Ross said. "Very funny, Johnson, but it happens to be the truth. I bet I have a hundred inventions right up here in the old noggin." He tapped his forehead with a finger.

"I really must go," Ivy said. "I've got to help with the linen."

"Take 'im with you, lass," one of the footmen called out. "He has nought to do but drive to the village and back—like a bleedin' omnibus!"

"Oh, is that so?" Ross said as he stood up and began to button his jacket. "I've got to drive Master Charles and his friend clear down to Southampton tomorrow morning. A relation of her ladyship is comin' in from America on the *Laconia*. You think *you* could drive a car to Southampton? Not bloody likely."

There was a sudden silence in the hall and everyone looked at him curiously.

"A relative? That's the first I've heard of it," one of

the assistant housekeepers said. "I'm sure that Mrs. Broome would have told *me*."

Ross smiled smugly. "All in good time, dearie. They'll get around to telling you."

"Well, really!" the woman expostulated. "You have your cheek."

"What sort of relative?" the valet asked. "Male or female?"

"A nephew, worse luck for you. Another pair of boots to shine."

No one appeared sorry to see the chauffeur leave. He strutted when he walked, and Ivy thought he looked very grand in his black breeches and highly polished black leather gaiters. Rather like a hussar. He walked her down the passage that led to the linen room.

"That bunch are nought but a gaggle of lackeys," he said. "They don't like me because I'm independent, see. I can go anywhere I feel like goin'. A man who knows cars can write his own bleedin' ticket."

"Do you like it here?"

"Oh, it's not so bad. His lordship's a proper sort, and the cars are right beauties—the Lanchester and the Rolls-Royce especially. I've been tinkerin' with the Rolls and found ten different things that could be done to make it run better. I might just write the factory and tell 'em about it. Yes, I might just do that one of these days."

They reached the linen room door, and Ivy held out her hand. "It's been awfully nice talking with you, Mr. Ross."

"Jaimie," he said, taking her hand and giving it a slight squeeze. "When's your afternoon?"

"Next Wednesday."

"Well, if I'm off duty I'll take you into Guildford on me motorbike . . . treat you to the pictures. Do you like William S. Hart? He's one of my favorites."

"I've never been to the pictures."

"What? Never? Lor', you don't know what you've been missin'. Well, take care of yourself."

He gave her hand a final squeeze and then walked jauntily off, whistling as he went.

"Was that you whistling in the hall?" the linen keeper asked when Ivy came into the large, sunny room.

"No, Mrs. Dalrymple, ma'am. It was Mr. Ross . . . the chauffeur."

Mrs. Dalrymple made a wry face. "I know who *Mr.* Ross is. You stay away from him if you've got any sense, and don't go fallin' for his blather, neither. He's ruined more than one poor girl's reputation, I can tell you." She took a stack of sheets and pillowslips from one of the shelves that lined the room and placed them on the long table used for folding the linens. "Take these up to the corner bedroom in the west wing. And make up the bed proper, mind. No sloppy edges."

"Yes, ma'am."

"And try not to get lost this time. It's the spare room down the passage to the left of Miss Alexandra's rooms. And be quick as you can. I'm shorthanded this morning. Doris took to her bed with the cramps."

Roger Wood-Lacy walked slowly along the corridor toward the breakfast room with a look of hazy abstraction on his face. He had been awake since dawn, seated on the window seat in his bedroom, watching the sun rise. The few moments between darkness and dawn had always been precious to him, a perfect time for creativity. The fifth stanza of the poem that he was writing on the legend of Pyramus and Thisbe was beginning to take shape in his head.

"Now hold the brittle garment of the night in jest—" he intoned softly, ignoring the portraits of seventeenth- and eighteenth-century Grevilles, who gazed stonily at him from their gilded frames, "—scoff the wearing of day's bright mantle rare."

Not bad, he mused, not bad at all. He could hear a low rumble of voices beyond the breakfast room door, and he paused in front of an ornately framed mirror to look at himself. The image pleased him: tall, imperially slender, the paleness of his face accentuated by his dark, unruly hair. He was wearing a well-worn pair of gray flannel trousers and his college blazer, a blue-striped shirt open at the neck, and scruffy tennis shoes with no socks. The image of a poet if he ever saw one. A Georgian poet—*New* Georgian, your lordship, if you please. The recollection of Lord Stanmore's faux pas made him smile.

"Good morning, all," he said, making an entrance, expecting Alexandra, Charles's sister, to be there as well as the Marchioness of Dexford and the Honorable Winifred Sutton. But only Lord Stanmore and, God forbid, Fenton were seated at the table.

"Hello, Roger," Fenton said.

The earl, Roger noticed with a flash of shame, was tucking a checkbook into his coat pocket and Fenton was slipping a folded check into his.

"Good morning, Fenton," he said tightly. "Good morning, sir."

"Ah, good morning, Roger," Lord Stanmore said. He took a final swig of coffee and stood up. "Got to be off. Must have a chat with that damn fool Horley before he strings any more of that bloody barbed wire across his field. The farmers know the rule, but they continue to ignore it. I suppose they want to see a good horse and rider cut up before they stop. Enjoy your breakfast, Roger. Is Charles up, do you know?"

"I tapped on his door, sir. He said he didn't feel too well and would breakfast in his room."

The earl only grunted and left the room scowling.

"Well, Roger," Fenton said, taking out his cigarette case, "how are you?"

"Fine. When did you get here?"

"Last night."

"Staying long?"

"A few days." He lit a cigarette and eyed his younger brother critically. "Your hair wants cutting."

Roger turned his back and walked stiffly to the sideboard, on which stood half a dozen silver serving dishes, their contents kept warm by tiny alcohol lamps burning bluely beneath them.

"As long as you're creating an atmosphere of criticism, Fenton, let me say that what you just did is frightfully embarrassing to me."

"Oh? And what's that?"

"Cadging more money from the old boy."

"It was a loan . . . not that it's any of your business. I've never said a word about your cadging from Charles, now have I?"

Roger flushed. "That's a beastly thing to say."

"Maybe it is, but it's true . . . not that Charles minds, I'm sure. It's just the principle of the thing . . . the pot calling the kettle and all that rot. Speaking of pots, try the kidneys. They're damn good."

Roger's anger began to dissipate, blunted by his hunger. He helped himself to a plate of kidneys, scrambled eggs, and a slice of gammon.

"Changing to more pleasant subjects," Fenton said. "My little brother has covered himself with glory at King's. First-class honors. I'm damn proud of you."

"Thanks," Roger murmured as he sat down to eat. It was impossible to maintain a grudge against Fenton. Like fighting feathers.

"How's Mother?"

"Very well last time I saw her. You really should try and go up there once in a while."

"The regiment's kept me busy, but I have some leave coming in September and I'll wangle a few days with her. Anyone staying here that I know?"

"House is rather empty for a change. Just that biddy Dexford and her daughter. You know, Winifred."

"Still as plump as ever?"

"Well endowed is the polite way to put it. And, let's see, one of Charles's cousins is due in tomorrow from Chicago, or some outlandish place. We're going to meet him at Southampton."

"And that's it?"

"Yes. Social activities will pick up no doubt when

they move to London next week. Charles and I hope to miss that though, thank God. We're planning a walking trip through Greece."

Fenton's smile was sardonic. "Young Winifred better work fast."

Roger nodded as he chewed. "Bit of a scene brewing, if you ask me. His nibs and Hanna are keen as paint about joining the Grevilles to the Suttons. They keep pushing poor Charles and Winifred into the rose gardens every night to walk under the moon. Rather like pushing a couple of puppies out of the house. Not a thing's come of it. Charles can't think of a word to say to her. Anyway, he's . . . well . . . he has other matters on his mind. It's all rather hopeless. *Omnia amor vincit*—unless you're the son of an earl. Going to Greece might be just what he needs. One's troubles seem terribly puny in the shadow of the Parthenon."

The door opened, and two servants came into the room, carrying more food on covered salvers. Lady Mary Sutton, Marchioness of Dexford, and her daughter, the Most Honorable Winifred Sutton, followed them, Lady Mary a tall, bony woman with a sharp, birdlike head, talking a blue streak in staccato sentences, hands waving to the rhythm of her words. Her daughter trailed after her in silent resignation.

"Ah!" Lady Mary shouted. "Both brothers Wood-Lacy! How nice! Fenton, you handsome rogue! I hear such naughty stories! My nephew Albert Fitzroy is in the Guards, you know. Grenadiers! Can't possibly be true, can they? Oh, dear, no! Well, here you are, and I shall get at the truth, never fear. Say hello to Fenton, Winifred."

"Hello, Fenton," Winifred said, almost in a whisper. "It's very nice seeing you again." Her soft unhappy eyes met Fenton's, and then she dropped her gaze quickly, a blush appearing on her plump cheeks.

Pretty, Fenton was thinking. A bit too buxom and padded at the hips, but she would bloom when the baby fat left her. She would be Alexandra's age—just turned eighteen. Ripe for the marriage block.

He smiled pleasantly at her. "I'm happy that you remember me, Winifred."

"How could she ever forget," her mother cried in her birdy squawk. "Gave the child her first kiss! Sweet sixteen! Most gallant of you, Fenton. Most gallant!"

He could barely recall the incident. An avuncular peck on the cheek at her birthday party. He had been invited by her eldest brother, Andrew, a good friend from Sandhurst. Now she was a woman, and a mate must be found. He felt sorry for her. The walks in the moon-drenched rose garden with Charles must be agony for her: a young woman longing to be loved; Charles silent and moody, wishing with all his heart that he were in the rose gardens of Burgate House walking beside Lydia Foxe.

"That's a charming frock, Winifred," he said. "It's very becoming."

"Th-thank you," Winifred stammered.

Roger choked on a piece of broiled kidney and coughed it up into his napkin. "Excuse me," he blurted.

Lady Mary dismissed the apology with a wave of her taloned hand. "Nonsense, dear boy! Better to cough than to strangle, I always say."

It would be a good match for Charles, Fenton mused, and he could understand Lord Stanmore's desire for it. The Marquess of Dexford was not only a rich man with an ancient title, but also a possible prime minister should the Conservatives ever regain power. Winifred was the marquess's youngest child and only daughter. He had four sons. No problem of handing down the title when he died. He would probably be content to see Winifred married to any man of good family and honorable profession. Her brother Andrew was a captain in the House Guards, and the marquess himself had served briefly with the colors during the Zulu war, something in which he took inordinate pride. There was food for thought there. He smiled warmly at Winifred, and she smiled shyly back. An easy bit of fruit to pluck from the tree, but of course he could do nothing positive about it unless or, rather, until Charles informed his parents that he would never become engaged to the girl, no matter what pressures they put on him.

Fenton stood up and gave a slight bow. "I leave you to breakfast. Perhaps we can form teams later for croquet."

"How marvelous! We will enjoy that, won't we, Winifred?"

"Yes, Mama," Winifred said.

"All right with you, Roger? You could team up with Lady Mary and show off your considerable skills."

Roger looked quizzical. "Fine. Although I must say, Fenton, I find your own skills to be downright humbling."

Ivy hurried up the back stairs cradling a stack of linens in her arms. The stairs were narrow and steep and the sheets and pillowslips felt like a ton weight by the time she reached the second-floor passage in the west wing. She opened the door slowly and peered hesitantly around it. The long corridor was empty. The housekeeping rules were emphatic: Maids must not draw attention to themselves, if at all possible. Should family or guests be seen standing in the halls, the maids should draw discreetly out of sight until the hallway is empty. There were so many rules that Ivy's head spun, trying to keep track of them all.

She looked to the left and to the right. The hallway that she was facing was known as the west wing gallery, an outer passage with tall mullioned windows on one side. She remembered those windows from the day before, when she had come this way to help Doris make up Miss Alexandra's bed. The room that she was looking for was to her left, past Miss Alexandra's suite and then down a short hallway which ran at right angles to the gallery. She stepped resolutely out of the stairwell, closed the narrow door behind her, and hurried toward her destination. As she passed Miss Alexandra's bedroom, the door flew open and the earl's daughter poked her head out.

"Velda?"

"No, ma'am."

"I can see *that*," the girl said petulantly. "I heard footsteps. Where's Velda?"

"I don't know, ma'am." She had never heard of anyone named Velda.

The Right Honorable Alexandra Greville took a step into the corridor and glanced up and down. "Oh, bother!"

Ivy stared at her in awe. She had only seen her from a distance before this. So pretty—like the portrait on a candy box. A slim, oval face . . . blue eyes . . . thick blonde hair curled into ringlets. And she smelled lovely, too—an odor of lavender soap and eau de cologne. Her dress was open down the back, revealing silk lingerie fringed with frothy lace.

"You must help me," Alexandra said quickly. "Hurry up, or I shall be late."

"What?" Ivy said dully, gawking at this girl who was prettier than any princess in a storybook.

"Don't just stand there! Help do me up. I shall be—" The sound of a car horn cut off her words, and she rushed across the corridor to the windows and looked out. "Oh, she's here! Drat that Velda!" She whirled in a fury of motion back toward the open doorway. "Quickly! Quickly!"

Ivy had no idea what she wanted her to do. She stood rooted, the linens in her arms. Alexandra disappeared from view for a second and then reappeared in the doorway, hands on her hips.

"I shan't ask you again. Now *please* do me up. Drop what you're carrying and come *here*."

"Yes, ma'am," Ivy blurted. Her arms parted as though they had a will of their own, and the clean sheets and pillowcases fell to the floor with a dull thump. She hurried into the room to find Alexandra standing impatiently in front of a mirror.

"The buttons . . . Do up the buttons. . . . Quickly, but don't miss any."

"No, ma'am." There seemed to be dozens of them, tiny ivory ones running from the waist of the dress to the neck. She began to button them, her fingers trembling. "There's ever so many," she whispered.

Alexandra tried to look down over her shoulder. "Don't start off wrong or you'll have to do them all over again."

"I—won't—ma'am." The fabric was a beige wool challis, of such fine quality that it felt like silk to the touch. "Oh, miss, it's ever such a lovely dress."

"Do you think so?" Alexandra asked anxiously.

"Oh, yes. So pretty."

Alexandra scowled and ran her hands over the dress, smoothing the fabric across the hips.

"I was rather worried about it. I'm going up to London and I do so want to look nice. You're sure that you like it?"

"Oh, my, yes, ma'am."

"I wasn't certain about the shade."

"It's . . . so nice against your skin, ma'am. Like . . . like a pale brown mist."

The young woman turned around and smiled. "Why, what a lovely thing to say. Quite poetic of you. A pale brown mist. Oh, I do feel better about it now!" She turned back so that Ivy could continue with the buttons. "I have a lovely hat that goes with it—a beige sailor with dark-brown velvet ribbons. You're new, aren't you?"

"Yes, ma'am."

"What's your name?"

"Ivy, ma'am. Ivy Thaxton."

"Well, Ivy," Alexandra began, then stopped as she noticed a middle-aged maid hurry into the room. "Well, Velda, it's about time. Wherever did you run off to?"

"I am sorry, Miss Alexandra. I . . ." The woman

hesitated when she saw Ivy, and her gaunt features clouded with anger.

"It doesn't matter," Alexandra said with a shrug. "I'm buttoned now. But do hurry and get my hat. I'm in a most awful rush."

"Yes, Miss Alexandra." Velda gave Ivy one final withering look and then hurried into an adjoining room.

Alexandra bent quickly toward the mirror and gave her cheeks a firm pinch to redden them. "I shall ask one final favor of you, Ivy. I must kiss Mama good morning. Please hurry downstairs as fast as you can and tell the lady who just arrived—Miss Foxe—that I shall be down in a few minutes and that we must drive like the wind or we shall miss our train." She spun away, pirouetting in front of the glass.

Ivy backed toward the door, her brain in a whirl. "A . . . Miss Foxe?"

"Yes, yes—quickly—quickly."

Ivy flew out of the room and down the hall. She gave no thought to taking the back stairs. There couldn't possibly be time for that. She was on a mission, the importance of which escaped her understanding, but a mission nonetheless. She ran full tilt, clutching her little cap to keep it from flying off her head, down the L-shaped hall of the west wing to the central corridor of the main house. It was exhilarating to run along such a broad carpeted surface. She felt like laughing out loud. It was like running down High Street early in the morning when all the shops were closed, racing Cissy and Ned and Tom to school. She nearly collided with a footman on the upper landing above the great hall.

"Sorry!" she called out, descending the stairway two steps at a time. The startled man stared after her in mute astonishment.

The astonishment was shared by Mr. Coatsworth and two other footmen standing in the entrance hall. They could merely gape at the young maid coming so rapidly toward them and could not have been more shocked if she had come sliding down the banister.

"What on earth . . . ?" Mr. Coatsworth blurted. "What on earth . . . ?"

Ivy almost slipped on the highly polished parquet floor and came to a skidding momentary halt in front of the butler.

"I . . . I must find a Miss Foxe. Have you seen her?"

Mr. Coatsworth could merely point in the general direction of outdoors. The front doors were open, and Ivy could see a shiny blue automobile parked on the drive. A young woman with red hair sat behind the wheel, a tall dark-haired man in riding clothes standing casually beside the car talking to her.

"Thanks awfully," Ivy said, making a dash for the door.

"Now, see here. . . ." the butler stammered. "See here. . . ."

Ivy slowed her frantic pace when she stepped out of the house and onto the hard-packed gravel drive. Her cap was askew and she straightened it, then tugged at her apron, which had begun to droop off one shoulder. She walked demurely toward the car, revealing the kind of deportment that the housekeeper had stressed.

"Are you Miss Foxe?" she asked respectfully.

Lydia Foxe looked past the tall angular form of Fenton Wood-Lacy. "Why, yes I am."

"I have a message for you, ma'am . . . from Miss Alexandra, ma'am. . . . She says for me to tell you that she shan't be but a minute as she has to kiss her mother and that . . . and that you will have to drive . . . like the wind to keep from missing the train."

"Oh, did she," Lydia Foxe said with a husky laugh. "Dear Alex," she said, looking up at Fenton, the presence of the maid ignored. "Honestly, that girl would forget her head if it weren't firmly rooted to her neck. I told her that we were driving up to London. I hate that smelly train."

"Driving, eh?" Fenton said. "Bit of a rough trip for you, isn't it?"

"Oh, Lord, no. The road's quite decent once you're past Dorking."

"Going shopping?"

"Alex has some dress fittings, and I have to see Daddy and then have the car looked at. There's a squeak of some sort in the differential."

"His nibs has a good man. Wizard with cars."

"I talked with Ross the other day in the village. He only knows English makes. And there's the question of tools. The Germans use different-size bolts or something. There's a Benz and Opel garage on the Edgeware Road."

"Won't break down on the way, will it?"

"No. It's just a noise—more annoying than anything else."

Ivy was at a loss over what to do—stand listening to the conversation until dismissed, or just turn and walk away? Not that she was in any hurry to leave. The woman in the shiny blue car fascinated her. She had never seen anyone so attractive—not pretty and soft like Miss Alexandra, a different kind of loveliness altogether. This woman had a hypnotizing, sensual beauty that caused Ivy to wonder if she might be on the stage. She certainly looked like an actress, not that Ivy had ever seen one except in the rotogravure section of the *Mirror*. Her hair was a deep chestnut red, coiled on top of her head and secured by a green velvet band. Her face was rather long, with high cheekbones and a slightly uptilted nose, the skin so fine as to be almost translucent. The mouth was large and full lipped, with a hint of wantonness in its moistness. Lip rouge? Ivy wondered. The woman's eyes were a luminous green that seemed to sparkle as she moved her head. Ivy gawked, spellbound, then pulled herself out of her momentary trance.

"Is . . . is there any message for Miss Alexandra, ma'am?"

A throaty laugh. "Oh, good heavens, no."

"Yes, ma'am . . . very good, ma'am."

"What an odd little creature," Lydia said as she watched the maid walk slowly back toward the house. "Did you notice her staring at me?"

"No, but then I was staring at you myself so I can't blame the girl. You're a damn attractive woman, Lydia."

She looked away from him, fingers toying with the heavy wood steering wheel, eyes narrowed against the reflection of the sun off the shiny bonnet of the car.

"Please, Fenton, we promised to talk only in generalities."

He touched her shoulder, sensing the warm flesh beneath the cotton motoring coat and the silk dress. "I find that nearly impossible to do."

She could see the reflection of the house in the car's paint—mellow brick and smooth stone, the faultless façade of Abingdon Pryory, home of the Grevilles and the earls of Stanmore for ten generations.

"I'm sorry, Fenton. Please don't make it difficult. You know how fond I am of you. You've been like a brother to me since I was nine years old and—"

His fingers tightened. "You can't look at me and say that, Lydia. But I shan't press you. I know what you're hoping to accomplish and I wish you luck. You shall need it."

Ivy made her slow way to the second floor of the west wing, taking the back stairs. The tableau on the drive lingered in her thoughts: the beautiful woman, the gleaming motorcar, the tall dark-haired man. What wondrous, exciting events lay in store for these people on this sunny June morning? Drive up to London, the woman had said. Ivy could not even imagine what that entailed or what Miss Foxe and Miss Alexandra would find when they got there. She had never been to London, although she had seen pictures of certain places in London: Buckingham Palace, St. Paul's, the houses of Parliament, and the Tower. A grand place, London, filled with pageantry—the Guards in their bearskin hats, the Beefeaters, the Lord Mayor with a great gold chain around his neck. Still, there must be more to it than that. A workaday sort of place, surely. Rather like Norwich or Great Yarmouth, only larger—more crowded. People doing ordinary things. Even some chaps repairing motorcars. It was all so curious. So far away. What fun it would be to be going with them, seated in the motorcar as it raced like the wind through the countryside, whizzing through the little villages that she had seen from the train on the way down from Norfolk. Would they pause for luncheon on the way? Cold meat pies and cider in a little inn? Or would they eat when they got to London, dining in one of those posh hotels with waiters in livery hovering around them? That would be the most fun. Would madam care to sample the cutlets? Would madam like a glass of bubbly champagne? The thought made her smile, and she was still smiling when she left the service stairs and walked down the hall. She was being served bubbly wine from a silver bucket when she suddenly became aware of a small crowd standing in the hall outside of Miss Alexandra's room. Mr. Coatsworth was there . . . and one of the footmen . . . and the maid, Velda . . . and Mrs. Broome. They were all of them staring at her and they were not smiling. Not at all.

"There she is, the little baggage," Velda said, sniffing back tears. "Oh, I'd give her such a thrashing if it was up to me."

Mr. Coatsworth and the footman nodded in agreement, their expressions like stone, but Mrs. Broome only sighed wearily.

"That will do, Velda. Kindly go about your duties."

"Yes, ma'am." Velda glared hatefully at Ivy before turning away and going into the room.

"If you need any assistance, Mrs. Broome," the butler said gravely, "I would be most happy to lend a hand."

"Thank you, no, Mr. Coatsworth."

"As you wish, Mrs. Broome. Come along, Peterson."

The butler and the footman walked stiffly away and Ivy was alone with the housekeeper, who was pointing down at the floor where the stack of linens were lying.

"Pick them up, Ivy."

"Yes, ma'am," Ivy whispered. She had forgotten all about them. She bent quickly and gathered them into her arms.

"We do not toss clean sheets and pillowcases on the floor in this house, Ivy."

"I . . . I'm sorry, ma'am. It's just that . . . that . . ." Events had taken place so quickly that she could hardly sort them out in her mind. Dropping the sheets had been the only feasible thing to do at the time, but how could she make that clear to Mrs. Broome?

"Mrs. Dalrymple sent you to make a bed. Is that correct, Ivy?"

"Yes, ma'am."

"Very well, child, go and make it."

"Yes, ma'am . . . right away, ma'am."

"And I wish to see you do it. I wish to make sure that you have not forgotten *everything* that you have been taught."

"Yes, ma'am." Ivy's face burned, and there was an awful sinking feeling in the pit of her stomach. She walked down the hall with the housekeeper keeping a slow, measured pace behind her, like a turnkey in a prison.

The bed that needed making was a large four-poster, and Ivy made it with painstaking care while Mrs. Broome stood silently watching. When the sheets had been stretched and smoothed and tucked in neatly, Ivy found blankets and a counterpane in a wooden chest at the foot of the bed. She spread them on, tucking in the blankets and straightening the corners of the counterpane and fussing with the folds so that it hung evenly, then she stepped back and waited for whatever comments the housekeeper might have.

"Very well done, Ivy."

"Thank you, ma'am."

"You were hired as an upstairs maid. I thought that I had made that clear. You were not hired as a lady's maid, nor were you hired as a messenger." Ivy opened her mouth as though to speak, and Mrs. Broome raised a hand in admonishment. "It would pain me greatly to give you notice. Your vicar has recommended many girls to us over the years, both at Abingdon Pryory and number fifty-seven Park Lane. The Reverend Mr. Clunes has always been a fine judge of character and I have never been disappointed with any girl he has sent us. Girls from Norfolk have always been level-headed, intelligent, scrupulously clean, and honest to the bone. I have never had a bit of trouble from one of them, but your shortcomings in the past half-hour have more than made up for so many years of perfection."

"I'm sorry, ma'am, but you see—"

"Please do not interrupt me," Mrs. Broome said sharply. "There is, apparently, something that you are not aware of yet, and that is *place*. Everyone has his or her place in life, Ivy. Your place, at least for the time being, is that of an upstairs maid at Abingdon Pryory. Velda Jessup's place is that of a lady's maid. Mr. Coatsworth's place is that of a butler . . . mine is managing the household staff. What do you think would happen if none of us knew our place? Chaos, Ivy. An upside-down queer sort of world. Can you imagine Mr. Coatsworth making beds or shining boots? Can you imagine me being told to empty chamber pots . . . and *complying* with such a request? Can you imagine cook and her helpers mucking out the stables? The mind rebels at such thoughts, but that is what you did, Ivy. You neglected—no, *ignored* your place and assumed the place of Velda. You then assumed the place of heaven knows what and went racing through the house like a wild Indian. Mr. Coatsworth nearly had a stroke when he saw you leaping down the main stairs. He thought you must have had a fit and lost your mind."

"But, Miss Alexandra . . ." Ivy stammered.

Mrs. Broome stiffened. "Miss Alexandra is very young and inclined to dramatics. It is up to the staff to take her current, and I trust transitory, spirits into consideration and to keep them from demolishing the orderly procedures of the household. Miss Alexandra should not, of course, have asked you to dress her in the first place. And she should not have asked you to run downstairs with a message for Miss Foxe. She should have waited for Velda to return, or rung down to me, and I would have sent someone up to her and dispatched a footman, who would have delivered her message in a proper manner. I cannot admonish Miss Alexandra, but I can, and must, admonish you or you may do something similar again. In the future, when asked to do *anything* that is not a regular part of your duties, you shall decline—in a polite and respectful manner, needless to say—and will immediately convey the request to one of your superiors—to a valet, a lady's maid, a footman, a parlormaid or, in the unlikely circumstance that no one of such status is available, to either Mr. Coatsworth or myself. Do you understand, Ivy?"

Ivy could only nod her head numbly. Mrs. Broome then reached out and patted the trembling girl on the cheek.

"I shall not give you notice, Ivy, never fear. You have a sparkle and a brightness that I find most engaging. If there are no more unfortunate lapses of mind, I shall start to train you as a parlormaid within the next six months. That will mean more pleasant duties and a bit more money to send home, which I'm sure will be appreciated."

"Yes, ma'am." The words were barely audible.

"Now, finish tidying up here. Check the towels in the drawer, open the windows and air the room. The countess's nephew is arriving from America tomorrow and will occupy this room. We wish it to be nice and pleasant. When you have finished, you will go downstairs and Mrs. Dalrymple will instruct you further."

And then she was gone, moving majestically out of the room, a tall black-clad, white-haired woman who held the power of life or death over everyone at the house with the exception of Mr. Coatsworth and the outside staff. Ivy held her breath until the woman was safely out of sight and hearing, then she sank down on the window seat and buried her face in her hands. She had come so close to losing her position, and then what would have become of her? She couldn't go home, not with the baby due any minute and Da having enough trouble putting food on the table and paying the rent and seeing to it that her brothers and sisters had decent clothes and sturdy shoes to wear to school. Oh, sweet Jesus, don't let me get the sack, she prayed, *ever*. She felt like blubbering, but the tears wouldn't come and so she rested her suddenly feverish face against the cool window glass. She could see the side garden, an old brick wall smothered by clematis, and part of the drive-way. The shiny blue car came suddenly into view, going very fast, Miss Foxe clutching the steering wheel, her red hair shiny in the sun. Miss Alexandra was looking backward and waving, one hand clamped on top of her straw sailor, the long brown velvet ribbons fluttering in the wind. "Goodbye," she was shouting happily to someone. "Goodbye . . . goodbye."

And that was *their* place, Ivy thought with a sharp pang of regret. It *was* a queer sort of world, come to think of it.

III

Hanna Rilke Greville, Countess Stanmore, sat at her writing desk fronting a deeply set bay window in the sitting room of her suite. The window overlooked a small formal garden, where ordered ranks of boxwood shrubs and roses formed precise geometric patterns when viewed from above. The countess was wearing a green silk peignoir with a downy fringe of marabou feathers around the collar, cuffs, and hem. Her long blonde hair was now unbraided and brushed into smooth, shiny waves that cascaded over her shoulders and down her back. She was forty-five, seven years younger than her husband, and, except for a slight thickening around the hips and the beginnings of a double chin, had retained the golden good looks of her youth. That she was Alexandra's mother there was no doubt. She was the mirror of her daughter's middle age.

Hanna listened to the stuttering roar of a car engine as the machine receded down the driveway toward the Abingdon road a mile away. That would be Lydia and Alexandra leaving for London, she reasoned correctly, refilling her coffee cup from a silver pot. She did not entirely approve of women driving cars, although more and more of them were doing so these days. There were advertisements in all the better magazines showing stylishly dressed young women seated happily behind the wheels of Vauxhalls, Benzes, Morrises, and other sporty makes. Alexandra had begged that she be given driving lessons, but the countess had refused to allow it. She was frightened enough by Charles having his own car.

There were so many accidents. One read about them almost daily.

She finished her coffee and set to work, pushing her sleeves back over plump white forearms. The top of the oval desk was nearly obscured by stacks of papers filled with her neat and almost microscopic handwriting. She had a formidable task almost completed—the schedule and guest lists for the many balls, fetes, entertainments, and extravaganzas planned for the balance of the summer, the "season" in London. The last two weeks in June and all of July would be spent at Stanmore House, the Greville mansion at number 57 Park Lane. The earl was not happy about it, of course, preferring to stay in the country. In previous years he had managed to avoid going up to London for the social whirl of those six weeks, but Alexandra had not been of age then and it hadn't mattered to Hanna whether he came up for the full time or not. This year was different. She had insisted firmly that he attend every function, meet every guest, for his daughter's future lay somewhere among the papers before her.

Somewhere. She sorted through the papers slowly, reading each name that she had written down, the guest list for each and every gathering. The list of names was long: two hundred for the ball on Friday, the nineteenth of June; three hundred and fifty for the gala on July Fourth—Independence Day . . . red, white, and blue bunting everywhere . . . the American ambassador as the honored guest. List after list: thirty for dinner on July 12; twenty-five for a picnic at Henley; forty seats reserved at the Drury Lane Theatre to see Chaliapin in *Ivan the Terrible*. On and on. Everyone who was anyone had found his or her way onto Hanna's lists and was grateful to be there. Stanmore House had always been the glittering focal point of the entire London season. It was a clever trap, for sprinkled liberally among the names of Lord and Lady this, and the Viscount and Viscountess that, were the names of a score of young men, highly eligible bachelors all, and one of those names—and, oh, how she wished she could point to it—would soon be Alexandra's betrothed.

"Who?" she wondered, whispering the word, her finger moving slowly down list after list as though reading Braille. "Albert Dawson Giles, Esquire . . . The Right Honorable Percy Holmes . . . Mr. Paget Lockwood . . . Thomas Duff-Wilson." She paused at that name. A barrister . . . Inner Temple. Twenty-five years of age. Wealthy from inherited money . . . a fine sportsman—Anthony would be pleased at that—a nephew of Lady Adelaide Cooper, one of the queen's ladies-in-waiting, and certain to be knighted in a year or two. The man's name fairly leaped at her. Yes, it stood out above all others, and she sorted through the lists to make doubly certain that he had been included on all of them.

"Terribly busy, my darling?"

She gave a little jump of surprise and turned on her chair to see the earl standing behind her.

"Oh, you startled me. I didn't hear you come in, Tony."

He bent his head and kissed her softly on the nape of the neck.

"Of course not. I'm quite skilled at sneaking into boudoirs."

"That isn't a skill a *gentleman* brags about."

He kissed her once more through the river of hair. "I am not always a gentleman, Hanna."

"No," she laughed, reaching up for his hand. "You're quite a rogue sometimes." She gave his hand a quick squeeze and then turned back to her work. "Pull that armchair over, Tony, and let me go over these guest lists with you."

"Heaven forbid. That's your province, Hanna . . . invite whom you like. You've never made a wrong choice yet."

"It's a little more important this year and you know it. Do you realize that these papers probably contain the name of our future son-in-law? That's a sobering thought, Tony, and I'd like to talk to you about some of these young men."

The earl frowned and walked slowly to the window and gazed down at the garden, his hands folded behind his back.

"I'm not concerned about Alexandra. I know that you will pluck just the right fellow out of the pack and that she will be happy over the choice. I have all the faith in the world in your ability to do that. No, I have no worries about Alex. It's Charles who disturbs me."

Hanna picked up a gold pencil and tapped it lightly against the edge of the desk.

"He's just going through a phase, Tony."

Lord Stanmore smiled wryly. "That's what Fenton said about Roger . . . going through a phase."

"Fenton? Is he here?"

"Yes. Got in last night. He'll be staying a few days. Damn glad to see him. Why is it that I can talk to Fenton and I can't talk to my own son? There's such a wall between us, Hanna."

"You were both chatting away at dinner last night."

"Oh, we *talk*. That is, we open our mouths and words come out . . . but that wall is there and we both know it . . . and we both know what that wall is. Or rather I should say *who* that wall is."

Hanna pressed the pencil against her pursed lips and then stood up and walked over to stand next to her husband.

"How pretty the garden is," she said quietly. "So wonderfully ordered and neat. It's a pity that lives can't be arranged in the same manner, but they can't and you know that they can't. We can merely guide people . . . train them . . . and I believe that we've trained Charles very well. He will never do anything that isn't the right and proper thing to do. He's infatuated by Lydia, and always has been, but I know in my heart that when it comes to a decision, he will make the right one, the one that pleases you and me."

"Perhaps," the earl grunted, eyes fixed on the geometric plantings below.

"But we mustn't press him . . . at least, *you* mustn't press him into building this wall you refer to any higher. It was a mistake inviting Mary and Winifred. I told you that."

"Winifred's father is——"

"A fine and honorable man," she cut in. "Yes, I know all that, and it would be wonderful if Charles fell in love with the girl and married her. But let me put in a little Yankee common sense, if you don't mind. You can lead a horse to water, but you can't make it drink. Charles feels nothing for Winifred. Nothing at all. In fact, he probably hates the poor girl by now and if he does we're to blame. I made up my mind last night when I saw the expression on Charles's face when you *suggested* that he take Winifred down to see the new gazebo. I shall have a quiet heart-to-heart talk with Mary and stop this nonsense before it goes any further."

"You can't tell the woman to leave and take her daughter with her. That wouldn't be right."

"I won't tell her to leave, just explain the blunt facts. She may be flighty, but she does have four sons who have minds of their own. She'll understand Charles's feelings and she won't resent it one bit. Mary's an old and dear friend and we've always been candid with each other."

"Well, all right," he said in a pained manner. "Perhaps you're doing the right thing."

"I will be doing the *only* thing." She touched him gently on the shoulder. "I'm a mother *and* a woman. I understand Charles far better than you do at this period in his life. And what's even more important, I understand Lydia."

"Oh, I feel so glorious!" Alexandra shouted, bouncing up and down on the car seat.

"Sit still," Lydia shouted back, "or you'll fall out."

Alexandra settled down firmly in the leather seat,

keeping one hand pressed on the crown of her hat. Lydia, frowning slightly, concentrated on adjusting the controls until the engine stopped its stuttering roar and settled into a smooth, powerful howl. They were past the village of Abingdon, racing along a narrow road which curved in a succession of lazy S's through dense old woods and sunlit patches of hedgerowed fields.

"Gloriously happy!" Alexandra cried into the slipstream of wind buffeting her face. "Oh, Lydia, do you realize that by this time next year I might be having a baby! That is, if we have a short period of engagement. I don't believe in long engagements, do you? Don't you think they're horribly old-fashioned?"

"Oh, do be quiet, Alex," Lydia said in vexation. "You're enough to make a saint swear. Honestly, you are."

The younger woman leaned closer to Lydia to keep from shouting over the noise of the engine.

"I went into Mama's sitting room last night after dinner and stole a long peek at her lists. Oh, Lydia, she's inviting every devastatingly handsome bachelor in London."

"How do you know they're *devastatingly* handsome?"

"I just know, that's all. Not a one under six feet . . . al! destined for greatness . . . And one of them will sweep me off my feet and into his strong ravishing arms."

Lydia rolled her eyes toward heaven. "What trash novel did you steal *that* line from?"

"Jane Bakehurst—you don't know her, she was my very best friend at school this year—well, she bought this book by Elinor Glyn. . . . Frightfully racy."

"Alex, you're impossible. The sooner you get married, the better."

"I couldn't agree with you more. I can't wait to have babies, dozens of them—well, five at least—all fat, pink, gurgling things, and I shall stroll into the nursery every night with my devastatingly handsome young husband beside me, and Nanny shall parade them in front of us."

"Are you planning on having all five at one swoop?"

"No, silly, one at a time . . . a decent interval between each. But seriously, I believe marriage and babies to be a holiness. I truly do."

The countryside gave way to the suburbs—Epsom, Cheam, Merton, and South Wimbledon, rows and rows of little brick houses, and semidetached villas of mock Tudor design. The traffic became heavier when they reached Lambeth and Southwark: cars, lorries, buses, and ponderous horse-drawn wagons. They crossed the river via Westminster Bridge and so on into Mayfair. The House of Ferris, couturier, occupied an elegant Georgian edifice in Hanover Square. Lydia stopped in front of it, and a doorman dressed in the livery of a Victorian coachman hurried from the entranceway to open the car doors.

"Good day, Miss Greville . . . Miss Foxe," he said, touching the brim of his hat. "Shall I have a boy park your motorcar, Miss Foxe?"

"Not today, thank you. I'm not staying."

Alexandra sprang from the car like a fluffy Persian cat. "Don't you dare pick me up before three. I don't want you to see my gowns until they're free of basting stitches. Promise?"

"Promise," Lydia said flatly. After the doorman closed the car door, she put the Benz into gear and roared off in the direction of Oxford Street.

Foxe House was one of the largest, most modern office buildings in England. It had been designed by an American architect and completed in spring 1912 to a flurry of controversy. Letters had poured in to the *Times*, the bulk of them decrying the erection of such a building within viewing distance of Nash's pristine Regent Street façades. But after a few months, Londoners began to grow used to, and then fond of, the oblong multistory limestone-faced building near Oxford Circus. It had long been Archie Foxe's dream to have all the varied departments of his vast enterprise under one roof instead of scattered hither and yon about the city. The efficiency of what Archie Foxe called "the Yank method" had been more than proved during the two years of the building's occupancy, and several of the larger British corporations were constructing massive office buildings of their own. The skyline of London was beginning to change, and that was just what Archie Foxe liked to see.

Lydia turned into the entranceway of the subterranean garage, where a boy in a smart blue uniform took the car from her. She removed her linen motoring coat and left it on the seat, then walked to a lift, which whisked her upward. The lift stopped at several floors and people got in and out—secretaries, office boys, mail clerks, men and women from advertising, marketing, the White Manor division, the Foxe's Fancy division, the legal and real-property departments. Lydia was instantly recognized by most of them and politely wished a good day, but she knew only one of her fellow passengers, a tall ruddy-faced man named Swinton, who was chief of the advertising department. He had gotten on at the first floor, a pipe jutting from his mouth and a large portfolio of drawings under his arm.

"Hallo, Lydia," Swinton said cheerily. "Come to take the guv'nor to lunch?"

It was a little joke they shared. Archie Foxe had never been known to have lunch. Once, long ago, Lydia had insisted that he join her at lunch at the Savoy Grill and Archie had sent Swinton in his stead.

"No," she said with a smile. "Just come to pay my respects."

"He's busy as a beaver. We're opening the new place at Charing Cross next week. Like to take a look-see at these?" He opened the portfolio to reveal a dozen watercolors, rough sketches for advertising posters.

"They're very good."

"Thank you," Swinton said. "We're attracting some first-rate artists these days. The Slade School has finally stopped turning its nose up at us and we're getting some damn brilliant chaps from there . . . women, too. Any particular one strike you?"

"That night scene is very eye-catching."

Swinton slipped it from the portfolio and held it up. It was an impression of a London street on a rainy night, great blobs of brilliant color shimmering in reflection on the wet pavement. People, heads bent against the wind-driven downpour, were scurrying shadows. Amid the gloom rose a brightly lit two-story building with the words White Manor illuminated across the front of it. At the bottom of the sketch—which would be even more effective when done in oils—was a slogan in black ink: GET OUT OF THE WET AND INTO A WHITE MANOR.

"Yes," Lydia said, "I like it very much."

"So do I. It's for the winter campaign. Well, ta-ta." He stepped out of the lift on the fourth floor and Lydia continue upward to her father's office.

Archie Foxe had an office of his own, complete with a desk that had once belonged to the Duke of Wellington when he had been Prime Minister, but he rarely spent time there. He was a roamer, a compulsive walker, going from office to office and desk to desk from the ground floor to the top, overseeing, supervising, suggesting, demanding, criticizing and praising, as the case might be, every one of his employees, from clerks to members of the board. Trailing after him would be one of his harassed stout-legged male secretaries, a shorthand notebook and a pencil constantly at the ready. One filled notebook represented a very slow day indeed.

Archie Foxe had been destined to make money and had never felt the slightest surprise that he had done so. He had never thanked God for his good fortune and was quick to point out that neither luck nor the Almighty had had anything to do with it.

"Hard work and a bloody good idea," was Archie Foxe's sole business philosophy. He was sixty years old and had been born in the slums of Shadwell in London's East End on New Year's Day, 1854. He would not talk about his childhood with anyone, not even his own daughter, nor had he done so with the woman he married late in life and who had died when Lydia was a child, an upper-class woman from Cumberland, who, had he told her, would not have comprehended his stories, or would have thought them mere Dickensian fictions. It had been a childhood of stinking hovels and workhouses, of a father drifting away in despair to gin-caused madness and a mother dying of consumption in a freezing attic. He could see the place of his childhood from the top-floor windows of Foxe House, the great serpentine stretches of the Thames below Blackfriars Bridge. It was not a distance that could be measured in miles.

Archie Foxe had been sent from a children's house of detention to Bethnal Green at the age of nine to be an apprentice in a butcher shop in Smithfield Market. The butcher's brother owned a bake shop, and Archie's job was to chop up scraps of near-putrid beef and veal, which the bake-shop owner turned into gelatinous meat pies. The vileness of those pies inspired Archie to make better ones, which he did after quitting his apprenticeship at the age of seventeen. He entered into partnership with a middle-aged widow who owned a tiny bakery near Covent Garden. The two of them made the pies at night, and Archie took them around to various eating establishments and public houses and sold them during the day. They couldn't make enough of them, and within a year they had rented a building and had ten meat cutters and pastry men working for them.

"It was just a question of pilin' one thing on another," Archie would tell a magazine writer many years later. The bakery growing, the acquisition of horses and delivery wagons, the expansion of product—beef and veal pies, beef pies with kidney, veal and pork pies, pork pies with currants and apple chunks. . . .

"And then the puttin' of the pies in tins, shippin' 'em

to India . . . Australia . . . all round the bloody world."

The widow sold her share of the partnership to Archie in 1880 to spend the balance of her days in a comfortable house in the country with four servants.

" 'Avin' it all to meself was really what did it. I could feel free like . . . just do what I ruddy well wanted."

What he wanted were a few shops in strategic places on the corners of major thoroughfares—clean, well-lighted places where ordinary blokes could have a cup of tea or coffee and something good and filling to eat and be waited on by a pretty young woman dressed in a blue uniform with a starched white apron and a white cap and all for very little money. He wanted all these shops to look exactly alike so that people would recognize them instantly. He thought up the idea of painting the exteriors a glossy white, and the first of all the subsequent hundreds of White Manor tea shops opened its doors on the northwest corner of Ludgate Circus on June 3, 1883, the shop at Holborn and Gray's Inn Road opening two weeks later.

"Men must eat, you see—that's only nature. A man can go years on the same pair o' boots, a woman can wear the same coat from one year's end to the other, or 'ave the same 'ousehold furnishin' for a lifetime, but they must eat, three squares a day and a cuppa char every few hours or so. That's the natural thing about it . . . that's why you can't 'elp but make a bit o' money at it, caterin' to that natural fact, you see. Can't 'elp it. . . . And the only trick to it is in givin' just ordinary people decent grub at a fair price, because those are the people you want to sell, the people who've got to watch their pennies, see. . . . Because there's a lot more of them kind of people than there are rich people, who don't give a damn 'ow much they spend for a meal. I don't care if they come into a White Manor or not—that is of no concern to me at all . . . not one bit . . . no. I built the White Manors with some bloke who clerks in an office in mind, with a shopgirl in

mind. Yes. Only, of course, it grew a bit from that, you
see. Got a bit more posh, you might say. Yes. There are
White Manors where a navvy can hop in for his tea and
two slices, and there's the White Manors that got a
ruddy six-piece orchestra and a duke couldn't find fault
with the Dover sole. But the price stays fair, you
see. . . . That's the whole bleedin' trick—the price
stays fair."

"Is my father about?" Lydia asked the pretty young
receptionist.

"He went below, Miss Foxe," the woman said. "But I
can ring down and I'm sure we can locate him for you."

"Oh, that's all right. I'll just wait in his office. But if
you hear from him, tell him I'm in there or I'll be waiting forever!"

"Of course, Miss Foxe. And may I compliment you
on your frock? It's very lovely."

"Thank you."

"Most becoming. Not English, surely."

"No. A Paris design."

"Oh, yes. It does show, doesn't it?"

Lydia could see the envy in the woman's eyes. She
was pretty, but her clothing was drab. A girl who
worked in an office and lived with other girls who
worked in offices in some crowded rooming house in
Holborn. It was quite pathetic.

She liked her father's office. It was what she imagined a judge's chambers would be like, or the study of a
dean at Oxford. The walls lined with oak, the flooring
oak as well, polished to a satin luster with a fine old
Oriental carpet to add the proper touch of color and
warmth to the room. Comfortable leather chairs. The
grand old Wellington desk. A few pictures on the walls.
A landscape by Constable. Two modern paintings of
London by Walter Sickert. And there were photographs
in silver frames, on the walls and on the desk. Photographs of herself, her mother, George Robey—a music
hall comedian of whom her father was very fond—
Herbert Asquith, and David Lloyd George. (Archie

Foxe's nearly bottomless bankbook had been of great help to the Liberal party in the general elections of 1906, and the prime minister and his chancellor of the exchequer would never forget it.)

The framed enthusiastically inscribed photographs of the prime minister and Lloyd George made Lydia smile. She wondered what Lord Stanmore would do if he were in her shoes, standing alone with the images of *those* men confronting him. Toss them out the window probably—or smash them with his riding crop in righteous Tory rage.

There were some magazines on a table, and she sat in a chair next to the window and leafed through a copy of the *Illustrated London News*. There were pictures of the king and queen at Cowes, the king looking trim and fit in an admiral's uniform, the queen looking beautiful and terribly austere in an ostrich-plumed hat. There were three pages of photographs of the rebuilding of a cottage in Derbyshire: an article by Mr. Hilaire Belloc on the French Revolution—the first of five articles— lavishly illustrated with old engravings of the period, and several pages on German army maneuvers in East Prussia: ranks of drably uniformed men with *pickle-haube* helmets marching across fields; squadrons of gorgeously uniformed uhlans and hussars passing the Kaiser and the Crown Prince in review. How operatic and *costumed* they all looked. She wondered which of the Kaiser's arms was withered. It was impossible to tell. She turned the page. An advertisement in halftone showed the newly completed White Manor in Charing Cross: "Three distinctly different restaurants for your dining pleasure . . . two orchestras . . . tango teas . . . saloon bar—"

"Well, this is a welcome surprise."

She looked up, and there was her father coming into the room, full tilt as usual, nearly running, a gaunt-eyed pink-complexioned young man at his heels.

"Hello, Daddy," she said.

"You can go, Thomas," Archie Foxe commanded

over his shoulder. "Get the Manchester directive in the post by five, that's all that's important. Give the rest to the typists."

The young man visibly brightened. "Yes, sir, I'll do that."

"Well, well." Archie Foxe rocked back and forth on his heels and gazed at his daughter with obvious pleasure. He was a stocky man who looked younger than his years, with reddish hair parted and combed carefully to help conceal a round bald spot, like a monk's tonsure. The East End was engraved on his puckish features, the face of a street imp grown old—and much wiser. "Well, well. What brings you up from the countryside? Money, I suppose."

She was looking at him through narrowed eyes, a critical stare.

"You promised not to wear checked suits. They make you look like a tout."

He touched the loudly patterned jacket with his heavy, blunt hands. "I like checks—an' touts. Smartest bloke I ever met in me life was a tout at Newmarket."

"Oh, Daddy," she sighed. "You're quite impossible." She stood up, walked over to him, and kissed him on the cheek. "I've missed you. Can't you come down for a few days?"

"There's been too much to do . . . but I'll try and manage. You keepin' busy?"

"Oh, yes, with one thing or another. I drove Alexandra up for a dress fitting."

"How is the girl?"

"Excited. Hopes to be married any minute."

"Oh? Who's the lucky gent?"

"She hasn't met him yet, but I gather any man will do as long as he's tall, handsome, and can walk on water."

"Seems to me that walkin' on water is *your* ruddy standard." He took a leather case from an inner pocket and extracted a long Cuban cigar. "That and curin' lepers and raisin' the dead."

She turned away from him and walked stiffly to the

windows. London had never looked so beautiful, almost
like a picture postcard rendition—a too-blue sky, a perfectly formed nimbus of white fleecy cloud framing the
dome of St. Paul's. How wonderful it would be to fly
above the city. . . . Not in an airplane—she had done
that and it was far too noisy for enjoyment—but as a
bird flew, on silent wings.

"I find your impatience with me depressing, Daddy."

"Oh, do you?" he snorted, biting the tip off his cigar
and propelling the fragment toward a shiny brass cuspi-
dor. "Well, my girl, it's normal for a man to want
kids—his own kids or grandkids. Natural fact that, ask
anybody."

"I wish I'd been born a boy," she sighed. "It would
have made everything so much simpler."

He came up behind her and rubbed the side of his
hand against her neck. "Yes, Foxe and son right from
the start. Only thing, see. He would 'ave looked like me
instead of his mother. I would 'ave 'ad a short, ugly,
redheaded nipper instead of a bloomin' ravin' beauty of
a girl."

She turned with a smile and put her arms around
him, hugging him, inhaling his scent of fine woolens
and good tobacco.

"You're a dear. I'll give you scads of little nippers
one day, Daddy. I promise."

"I've never doubted it, but I wish you'd hurry up and
get started."

"I have plans," she said quietly. "Really quite wonderful plans."

Hanna gave some thought to her nephew as a maid
brushed and combed her hair for her.

"Would her ladyship like it swept up this morning?"
the maid asked. "With a few curls on the sides?"

"I think so, Rose . . . yes, the way you did it the
other day."

"Very well, your ladyship. I'll just heat up the iron."

The cablegram, sent from New York, was in the center of her desk: WILL ARRIVE CUNARD SS LACONIA DOCKING SOUTHAMPTON FRIDAY JUNE 12 STOP EAGERLY AWAITING SEEING YOU AGAIN REGARDS TO ALL MARTIN RILKE.

Just thinking of the wire made her smile. It was so *American*. So filled with uninhibited eagerness and friendliness, a pat on the back and the big hello—the Chicago manner. *Give my regards to all.* Only a midwesterner would cherish such presumptions toward people he had never met, nor even corresponded with, simply because they were *family*. She could understand his attitude, because although she had left Chicago at the age of nineteen, to return there only once for the briefest stay, she had never lost her awareness of American attitudes. It would have seemed perfectly natural and right for him to send such a wire—"give my regards to all"—to Uncle Tony, cousins Charles, Alexandra, and William. Indeed, it would have seemed wrong, in his mind, not to do so. The unfortunate fact was that her husband and her children would have been bewildered had she passed on such sentiments to them. She had merely said, after receiving the wire, "My nephew will be arriving on the twelfth. He is looking forward to meeting all of you." That, of course, was understandable. They were, in a mild fashion, looking forward to meeting him. (William, not having been home and knowing nothing about it, was excluded.) She had told them two months before that Martin would be coming to England, to stay for a week or two before traveling on to France, Germany, Austria, and Italy, so that the announcement of a specific time and place of arrival had come as no surprise.

"Is he, now?" her husband had said. "So soon. Well, we shall have to send Ross down to the docks to pick him up . . . and one of the footmen to help with the luggage."

"I think it would be nicer if Charles went also."

"Yes, quite so, my dear, by all means."

Charles had shown a certain reluctance: "It's not as

though I knew the chap, Mother. . . ." But her will had prevailed.

"I just hope to heaven he's not like that other Rilke who descended on us last year."

"No, dear," she had said, "I'm sure that he isn't. He's my brother William's son. You remember my telling you about him."

Charles had nodded in the affirmative, but she doubted whether he remembered very much of what she had told him in bits and pieces over the years, of her brothers William and Paul and of the polar distance between them. Paul successful and rich, William a failure, poor—and now dead. It had been Paul's son, Karl, who had come over the previous summer for a brief visit before going on to Paris and Berlin. A contentious, brash young man, who had prefaced almost every sentence that he uttered with the words, "Well, at Yale we . . ." They had all grown rather irked at the Yale standard for everything by the time he left. Now another young Rilke was coming from across the sea and she could not guarantee that he would be any different from the last one, although she had sensed by the letter he had written to her in March telling her of his plans for travel in Europe that he was very different indeed. Willie's son. They had met for the first time in Chicago when she had gone back for Aunt Ermgard's funeral in the summer of 1903. He had been twelve years old then, a month younger than Charles. A quiet, polite boy who had rather startled her by quoting a passage from Goethe in a German untainted by New World idiom or accent. But why should that have been a surprise? Willie's son, after all. It was impossible to think of her dead brother without feeling a tug at the heart.

"Keep steady, madam," the maid cautioned. "The iron is quite hot."

After her hair was fixed to her satisfaction, the maid helped her into a morning dress of white lawn, and she left her room and started down for her breakfast, passing her son's room on the way. The door was closed, and she hesitated in front of it for a moment, then rapped gently. She distinctly heard him call out, "Go away," but she ignored the directive and opened the door.

"Good morning, Charles," she said cheerfully.

He was on the bed, fully dressed, his back against the headboard. A breakfast tray, the food barely touched, was on the bedside table. He closed the book he had been reading and smiled in apology.

"Sorry, Mother. I didn't know it was you."

"I'm going down for breakfast. Have you eaten?"

"I was brought something, but I'm not hungry."

"Don't you feel well? You look a bit pale."

"I'm fine."

"Are you sure?"

"Yes, Mother, quite sure."

How gaunt he has become, she was thinking, his face like that of a troubled man. She could see the unhappiness in his eyes and that hurt her deeply. He was her firstborn, and they had always had a special relationship, a closeness.

"Can we have a little talk, Charles?"

He looked away from her and tossed the book onto the bed.

"What about?"

"Winifred Sutton, among other things."

"Ah," he said with a thin smile. "Winifred."

"I convinced your father this morning that there is no possible chance of your becoming attracted to the girl and that any dreams he may have had about the two of you are simply that—his dreams, not yours. I intend to be quite candid about the situation with Winifred's mother."

"Well, that's a step in the right direction, I must say." He sat on the edge of the bed and placed his hands on his knees, a pose that always reminded her of her husband. They were so alike in looks and mannerisms—the same long legs and slender body, the same clean features—and yet so opposite in character. The room re-

flected his tastes, just as her husband's apartment reflected his. Books were everywhere—stacked, piled,
some open, some closed with scraps of paper jutting
from the leaves. She had no idea of his purpose in all
that reading. He had mentioned in an offhand manner
his interest in the Seven Years War and the expansion
of the British Empire. Did he intend writing a book? It
seemed to her like an odd subject to devote one's time
to.

"You look instantly better," she said.

"Yes, as a matter of fact I am." He grinned at her.
"And I'm quite sure that Winnie will feel better as well.
I frighten her. Do you know that? It's true. She told
me . . . last night down at the gazebo. She called me
moody and intense. There's quite a simple, passionate
soul beneath all that *embonpoint*. I'm not the man to
bring it out and she knows it."

"That's a pity . . . in some ways."

He nodded emphatically. "The dynastic blending of
two fine old names. A gilding of coronets. I feel a bit
of a rotter disappointing everyone . . . except Winnie,
of course. I wouldn't say a word to Lady Mary, though.
I'll take Winnie for a drive into Guildford, treat her to
a cup of chocolate and an éclair at the sweetshop, and
break the terrible news to her. That's the gentlemanly
thing to do, isn't it?"

"Yes, I suppose it is."

"Then she'll tell her mother whatever she feels like
telling her—that she's fallen in love with the Prince of
Wales . . . or discovered in the nick of time that there
is galloping insanity in the Greville blood—and in a day
or two they will both depart, seeking more receptive
game. I'm sure that Lady Mary has a list that beggars
the one you've compiled for Alex."

"Charles! What an awful thing to say!" Her indignation was so patently artificial that they both laughed.
"Very well, you handle the entire matter . . . but
don't put it off."

"First thing this afternoon."

She walked further into the room and stood looking about with a wistful expression.

"You used to keep this room so neat at one time. Everything in its place. It must be the despair of the maids now."

"I won't let a maid in it. They have a compulsion for tidiness."

"I think the room reflects your state of mind, Charles. A topsy-turvy confusion."

Their eyes met and he looked away. "I sense the preamble to a motherly lecture. I think I can guess the subject matter and I'd rather you didn't get started. Not now."

"If not now, then when?"

He turned to the book he had tossed aside and riffled the pages idly.

"Soon. When . . . when I get it all clear in my mind as to just what I want to say."

Hanna's face seemed suddenly drawn and tired as she looked pityingly at her son.

"I know what you're going to say, Charles. I can hear every word of it . . . and I can hear your father's reply. He's a proud and inflexible man. No need to tell you that. Yes, Charles, I can hear his reply . . . anticipate his actions. I should like to leave you with just one thought, and I want you to face that thought and dwell upon it honestly. Will you promise me that?"

"Of course," he said, frowning at the pages.

"I hope you won't think me cruel."

"No."

"I've known Lydia since she was a child and I'm fond of her. Her mother was a dear woman, and it was a great tragedy that she died when Lydia was so young. I think she would have grown up to be a more . . . well, a more *traditionally* minded woman had her mother lived." The branch of an elm moved gently in the wind outside one of the windows. Charles used to climb out of that window when he was a little boy and clamber down the tree into the garden below. "The question

I raise is this. Should you marry Lydia without your father's blessing he might publicly disavow her as his
daughter-in-law. The social implications of such an action would be devastating. I ask you in all honesty,
Charles—if Lydia knew for certain that your father
would ignore her in such a drastic fashion, would she
have quite the same affection for you as she does now?"

Twilight lingered until past nine o'clock, a soft blue
glow in the sky with cobalt shadows lying across the
fields. On Burgate Hill, the top branch of the tallest tree
caught the last ray of sun from the west: a golden
bough turning slowly to black.

Lord Stanmore leaned back in his chair and waited
for Coatsworth to pass the cigars around the table. The
ladies had left for the drawing room, the younger wom-
en to the music room off the conservatory, where re-
citals were sometimes held and where Alexandra
kept her Victrola. He could hear the steady far-off beat
of music. He felt satisfied, with just a small tinge of regret. Satisfied by the dinner, an exceptionally fine baron of beef, the company—old and dear friends—but
regretful over the way things had turned out between
Charles and Winifred Sutton. He had allowed Hanna
her way and the situation had no doubt been resolved.
Charles had been a little less moody, although that
could have been because Lydia had been at the table,
and Winifred, acting as though a great weight had been
lifted from her shoulders, had chatted away to Alexandra and Roger Wood-Lacy like a plump magpie. The
young knew what they wanted, and didn't want, he
supposed. Still, it was a pity. It would have been a
damn fine match for both of them.

Coatsworth had decanted a fresh cask of port, the
first of the shipment from Messrs. Lockwood and Grier,
Lisbon, and he stood expectantly beside the earl's chair,
waiting for him to taste the first glass poured.

"Nice color, Coatsworth," the earl said, holding the
glass up to the light.

"Yes, m'lord, it is."

He sniffed the rim. "Aroma, too." He tasted, holding the wine in his mouth for a moment before swallowing. "Ah!"

Coatsworth took the sigh as a signal of approval and placed the crystal decanter on the table to the earl's right, where Mr. Cavendish, a local squire and one of the earl's oldest friends, was seated. Cavendish filled his glass and passed the decanter on to Fenton, who filled his glass and handed it down to a florid-faced man who was the Conservative MP from Caterham. And so the port went the rounds of the ten men at the table, only Roger Wood-Lacy, who could not physically tolerate spirits in any form, declining.

"Well, Fenton," a retired brigadier, and one of the leading horse raisers in the county, called out from the far end of the long oak table. "Well, sir, what do you hear from Ireland? You chaps still standing pat at the Curragh?"

Fenton dipped the end of his cigar in his port. "One never knows from one day to the next, sir. But I believe it's all rather more sound than fury . . . like Irish politics in general."

There was a muted chorus: "Hear, hear."

"It's all the newspapers, if you ask me," a tall bald-headed man said. "You can always rely on Northcliffe or Lord Crewe to toss kerosene on a fire. I'm certainly against this damn home rule bill as you all know, but I do believe that it's irresponsible journalism to intimate that the British Army is on the verge of mutiny over it."

"Only the Irish garrison," someone remarked in clarification.

"Quite so . . . still, you get my drift."

Fenton lit his cigar and blew a contented puff toward the high-beamed ceiling. "Oh, a few officers might resign rather than use force against the Ulster volunteers, but I'd say that would be the size of the so-called mutiny. And if push comes to shove, you'll see the Orangemen back down. They'll have to settle this home rule business around a table, not by taking potshots from the bogs."

Lord Stanmore shook his head. "That's giving the Irish too much credit for common sense, Fenton. I'm sure they could work out a solution if they tried—or if they wanted a solution badly enough—but they have dug themselves into fixed positions."

"Oil and water, Tony," the brigadier said. "Two things that simply will not mix. The whole concept of home rule for Ireland is as foolish as trying to tamper with God's design."

"That's the Liberals for you," Mr. Cavendish said. "They feel above the laws of God or physics. Take Lloyd George and his home rule for Ireland . . . home rule for Wales . . . home rule for Scotland. He'll be wanting home rule for India next."

"I met Parkhurst at the Carlton Club last week," the brigadier said with a chuckle. "He quipped that one sure way to get that randy Welshman out of office was to offer him an earldom in Glamorganshire and half interest in a coal mine. He'd be off like a shot!"

"There might be something to that, sir," Charles Greville said solemnly. "I have no doubt that the man's ambitious, but I rather think he fancies himself above material gains or honors at the moment."

"A leader of the people," Roger said. "A sort of Celtic Napoleon or benevolent tyrant in the Greek manner."

"Friend of the common man," someone scoffed. "Quite an easy matter to make friends if one is in the position of sending five bob a week to every old duffer in the country. But the people who thank Lloyd George and Asquith for their pension money should really thank me, and the rest of us at this table. The money comes from *our* pockets."

"No politician ever lost support by taxing the rich," Mr. Cavendish remarked dryly.

Fenton let his attention wander, distracted by the ragtime music coming from the Victrola, which he could barely hear. He was a good dancer, an attribute that was an outright necessity for any officer garrisoned in London. The regimental adjutant insisted that all new subalterns attend dancing class, conducted three evenings a week by C Company's Corporal Booth, who had been a professional dancer in the music halls before enlisting. An inept dancer would have socially disgraced the regiment. It was Corporal Booth who had taught Fenton to dance the Castle walk, turkey trot, and the Texas Tommy, and to keep abreast of all the latest steps coming out of America. His right foot began a soundless tap-tap-tap on the carpet.

"I'd gladly have them double my taxes," the brigadier declared stoutly, "if it meant another dreadnought or two."

"Nonsense," the MP from Caterham said. "Let Germany pour millions into saber rattling. War is being fought now, today, and we're winning it hands down. The British merchant navy is the most powerful on earth and getting more powerful minute by minute. By jove, it seems only yesterday that the *Lusitania* and the *Mauretania* were being touted by Cunard as the grandest ships afloat, and now they come up with the *Aquitania,* which simply beggars them. North German Lloyd and the Hamburg-American line will never be capable of building, or operating, anything like it."

An elderly surgeon from Guildford, a well-known hunting man, cleared his throat. "Still, it isn't simply a question of merchant bottoms, is it? It's a question of production. Fritz may be trying to imitate his betters by venturing out into the sea lanes, but they outproduce us in steel and chemicals. One simply can't argue about that."

"The *manufacture* of chemical products," the MP said firmly, as though making a point in the House. "They must import every ounce of nitrate and other raw materials. You know a bit about that, don't you, Tony?"

"Yes, quite so," the earl said. "My wife's relations in

Mecklenburg and Waldeck, the von Rilkes. Very heavily involved in the chemical industry. Import a great deal of nitrate from South America, I believe. Still, rather amazing how many things they can make in Germany out of coal tar. A cousin of my wife's . . . Baron Heinrich von Rilke, you met him last year, Percy, the scientific chap."

"Yes, of course," the Guildford surgeon replied.

"Well, he told me of some truly remarkable things that they were doing at his laboratory in Koblenz. Quite astonishing. One mustn't sell the Germans short."

The Caterham MP blew a stream of cigar smoke past the candelabrum, the smoke curling above the steady candle flames.

"My point exactly! We must rise to their challenge, not with more battleships, but with increased productivity and better technocracy—bicycles, motorcars, farm tools. Fight them to a standstill in the marketplace with better and *cheaper* goods."

Fenton stifled a yawn. How many hundreds of hours had he suffered through listening to after-dinner conversations? It wasn't so bad at the Guards' Club, where they could talk shop or sports—but not sex—or at the battalion mess, where they could talk sex or sports—but not shop. He couldn't think of one brother officer who cared a tinker's damn about Germany, or England's social, political, or economic affairs. Cheaper goods indeed! That was the province of America, wasn't it? Ford cars and buying one's clothes through the post from an illustration in a catalogue.

"I say, sir," he said, hoping to sidetrack any further discussion of English technocracy, or lack of it, "Roger tells me that one of her ladyship's relations is arriving from America tomorrow."

"Quite so," Lord Stanmore said without enthusiasm. "From Chicago. Newspaper wallah of some kind. Never met him." He stood up, an Augustan figure in his evening clothes. "Gentlemen, let's join the ladies."

Roger, Fenton, and Charles lingered in the dining

room until the older men had left, trailing cigar smoke down the corridor toward the drawing room. Charles drew a silver watch from his waistcoat.

"Not bad, a damn sight shorter than usual. A master stroke, Fenton, or we'd have been stuck in here for another quarter-hour at least."

Fenton looked puzzled. "What are you talking about?"

"My cousin from Chicago. Father wished to avoid any probing questions about the fellow from his cronies."

"What on earth for? Is he some kind of desperado, like Jesse James?"

Charles laughed. "I hope so, but in all seriousness, no, he's just a chap who works on a newspaper. But there's some kind of skeleton in Mother's closet . . . the chap's father, her brother William. I forget the story. All I know for sure is that he died years ago . . . of drink . . . or suicide. Something rather nasty. She named our William after him."

Fenton grimaced and flicked cigar ash into a plate. "I'm sure young Will appreciates *that*."

"Well, they couldn't change his name, could they? It happened after he was born. Poor chap is stuck with it. Are they gone, Roger?"

Roger had been peering down the corridor. "Yes, safely turned the corner. Let's hop to it before someone comes back and insists we form bridge fours."

They left the dining room by way of the French doors, which led onto the terrace. The phonograph grew louder as they passed the domed glass structure of the conservatory, designed by Sir Harold Wood-Lacy as a scaled-down replica of the Crystal Palace. Beyond the carved-stone balustrade of the terrace lay the Italian gardens, bright under the rising moon, the topiary elephants and giraffes bobbing their cypress heads in the warm wind.

Alexandra and Lydia were dancing together to the trombone, cornet, and snare-drum beat of a Texas

Tommy. Winifred stood beside the Victrola, one hand on the crank, her hips moving slightly to the syncopated sound.

"Charming!" Fenton said loudly, watching the girls prance about the room. Their images reflected back from the mirrors on the walls—mirrors installed when Alexandra had been twelve and avid to study ballet. "Most inspiring!"

Roger stepped fully into the room, arms spread wide. "All hail the antic Bacchae . . . chaste and fair!"

"Oh, don't be an ass, Roger," Alexandra called out over her shoulder. "Dance with Winnie."

Winifred looked startled. "Oh, no . . . I don't know how."

"Of *course* you do," Alexandra said breathlessly. "Don't be a frump."

The frantic music came to an end and the two girls broke apart, flushed and laughing.

"Oh, I did enjoy that," Alexandra said. "I could do the Texas Tommy all night."

"I prefer a waltz myself," Roger said.

"That's because you're staid and dull."

Roger stiffened with indignation. "I am not."

"Yes, you are."

"All right, play a tango then. I'll show you how staid and dull I am *not*. I dance the tango with a great deal of *sensuality*."

Fenton helped Winifred find a tango record among the stack in the Victrola cabinet. The girl's hands, he noticed, were trembling slightly.

"Don't you really know how to dance?"

"No," she whispered. "I never learned . . . at least not properly. I have no ear for music . . . that's the trouble. I can't keep time."

"I'm sure I could teach you in a few minutes. It's really quite simple. No trick to it at all."

"Which tango are you playing?" Alexandra asked.

Fenton glanced at the label. " 'The Sans Souci.' "

"Fine. I like that one." She held out her arms.

"Come on, Roger . . . and try not to step on my toes."

Charles bowed to Lydia with exaggerated formality. "Miss Foxe, may I have the pleasure?"

She curtsied. "You may indeed, Mr. Greville."

He put an arm about her waist and she moved closer to him. Their hips touched and his body became tense. When he took her right hand in his left, she could feel the dampness of his palm.

"Relax," she said softly.

"We must talk, Lydia."

She smiled coquettishly into his taut, pallid face. "Why, Mr. Greville, whatever about?"

The music began, the pulsating Latin rhythm that had all Europe in thrall. Charles stumbled slightly, as though his knees had become locked from tenseness, and she had to lead for a moment until he was able to coordinate his body to the throbbing sound.

Fenton took Winifred by the hand. "Shall we try it?"

Her smile was wan. "I . . . I don't think I can."

"Nonsense. I saw you swaying to the Texas Tommy when I came into the room. You were keeping perfect time."

"Oh, I can dance by myself. It's just that . . . when I . . ."

"I quite understand." He held her firmly, one hand in the small of her back. "It's simply a question of practice . . . and confidence in oneself. I know I could teach you to tango in a very short time."

"You don't mind?"

"Why, of course not, Winifred. It would be a pleasure."

She was really quite pretty, he was thinking, smiling down at her. She smiled back, shyly, a pink glow spreading across her cheeks and throat. She had been casting glances at him all day. A young girl's sudden infatuation, a crush—he had done nothing to encourage her. Always he had been the correctly formal officer and gentleman, her brother Andrew's friend. He guided her expertly through the steps, the sensual movements of the dance.

"You're doing very well," he said. "Just follow me . . . don't look at your feet."

She had little grace, but that was probably nervousness. Her hand clenched his tightly and the hand on his shoulder kept straying down as though she were not sure where it belonged. Her eyes were hazel, he noted, and her hair the palest shade of brown. Yes, a very pretty girl, and if she lost a stone or so in weight she would have quite a fetching figure. The Most Honorable Winifred Sutton, only daughter of the Marquess and Marchioness of Dexford. A substantial yearly income when she reached the age of twenty-one. A dowry of—ten thousand pounds?

"Are you going up to London for the season, Winifred?"

"Oh, yes," she blurted, staring down at her feet. "Mama will open the house next week. Number twenty-four Cadogan Square." She looked up at him, and there was a wistful look in her eyes. "That isn't very far from the Guards' barracks, is it?"

"No. And it's just a short walk from my flat on Lower Belgrave Street."

He detected a sudden change in her breathing. The exertion of the dance? Hardly, she was barely shuffling her feet across the floor. A faint line of perspiration had formed on her upper lip.

"Perhaps . . ." she said hesitantly, "perhaps . . . you could attend one of our . . . entertainments. That is . . . if . . . if your social schedule isn't completely filled."

"Why, no, it isn't. I'm quite flexible this season. Quite flexible indeed."

Her hand tightened on his arm. "My debut ball is on the twenty-second of next month. Alexandra will be there, of course . . . and Charles . . . and I know that Mama would be pleased if you could come, also. Do you think that you could?" she added anxiously.

He appeared to think about it. "Why, I believe so, yes. You can tell your mother that I'd be honored to receive an invitation."

She smiled brightly and her dancing improved to a remarkable degree.

Passing them, Lydia caught part of the exchange and the smile and decided that Fenton was toying with Winifred. The Fenton charm. Was it just for her benefit, Lydia wondered, or did he have a serious motive in mind? Winifred Sutton was rich, as Fenton well knew. Rich and dowdy, with a good deal of poundage and not an ounce of chic. No one knew that more than her mother and father. A dashing, handsome man like Captain Fenton Wood-Lacy, son of the late Sir Harold, nephew of Major General Sir Julian Wood-Lacy, would hardly be ignored if he asked permission to call on their daughter. Would he do that? He was smiling at her and Winifred was smiling back. Lydia looked away.

Charles bent closer to her. "Let's dance out onto the terrace."

"Oh," she said, forcing her attention back to him, "if you wish."

They stopped dancing as soon as they had tangoed out of the music room. Taking Lydia by the arm, Charles led her across the terrace and down the stone steps into the Italian garden.

"You've been practically ignoring me all evening," he said, his hand pressing into her bare arm. He stopped at a stone bench and pulled her down on the seat beside him. "You look so beautiful tonight, Lydia . . . that dress . . . your hair . . . everything about you is like music . . . poetry. You knew I wanted to talk to you alone before dinner, but you deliberately stayed in . . . in *groups!*"

"It would have been rude not to mingle."

"So much has happened today," he said excitedly, running a hand through his hair. "I told Winnie, in a very nice way, that I could—well, that I could never become *emotionally* involved with her. She took it quite well."

"So I noticed," she said stonily.

"But that doesn't really solve anything, darling. I'm afraid that Father is going to be as intractable as ever as far as we're concerned."

She smoothed her dress over her knees. It was a long evening dress of pale-green silk embroidered with seed pearls, the bodice cut with a discreet plunge.

"Charles, I think that the time has come to be honest with each other. I love you and . . . I *think* you love me."

He stared at her with his mouth open. "You *think*? Good God! You dominate my thoughts day and night. I wake up in cold sweats a dozen times a night because I have nightmares of losing you. There's not another woman on this earth that I would care to even *look* at, and you *think* I love you!" He put his arms around her and pressed her close to him. Her perfume made his head reel. "Oh, Lydia, how can you question my feelings?"

She pulled back from him slightly and placed a slim, cool hand on the side of his face. He was gravely handsome, with a noble, intelligent face that reminded her somehow of the portrait of Shakespeare—the engraving in most editions. He was much younger, but had the same high-domed brow, the soft eyes—an Elizabethan man, courtly and gallantly romantic.

"You had a talk with Winifred, and I'm sure that you were very tactful and considerate."

"And direct," he cut in.

"Yes . . . direct. But tell me, Charles, are you ever that direct with your father regarding us?"

He looked away from her, toward the house, which reared up against the moon-streaked sky; most of the rooms were lighted, and yellow squares of light fell across the dark lawns.

"I . . . I intend to . . . have a long talk with him."

"You might begin by reminding him that we're living in the twentieth century."

He smiled sardonically. "The twentieth century? Father doesn't recognize it socially."

"Perhaps he doesn't, but most people are beginning to. I don't think he would be ostracized in the House of Lords if I married into the family. After all, it would be apparent to everyone that I hadn't *bought* my way into the peerage. Now, if I should marry Lord Peter Manderson, or the Earl of Cromer, that would be quite a different story, wouldn't it? There are a number of impoverished peers in this country, Charles. You'd be utterly amazed at how easy it would be for me to marry one of them if that was all I wanted . . . as your father seems to think."

He was staring at her with a look of dread. "Lydia . . . you . . . you'd never marry a rotter like Cromer. My God . . . I—"

"Of course I wouldn't." She draped her slender white arms about his neck and pulled him gently down to her. Her lips roamed teasingly across his face. "You're my own, sweet darling and I love you very much. I want to stop being *Miss* Foxe and start being *Mrs.* Charles Greville. I want to experience all the joys of marriage . . . and I want to experience them with you . . . no one else."

He held her tightly, kissing her lips, her neck, the soft hollow of her throat. He could feel her firm breasts against his chest.

"Lydia . . . Lydia . . ." he murmured.

She stroked the side of his head and traced a finger tip across his earlobe. He was really such a boy, she was thinking, so torn between duty and desire, so deferential to the Victorian codes of his father. The future Earl of Stanmore pressing trembling kisses on her skin.

"I've thought of a way to approach your father, Charles," she said quietly, stroking his soft hair. "It will require a positive attitude on your part, darling. You'll have to beard the lion in its den . . . but I've given quite a bit of thought to this—"

"Whatever you say, Lydia," he mouthed against the narrow opening of her dress, the deep cleft between her breasts.

"But we must talk it over thoroughly first. Spend the day with me tomorrow. Daddy's still up in London . . . we can be alone . . . have the day to ourselves. . . . Perhaps take a luncheon basket to Leith Woods and talk . . . talk . . . talk . . ."

"Lovely," he murmured, "lovely—" He suddenly stiffened and pulled away from her, his face even more pallid than it had been before. "Oh, God! I can't. . . . I . . . I have to go to Southampton tomorrow and greet some bloody cousin from America. Oh, damn . . . I'm sorry, darling, but . . ."

Her smile was cryptic. "I understand, Charles. There's no need to explain. I quite understand."

IV

Martin Rilke double-checked his tiny cabin to make
sure that he had left nothing behind. He had packed in
a hurry, having spent the entire morning on deck gawking at the coast of England as the S.S. *Laconia* moved
up the channel toward Southampton.

"You won't see a better day than this in a long
while," one of the ship's stewards had told him. "We
'ave quite a bit of mist most days, sir."

Not a speck of mist that morning. Martin had gulped
down his breakfast and had gone on deck to share a
pair of binoculars with a fellow passenger, a Dr. Horner
from Cincinnati, who was on his way to London for a
month's seminar on neurosurgery. Both men had been
fascinated by the vivid greens and whites of the land,
the sparkling blue of the sea. The passage had been
marred by a summer storm on the second day out of
New York, gray seas and a clammy rain staying with
them as far as the coast of Ireland. Of the Emerald Isle
they had seen nothing but great banks of cloud, but the
clouds had parted when they entered the English Channel and there was not so much as a scrap of vapor to
mar the scenery.

" 'This royal throne of kings, this sceptred isle
. . .' " Dr. Horner had recited grandly as he leaned
against the rail, the binoculars cradled in his hands.
"Shakespeare, *Richard the Third*."

"*Second*." Martin had corrected. "*Richard the Second*. 'This precious stone set in the silver sea.' It does
look like a precious stone, doesn't it?"

"Fire opal, Martin. Gosh, I wish my Agnes had been able to make this trip. And she thought *New* England was beautiful when we went up to the Berkshires last summer. Can't hold a candle to the old." He had handed over the glasses. "Take a squint at that little village beneath those cliffs. If that doesn't put the icing on the cake, I don't know what will."

The landscape had at last given way to less pastoral views, reminding them both that England was not all quaint villages and rolling hills. By noon they were steaming up the Solent into the crowded roadstead of Southampton, whose shoreline was cluttered with iron cranes, docks, wharves, and warehouses.

"It's been a pleasure traveling with you, Martin," Dr. Horner had said before going below. "Perhaps we can have lunch one day in London. I'll be at Guy's Hospital . . . the Sir William Osler seminar group."

A seaman with a handcart waited impatiently outside the cabin door. Martin hoped that the good doctor had been better organized than he.

"Okay," Martin said. "You can take the steamer trunk and the suitcase, but leave the leather attaché case."

"Yes, sir," the sailor grunted as he pushed his cart into the cabin.

Martin took one last look around—under the bunk, in the dresser drawers, the closet. He suffered from a vague absentmindedness at times, and it wouldn't have surprised him to have come across a drawer filled with socks and underwear. But everything had been packed. Though rushed, he had been thorough. There was nothing of his left in the cabin except the attaché case, a brown wool jacket, and a Kodak folding camera in a leather carrying case. He put on the jacket and checked his appearance in the mirror. He wasn't all that happy about the fit of the jacket. It had been bought off the rack at Marshall Field and was a bit too tight across the chest. He solved that problem by leaving it unbuttoned.

Well, he thought, as he slung the Kodak over one

shoulder, you look every inch the world traveler. He was, finally and irrevocably, a long way from Chicago.

Jaimie Ross managed to find a parking space for the big Lanchester touring car, but they were a good distance from the Cunard dock.

"Can't you get a bit closer, Ross?" Charles asked.

"Afraid not, sir. Take us an hour to crawl through that mess."

The mess he referred to was a nearly solid line of cars, lorries, and taxicabs jamming the narrow approaches to the Cunard and White Star Line piers.

"Looks like three big ships came in at once this afternoon, sir," Ross said as he slipped his driving goggles from his face.

"So it seems," Charles said, suppressing an urge to swear. He picked up his straw boater from the seat and placed it squarely on his head.

Roger Wood-Lacy did the same. The hats of both men bore the Cambridge colors on a silk band around the crown. "Nothing for it, old boy, but to plod resolutely ahead."

"I hope we can snare a porter, Ross."

"I'm sure we can, sir," the chauffeur replied as he got out of the car and hurried to open the passenger doors.

"A thought just struck me," Roger said as they walked away from the car, the nattily uniformed Ross keeping a respectful six paces behind them. "How do we go about finding the chap? Do you have any idea what he looks like?"

"Haven't a clue. My age . . . a bit Germanic, I expect. I suppose we shall have to have him paged."

Charles glared balefully ahead. The street was narrow, dingy, lined with small shops and eating places. The fumes from the backed-up vehicles poisoned the air. He was in a bitter mood; the thought of what he would have been doing at this moment galled him. But for Martin Rilke's inopportune arrival, he would have been resting his back against an oak tree in the cool glades of Leith Woods while Lydia, her body uncorseted beneath a light summer dress, served him watercress and ham sandwiches from a wicker basket. Damn!

Both young men found the jumble of large wooden structures along the wharf bewildering. Beyond the roofs of the buildings they could see the tall funnels of the *Laconia,* wisps of smoke still trailing after them. Ross stepped forward and suggested that they head for an enormous, open-sided structure which bore a sign marked BAGGAGE DISPERSAL—CUNARD LINE. Hundreds of people could be seen inside milling about under twenty-six large metal shingles which dangled from the roof beams and had the letters of the alphabet painted on them. A regiment of stevedores in blue coveralls trundled carts filled with luggage into the building from the ship.

"Good thinking, Ross," Charles said. "The chap's bound to be under the 'R' sign sooner or later."

There were a great many people under the "R" sign, roaming through canyons of steamer trunks and stacked suitcases. Several officious-looking men representing various tour organizations walked about calling for their groups to stay together.

"Raymond Whitcomb people over here, please!"

"Will all passengers on Cook tour number seven please wait at the customs shed. Will all passengers . . ."

"Is that him, do you suppose?" Roger asked, pointing discreetly down one of the aisles of baggage.

Charles contemplated the man Roger had pointed out, seeking a family resemblance. He saw a man in his early twenties, of medium height and stocky build, blond-haired and square-jawed. His nose was long and high bridged, the eyes blue and merry. Very much a masculine version of his mother's face. And he certainly had the Rilke mouth: wide, full-lipped, and quick to smile—as it was smiling now in his direction, a warm, faintly lopsided grin.

"Say," the man called out, "you wouldn't happen to be Charles Greville, would you?"

"Why, yes, I am," Charles said, taken slightly aback. He hadn't expected to find him so quickly.

Martin came toward him with his right hand thrust forward. "Don't ask me how I knew," he said, grinning more broadly. "I guess you just look like I thought you'd look." He took hold of his cousin's hand and pumped it vigorously. "Gosh, it's nice of you to meet me. Is Aunt Hanna with you?"

"No," Charles said, managing a weak smile—his hand felt as though it had been gripped in a vise. "I came down with my friend." He gestured toward Roger. "Martin . . . Roger Wood-Lacy. Roger . . . my cousin from America, Martin Rilke."

Roger tipped his hat. "How do you do?"

"Very well, thanks," Martin said. "Had a swell trip . . . a bit rough for a few days, but all the passengers were good eggs. Had a really great time."

"Glad to hear it," Roger said. A pleasant-looking fellow, he was thinking, although a bit on the boisterous side—like most Americans. Not one of the millionaire Rilkes, he remembered Charles remarking. Some kind of poor relation. The jacket he was wearing certainly confirmed that fact. "Welcome to Merrie England."

"Thanks." He let go of Charles's hand and stood facing them, arms folded, grinning like a fool. "I just can't believe I'm *here*—that I'm actually on the other side of the Atlantic. Travel is really fantastic when you think about it. Just a week ago I was in Chicago and now I'm in the Old World."

"The *old* world?" Roger repeated dully.

"Takes some getting used to," he went on blithely. "But here I am, Martin Rilke in the flesh . . . or on the hoof, as they say on the South Side. Maybe you guys wouldn't mind helping me find my trunk. It's dark brown leather—a bit scuffed—and it has my name painted on the side."

The two inhabitants of the Old World exchanged bleak glances and then helped Martin in his search. The trunk and suitcase were soon located and Charles had Ross collar a porter, tipped the man half a crown, and the luggage was soon safely strapped to the rack on the back of the Lanchester.

Martin sat between Roger and Charles in the back seat, his attaché case on the floor between his feet, his camera case on his lap.

"Beautiful scenery," Martin said as they left the outskirts of Southampton and drove into the open countryside. "I hope you won't mind if I ask your driver to stop now and then. I'd sure like to take some pictures of this."

Oh, God, Charles groaned silently. He couldn't look at Roger. "Well, it's rather a long drive, and we'd like to get there before dark. But we shall stop soon at Taverhurst for lunch. A quite ancient inn—the Three Talbards—and you can take all the pictures you want."

"That'd be fine. Thanks a lot. Where are we now? The county, I mean."

"Hampshire," Roger said.

"Hampshire? Near Thomas Hardy country . . . well, I'll be darned."

"The edge of it, yes," Charles said. "Dorset more than Hampshire, of course."

Roger arched one eyebrow. "I suppose Hardy's novels are required reading everywhere. *Tess of the D'Urbervilles* and *Jude the Obscure.*"

Martin nodded. "That's right, but to be honest, I never could get into the novels. I prefer Hardy the poet."

"Oh, I say," Roger said with exuberance. "Jolly good for you. I feel the same way about him. Have you read 'Channel Firing' yet?"

"Yes, just before I left home. I especially liked the last stanza, where he talks about Camelot and Stonehenge." He glanced wistfully at the green hills of the South Downs. "I'd sure like to see those places."

"But you shall, old boy," Roger cried. "We'll see to that, won't we, Charles? Oh, I say, this is absolutely marvelous. Think of old Hardy's poems being read in *Chicago*!"

Their accents and mannerisms began to grate on Martin's nerves a little. They seemed so affected, like certain theatrical people he had known. But unlike actors, Charles and Roger were not trying to be something they were not. They were, in the slang of the city room, "genuine articles." He knew enough about England to recognize that, and so he did not inwardly sneer at their way of speaking, their attitudes or their posturings. They did everything and said everything in a manner designed, consciously or unconsciously, to set them apart. It was something they had been born to practice, a manner carefully nurtured by their parents, steadily built upon at Eton, and then honed to a silver perfection at Cambridge. They were, by every gesture, every nuance of speech, English gentlemen. They could have been set down in rags in the middle of the Arabian desert, and that fact would have been apparent to the lowliest bedouin, just as it was apparent to the chauffeur, the porter at the docks, and the young woman who waited upon them at the Three Talbards inn in the village of Taverhurst. Driver, porter, and barmaid treated these two young men without the slightest sign of servility, but with a natural deference. This he knew was what the English called "class," the lower class recognizing and accepting without resentment the superiority of the upper class. It was not an exportable commodity, like English woolens, although a great many rich Americans had tried to import it. He thought of his uncle Paul and aunt Jessica Rilke in Chicago, their huge palace of a house—referred to as the North Side horror by many of Chicago's younger architects—staffed with footmen in knee breeches, butlers, and grooms. A façade of upper-class splendor, no more than that. The servants needed the money they were paid, but they had no ingrained respect for their master and mistress. None at all. They felt degraded by their costumes and saw the difference between themselves and the Rilkes not in terms of "class," but in terms of money. Paul Rilke owned breweries, a brokerage house, real estate in the Loop, iron foundries in Gary, Indiana, Toledo, and Cleveland, and held half ownership in a baseball team of the American League. That made him rich, even powerful, but did not insure by right of heritage or custom that a porter would tip his cap to him and say sir.

"Here you are, sirs," the barmaid said as she approached their table with a loaded tray. "All piping hot."

"And very good it looks, too," Roger said, rubbing his hands. "I tell you, Rilke, it's steak and kidney—in pudding or pie—that is the true secret of British fortitude."

"Has my man been taken care of?" Charles asked.

"Oh, yes, sir," the barmaid said. "He's out back, sir."

She placed the steaming beef and kidney pie on the table along with mugs of dark brown ale, curtsied, and departed.

"I understand you work on a newspaper, Rilke," Roger said after a few minutes of silent eating.

"That's right—the Chicago *Express*. I joined the paper when I left college last June."

"Where'd you go?" Charles asked. "Yale, I suppose."

"No. University of Chicago."

"Thank heaven for that. We had our fill of Yale men when cousin Karl was over here."

Martin laughed. "Yeah, I know what you mean. We have a saying in the States—you can always tell a Yale man, but you can't tell him much."

"Oh, I say," Roger chuckled, "that's rather good. I must remember that."

"Anyway," Martin said, "I joined the paper hoping

to become a reporter—on the police beat. You see, I'd like to become a novelist, and I thought a year or two of seeing the seamier side of life would be a big help. That's how Theodore Dreiser started . . . and Frank Norris and . . . oh, a lot of good writers. But they stuck me in a little office of my own and have me writing book reviews and theater reviews. I'm getting sick of that and may quit when I get back unless they give me a more challenging job."

"Jolly good for you," Charles said. "There's nothing worse than being stuck in something you don't like."

"Well, I liked it okay at first, but I'm not going to learn very much about life reviewing the novels of Gene Stratton-Porter or Harold Bell Wright."

He wondered if he should mention that he had the first sixty pages of a novel in progress with him—a saga of Chicago, men struggling to break the power of the street railway barons. The manuscript was in his attaché case, but he decided against it. He was apprehensive about the direction the book was taking. It was—although he hated to admit it even to himself—too imitative of the "class struggle" novels of others. And besides, looking at the two faultlessly dressed men, he doubted whether they would have the slightest empathy for the problems of poor Chicago streetcar motormen.

"What are your plans, Martin?" Charles asked.

"Well, let's see. . . . Ten days here in England, then I go to Paris . . . Berlin . . . Zurich . . . Milan . . . Rome. . . . Then home on the Red Star liner *Majestic*, from Naples. Six weeks in all. Not exactly the grand tour, but the limit I could afford."

"We may go to Greece in July," Roger said. "Pity you couldn't hop over for a week or two and join us. But you must at least make a point of seeing Perugia and the Abruzzi. That's the true Italy, Rilke, the true Italy."

They arrived at Abingdon Pryory in time for tea, which was being served on the terrace. It was a hectic moment for both Martin and Hanna, he trying to remember the names of the people he was introduced to, and she trying to greet him in a proper "auntly" manner while not neglecting her guests. Two of the guests were leaving for London—a lady somebody or other and her daughter, a Winifred something—and their departure added to the confusion.

"We shall have a long talk later, Martin," Hanna whispered, giving his arm a little squeeze. "I'm sure you'd like to freshen up before dinner. I'll have one of the servants show you to your room. And it *is* your room, Martin, to stay in as long as you wish."

He blurted his thanks to her and then excused himself to the dozen or so people whom his aunt had invited for tea. "My fellow members in the Abingdon Garden Club," Hanna had explained to her nephew before introducing him to them. They had seemed pleasant enough people, but they had studied him with unabashed curiosity, as though he were some rare breed of plant that was entirely foreign to them. He was grateful when a footman arrived and ushered him into the house.

His trunk and suitcase were in his room, looking shabby against the pristine furnishings, but he only had eyes for the bed and flopped wearily onto it. He wondered what time they served dinner and whether he could take a nap for an hour or two. He had just closed his eyes when someone coughed to draw his attention. A middle-aged man wearing a black linen jacket and gray striped trousers stood just inside the room, one hand on the handle of the door.

"Yes?" Martin said, raising himself on his elbows.

"Beg pardon, sir," the man said. "I'm Eagles, your valet. If I may have the trunk keys, sir, I shall unpack and give your clothing a press-up."

He wanted to tell the man not to bother, but his aunt had obviously ordered the valet to come and she might feel offended if he told him to go away. He got off the bed and searched his pockets for the small flat keys.

"Here you are," he said, handing them over.

"Thank you, sir. Shan't take but a moment. Travel is terrible hard on clothing, sir."

"Yes," he said lamely. "I guess it is."

"Oh, terrible hard, especially a sea voyage, sir. The salt air sets the creases."

It was embarrassing to Martin to watch the man go through his luggage, like standing by and watching a total stranger sort through his dirty laundry, piece by piece. And that was what most of his suitcases seemed to contain: soiled shirts, underwear, pajamas, and socks. The valet did not actually cluck his tongue, but his lips remained pursed as he sorted out the dirty clothes and removed wrinkled suits and jackets from the steamer trunk. It was obvious even to Martin that everything needed a good "press-up," but the valet singled out one article of clothing for immediate attention as he held up a particularly wrinkled tuxedo.

"I shall give this a sponge and press immediately, sir. Dinner is always black tie—at least."

The "at least" had an ominous ring. He didn't own tails. The tuxedo was his only article of formal wear, and it was nearly two years old, bought for a fraternity dinner in his senior year and not worn since. It would be tight, but maybe a sponge and press would stretch it a little.

"Thank you . . . Eagles?"

"Eagles, yes, sir. I shall get right on to this, sir, and have the rest of your clothing back in the morning."

After the valet had gone, Martin sat on the edge of the bed and debated whether to flop back and go to sleep or take a hot shower. A shower sounded good, but it was obvious that the room didn't contain a bathroom. He was puzzling over that dilemma when there came a gentle knock on the door.

"Come in," he called out.

The door opened and a slender dark-haired girl in a maid's uniform came into the room, bearing a large bouquet of flowers in a glass vase. She seemed to shrink into the room like a scared doe.

"Hi," Martin said cheerfully. "Who sent the flowers?"

The girl mumbled something inaudible and set the vase down on a table next to the windows. She barely glanced at Martin before turning to go.

Martin stood up and blocked her exit to the door. "Wait a minute . . . maybe you can help me."

"Help you, sir?" the girl whispered, almost shrinking away from him.

"Well . . . I'd like to take a shower. Where's the bathroom?"

"The bath, sir . . . or the WC?"

He wasn't sure for a moment what she meant by WC. Then he recalled all the tales he had heard about primitive British plumbing facilities. An English mansion might have thirty bedrooms but only two baths and a couple of water closets, almost as an afterthought. There would be, he felt certain without taking the trouble to look because he'd be damned if he'd use it, a chamber pot under the bed.

"Well," he said, "both, I guess."

"Yes, sir," the girl said, looking past him toward the door. "The WC is the last door at the end of the corridor, sir, and the bath is the third door to your left—no, to your *right* as you leave the room, sir."

She was a daisy of a girl, Martin was thinking as he looked at her. Seventeen or eighteen. Skin like the proverbial peaches and cream and eyes that were almost violet, with the thickest and longest lashes he had ever seen.

"My name's Martin," he said impulsively. "Martin Rilke. What's yours?"

"Ivy, sir."

"Ivy what?"

"Thaxton, sir."

"Thaxton." He repeated the name slowly, savoring it. "*Thaxton.* That's really a good *English* name, isn't it?"

She was looking squarely at him for the first time, and a smile appeared to be lingering just below the surface of her face.

"Yes, sir . . . I suppose."

"I guess that's because it rhymes with *Saxon*."

"It does . . . yes." The smile came, faint, curious. "You're from America, aren't you?"

"That's right. Chicago."

She nodded. "Chicago, the state of Illinois . . . situated on Lake Michigan . . . Railroads . . . stockyards . . ."

"Say, you've really done your homework, haven't you?"

"My what?"

"You know . . . study. You seem to know a lot about Chicago."

"I was very good at geography, sir . . . at school. It . . . it was my favorite subject. . . . That and arithmetic."

"Arithmetic? You're the first good-looking girl I've ever met who liked arithmetic."

A bright crimson glow appeared suddenly on her cheeks. Lowering her eyes, she started past him toward the door.

"If you need anything, sir, just ring the bell. . . . The pull's on the wall, sir."

"Hey, wait a second." But she was gone, and he could hear her footsteps going rapidly off down the hall.

The bathroom was large, its walls and floor covered with tiny white tiles. There was nothing in the room but a mammoth cast-iron porcelain-enameled tub and an oak cabinet containing fresh soap and extra towels. There was no shower. The hot water came in fits and starts, rattling the pipes and belching occasional puffs of steam, but eventually the water rose in the tub and Martin sank gratefully into its warmth. Odd, he thought as he soaped himself and lathered his hair. The room was totally out of proportion to its use. Ten bathtubs could have been placed in the room along with half a dozen stall showers. On the other hand, the WC had been no larger than a closet, a dark, evil little place to get out of as quickly as nature would permit. The bathroom had four wide windows along one wall with a view of trees and distant hills. The WC had only one tiny window near the ceiling, which had emitted the palest shaft of light—like the window in a dungeon far above the prisoner's reach. Odd. Well, the English were an odd race. No question about that. Everyone on the paper had warned him about what to expect—although only Harrington Comstock Briggs, the managing editor, had ever been to England, and that had been during the Boer War. "Primitive." That had been the most common word bandied about. "A cultured but primitive race." Trying to pin people down as to their interpretation of the word "primitive" had led to little or no elucidation. To Briggs, primitive had meant warm beer and boiled food. To others it had meant king worship, the class system, and the bullheaded preference for cricket, when it was obvious to anyone with even a grain of sense that baseball was a better game. So far, the only area of criticism he could find was in their plumbing.

The tuxedo was back, hanging from a peg on the closet door when he got back to his room. Its appearance had been bettered, but not by much. Martin eyed it dubiously and prayed that he could get into it without popping any buttons. He dressed gingerly, but, Glory be, the suit fitted quite well. He was struggling with a black tie when there came a tap on the door. It was one of the liveried footmen informing him that whiskey would be served in the library at six-thirty.

Lord Stanmore set down his glass of whiskey and soda and walked toward the door as Martin entered the room.

"My dear fellow," he said, advancing with hand outstretched in greeting. "I'm delighted to meet you. Pity we've never met before this, but your aunt talks of you often."

Martin could only assume that the tall ruddy-faced man with the iron-gray hair advancing on him was his uncle. He had never seen a photograph of him. How did he greet him? Uncle Tony sounded too familiar, your lordship too formal.

"How do you do, sir?" he said, shaking the man's hand. The grip was strong, friendly.

"Come," he said, placing an arm about Martin's shoulders. "You know my son and his friend, Roger. . . . Let me introduce you to the others." He steered his nephew toward a small group of men standing at the far end of the room with glasses in their hands. Charles and Roger were among them. Their dinner jackets, Martin noted with a touch of envy, were faultless—as was the jacket of every other man in the room.

"Gentlemen, my nephew from America, Martin Rilke. Martin, may I introduce Mr. John Blakewell, Master of the Doncaster Hunt . . . Major Tim Lockwood . . . retired, I'm afraid . . . a great loss to king and country . . . Sir Percy Smythe . . . finest barrister and the best equestrian in the county. . . . And Captain Fenton Wood-Lacy."

Martin shook hands and greetings were exchanged. Then Charles Greville put a drink in his hand, and he was on his own, the earl rejoining an interrupted discussion about horses with Blakewell, Major Lockwood, and the barrister.

"Well, Martin," Charles said, "did Eagles look after you all right?"

"Yes . . . thank you."

"By far the best valet I've ever had. Just take his word on all sartorial matters and you won't go wrong."

"I'll remember that," he said, thinking of his pile of laundry.

Roger sipped a ginger beer and pointed at the towering shelves of books that lined two walls of the room.

"As a budding novelist, I'm sure you find this father

interesting." He bent closer. "Though I doubt that a tenth of them have been read. Charles is the only reader in the family, and he keeps his books quite separate. You won't find much in this room written after eighteen eighty."

Charles laughed. Some sort of private joke, Martin supposed.

"So you're from America," Fenton said.

"That's right, Chicago."

"Ah, Chicago. And how do you like England so far?"

"Very much. Beautiful country."

"And by far the best time of year to see it. Planning on playing the tourist?"

"Yes . . . I suppose so."

"Then you must see the lake district. . . . Stratford, of course . . . Bath . . . the Chilterns."

"I'm sure he knows where to go, Fenton," Roger said.

"Just thought I'd be helpful. If you care to see the changing of the guard, I'll get you a first-rate view."

"Are you a captain in the army?"

"Yes. Coldstream Guards."

"That must be exciting."

Fenton took a long pull on his Scotch before answering.

"Well, if you want to know the truth, it's deadly dull most of the time. The only excitement is when we're off duty. London is not without its perils."

"Women and cards," Roger said.

"Yes," Fenton said. "Quite so. They've cut more than one promising fellow down in his prime."

Martin caught the twinkle in the tall hawk-faced man's eyes and they both grinned.

"We have those kinds of perils in Chicago, too. But getting back to the army, don't you serve a good deal of time in India?"

"No such luck. The Guards don't leave the country without the king's permission. We're his household troops, and he's not about to squander us on the Northwest Frontier keeping the wild and wily Afghan in line."

"Saving you lads for the big one," Roger said.

Fenton nodded. "Right you are. The next Hundred Years' War."

After dinner, Martin played one game of pocket billiards with Fenton and then excused himself and went up to his room. The cover had been removed from the bed and the sheets neatly turned down. His last clean pair of pajamas had been laid across a chair along with his robe and carpet slippers. The quiet efficiency of the house impressed him. All of the servants moved about without, at least apparently, anyone telling them what to do. He had seen quite a few maids during the course of the evening, but the pretty Ivy Thaxton had not been one of them. Had she turned down his bed? he wondered. He hoped that she had, not knowing why he hoped so.

There was a good bedside lamp, and he sat in bed and placed his leather attaché case beside him, opening it and rummaging through it for one of the new notebooks he had brought along. The first section of the novel-in-progress lay at the bottom of the case—like a flat corpse in a flat coffin, he thought ruefully. *City of the Broad Shoulders*. He didn't even like the title anymore.

"Write out of your own personal experiences of life."

Theodore Dreiser had told him that—and all the other memebers of the Pen and Quill Club at the university. That had been during the fall term, 1912, and Dreiser had been the guest speaker. The big slow-speaking gloomy-faced man had told of the difficulties he had faced in the publication of *Sister Carrie* and *Jennie Gerhardt*, and had spoken to them about the need for truth in writing—honesty and realism. They had spoken afterward in German, their common heritage as German-Americans creating an instant bond, although their childhoods and upbringing had been poles apart. It

had been Dreiser who had advised him to work on a
newspaper so as to see life as it truly was—the raw,
hard, often ugly side of the human condition—and it
had been Dreiser who had told him to write down his
thoughts and observations every day and to keep them
for reference later. He had followed the suggestion,
keeping a free-flowing sketchbook written in Pitman
shorthand.

He took a notebook and a fountain pen from the case
and then placed the case across his legs to serve as a
desk. Opening the shorthand notebook to the first page,
he began to write.

Friday night, June 12, 1914
Observations and Reflections. Here I sit, feelin
like every one's country cousin come to stay with
rich relatives. The country mouse and the city
mouse fable. A paradox there as I come from Chicago—which is about as big a town as you can
find—and the cousins come from Abingdon, Surrey, which is about as hick a place as you'll find
anywhere. But, oh, Lord, do they ooze sophistica-
tion! Debonair. What an overworked word that
was during my last year in school. Any guy who
smoked Murads was debonair—or wore a wrist
watch, or took a girl up to the Loop in a taxicab.
Well, we never really understood the meaning of
that word. If the fellows in the frat house want to
know what debonair means, they should watch
Captain Fenton Wood-Lacy for about ten minutes
and then crawl off somewhere and write UN-
COUTH across their foreheads.

I feel depressed—by my clothes. I caught my
uncle— No, I shall clarify my thoughts on that
subject first. The Earl of Stanmore is not my uncle. He is the man my aunt married. An uncle
should have at least some common ground to share
with his nephew. Uncle Paul and I have little in
common, but we can at least get into a roaring ar-

gument on the subject of Cubs versus White Sox.
Returning to the matter of clothing. I could see the
earl glancing with definite disapproval at my dinner jacket at least five times during the course of
the evening. This was true also of my cousin
Charles and Captain Wood-Lacy. Roger Wood-
Lacy does not appear to share the others' fixation
about clothes. He looked a bit rumpled himself,
but then he appears to go out of his way to "play
the poet." Have not read any of his verses, but,
judging by the number of Greek and Latin phrases
he drops like pearls, I imagine he is not a budding
Carl Sandburg or Vachel Lindsay.

House is magnificent. A mixture of architectural
types: Tudor, Queen Anne, Georgian, and Victorian. But there is a unifying cohesion to the style,
the entire façade having been rebuilt, or recon-
structed, by the Wood-Lacys' father, a prominent
architect now dead. Charles told me something
about the house's history. The Normans built a
priory here in the twelfth century, and it was written into the Doomsday Book as pryory, with a
"y" instead of an "i." The structure was torn
down in the fourteenth century, and the Duke of
Abingdon built a manor house here and retained
the name, poor spelling and all. The dukes of
Abingdon, a family named de Guise, died out during the War of the Roses, and the property was
bought by the first of the Grevilles during the reign
of Henry VII. The Grevilles had been firm back-
ers of the Tudor cause and were given knighthoods
and land, but the first earl was not created until
1660 at the restoration of the monarchy, the Grevilles having weathered the political turmoils of the
struggle between king and parliament. The first
earl had been a Greville who had hitched his star
to the king and had gone into exile with the future
Charles II. They are a landowing family that has
always been blessed with sons. Country gentry.

One earl had fought with the Duke of Marlborough and lost an arm at the battle of Blenheim, but, from what I can gather, soldiering has never been a family tradition as it is in some great English families.

The earl is a political conservative, but not rabidly so. He had some good things to say about the prime minister, Mr. Asquith, but his bête noire is Lloyd George, a Welshman who used to be a solicitor—lawyer. Lloyd George is chancellor of the exchequer, and the earl blames the man for the rise in taxes and for pressuring the prime minister into taking an inflexible stand on the question of home rule for Ireland. The Irish question did not come up at dinner—no politics are discussed until the ladies have left the room—but it was woven into the general conversation when port and cigars were passed around after the women had left. I say woven, because politics takes a decided back seat to talk about the coming hunting season and horse riding in all of its phases—point to point, jumping, dressage. I was asked if I rode and I said yes. Not a total lie because I have been on a horse a few times, not enjoying the experience any more than the poor animal beneath me.

Hanna has three children. William—named after my father—is sixteen and will be home from Eton for the summer holidays any day now. Charles is my age. He seems like a nice enough sort of guy but vaguely indecisive about things. I have no idea what he wants to do in life, but I gather that that isn't terribly important to him or to his parents. Young men of his class—he will inherit the title one day—are not expected to do anything except ride a horse and look after the lands and the tenantry. A friend of Charles from Cambridge, the son of a lord somebody or other, had shocked his friends by "going into trade." He had taken a job with a company that makes automobile engines. I gathered by the way they talked about him that he had committed some kind of sin against the peerage. Peers, or the sons of peers, may serve on the board of directors of business concerns, but they don't get involved in the day-to-day grind of making or selling the product. This class structure is arcane, but I shall fathom it out in time. A million and one taboos. Alexandra is eighteen and just about the prettiest girl I've ever seen in my life. Honey blonde. Blue eyes. Angelic face. Not too much behind it, I'm afraid. The kind of girl who has no room in her head for anything but boys, clothes, parties, and sugar-whipped dreams of perpetual happiness.

Aunt Hanna. She took me aside after dinner and we walked for a quarter-hour on the terrace. She talked about my father—her beloved Willie—and how much I reminded her of him. Perhaps we were alike when she last saw him. He left home at twenty. She would have been seventeen. She never saw him after that time. In other words, her image of him is vastly different from my own. She referred to him, in rather schoolgirlish French, as *le beau bohème*, as though his act of leaving home and finally being disinherited had been romantic. She should have come to Paris and seen him in his final days, drugged with absinthe, our apartment filled with mad paintings that would never sell. God forgive me, but his death was a blessing. Aunt Hanna feels a certain sense of guilt for not having come to Paris after Father died. She was ill at the time, she says. Perhaps she was, or perhaps she couldn't face seeing her beloved Willie in the awful light of truth. Anyway, she let Uncle Paul pick up the pieces, which is just as well in retrospect. I can't imagine the Earl of Stanmore being overjoyed at taking into his ancestral home the Catholic daughter of a Paris shopkeeper and her eight-year-old son. In all fairness, Aunt Jessie wasn't

that overjoyed either—nor Uncle Paul. But he
bought Mother the house on Roscoe Street and
paid all the bills and gave her a generous allow-
ance and— But why are my thoughts roaming so
far afield tonight?

His eyes began to blur, and he capped the pen and
closed the notebook. He had a pair of glasses in the
case, but he was tired of writing. His heart wasn't in it.
Thinking about the house on Roscoe, only five blocks
from the home of the ever-glorious Cubs, the palace of
Frank Chance, the domain of Frank Schulte, triggered
too many memories. They flooded in upon him and he
shut them out. The novel that Dreiser had advised him
to write was in *that* Chicago, not the Chicago of stock-
yard workers and striking trolley motormen. If he was
serious about becoming a novelist, he must attempt to
weave the tangled threads of his childhood into a cohe-
sive pattern. The plight of Chicago's working poor was
not his element. Neither, of course, was Europe.

He turned off the lamp and sat in the darkness,
watching the window curtains float gently in the night
wind. The silence was almost unnerving. He wasn't used
to it. A big-city boy, born in Paris, raised to manhood
in Chicago. He missed the muted thunder of traffic, the
distant rumble of trains. He felt a pang of homesickness
for Pastor's saloon on Clark Street: the sawdust and the
shots of rye with beer chasers; the pool and the poker
games; the lean, hard-boiled talk of newspapermen.

He got off the bed and placed his attaché case on a
table, then stood in front of the open windows. A long
way from home, but maybe this was the perspective he
needed. Europe was the past, changeless, drowsy, and
content with its old glories, fiercely proud of its ancient
traditions. Nothing stood still in Chicago. The city was
bursting outward and upward. Even the old house on
Roscoe was gone to make way for the new apartment
houses being built on the North Side. Looking out on
the ordered patterns of the garden, he could see the lit-

tle house much more clearly than he could have in the Windy City. He had debated with himself about coming to Europe, blowing the bulk of his savings, putting his job in jeopardy (for there was no guarantee that Harrington Comstock Briggs would take him back after being away for six weeks—the hard-nosed little editor's idea of a vacation for his staff was three days in Waukegan), but he was here and by God he'd make the most of it. He'd let himself drift to Europe's stately music and then go back to the New World's ragtime clear-eyed and refreshed.

"I wrote *Jennie Gerhardt* out of love and pain . . . facing my ghosts," Dreiser had said. It was what he must do. He would scrap *City of the Big Shoulders* and begin another novel, one rooted in his own heritage. He would take his time, plan the book carefully, write it with honesty. The saga of the Rilkes, which was the saga of America over the past half-century—money, power, success and failure. Uncle Paul would be fictionalized in the book, as well as his father, mother, and even Aunt Hanna and the Grevilles. The awesome scope of it stunned him for a moment. Was he up to the challenge? Well, he thought, turning away from the window and getting into bed, he had six weeks in the tranquillity of Europe to think about it, to make notes and plan the outline. He felt both awed and excited and wondered whether he would be able to fall asleep, but the moment he closed his eyes that question was no longer in doubt.

V

Captain Fenton Wood-Lacy walked across a stubbled field with a light fowling piece under his right arm, the gun uncocked and, for that matter, unloaded. He had brought a game bag, which dangled from his left shoulder, but no shells.

"I might try and bag some of those jackdaws," he had told Lord Stanmore after their early morning ride. It was the type of shooting that the earl felt was beneath his dignity as one of the premier grouse hunters in the British Isles, but he did not discourage other men from killing the grain-scavenging birds.

"Try and get a pigeon or two while you're at it."

"I'll try," the captain had said.

He was now within sight of the crows. They were in the same spot as the morning before, wheeling and cawing above the chimney stacks of Burgate House. He wondered if the raucous noise disturbed Lydia's sleep. He walked on slowly, and it was nearly nine o'clock when he reached the edge of the formal gardens that were spread out on both sides of the house like pruned wings. A gate to the east gardens was open, and he sauntered through, leaving the gun and the game bag on a carved stone seat. He followed a path that meandered through groves of yew and willow to the terrace that encircled the house in a broad stone ring. A maid washing an upstairs window waved at him and he waved back. The servants at Burgate House reflected their master. They were all Londoners, as cheery and cheeky as sparrows.

As he approached the tall bow windows of the morning room, he could see Lydia inside, just as he had hoped, seated at a table, having her morning coffee. She was wearing a pale yellow peignoir and her hair hung loosely to her shoulders. He tapped gently on the glass, and she looked up, first with a frown, then with a bemused smile. He waited patiently until she got up from the table and opened a side window.

"Good morning," he said.

"What on earth are you doing here? Don't they serve breakfast at the Grevilles'?"

"They do, but the company can't compare to this place. May I come in?"

"Through the front door or through the window?"

"Which would you prefer?"

She stepped back. "The window, by all means. But take care Harker doesn't mistake you for a burglar and put buckshot in your backside."

"I'll take the chance." The casement window was narrow, but he managed to squeeze through after stepping up on a ledge. "*Voilà!*" he cried, stumbling into the room. "Amazing the skills one learns in the Guards."

She returned to her coffee, and he could tell that she was not overjoyed to see him. She would be polite, of course. Lydia was always polite, even when she was on the verge of being her most shrewish.

"Well, now," he said, straddling a chair and folding his arms along the back of it. "I just happened to be passing by—"

"Please, Fenton, don't be any more ridiculous than you are already. Want some coffee?"

"Wouldn't mind."

Her foot sought the buzzer bell under the table. "Jenny baked a seed cake. You can have a slice." She sipped her coffee without looking at him. "The Rilke cousin get in all right?"

"Yes. Pleasant chap. Open faced and honest . . . hardly your type."

She finished her coffee and set the cup down with

great delicacy, as though it might shatter if she did not.

"That was a crude remark, Fenton. Quite beneath you."

"I feel a bit crude this morning, to tell you the truth. Had a rotten sleep. By the way, Charles telephoned you at least five times last night that I know of. He kept ducking out to the hall while we were playing snooker. Were you out?"

"No. I didn't wish to be disturbed."

"Well, you certainly disturbed *him*. I think you'll be getting quite a few more calls today. Going to speak to him?"

"Does it matter to you?"

He shrugged. "Yes and no. Is Archie here?"

"You do jump around, don't you? What's Daddy got to do with it?"

"I wanted to tell him that I'm serious about joining the old firm. I sat up most of the night, if you want to know the truth . . . writing my resignation-of-commission letter." She was looking at him now, and he smiled into her narrowed, questioning eyes. "It's a great deal easier getting out of the Guards than getting in. It took Uncle Julian at least six letters to get me posted from Sandhurst . . . and God alone knows how many lunches at his club for old comrades-in-arms. Must have cost the old boy a tidy sum, depending on his choice of wine, of course."

"Don't be facetious," she hissed. "What the hell are you up to?"

The door opened before he could answer, and the Foxe butler stepped into the room.

"You rang, Miss Lydia?"

"I'm sorry, Spears . . . must have hit the button by mistake."

The butler was a huge florid-faced man who had once been a publican in Cheapside. He had known Lydia from the day of her birth, and Captain Wood-Lacy from the age of nine. His gaze at the moment went over both of them.

"Very good, miss," he intoned and then departed, closing the door silently behind him.

Fenton chuckled and took a tin of cigarettes from the breast pocket of his Norfolk jacket.

"Poor old Spears. He probably thinks I spent the night."

"Stop grinning," she said icily.

The telephone began to ring far down one of the halls, the sound muted by the walls. Fenton lit a cigarette, and Lydia sat motionless, one hand toying with a silver spoon. The ringing stopped, and after a few moments there was a tap on the door and the butler appeared again.

"Mr. Charles Greville on the line, Miss Lydia."

Fenton blew a passable smoke ring. Lydia played with the spoon.

"Thank you, Spears. Tell him . . . tell him that I'm still sleeping."

"Very good, miss."

They sat in silence until the butler's footsteps had receded down the hall, then Fenton stood up and sought out an ashtray.

"When *are* you going to speak to him?"

"I'm going to invite him for dinner," she said. "Not that it's any of your bloody business."

"My, my, aren't we touchy this morning . . . and after I walked all the way over here to ask you to marry me."

He was standing very close to her, reaching across the table to snuff out his cigarette in a crystal plate. Her hand was on the spoon, and he noticed that it trembled slightly.

"Anything the matter with your hearing?"

"No," she said softly. "Please go away, Fenton."

He straightened up and stepped behind her, placing his hands gently on her shoulders.

"We could hop into your spiffy little motor and drive up to Scotland. Get married in Gretna Green. I know an inn overlooking Luce Bay with a magnificent view of the Solway and the deepest, softest feather beds one ever sank into." His fingers slipped through her hair and stroked the back of her neck. "Give up on Charles. Nothing can ever come of it. You know that, if you're honest."

"He'll marry me," she said, so quietly that he could barely hear the words.

"I'm sure he *wants* to, but his nibs has something to say about it and that's an obstacle you'll never get around. And Charles won't be much help. He'll never take any step that isn't *right* and *proper* . . . according to the unwritten code of the Grevilles and the untainted earls of Stanmore. Christ, is marrying into the peerage so damn important to you? Of course, you could always pick up a lord on the cheap . . . pay off his debts and add a title to your name. But you don't want that, do you? People would only make jokes about how one can buy anything at a White Manor Tea Shop these days."

She jerked her head away and turned quickly, lashing out at his face with her right hand. He grabbed her wrist in full swing and pulled her roughly to her feet, knocking the chair over.

"You bastard!" Her lips were taut, bloodless.

He held her wrist tightly and pulled her against him, bent his head, and kissed her mouth. She didn't struggle—he hadn't expected that she would—and he could feel her body relax, submit, bend into him.

"Marry me," he said, pulling gently away. She shook her head, eyes closed, lips parted. "You love me and you damn well know you do. But then love doesn't count, does it? Marriage is too important for that."

She stiffened, as though slapped in the face, and stepped back. Her eyes smoldered, passion and rage mingling.

"You're a fine one to talk. You and Winnie Sutton . . . what a fine exhibition that was. The Fenton Wood-Lacy prelude to seduction." She mimicked his voice: " 'It's so easy to tango . . . let me teach you.' What else do you plan to teach her?"

"I felt sorry for her."

"Yes, that's easy to do. She's such a dowdy, awkward creature. Simply makes your heart bleed to look at her! Don't insult my intelligence. You weigh your charities very carefully. You looked at poor Winnie as just so many pounds sterling to the ounce. Is that how you look at me?"

He smiled sheepishly and rubbed the side of his nose. "Touché. Yes . . . I admit part of that. I feel a bit of a cad about my behavior the other night. I'm a good sportsman. Never shoot ducks on the ground. You're quite right. I'm in a rather nasty spot at the moment, and endearing myself to Winnie and her loving parents would pull me out of it . . . very nicely, too, I might add."

"I'm sure it would, but that would be nothing to how nicely you'd be 'pulled out' if you married *me*. Daddy would be so happy, he'd probably thrust a million pounds into your hot and greedy hand!"

"Hands," he said, holding them up to her, palms out. "Two hands. Drive a spike into each if I'm not speaking the truth. I'm not after Archie's money. If I thought you'd be content living on my twelve-shillings-and-sixpence-a-day pay, less mess fees of course, I'd never ask the old boy for a farthing. But you couldn't live on it, and so I'd be willing to go to work on civvy street. It's as simple as that. I'd make you a damn good husband, in bed and out, and you bloody well know that, too."

She nodded solemnly. "Yes, I know it."

He placed his hands on her hips, feeling the softness of the flesh beneath the silk morning gown.

"We're very much alike. We both want things that are just a shade beyond our grasp. I'm in a regiment that I can't afford, and you want a social standing that all the money in the world won't buy. I have a minor confession to make. I didn't sit up half the night drafting a letter to my colonel. I just couldn't sleep. My mind was a jumble of thoughts. I kept seeing the expression on poor Charles's face after trying to reach you on the telephone. Did you have a tiff with him?"

"No. Nothing like that."

His smile was knowing, a bitter twist of the lips. "Letting him dangle on the hook?"

"That's unkind," she said stiffly.

"Perhaps, but I know the game. He might just become desperate enough to take a positive stand with the lord of the manor—an ultimatum that he may or may not win . . . that *you* may or may not win. You're a reckless gambler, Lydia, and for what? There has to be more to life than living in Abingdon Pryory and becoming a countess one day. And more to life than my strutting around Buckingham Palace in a red coat. Do you remember when you were eight or nine years old and my father was working at the Pryory? You used to follow me up the scaffolding and do every dangerous thing I did. Charles and Roger were afraid, but you weren't. You used to say that you'd follow me anywhere. Well, I wish you'd follow me now."

He was very handsome in a dark, piratical way. A swash-buckling bounder with fine manners. His hands on her hips had a strong surety, as though they had a right to be there, or anywhere else they wanted to rest on her body. It would have been easy to succumb, to rush upstairs and pack a bag, to drive to Scotland and then to follow him anywhere. But it wasn't what she wanted. It wasn't enough.

"I'm sorry, Fenton. I'm not a little girl anymore."

He let go of her hips. Not with any obvious reluctance. He simply allowed his hands to drop away from her body.

"No need to apologize. It was a forlorn hope anyway." He held out his hand. "Still friends?"

Her fingers brushed his. "Always."

"May I leave by the front door? I'm not too adept at going *out* of windows."

"Of course. What are you going to do? About Winnie, I mean."

"Oh," he said vaguely, "I haven't really given it much thought."

"Are you horribly in debt?"

"That's one way of putting it."

"I can give you a check, or would that be too painful to bear right now?"

He bent stiffly from the waist and kissed her on the forehead. "As a matter of fact, it would be. No, I'll land catlike on my feet as usual. I have some plans afoot . . . prospects in mind."

She winced and looked away from him. Gardeners in dark-green smocks could be seen through the windows moving down one of the paths toward the rose trees. They carried spades and hoes over their shoulders and looked like medieval soldiers going off to the wars. She had a vivid mental picture of Fenton and some featureless debutante walking beneath an arch of drawn swords, strewn rose petals at their feet. The image pained her. She looked past the gardens at the distant chimney tops of Abingdon Pryory faintly visible above the green frieze of Leith Woods.

"Let's wish each other good fortune," she said tonelessly. "And much happiness."

Martin slept late and was the last one down for breakfast, but there was plenty of food left and he was amazed by the variety. He heaped his plate with scrambled eggs, broiled kidneys, two slices of a hamlike bacon, grilled tomatoes, and thin fried potatoes. He also had some hot scones and a fruit compote. There was a humidor filled with slim, mild "breakfast" cigars on the table, and he lit one after finishing his meal and strolled contentedly out onto the terrace. He was walking slowly around the house, admiring its architecture and the view of the gardens, when a ground-floor window suddenly opened and Lord Stanmore leaned out.

"Good morning, Martin. Had your breakfast yet?"

"Yes, sir," he said, removing the cigar from his mouth. "More breakfast than I should have eaten."

"Have some coffee with your aunt and me. See that door? Just follow that passage to your right."

The earl was waiting for him in a corridor and led him into a room which contained a rolltop desk, several filing cabinets, a leather sofa, and some chairs. Hanna was seated at the desk, papers strewn in front of her.

"My office," the earl explained. "The heart of Abingdon Pryory."

Hanna glanced up from her work. "Good morning, dear. We were just discussing you." She tapped some papers with a pen. "We have so many functions planned for later this month and all through July. I don't believe you'd find all of them interesting, but I've written your name down on every list containing lots of pretty girls."

"That's swell of you, Aunt Hanna, but—you see, I'm only planning to be in England for two weeks or so and I—well—I was hoping to see as much of the place as possible—travel around—leave my steamer trunk here, if you don't mind, and just pack a suitcase." He felt embarrassed, hoping he wasn't insulting her. Then she smiled, almost with relief, it seemed to him.

"That's a wonderful idea, Martin! Isn't that wonderful, Tony?"

"Yes, it is," the earl agreed, nodding his head vigorously. "When I was your age, I went on a walking tour—all around the isle, from the channel to Thurso Bay in Caithness, then back along the west coast of Scotland, through Wales. . . . Glorious time I had, too. An ash walking stick in my hand, a rucksack on my back. Yes, my boy, a capital idea. The London season may be heaven for the ladies, but it's hell on us men."

"Now, Tony," Hanna chided.

"It's true. A nonstop round of parties and balls. I require two valets in London, and I wear them both out before the season is half over. And I shan't even mention the effect of all that partying on one's liver."

"Oh, Tony!" Hanna laughed. "What a dark picture you paint. But in all seriousness, Martin, I think your plans are splendid. When do you want to get started?"

"The sooner the better. There are so many places I want to go to. I thought I might take the train up to London today and make arrangements with Cook's—you know, join a tour group of some kind. Maybe I could take off Monday or Tuesday."

Lord Stanmore drew a silver watch from his waistcoat and flipped the lid open. "Jolly good way to go about it. Those chaps make all the arrangements in advance for accommodations in decent hotels and inns. Let's see . . . you could catch the eleven-thirty from Godalming. I'll have Ross drive you to the station. Get a taxi at Waterloo to Thomas Cook's. They're in the Strand, I believe."

Hanna sorted her lists back into order with an air of finality. "Of course, I am a bit disappointed. I was looking forward to showing off my handsome nephew. But I will have you meet some of my friends before you travel on to Germany."

"I would like that," Martin said politely. He understood her approval of his plans. Aunt Jessie had found him socially redundant on more than one occasion. It was probably his destiny, he thought ruefully, to go through life messing up people's seating arrangements.

Lord Stanmore clapped him on the back. "And we must get in a day's riding. The only way to truly enjoy the English countryside is from the back of a horse."

The earl walked with him to the main hall, talking ecstatically about the joys of horseback riding, a subject that Martin was incapable of warming up to.

"I shall inform Ross and he'll bring the car around. Do you have any English money?"

"I have a pound or two, sir. I imagine I can cash some traveler's checks at Cook's."

"Yes, they provide that service, but I'd better give you a fiver just to be on the safe side." He was reaching into his jacket for his wallet when he spotted Fenton entering the hall from the direction of the conservatory. "Ah, Fenton, have a good shot?"

Fenton, walking slowly and apparently lost in thought, seemed startled by the question.

"What?"

"The bloody jackdaws. Get any?"

He had left shotgun and game bag on the seat in Lydia's garden. Well, someone would find them. "Bagged a couple."

"Jolly good for you. Young Rilke here is going up to London . . . book a Cook's tour of the British Isles. Sensible way to go if one doesn't know the country."

"Yes . . . I suppose it is. Are you going up this morning?"

"Yes," Martin said.

"I'll go with you, then." He smiled apologetically at Lord Stanmore. "I ran into the telegraph boy as I was crossing Fern Lane. The adjutant needs me back."

"Whatever for?"

"A battalion matter that could easily have waited until next week, but he's a nervous old aunty of a man."

"Damn. Well, at least we got in a couple of decent rides."

He sat in a moody silence half of the way to London. Martin had made an attempt at conversation, but Fenton had responded with a few grunted monosyllables so he gave up trying. He sat opposite the tall officer in a first-class carriage and contented himself with watching the scenery. As the train entered the suburbs of South London, Fenton emitted a deep sigh and reached into his pocket for cigarettes.

"Do you smoke, Rilke?"

"Yes, thanks." He preferred cigars, but he took the offered cigarette, grateful for the breaking of the ice.

"Rather a blistered landscape, isn't it?" Fenton said, gesturing toward the window. "I suppose all England will be like that one day—every scrap of turf paved, every hill crawling with brick villas. I really detest progress."

"So do I—sometimes. It's the same way in Chicago.

New things going up all the time, the city growing like a weed."

"Yes, I dare say. Still, in America there is so much land to expand into. I mean . . . all those prairies and deserts and things." He puffed on his cigarette and eyed Martin narrowly through the smoke. "I really hate to bring this up, Rilke, but that jacket doesn't fit you at all. Who the devil is your tailor?"

"Marshall Field," he blurted.

"The man should be shot. Look here, old chap, I hope you won't take offense, but a gentleman is judged by his clothes and you're too nice a fellow to be snubbed. My tailor is a wizard. He could make you a couple of outfits in no time flat, a few days. He's in Burlington Street, just off Savile Row. What do you say we pop around there after you leave Cook's?"

"Well, I . . ." He felt like ripping the offending jacket from his body and tossing it out of the speeding train.

"And if ready cash is a problem," Fenton went on blithely, "don't give it a thought. Old Purdy wouldn't expect an earl's nephew to fork over vulgar coin. Just pay him when you get around to it. And you'll find him surprisingly reasonable." He sat back with the contented air of a man who had just settled a question once and for all. "Yes, we'll do that straightaway."

Martin squirmed. He felt humiliated, but the man had only been speaking honestly. The jacket was terrible, there was no question about that.

"But . . . don't you have to report to your unit?"

Fenton brushed a fleck of cigarette ash from the knife crease of his gray flannel trousers. "As a matter of fact, I pulled a slight deception on his lordship. There never was a telegram from the adjutant. It was an excuse to get out of staying for the weekend. I hope you won't say anything."

"Of course not."

"Thank you. I just felt like getting back to London for . . . personal reasons."

They took a taxi from Waterloo Station to the Strand. The office of Thomas Cook & Sons was found and arrangements quickly made. Martin would join a tour group leaving Euston Station on Thursday morning for "ten days of wending one's way slowly through the beauties of the British Isles. The pageantry of her great castles . . . the historical significance of Stratford-on-Avon . . . the Roman wall . . . Bath . . . the lake district, where the great poets roamed . . ."

The clerk had spoken with evangelical zeal and had congratulated Martin on his foresight in choosing Cook's. He had then cashed one hundred dollars in traveler's checks for him and handed him a printed sheet detailing the schedule for his trip, British Isles Tour Number 32.

"Rather painless," Fenton remarked as they left. "Though Lord knows what your fellow tourists will be like. One should at least be given a choice of traveling companions."

The two hours spent with Fenton's tailor, the firm of Purdy & Beame, were equally painless. Both Mr. Purdy and Mr. Beame looked on Martin as a challenge to them as makers of fine gentlemen's apparel. They exchanged knowing glances and raised eyebrows as they divested Martin of his clothes, clucking their tongues over the shoddiness of Yankee cloth and workmanship. Martin was so much clay in their capable hands. He ended up purchasing three outfits, which, according to Fenton and the tailor, would see him through the day in impeccable style. They would be ready Wednesday afternoon.

"Two fittings on Tuesday, Mr. Rilke—in the morning and again in the afternoon. It is not customary for Purdy and Beame to work under such pressure of time, but we will be, I can assure you, equal to the task."

Martin was then helped back into his offending garments and that was that.

"A decent bowler and an umbrella with a silk slip-

case and you'll look like the Duke of Norfolk," Fenton
said as they stepped out of the shop. He pointed in the
direction of Old Bond Street. "My hatter's a short walk
away. Come along."

As they turned into Bond Street, Fenton suddenly
stiffened and then faced about to peer intently into a
window displaying pipes and tobacco.

"Christ," he said under his breath. "I hope he didn't
see me."

"Who?" Martin asked, looking around.

"Don't look. Just stand beside me. Perhaps he'll pass
on by."

Martin stared at the racks of pipes, the tins of tobacco, and then he sensed someone approaching and
looked to his left. A young man was coming toward
them, somewhat hesitantly. Martin's first impression
was that it might have been a girl in man's clothing. The
body was slim, almost willowy, and he was more pretty
than handsome. Black curly hair framed a narrow high-
cheekboned face, with skin of a pale olive-ivory complexion. The man's nose was thin but prominent, the
eyes large, oval, and soft brown, like the eyes of a fawn.
But the fawnlike characteristics were negated by the
mouth, a wide slash that seemed to be fixed in a permanent sneer.

"Captain Wood-Lacy, I presume," the man said.
"And companion."

"Why, hello, Golden," Fenton said, doing a poor job
of imitating surprise. "Fancy running into you."

The man's lips curled even tighter in derision.
"Fancy! And on Bond Street to boot. I never knew you
to be taken by pipes."

"I'm not, as a matter of fact, but any port in a
storm."

The man threw his head back and laughed, a rollick-
ing peal of such depth and timbre that it was difficult to
associate it with so delicate a throat.

"Oh, Fenton, I do admire you. You are positively the

most candid man I've ever known. But mind your manners, introduce me."

"Golden . . . Martin Rilke from Chicago. Rilke, Jacob Golden, the Fleet Street gadfly. Rilke is a fellow journalist, by the way."

"Oh?" Golden said, peering at Martin intently. "What paper?"

"Chicago *Express*."

Golden closed his eyes for a second. "*Express* . . . Republican attitudes . . . hostile to President Wilson . . . distrustful of organized labor—"

"Hey," Martin said with a nervous laugh, "lay off. I only write book reviews."

"That's what you should be doing, Golden," Fenton said dryly. "Might keep you out of mischief."

Golden sighed deeply and pulled a long face. "My father feels the same way, I'm afraid. No more reporting on the Ulster farrago or Balkan intrigues. It's nothing but murders and crimes passionels for the immediate future. I'm covering the Goodwin case at the moment . . . you know, the Birchington dentist who drilled his sister-in-law to death because God told him to do it. Very nasty business, but I believe God knew what he was saying. The victim was an absolute horror. Everyone in the family is overjoyed that the biddy is gone. The paper is paying for his defense."

"And if it wasn't," Fenton drawled, "I'm sure you'd be just as enthusiastic over his hanging."

"Yes, I dare say I would." He spread his hands outward in a gesture of helplessness. "But that's the old newspaper game, isn't it? One must cater to the public tastes . . . or even create tastes to cater to." He winked slyly at Martin. "But then I'm sure you know all the devious ramifications of our noble profession. It must be rather pleasant being a soldier. At least one is *told* who to shoot. No inspired judgments in the thin red line."

Fenton faked an exaggerated yawn. "Same old Golden. No wonder your friends duck into shop doorways." He pulled a watch from his waistcoat pocket and glanced at it. "Time for tea. Let's hail a taxi and go to the Marlborough."

"My dear Fenton," Golden said, "they don't like Jews at the Marlborough."

"I know. An odious rule. It should merely be *certain* Jews." He scowled at his watch. "Bother, we're a bit late for tea there anyway. Where do you suggest?"

"A White Manor by all means. The two-shilling de luxe. And speaking of White Manors, have you seen the beautiful Lydia Foxe lately?"

Fenton appeared preoccupied as he scanned the busy street for a vacant taxi.

"No . . . not for some time."

"I saw her in Paris two months ago. At the opera, clinging to the arm of a major in the cuirassiers. She seems to have a penchant for military men."

The captain turned slowly and gazed down into the smaller man's blithely innocent face.

"Why in God's name did I ever befriend you in school, Golden? You are truly the most insufferable—"

The laugh came again, deeper and louder than before. "It was an act of pure Christian charity, old boy. And like any worthwhile Christian act, it needs to be paid for with a modicum of suffering. Ah," he cried, dashing suddenly into the street, "there's one. . . . Taxi! Taxi!"

Martin arrived back at Abingdon Pryory at ten-thirty that night, taking a rattletrap taxi from Godalming station to the house. The butler informed him that his lordship and the countess had retired early, that Master Charles was not at home, and that Mr. Wood-Lacy had also retired for the night.

"But if you care for supper, sir . . ."

"Perhaps a sandwich and a glass of beer, if it's no trouble."

"Not at all, sir."

"In my room, if you don't mind. I'm pretty tired."

"Indeed yes, sir," Mr. Coatsworth said with genuine understanding. "A trip up to London is always most fatiguing."

He wasn't sure if it had been the trip or the company that had been fatiguing. A bewildering day, he decided as he put on his pajamas. A footman brought ham sandwiches and a tankard of pale ale, which Martin wolfed down before getting into bed, placing his attaché case on his knees, and taking from it a notebook, pen, and his eyeglasses.

Saturday night, June 13, 1914

Observations and Reflections. The upper-class Englishman's attitude toward "trade" is an interesting one. Fenton is probably not "upper class," in the strictest meaning of the term, but as an officer in a socially prestigious regiment, he is entitled to all the prejudices of that class. "Trade" is, loosely speaking, the province of purveyor of services or products—haberdashers, wine merchants, boot makers, tailors, etc. Doctors are not in "trade," nor are journalists, the military, professional sporting people, et cetera. Upper-class Englishmen rely on "trade" for their comfort and well-being, but consider it proper form to delay paying their bills for as long as possible. Cash, it seems, is vulgar. After tea, Fenton took me to his hatter, where I was measured for a derby; the hat will be ready Wednesday afternoon. I insisted on paying cash in advance, and both Fenton and the hatter appeared slightly nonplussed.

We had tea at a White Manor on Oxford Street near the Marble Arch. It was a huge multistoried place with several dining rooms, a string orchestra, bakery shop, and Continental delicatessen. The food—small tea sandwiches and a variety of cakes—was both good and inexpensive. The service is first rate: hordes of young women in crisply starched blue uniforms, taking orders and carrying trays, all of them pretty and cheerful. Fenton told me that they are well paid and that they live in hostels owned by the company, are charged very little for their rooms, practically nothing for their meals, the bulk of their wages going into a savings plan. Golden added that this benevolence has resulted in a shortage of maids for the gentry. Girls prefer the short hours and fine working conditions at the White Manors to going into service—like Ivy Thaxton—where they must work long hours and receive practically nothing for their labors. Maids in big houses get one afternoon off a week and are on call twenty-four hours a day. I wonder if Ivy Thaxton has ever heard of the White Manors? Probably must have. Fenton said they are all over England, but not all of them as splendid as the one on Oxford Street. It seems to me that it would be a far better place for a young girl to work. Being a maid in a place like Abington Pryory must be grueling. So many rooms to clean, beds to make, chamber pots to empty. I have a horror of that white ceramic bowl under the bed, but I can readily understand why one would use it, especially in the winter. That little room down the hall is as cold as death, and it's only June! I imagine that if I were living here in December I'd think twice about getting out of a warm bed in the middle of the night and trotting down the hall to that icy cubicle.

Brief impressions. Jacob Golden is twenty-four, about a year younger than Fenton, a year older than me, but wise beyond his years, as the saying goes. From conversation at tea, and from what Fenton told me about him later, I can piece together a sketchy biography of the man. He's the only son of Harry Golden, the great Lord Crewe. Crewe is as well known in Chicago as William Randolph Hearst is in London. Publisher of the London *Daily Post*, largest daily circulation of any newspaper in the world. A rag. Yellow journalism at its most blatant, a paper catering to the lowest common denominator of mass interest—lots of pictures, short texts, stories of murders and other crimes, falls of the mighty from grace, lives and loves of theatrical people and moving-picture performers, scare stories of civil war in Ireland, damnation of the German empire for having the temerity to compete with Britain in the building of a war fleet and the maintaining of colonies. Jingoism and sensationalism in a heady mixture.

Jacob Golden is amused by the paper his father built up from nothing, but I can detect an air of gravity beneath his cynical posturings. The paper, he says, wields a far greater influence on the masses than the Bible. The Gospel according to St. Crewe. Golden sees the world as being divided into two distinct classes, yahoos and nabobs—a few nabobs who rule, millions upon millions of yahoos who do what they're told and believe what they read. He can see nothing wrong in this division, provided all the nabobs are intelligent, compassionate, and enlightened men—which, of course, they are not. The nabobs, he says, are donkeys sprinkled with a few apes. He says all of these outrageous things with a smile; a perverse pixie gleefully watching humanity stream toward the edge of a cliff. Fenton referred to him as an ass several times, and I'm half inclined to second the motion. And yet, I wonder.

Jacob and Fenton went to school together, a well-known preparatory school near London that sends the vast majority of its pupils on to Eton or Harrow. There were only a couple of Jews in the school, and Jacob had a miserable time until Fenton took him under his wing. From what I could gather, Fenton's father had designed the Daily Post Building in Whitefriars Lane off Fleet Street and was a good friend of Jacob's father. Jacob went on to Eton and then to Balliol College, Oxford. Fenton went to Sandhurst and the army, but there has been a tenuous bond between them since their prep-school days.

Jacob was expelled from Balliol and seems proud of the fact. He didn't say why he had been "sent down," but I'm sure the powers at Oxford University didn't lack for reasons. His father gave him a job on the paper as a roving correspondent, and he has been to a great many places. I felt a pang of envy as he talked about the Balkan wars, tramping along with the Servian Army during its thrust across Albania to the Adriatic in 1912. An interesting anecdote, one that illustrates Jacob's theory about the nabobs. It seems that Lord Crewe objected to reportage on the "Servian" Army. He felt that the word sounded too much like "servile," and so he ordered his editors to substitute a *b* for a *v*. So Servia became Serbia overnight, at least to the readers of the *Daily Post*. Nabob power! The changing of a nation's name by the mere stroke of a blue pencil.

Reflections. Jacob Golden is a newspaperman. I work on a newspaper. What a gulf separates our occupations! While I was toiling over a review of Frances Hodgson Burnett's latest novel, Jacob was sending dispatches from Ireland suggesting that Germany was supplying rifles to the Ulster volunteer army. He went a bit too far, I gather, and accused a British general of corresponding with the Germans in order to equip the Protestants with Maxim guns. Lord Crewe wouldn't print that story, and Jacob was brought home to cover local events. Still, even the reporting of murder trials is far and away more exciting and meaningful than anything I have done on a newspaper. Jacob made a suggestion to me. He said that his paper might be interested in half a dozen articles about England as seen through the eyes of a visiting American—"A

Yank's View of Britain," he suggested as a lead
title. Advised me to make the pieces short and laudatory, although a gently chiding humor would be
okay. The paper would pay three to five pounds
per article. That won't pay for my trip, but it will
make a slight dent in the tailor's bill. It will also be
good training. The observation and reporting of
life around me—people, places. . . .

A gentle tapping at the door interrupted his train of
thought. He assumed it was the footman coming back
for the tray and called out for the man to enter. He was
surprised when Charles opened the door and stepped
into the room, dressed in evening clothes and carrying a
bottle of champagne.

"I hope I'm not disturbing you," Charles said.

"No . . . not at all." He capped the pen and closed
the notebook.

"I saw your light as I came up from the garage.
Thought you might enjoy a nightcap." He held up the
bottle. "Found this in the butler's pantry. Still reasonably chilled, and a truly decent year. My father has impeccable taste."

Martin shoved notebook and pen into the attaché
case, got out of bed, and put on his robe. Charles found
two glasses on the dresser, one of which had a toothbrush resting in it.

"Just right for swizzing out the bubbles," Charles remarked as he undid the wire around the cork. There
was a tiny, satisfying pop, and then the pale amber wine
flowed into the water glasses. "Enjoy your trip up to
London?"

"Yes," Martin said, taking one of the glasses. "I'm
going on a Cook's tour of England next week. Leave on
Thursday morning."

"That should be pleasant. You'll probably see a good
deal more of old England than I've ever seen. But that's
always the way, isn't it? The traveler sees more than the
native."

There was only one chair in the room and Charles sat in it. Martin leaned against the bedpost, feeling self-conscious in his bare feet.

"Well, here's how," he said, raising his glass.

"Yes, to your health." Charles sipped the wine, staring moodily into the glass. "Nice and dry, don't you think? One of the few things the French can do well."

It seemed to Martin that something was troubling his cousin and that he had come to the room for more than a friendly nightcap, but what it could be or why he had come was a mystery to him. He endured five minutes of small talk, and then Charles said:

"Odd, come to think of it. Here we are cousins—blood relatives—and yet I know next to nothing about you. Oh, just a few things that Mother has told me."

"I know very little about *you*," Martin said.

"There isn't that much to know. I went to Eton and Cambridge. Would like to be an historian . . . or teach history. I've been to France, Germany, Italy, and Greece. Enjoy good music . . . books . . . used to enjoy hunting. Rather an ordinary, uneventful life."

There was a long pause, and Martin struggled to think of something to say.

"Were you born here?"

"In this house, do you mean? Yes. You were born in Paris. Is that correct?"

"In Montparnasse."

"Is your mother French?"

"Was. She died four years ago."

"I'm sorry. That's my point. I should have known that."

Martin drained his glass, and Charles stood up quickly to refill it.

"I don't know why you should," Martin said, sitting on the edge of the bed. "Your mother only met mine once. And besides, her death wasn't really a family matter."

"The disinheritance, you mean?"

So he knows about that, Martin thought without bitterness. The midnight conversation was becoming curiouser and curiouser.

"Yes . . . the disinheritance. That took place before I was born, so I don't know too much about it. I never knew my grandfather, but I gather he was a tough old bird . . . very old-fashioned and puritanical." He paused to drink some more champagne. Charles was watching him, hanging on to every word with taut-faced concentration. "I guess my father was a rebel. He was the second son, five years younger than Uncle Paul and three years older than Aunt Hanna. Paul was in the family business—half a dozen breweries—but my father didn't want any part of it. He wanted to paint. I guess my grandfather gave him a choice. It was as simple as that. Anyway, when he died, he'd cut my father out of his will. A dollar. I think he left him that much." He felt dispassionate about the whole thing. It was like telling the life story of a total stranger.

Charles wet his lips with champagne. "I wonder what my mother felt about it. She was very fond of your father. At least, I've always had that impression . . . that he was her favorite."

"I think he was, when they were kids. But my father alienated people. He had a talent for that at least."

"Not much of a painter?"

"I couldn't say." Martin shrugged. "He died when I was eight, and I don't remember his work . . . except that it didn't sell. My mother was a modiste, and a good one. That's how we lived. I remember my mother telling me that Aunt Hanna and Uncle Paul used to send Father money from time to time, but he always mailed the checks back—torn into scraps. He cut himself off totally from them . . . getting back at them for being cut off himself, I guess. Although Uncle Paul and your mother had had nothing to do with it. I suppose they gave up trying to help him after a time . . . as did everybody he knew in Paris. He had a terrible reputation, and I don't think anyone was sorry when he died. I'm sure you know your Conrad. I can't read *Heart of*

Darkness without thinking of my old man. Paris was his Congo. It found him out early . . . the way the jungle found out all there was to know about Kurtz. 'It whispered to him things about himself that he did not know' . . . or hadn't known in Chicago. I often wondered if he died like Kurtz, whispering, 'The horror . . . the horror.' " His mouth was dry as stone, and he reached down for the bottle, which was on the floor next to the chair. Charles picked it up and handed it to him. His face was pale, and tiny beads of sweat clung to his wide, smooth brow.

"How did he die?"

Martin took his time answering. He filled his glass and drank half of it.

"He cut his wrists. He spared my mother and me the sight, thank God. It was his most noble act. He did it in the apartment of one of his models in Montmartre. My mother believed he was just trying to scare the woman, but he'd been drinking heavily and I guess he lost his sense of caution. Anyway," he continued in a flat monotone, "he died."

"That's horrible," Charles whispered.

"Yes. A wasted life."

"It seems so cruel to be disinherited for such a trivial thing . . . wanting to be an artist."

"I guess it wasn't a trivial thing to my grandfather. He expected obedience from his children. That was over twenty-five years ago, remember. A different age. And he was very Germanic. Never bothered to learn English properly or to assimilate American customs. I suppose he felt it was his duty as supreme head of the house to punish a prodigal son."

Charles stood up abruptly, as though shaken by what he had heard.

"I'm glad you told me all this. I've always had the feeling that my mother wanted to tell me how her brother died. She started to tell me once. But perhaps she found me unreceptive . . . or the matter was too painful to discuss in any detail."

"Could be," Martin muttered into his glass.

"Anyway, I appreciate your candor." He combed a stray lock of hair from his forehead with stiff fingers and began slowly pacing about the room. "One wonders what effect all that had on her. It must have been a shock to see her favorite brother destroyed by such a harsh, uncompromising directive and be unable to raise a voice in protest or, anyway, be unable to alter the outcome."

"Being disinherited was a lousy break, but that wasn't what destroyed my dad. If he had been a different sort of man—"

"Perhaps, perhaps," Charles cut in, speaking rapidly. "Still, that patriarchal edict was the first blow. If that blow could have been softened . . . If there had been someone in the family willing to take your father's side . . . to arbitrate . . . to conciliate—"

"But there wasn't. Uncle Paul told me quite a lot about my grandfather. His word was law. But that was a long time ago. There's not much point in talking about what could or could not have been done. Or is there? You won't mind if I'm blunt, will you? A little Chicago spade-calling. Is there anything bothering you?"

Charles stood very still, eyes fixed on the windows, where the curtains fluttered in the night wind. Then he returned to the chair and slumped wearily into it.

"I asked a woman to marry me . . . a positive, irrevocable commitment."

"Congratulations. But you don't look very happy about it."

Charles stared down at his hands, folded tightly in his lap. "It's something we both want. Something we've talked over many times. The final decision rested with me . . . not in asking her, but in facing my father squarely and resolutely."

"And did you?"

He looked up, his expression carved into a mask of firm resolution.

"I intend to tell him in a few weeks . . . on my birthday. It seems like the best moment. I'm terribly afraid that he might withhold his blessing. It's not the girl—Father likes her—it's what her father does, and what his political views are, that my father finds totally unacceptable. Having him as an in-law would be a constant source of embarrassment." His resolution appeared to waver and Martin could detect a slight trembling of the lower lip. "I'm certain Father would resign from some of his clubs because of it. What else he might do I . . . I . . ." His voice trailed off into silence.

Martin bent down for the champagne. The bottle was half empty, and he divided the contents between his glass and his cousin's.

"I think I understand what you've been driving at. Are you trying to say that your father might disinherit you? I mean, could something like that happen these days?"

"No, I can't be legally disinherited, but he could turn his back on me, disclaim me as his son. That might sound harsh, but it could happen. There's nothing to prevent him from doing that, except my mother. She's always had a great influence over him and would probably take a firm stand. I think she'd remember your father, how he was cut off from the family and what it did to him—or what she believes it did to him. I'm banking on that."

"Jesus," Martin said softly. He took a swallow of champagne. "Maybe you'd better talk to her first."

"No. She'd just tell me to think it over . . . to wait. She's hoping my feelings for Lydia will undergo a change, or hers for me. That won't happen." He drained his glass and leaned forward. "God, she's lovely. She's leaving for London tomorrow, but when you get back from your trip I want you to meet her. When you do, you'll understand my feelings about her. Lydia Foxe is the most beautiful, most captivating, most exquisite creature that God ever gave the breath of life to."

Martin avoided looking Charles in the eye. He drank his champagne, the wine tasting musty all of a sudden. He was thinking of Jacob Golden and his remark to Fenton about seeing Lydia Foxe in Paris. Could there be two Lydia Foxes? It didn't seem likely.

"I sure hope it all works out for the best."

"I have a strong feeling that it will," Charles said a little too fervently. "Yes, I really believe it will."

He became euphoric and wanted to go downstairs and bring back another bottle of champagne, but Martin talked him out of it and persuaded him to go to bed. He wasn't in any mood for an all-night bull session. After Charles had gone, he turned out the light and flopped wearily into bed, but it was impossible to get to sleep.

"God damn it," he whispered, staring at the ceiling. His father wasn't a ghost that he couldn't face; it was just that he preferred not thinking about him. The image was blurred by time. He thought of him as a tall man who had slipped in and out of the apartment on the rue Dupin like shadow and smoke.

He tossed and turned under the light blanket for a long time and then got out of bed and stood in front of the open window. He gazed down at the gardens, so ordered and geometric, so faultlessly pruned. Their serenity seemed ironic when he thought of his cousin's problems. Perhaps that was symbolic of England. A carefully nurtured façade of grace and tranquillity, behind which emotions seethed as strongly as they did in New York or Chicago. He had been falling into an artful trap. England could do that to visiting Americans. The old stones and the imperial customs tended to overawe Yankee common sense and lull one into a misty shortsightedness. Even the perceptive Henry James had fallen into that trap at least once, writing a book that had been filled with rhapsodic descriptions of buildings and sylvan glades but devoid of people. England was more than Gothic spires and Roman ruins, Tudor castles and Georgian spas; it was a country of people, rich and poor, with all the vices and virtues that human flesh was heir to. He would keep that in mind when he wrote his articles for Jacob Golden's paper. He would be a true reporter and write what he saw and felt and heard, and if the editors of the *Daily Post* didn't like it, that was just too damn bad.

VI

Jaimie Ross was happy to be in London. Every day there helped to brighten his spirits. Strolling up and down the narrow cobblestoned mews behind Stanmore House, he inhaled the aroma of burned petrol wafted by the morning wind from the motor traffic on the Bayswater Road and nearby Oxford Street. That aroma was sweeter to him than any country wind. London was motorcars and the company of his true peers, the men who drove those motorcars and made them run. London was a pub near Paddington station where chauffeurs, garagemen, and mechanics met over a pint or two and talked seriously about magnetos, carburetors, fuel pumps, and horsepower. London was also pretty girls, droves of nursemaids and housemaids, typists, and God knows what else in Hyde Park, Piccadilly, and the Strand. It was heaven for a bloke like him, he was thinking, as he walked up and down, the heels of his boots ringing sharply on the stones. He was wearing a new uniform of dove-gray serge, black boots and leggings, a gray cap with a black leather bill, and tight-fitting black leather gloves. He strutted a little, feeling certain that a maid or two would be peeking through the window curtains of the big house. Up and down he walked, past the old limestone buildings that had once been coach houses but were now garages with living quarters above them for the servants. The rear of Stanmore House rose four stories on the other side of the alleyway, a grim stone block of a building, its marble-columned front facing Park Lane.

One of the garages was open, its wooden doors folded back to reveal the Rolls-Royce parked there. Ross paused for a moment to look at it. A good car. Polished to a rich silver sheen. Fine bit of machinery beneath the bonnet, but it could be better. He had written a letter to the Rolls-Royce company suggesting a method for improving the carburetion system and had posted it that morning in the letter box on Brook Street. He wondered idly if anything would come of it.

"Morning, Ross. Care for a fag?"

He looked away from the car to see one of the elderly footmen coming toward him. The man was in his braces and wore carpet slippers. He took the offered Woodbine, and the footman lit it for him.

"Keepin' banker's hours, aren't you?"

The footman made a sour face. "Didn't get to me bed till after three this mornin'. They had thirty-five people for dinner last night. Nothin' on for tonight, thank the Lord. Goin' to the theater."

"I know," Ross said.

The footman sat down on a stone step and unfolded a newspaper that he had been carrying under his arm. Ross leaned against the edge of the garage door and looked over the man's shoulder.

"What happened at Newmarket yesterday?"

The footman turned the large pages of the newspaper. "Let's see. . . . Ah. Kennymore took the Prince of Wales stake. . . . No surprise there."

"Who took the second race?"

"Sheba . . . Went off at seven to one."

Ross whistled softly through his teeth. "Wish I'd had a quid on her." He leaned closer to see the paper better. "That Jack Johnson. No one's ever going to whip that lad."

"Well, it's for sure Frank Moran was never the one to try, but it says here the darkie was in poor form. He's not what he used to be an' that's for certain."

Ross squinted down at the sporting page through a haze of cigarette smoke. There was nothing much there that interested him. Cricket scores mostly: Winchester over Eton, Navy beating Army at Lords. He hated cricket, a bloody soppy boring game. America's Cup trials at Torbay . . . Shamrock IV wins . . . doubles play at Wimbledon . . . polo at Ranelagh. There would be nothing to interest him until football started. Queens Park Rangers . . . England versus Wales.

"Did you hear about the archduke?" the footman asked, turning the page.

"What archduke?"

"The Austrian one."

"What about him?"

"Got scuppered yesterday. Him and his missus."

Ross removed the cigarette from his mouth and tapped ash on the ground.

"Go on," he said. "Who'd do a thing like that?"

"Anarchists. Tossed a bomb at him. Then shot the poor blighter dead . . . and her, too."

"Get off it," Ross said with a tone of disbelief.

"It's in the paper." The footman turned pages until he found the one with the archduke's photograph on it. "See. Archduke Franz Ferdinand . . . heir to the Austrian throne—and his consort—murdered in Sarajevo. A student's political crime, it says here."

"I can read." He leaned over the man's shoulder. "Where's Sarajevo?"

"Bosnia."

"Never heard of it. One of them queer penny-farthing countries. Couldn't happen here. Too bloody civilized."

"The king's puttin' the court into mourning for eight days."

"Our king? Why? The booger wasn't a relative, was he?"

The footman closed the paper in disgust. "You don't know a bleedin' thing except motorcars . . . and care less. It's just common courtesy, that's all. Just plain common decency. One king to another."

Ross straightened up and walked slowly away.

"Thanks for the fag, mate." He didn't much like the footman—or any of the male staff, for that matter. Not a drop of spirit in any of them. Content. That was their problem. Content to walk around in knee breeches and powdered wigs like a packet of bleedin' Drury Lane fairies. He took a final drag and flipped the cigarette away. It was starting to get hot, the sun bouncing off the walls of the old stable houses, their slate roofs intensifying the rays. The high, tight collar of his jacket was beginning to feel uncomfortable, and his hands felt sweaty in the gloves. Well, what the hell did he expect on the twenty-ninth of June, snowflakes? The church on South Audley Street began to toll the hour of eight.

"Thank God," he muttered as he walked quickly to the open garage and got into the Rolls. Before the bell had finished ringing the hour, he had driven out of the mews and had turned onto Park Lane. Lord Stanmore was just coming out of the front door, preceded by a footman.

"Bloody good timing." He drew the car up to the curb, the footman opened the rear door, and the earl got in.

"Good morning, Ross."

"Good morning, your lordship."

Lord Stanmore sank back against the seat with an audible sigh.

"Ah, a perfect morning, Ross."

"Indeed it is, sir," he said, watching the traffic streaming down from Marble Arch, waiting for his moment to slip the car into it without causing any other driver to brake or sound his Klaxon.

"Too nice a day to waste in the city. Should all be back in Abingdon, eh, Ross? Breathing that fresh country air."

"Indeed we should, sir."

"I have to go to the House, Ross. Shan't be too long, though. Drafting a message of condolence. That beastly assassination of the Austrian archduke."

"I was just now reading about it, m'lord. Told Mr.

Picker that it would never have happened in England, sir."

Lord Stanmore leaned forward to make conversation easier over the hum of the traffic. He was fond of young Ross. A bright, intelligent man. Bit of a diamond in the rough. A good example of what was admirable among the lower classes.

"Quite right, too. Jolly well put. We may have our anarchists in England, but they have a sense of fair play. And shooting the man on a Sunday, too. But the deed was done and that's the end of it. I shall tell you something, Ross, that you won't read in the newspapers. They won't be shedding many tears in Vienna."

"You don't say so, m'lord."

"The fellow was neither liked nor trusted." He was about to add that the archduke's morganatic wife had been déclasée, no better than a housekeeper, but thought better of it. "Well, *de mortuis nil nisi bonum.* One shouldn't speak ill of the dead."

Ross drove the earl to fhe Houses of Parliament and found a parking space in Parliament Square. He spent the next two hours in enjoyable conversation with the other drivers who had parked their cars there, and he told them about the carburetor fuel mixture device he had thought of and of the letter he had written to the Rolls-Royce company. Lord Curzon's chauffeur, a tall, whitehaired man, spoke up:

"I say, Ross. Did you take out a patent?"

"No. Why?"

"Why? To keep anyone from stealing your idea."

Ross winked broadly at the other men. "Well, if someone does, I'll know who to thank."

"Don't be daft," Lord Curzon's man said with some annoyance. "I hope you didn't mail a set of drawings to Rolls-Royce."

"No . . . just wrote 'em." He was beginning to feel a bit uneasy. "Told 'em enough to wet their whistle like."

"Good." The man drew a piece of paper and pencil

from his coat and leaned against a fender to write. "I'm going to give you the name of my brother-in-law and his establishment. He's chief clerk for a firm of solicitors in New Fetter Lane near Lincoln's Inn. Go have a chat with him soon as you can. He'll tell you how to go about getting a patent."

"I've got dozens and dozens of ideas."

"Do you, Ross? Well, lad, put a patent on the best of them. It could turn out to be a good deal more rewarding than spending your money on skittles and beer."

"Hop to it, lads," a driver warned, flipping away his cigarette. "Here they come."

Lord Stanmore and a dozen other peers could be seen crossing Palace Yard, all of them smoking cigars and chatting away in high spirits. Hardly the proper mood for men who had just drafted a message of condolence, Ross was thinking. He straightened his cap and walked toward his car.

"Mind what I said," Curzon's chauffeur called out. "Go see him straightaway."

There was a faint aroma of sherry as Lord Stanmore got into the back of the Rolls.

"Pall Mall, Ross. Drop me at the club and then see to her ladyship's needs . . . or my daughter's." He chuckled wryly and contemplated the ash on his cigar. "I can well imagine how they've been keeping you hopping the past ten days or so."

He doubted that, as he turned the gleaming silver car into Whitehall. The earl had only to attend the various parties that were almost a nightly feature at Stanmore House—he didn't have to prepare for them. Ross estimated that he had been on duty an average of fourteen hours a day since the family and most of the servants had moved up from Abingdon Pryory. For the maids, cooks, and footmen, the hours had been even longer and more taxing. As he drove sedately toward the hurly-burly of Charing Cross, he wondered what the countess or the Right Honorable Miss Alexandra would have in store for him the rest of the day. The countess's passion was for hand-delivered invitations. That meant driving all over London with one of the footmen, in full livery, powdered wig and all, seated beside him—to the hooting delight of every passing lorry driver. Miss Alexandra was party-mad, which meant long hours waiting outside the Cafe Royal or any number of houses in Belgravia and Chelsea, jawing with other chauffeurs while tango music drifted into the dark street. It was such a bloody waste of time. Somehow, he had to find a spare hour to visit the solicitors' office in New Fetter Lane. A patent with his name on it. The thought awed him. Of course, it would take a bit of money, perhaps every penny he had saved up. He might be forced to sell his motorbike, but that was not a great sacrifice. And he'd have to give up his pleasures for a bit. No more walking out with girls and taking them to pictures. A penny saved was a penny earned.

"I say, Ross," Lord Stanmore called out, "turn into the Strand."

He obeyed without question, although it meant cutting in front of other cars, ignoring the squeal of brakes and the irate blowing of horns. Lord Stanmore was leaning forward and pointing across the lowered glass partition, which, when raised, isolated him from his chauffeur.

"There, Ross . . . in front of Cook's. Yes, by Jove, thought I'd spotted the fellow. Pull up in front."

There was a great press of traffic inching toward Charing Cross Station, but Ross sliced neatly through it to the curb and parked behind a touring bus.

"Martin!" The earl rolled down the rear window and poked his head out. "Martin, dear boy!"

Martin Rilke was standing on the pavement talking to the tour director. His attaché case was under his arm, an old leather suitcase beside his feet. He turned at the sound of his name and walked over to the car.

"Hello, sir." He still couldn't find the courage to call the man "Uncle Tony." "This is a surprise."

Lord Stanmore extended his hand through the window and squeezed Martin's arm. "And a very pleasant one at that. All done with your tour?"

"There are two more days of it—the sights of London—but I'd rather see those on my own. I was just saying goodbye to the guide."

"Just get back in town?"

"Yes . . . drove in from Cambridge this morning on the bus. It's been a good trip, but tiring. They keep up a fast pace."

Lord Stanmore opened the door. "Hop in, lad, and we'll take you to the house. All your gear's up from the country as promised and there's a room waiting for you."

Martin hesitated. "Thank you, sir, but I wrote a few articles about the trip that I think I can sell to the *Daily Post*. I'll hail a cab."

"Busman's holiday, eh? Jolly good for you, but hop in anyway. I'm just going to my club, and then the chauffeur will drive you to the Post building." He shifted over on the seat. "Won't hurt your chances for a sale if you arrive in style."

New Fetter Lane was practically around the corner from the Daily Post Building. Ross was out of the car with alacrity, not giving Martin time to refuse the offer of a ride.

"I'll get your luggage, sir," he said, hurrying across the pavement. "And may I say that it's nice to see you back again, sir . . . very nice indeed."

The Daily Post Building was an architectural melding of Gothic cathedral and Victorian railway station. Slender Ionic columns of soot-blackened stone and dull-green copper flutings bound myriad windows into an awesome monolith designed to impress even the most casual observer with the power of the press.

"Do you want me to wait for you, sir?" Ross asked as he stopped at the main entrance.

"No, thanks," Martin said. "I'll get a cab. Fifty-seven Park Lane. Is that right?"

"Yes, sir. Stanmore House."

And then the chauffeur was gone, and Martin, clutching his attaché case under his right arm, mounted broad stone steps and entered the palatial lobby of the newspaper building. A uniformed page escorted him up to the second floor to a vast room filled with oak desks and shirt-sleeved men. Taut steel wires were suspended horizontally from the ceiling, crossing and crisscrossing the room. Small metal canisters rocketed back and forth on the wires like artillery shells whizzing from one target to another. Typewriters clattered, men shouted over telephones or cried out for the copy boys, the message containers hummed over the wires, and a bank of teletypewriters added their own chatter to the din. It was a room that made the editiorial offices of the Chicago *Express* seem like the parlor of a funeral home.

"Mr. Golden's down there, sir," the page said in a cockney accent so thick as to make his words barely intelligible to Martin. "Fourth desk in the center past the glass cubicles."

Martin pondered what "glarssubles" were, but he could see Jacob Golden, bent over a desk, a green eye-shade pulled low on his forehead, and so he thanked the boy and made his way through the aisles, walking ankle deep in scrap paper at times. A harried-looking man at one of the desks looked up as Martin came abreast of him.

"How in God's name do you spell Count Marish Szogyeny? My bloody mind's gone blank." A metal tube whizzed overhead and then plummeted down a curved track that jutted up from a corner of the man's desk, coming to rest in a little contraption that looked like the breach of a gun. The man flipped a lever and the canister plopped into his hand. "Oh, God! Not more memos! The chief's gone bloody bonkers!"

Martin left him to his troubles and walked on to Golden's desk.

"Hello, Rilke," Golden called out cheerfully. "Pull up a scrap-paper basket and sit down."

"I think I'm intruding. You guys seem pretty busy."

"Not me, *they*." He leaned back in the chair and locked his hands behind his head. "I'm polishing an item about a clerk who made off with five thousand pounds of his firm's money and is now living in splendor in Brazil. The other lads in this room are not so much busy as they are confused. Austro-Hungarian internal affairs have never been their long suit, and now the chief, meaning my dear old man of course, is demanding reams of articulate, incisive prose in order to explain Bosnian political aspirations to a multitude of unwashed, unlettered readers. I have my own views of that dark corner of the world, but no one around here is interested in hearing them expressed."

"That was a terrible thing. But there doesn't seem to be any major crisis over it."

Golden's slash of a mouth twisted in derision. "Precisely, my dear Watson. It's the case of the dog that didn't bark all over again."

Martin scratched the side of his jaw. "Sorry, Holmes, but that's a bit too cryptic for me."

Golden uncoiled his hands and reached to the desk for a tin of cigarettes.

"A bit backward in our knowledge of the European ant heap, are we?"

"A bit . . . yes."

"A common enough fault, I'm afraid, but don't despair. Professor Golden is at hand with pungent commentary and a full assortment of descriptive material." He tapped the cigarette tin after removing two cigarettes and handing one to Martin. "The Austro-Hungarian empire, a simple tin of Abdullah smokes— only not so simple in real life. A hodgepodge of Germans, Magyars, Croats, Slavs . . . corrupt and monumentally stupid, exceeded in stupidity and corruption only by the Russians, who border them to the east." He shifted an inkwell into position. "The mighty Russian inkwell, murky with serfs, Cossacks, mystics, and dark plots . . . most of them hatched in Viennese coffee-houses."

"I'm not totally ignorant of European politics," Martin drawled in his best laconic Chicago manner.

"No, I'm sure you're not, Rilke, but you've watched it all from a long distance, across a wide ocean. I've seen it from the gutters of every capital. Hate. That's the binding word on the Continent. Everyone hates everybody."

Martin picked a match off the desk and lit his cigarette and Golden's.

"I know that, too. My mother was French . . . from Lorraine. She mourned the lost province to the day of her death."

"And your father was German?"

"German-*American*. She never held the Franco-Prussian War against him. They had more personal wars to fight."

Golden's smile was arcane. "French hatred for Germany is a normal hate, almost quaint. To see true hatred, one must go to Serbia, to the little cafés in Belgrade, and, casually, over a glass of slivovitz, bring up the subject of Austria and whether or not she has a legitimate right to keep all those Slavic people in Bosnia and Herzegovina enfolded in the Hapsburg wing. *Then* you will see hate, my dear Rilke. A violent, hot-blooded people, those Serbs. They cut one of their kings down nine years ago and most of his household. Sliced them up like dog meat and tossed the scraps from the palace windows. The king they have now is very imperial looking—tall and straight, a rather kindly face. Only one minor deficiency in the man—he's insane. It's a country ruled by a weak regent and strong-armed ministers. Plot and counterplot . . . Pan-Slav radicals . . . the Black Hand. Oh, quite a charming little country, Serbia, but we love them because they're so small and plucky and Austria is such a big bully."

A man darted over from an adjoining desk. "Do you have a pen I can borrow? I just broke my last nib."

Golden pulled out the center drawer. "Help yourself. Care to hang about for a few minutes? I'm explaining the Balkan crisis."

The man grabbed two pens from the drawer and turned quickly away. "Good Lord, no."

"I have few listeners," Golden sighed, puffing smoke. "The reason being that no one can conceive of a world that isn't neatly divided into villains and heroes. Well, they're *all* villains across the channel, every bloody one of them." He moved a box of paper clips into position below the flat tin of cigarettes. "Serbia. On Austria's southern flank. That's why the Russians love them. They keep the Austrians off-balance and tie up half their army. Austria could never go to war against Russia, not with all those Serbs facing their soft underbelly. Well, now, what have we got right at this moment? One dead archduke. Not much of a loss. A typical Hapsburg, who had a girdle on his belly and one around his brains. But his death will give the Austrians an excuse to crush Serbia, if they can prove it was a Serbian activist who committed the crime, and there's no doubt in my mind that one did." He pushed the tin sharply against the box of clips. "Austria moves against Serbia, but not in swift anger—a dog that doesn't bark can't be heard, can it? Oh, no, they'd never cross the Danube unless they can be assured that Germany will keep the Russians in check, and they'll be given that assurance in due time. That will anger the Russians no end, and so we can move the inkwell against the smokes. Hordes and hordes of bearded Russkies, more than enough to deal with Austria and the Germans, too. And what will France do if war flares from the Baltic to the Adriatic? She has a treaty with Russia, just the excuse la belle France needs to avenge 1870 . . . Alsace and Lorraine, the holy names. With the Russian bear scaring the wits out of the Germans in East Prussia, the French will attack across the Rhine and storm Berlin with their magnificent élan, march in triumph down

Unter den Linden the way the Germans marched on the Champs-Elysées forty-four years ago."

He leaned forward with a gleeful smirk and pointed his cigarette at Martin's face. "But the Germans are such clever chaps. They know all this . . . they've worked it out on paper years ago. They prize and honor generals with brains while we despise ours and the French ignore theirs. Rather a sad omen, that. Anyway, the Germans have a plan to deal with French moves. It's not a secret. Every *sous-lieutenant* in the French army scoffs at the details. It calls for a massive flanking sweep through Belgium in order to fold the French armies into a net . . . to crush them in less than three weeks, before the Russian bear can even stumble out of its cage. Not a plan without its flaws, dear Rilke, but it might well work and even work well. The French refuse to believe that Germany would violate Belgian neutrality. So do we. It wouldn't be sporting, would it? Not playing the game. Belgium is sacred and inviolate. There's a paper to prove it, signed by us and all the great powers years and years ago. One more holy relic to toss on the scrap heap."

"Oh, shit," the man at the next desk cried out in exasperation. "Put a sock in it. I can't hear myself think."

"You can't hear what you can't do, old boy." Golden sighed wearily. "Oh, well, I suppose all prophets are without honor in their own countries."

The man leered at him. "That makes you rather unique, Jacob. You're without honor in every bloody country. Bar none. But thanks for the pens. You're a generous soul at heart."

Golden leaned back in his chair and stared into space, the cigarette drooping from his lips.

"Where was I?"

"Damned if I know." Martin laughed. "Bucketing along through Belgium."

"Yes. Crying havoc as usual. I don't really blame people for ducking under tables when I come into a room. Hope I didn't bore you."

"Not at all. I'm glad you brought me up to date."

Golden stabbed out his cigarette and tidied up the European scene by moving the inkwell to its proper place and dropping the box of paper clips into the top drawer. "Back to more pleasant subjects. So the Yankee tripper has returned safe and sound. How did you find little Britain? No revolutions in Manchester, I trust. Is the wild and hairy Scot still keeping to his side of the border?"

"I had a grand time." Martin laughed. He placed the attaché case on the desktop. "Wrote half a dozen sketches. In shorthand, I'm afraid. If I could borrow a typewriter—"

"No need for that. I learned Pitman at my old dad's knee. It *is* Pitman, I hope, not that awful American stuff."

"It's Pitman."

"Good." He lit a cigarette and pushed the tin toward Martin. "Leave your copy and go wander about for a bit. You'll find a canteen of sorts down that corridor to your right. Acidulous tea and stale buns . . . all profits to a home for venereal mill girls in Huddersfield. Ta-ta and leave me to it."

The tea was fresh, the buns were soft, and the charity was a trade school for orphaned boys in Southwark. Martin sat at a small table next to a window with a view of the Temple gardens and the river. He was finishing his second mug of tea and his third bun when Golden came into the canteen with the travel-copy papers rolled into a tight cylinder. He sat down and tapped the roll against the edge of the table.

"Spend much time on these, Rilke?"

"No . . . not much."

"Just off the top of your head?"

"Sort of . . . yes." He could feel his face beginning to burn.

"Well, they're bloody damn good. You have a sharp eye and a finely tuned ear. I laughed out loud over the Yorkshire cattleshow piece. The judges were right out of Dickens. Gentle satire. Just the ticket." He looked thoughtful. "When are you leaving for the Continent?"

"The day after tomorrow."

"Is it absolutely vital that you go?"

"No . . . I guess not. Why?"

"Because perhaps you could postpone it for a bit. I think your style of writing would go over very well with our readers. A Yank's-eye view of Britain . . . with the emphasis on the upper-middle-class types . . . mildly satirized, like the Yorkshire squires. It'd probably be good for eight weeks at least, and being a roving feature writer for the *Post* would be jolly good experience for you. Or do you have to be back in Chicago by any fixed date?"

"No. As a matter of fact, I don't even know if I'll have a job when I get back."

"Does that mean you're interested?"

"Sure."

The sardonic mouth softened into a warm smile. "Jolly good. Let's hop upstairs and I'll introduce you to the chief. . . . Give the old boy the pitch, as they say in America."

The top floor of the building formed an awesome contrast to the lower depths. No harried men there, no nerve-racking typewriters. Deep carpets and oak-paneled walls subdued all sound. Massive oak doors lined a broad carpeted corridor, all of them closed, all of them bearing discreet brass markers with engraved names: MR. KEENE. MR. UPSHAW. MR. ROSENBERG.

"The real powers," Golden whispered as though in church, "reside here as the prophets reside in heaven. Policy makers all." The hooked little smile returned. "A terribly difficult job. Does one advocate votes for women now, or wait and see how the wind's blowing? And what stand do we take on birth control? Ribald plays? The income tax? Should décolletage be more or less this season? If one stands very still and listens hard, one can hear the brains creak like rusting gears."

The corridor ended in a double set of oak doors. No

brass nameplate. None was needed. The doors opened
into a vestibule in which several men were seated in
leather armchairs, all of them with the resigned expression of men who had waited a long time and knew they
would wait a good deal longer. A male secretary sat behind a small desk adjacent to another set of double oak
doors.

"Is he busy?" Golden asked.

"Naturally," the secretary drawled in Oxonian tones.
"You know better than to ask, but he'll see you if it's
important."

"It is," Golden said. He leaned toward the man and
spoke in a stage whisper. "The chap I'm with fired the
fatal shot yesterday and is willing to tell all for fifty
quid."

A few nodding heads stirred. The secretary faked a
stage yawn.

"Go in, Jacob, and take your assassin with you."

Beyond the doors was a cavernous room that seemed
to be part office and part museum. Glass cases filled
with Egyptian artifacts stood next to teletypewriters enclosed in soundproof glass domes. Paintings by Rey-
nolds, Gainsborough, and Turner competed for wall
space with two-shilling maps of Europe, Russia, Africa,
and other sections of the world that were pinned to the
oak panels with thumbtacks. Secretaries and typists,
both male and female, abounded, scurrying in and out
of glass-enclosed cubicles, all of them moving in a
soundless frenzy. At the far end of the room was a
broad oak dining table used as a desk, and behind it, in
a Biedermeier chair, sat Harry Golden, Lord Crewe.

"Guv'nor," Jacob said, "meet Martin Rilke . . .
from Chicago. An eminent journalist on the *Express*."

There wasn't even the remotest family resemblance,
Martin was thinking as he extended his hand across the
table. If Jacob was a willow, his father was an oak, and
a substantial one at that, the king of all oaks, a dark
brown trunk of a man, with arms that could truly be
called limbs. A sailor, Martin dimly recalled, a constant

contender for the America's Cup races, and as constantly fated to lose in the trials to Sir Thomas Lipton. The hand that reached out and took hold of his own was as hard and horny as a sailor's foot.

"Rilke, did you say?" The voice fitted the man, deep and growling like a storm at sea. "Any relation to Paul Rilke of Chicago?"

"My uncle, sir," Martin said, tensing, expecting a vise squeeze. The big, brown hand was surprisingly gentle.

"One of my good friends. Saw him two years ago, come to think of it. Right in this room. How is he?"

"Fine, sir . . . just fine."

The brown hand slipped away and joined its mate in a lock-fingered grip across a waistcoat broad as a sail. A hawser of gold chain dangled in a loop from the pockets.

"Then you'd be Hanna Rilke Greville's nephew as well. Yes. I can see the resemblance."

Martin could detect a likeness to Jacob now. It was in the mouth. The same slash of lips. Nothing else was the same, only that. Jacob's eyes were large and luminous, his father's tiny, like black beads almost lost in a great meaty, sunburned face.

Jacob leaned across the table and placed the tightly rolled sheaf of articles in front of the press lord.

"Young Rilke here took a Cook's tour of jolly old England and came back with some very amusing observations of about a thousand words each. I'd like you to read them."

Lord Crewe merely glanced at them. "If you say they're good, Jacob, give them to Blakely."

Jacob scooped up the articles and shoved the roll under his arm like a baton. "Right. My idea is to run a short column every day by Rilke . . . his unjaundiced view of the London social and sporting scene. Use a nom de plume . . . Yankee Cousin, or something on that order. He's staying with the Grevilles, which gives him an inside look at society high jinks. . . . Thus the nom de plume, Rilke. Can't have you being accused of biting the hand that feeds you, can we?"

"He can feed himself," Lord Crewe rumbled. "We've never been accused of underpaying our correspondents."

A harassed-looking young man darted up to the table with handfuls of paper torn from the Teletype machines.

"Berlin and St. Petersburg reports, sir."

Lord Crewe snatched them from the man's hand and read through them rapidly. His face was expressionless, the carved figurehead on a ship's prow. When he was through with them, he tossed them casually aside.

"I'll have a few memorandums to shoot down. Ask Miss Fisher to come over."

"Yes, sir," the young man said, hurrying away.

Lord Crewe looked at his son with a faint smile. "All your fears are proving groundless. Serenity reigns. The world is used to Hapsburgs getting themselves murdered. The new heir apparent is well thought of. Not a ripple in the European pond."

"Still waters run deep," Jacob said. "I do believe."

Lord Crewe settled back in his chair. "Get on with your work, Jacob. And have the decency to telephone your mother once in a while."

They returned to the bedlam below.

"Well, Rilke," Jacob said, "how does it feel to be' writing for the most powerful newspaper in the world?"

"Pretty good . . . but I can't stay with the Grevilles. It wouldn't be right."

"You'll have a hard time finding suitable lodgings, old boy. This is the height of the season and London's bursting at the seams. Tell you what, I have more rooms than I know what to do with . . . a big old flat in Soho above the finest Hungarian restaurant this side of the Danube. And I know you'll like the digs, Rilke. Every chorus girl in London has a key to the place."

By leaning out of the garret window and craning her

head to see around a chimney, Ivy Thaxton had a fine view of Mayfair. True, a bit lopsided, more roofs than streets to be seen, but, still, it *was* London and she *was* there.

> Dear Mum and Da and my own dearest sisters Mary and Cissy and brothers Ned and Tom and our own dear baby Albert Edward. I am penning this to you all in London town. Oh, it is the grandest place you ever did see.

Just below the window there was a flat, secluded spot near the base of the tall chimney that had probably been used during the building of the house to stack slates for the roofers. It was an easy matter to climb out the window with notebook and pencil and to sit with her back against the chimney. The roof was a wonder that she would have loved to explore, a vast place of triangular slate hills running in all directions, with narrow valleys in between to catch the rain. In the winter, those valleys would be rushing torrents of black water tumbling to the drains. Rising amid the sharp ridges was a forest of chimneys and vents, some of them emitting clouds of steam or black smoke like thin volcanoes. Her happiest moments of the long day were the few minutes she could sneak in total aloneness by popping out the window with the sureness and silence of a cat.

The sun was hot, and she turned her face to it for a moment and closed her eyes. The sun was thought to be death to a woman's beauty—she had read that somewhere—but Norfolk girls loved the sun because there was so little of it to be seen in the watery, misty fens.

The letter had been started days before, but she had so little time to complete it. Velda Jessup had thrown a fit of some kind shortly after they arrived in London, falling to the floor and frothing at the mouth. She had been carried out of the house on a stretcher, her body rigid as a broomstick. Her inopportune departure had created a crisis, as Miss Alexandra was left without a lady's maid at the hour of her greatest need for one. Mrs. Broome, who ran the Park Lane house with the same calm sureness with which she ran Abingdon Pryory, had given the job to Ivy.

"It's a big step up the ladder, my girl."

It was also hard work. Alexandra was in a perpetual fever of activity, her days and nights spent at parties, balls, fetes, luncheons, garden-party teas, dinners, dances, riding in Rotten Row, attending fashion shows, concerts, and plays. Each activity required a new costume, from shoes to hat, and she could never make up her mind about just which dress she wanted to wear. She would try on a dozen before settling for one that halfway pleased her. And talk! The girl never ceased. A constant stream of chatter about this boy and that boy, and should she marry a barrister or should she give her hand and heart to a dashing hussar who was the youngest son of a duke? And gossip, gossip, gossip, as Ivy struggled to turn up a hem or sew on a button. Lady Jane Blake, it was rumored, was seen at the Cafe Royal with a devastatingly handsome Russian ballet dancer, while Lord Blake, surely the ugliest little man in London, was away in Dublin. And had Ivy heard the hilarious bon mot that George Bernard Shaw had uttered to Granville-Barker in the foyer of the Lyceum?

Ivy smiled in the blessed sun-filled tranquillity of the rooftop, lulled by the muted rumble of traffic and the cooing of a pigeon preening itself on a chimney pot. George Bernard Shaw indeed! How could she have possibly heard what the man had said. And who was Granville-Barker? She truly liked Miss Alexandra, but she was a flibbertigibbet if there ever was one.

> Dear Mum and Da and my own dearest sisters . . .

The words seemed to wriggle across the page in the heat. She licked the point of her pencil and placed it against the notebook, but she couldn't get her thoughts together.

> I am penning this to you all in London town. Oh, it is the grandest place you ever did see.

That was true enough—what she had seen of it on a few shopping trips with Miss Alexandra and one afternoon off, which she had spent sitting in Hyde Park watching the rowers on the Serpentine. Ross had offered to take her to the pictures, but she had overheard one of the parlormaids telling another maid what Ross liked to do in the dark of the picture palace.

"Put his hand clear up me knickers," the girl had said, tittering. Tittering! Ivy glared up at the pigeon. If any man did a thing like that to her, she'd make *him* titter, right out the other side of his mouth. She began to write in a slow, precise hand:

> I have been given a much more enjoyable and responsible job here, quite a rung up for your Ivy . . .

Was it? She stared thoughtfully into space. What was she? A lady's maid. Ironing and sewing and smoothing, folding things into drawers and hanging things in closets all day and half the night, too. Miss Alexandra never put so much as a stocking in its proper place, but then one didn't keep a dog and expect to do the barking.

How cheeky the pigeon was, strutting back and forth as though it owned the house beneath its tiny feet. The true London spirit all right. She had noticed that in the park, the London air, everyone strutting along the paths, rich and poor alike, cocky as lords. She had sat on a bench in her plain brown dress, one hand pressed to the crown of her straw sailor hat to keep it from spinning away across the pond in the wind. Three girls had come along the path, sharing a bag of sweets between them, nice-looking girls, her age or perhaps a bit older. Well dressed. Nice linen skirts, white shirtwaists. They had sat for a moment on the bench, talking and laughing, and then one of them had drawn a silver watch on a silver chain from a small pocket in her shirt and had glanced at it and said: "Oh, my, we'd best get back to the office or Mr. Parrot will be ever so upset."

The other two girls had laughed merrily, and one of them had replied, cheeky as can be: "Well, you know what Mr. Parrot can do!"

Then they had walked on, not hurrying one bit, down the path toward Stanhope Gate and on into the great city to work in an office somewhere—and surely no later than six in the evening. Typing, she supposed. They hadn't taught typing at school. Hadn't taught much of anything, if it came to that. How to do sums, read, and spell. The library in Norwich had been her real school. The books of Dickens, Thackeray, Galsworthy, Austen, and, oh, all the building contained, but nothing of any practical use.

> . . . quite a rung up for your Ivy, and Mrs. Broome said that I'd be making an extra shilling a week from now on.

It was too much of an effort to write. Her heart wasn't in it and she couldn't keep her thoughts from wandering all over the landscape. It was almost with relief that she heard the sound of Mrs. Broome's voice calling for her.

"Ivy? Jane, where is Ivy Thaxton?"

The girl was sure to tell. She shared the garret room with four girls. Sneaks all.

"Out the window, Mrs. Broome. I told her. I said, 'Ivy,' I said . . ."

Ivy sighed and closed the notebook. Looking up, she saw Mrs. Broome's incredulous face in the garret window.

"Ivy Thaxton! You come up from there this instant before you fall to your death!"

"It's impossible to fall, Mrs. Broome."

"Perhaps. It is also impossible to permit one of his lordship's staff to scamper across the rooftops like a common chimney sweep! Come up! Come up *at once!*"

She returned to the small stuffy garret, climbing in the window with the same agility with which she had climbed out of it. She brushed dust from her skirt while Mrs. Broome stared coldly at her and the other girl in the room pressed a hand to her mouth to keep from laughing.

"Honestly, Ivy," Mrs. Broome said, "you are incorrigible. Never let me see you out there again."

"No, Mrs. Broome . . . you won't."

The housekeeper appeared dubious. "Well, we shall see what we shall see. At least I won't have to concern myself with your extraordinary behvaior for the next few days. Miss Alexandra has been invited to Arundel. You will go with her, of course. So hurry along and begin packing. Your mistress will choose her dresses, but you can get started on the underthings and accessories."

"Yes, Mrs. Broome."

"Take an extra dress for yourself and plenty of clean aprons and caps."

"Yes, Mrs. Broome."

"And don't look so penitent, girl. You're not fooling me one bit. Sitting on a roof indeed!"

They would be leaving first thing in the morning, the eight-thirty train from Victoria. Miss Alexandra was more bubbly and talkative than usual as she agonized over her selection of clothing. The occasion was a three-day house party at the Duke of Avon's ancient, beautiful, but restored (all the modern conveniences) castle. She had gone to school with the duke's daughter, and all the *most* eligible bachelors in England, perhaps in the *entire* empire, had been invited.

"Oh, Lord, I can't possibly be seen in this rag!"

By eleven o'clock that night, the clothes had been selected and carefully packed away. Supper had been brought up on a tray—sandwiches and tea. Ivy barely had two bites of a ham sandwich, being too busy smoothing dresses and skirts.

"Should I take the taffeta? Do you like the yellow silk from Worth's?"

A hem or two needed a few stitches, a button or so was gone and had to be replaced. At last all of the work was done, the cream-colored leather trunks with the Greville coat of arms embossed upon them in gold leaf closed and ready for the footmen to take downstairs in the morning. A three-day house party! Ivy shuddered to think what would have been involved if her mistress had decided to take a world cruise.

"Good night, Ivy. Be up bright and early in the morning."

"Yes, miss."

She walked wearily down the corridor and then up the curved staircase to the third floor, where a narrow stairway led to the garret rooms. As she passed one of the doors that faced the landing, it opened and Martin Rilke stepped out. He was wearing a bathrobe and was holding a toothbrush and a tube of Pepsodent.

"Ivy . . . Thaxton?" he asked, smiling.

"Yes, sir," she said, staring blankly at him.

"Don't you remember me?"

She nodded. "Yes, sir. Mr. Rilke from Chicago."

"Right! Stockyards and railroads." She was looking at him curiously, and he suddenly felt at a loss for words. He wanted to say that he'd been hoping to run into her again, that she was just about the prettiest girl he'd ever seen, but he knew that would only confuse and embarrass her. In England, gentlemen didn't speak to maids that way. Maybe they didn't do it in America, either. But then he'd never grown up around maids.

"Well," he said helplessly. "How do you like being up here in London? Do you miss the country?"

"No, sir."

"Do you come from here? I mean, are you a Londoner?"

"No, sir. I come from Illingsham, near Norwich."

He hadn't been to either place on the tour. He was starting to feel silly standing in the hall in his robe, holding toothbrush and paste. He couldn't think of another thing to say to her.

"Are you going back to America soon?" she asked.

"No," he said quickly, glad that she had broken the impasse. "I've got a job on the *Daily Post*. I'll be in England for another couple of months, but I'll be leaving here tomorrow . . . moving in with a friend in Soho."

"That should be nice. I'm going down to Arundel tomorrow with Miss Alexandra."

"That should be nice, too."

"Yes, sir," she said, looking away from him and starting off down the hall toward the garret stairs. "Good night, sir."

Two of the girls in the room snored—loudly. Great fleshy lumps of girls, both Scots, strong as horses. They worked in the kitchen and their hands were beet red from being in water so much. They labored like navvies, and she didn't have the heart to wake them and tell them to turn over on their sides. The other two girls were Irish, parlormaids, sisters from Belfast. God's wrath couldn't have wakened them.

Ivy sat up in her narrow bed and then got out of it to stand by the window. She could see the dark shapes of a dozen pigeons on the chimney, huddled against the tall pots. There was hardly any sound of traffic. The city was asleep—or holding its breath on the brink of July.

Dear Mum and Da and my own dearest sisters Mary and Cissy and brothers Ned and Tom and our own dear baby Albert Edward. I am penning this to you in my thoughts on a hot night in London town. Tomorrow I go to Arundel to stay at the castle of a duke. I have met a very nice young American who is from Chicago, in the state of Illinois, on Lake Michigan as Tom will understand because we both know the atlas better than we know the streets of Illingsham. He is quite taken by me, I think, but bashful and shy and he knows his place. He wouldn't dare say, Ivy, may I go walking with you tomorrow? Or, Ivy, may I take you to the pictures on Saturday? After all, he is really nothing but an American boy with shabby suitcases and pajamas that are a bit thin in the knees. Tomorrow I go to Arundel to the castle of a duke. The plumbing, I believe, is sound. Every eligible bachelor in the world will be there, and I will startle them with my inexhaustible supply of starched aprons and crisp caps.

"Damn," she said softly, staring out across the shadowed roof, the sleeping city. "Damn . . . damn . . . damn."

VII

Charles Greville emerged from the cool foyer of the Carlton Club and waited patiently in the afternoon heat for the doorman to signal a taxi. To anyone passing by he looked elegant, cool, and detached—attributes that one would expect of any man leaving the Carlton. Inside, he was seething. He had just left his father, and absolutely nothing had been resolved. They had had lunch together: Scotch grouse and a superb bottle of hock followed by fruit, cheese, and a hundred-year-old brandy. His father had waited for the brandy before toasting his birthday.

"To the twenty-third of July. The date of my son's birth. May it always be a day of sunshine."

"Thank you, Father."

"Drink up, my boy. A true Napoleon."

His father had been in a good mood. The season was beginning to wind down, more and more people were moving out of London, back to their country estates. He could decently do the same. Abingdon Pryory would be back in full swing by Bank Holiday.

"I tell you, Charles, I miss the horses, damned if I don't. Banks will have 'em in shape to suit Banks, but I like 'em a good deal leaner. I'll have to run the fat off them. And speaking of horses, my lad, why don't you come with me in September and ride in the Tetbury? Be like old times."

"Perhaps I'll do that, Father."

"Happy to hear it. By the way, thought you and Roger were planning to go to Greece this month."

"We decided against it. Roger is preparing a book of his poems for publication . . . a slim book."

"A fruitful summer, what? Did Alex tell you that she's finally made a choice?"

"No. How did she do it? Stick a pin into a list?"

"Something like that, I'd say. The chap's name is Saunders. Good-looking fellow. Went to Trinity. He's in the Foreign Office . . . Lord Esher's nephew and heir. Of course, that's her choice for *this* week, but I hope she stays with it."

"So do I. And, Father, I've made up my mind to marry Lydia."

How soft those words sounded to his ears, a melody. They had rung a different tune for his father, but he had said little. Merely sipped his brandy. Lit a cigarette.

"Oh? You know my feelings on that subject, Charles. The thought of your being Archie Foxe's son-in-law is most painful to me."

"Because Archie's in trade?"

The earl had cradled his glass of brandy between his hands, sniffing the aroma. "Archie Foxe is an extremely successful shopkeeper. More power to the man. I don't hold that against him to any great extent. What I simply cannot abide about him is his contempt for the British class structure. Damned if I don't believe the man's a socialist at heart. And his closeness to Lloyd George and all that scruffy bunch of icon-smashing liberals is repellent to me. I'm sorry. Lydia has been welcome in my house since she was a child. I would never by thought or deed snub her because I disapprove of her father's views. But marriage? That is out of the question."

"And if I marry her anyway, Father?" His voice had sounded tinny and ineffectual in the vastness of the dining room. He had studied his father's face but had discerned no drastic change of expression. He had looked, if anything, slightly bored.

"I do not wish to discuss the matter any further, Charles." He had set his glass on the table and reached for the bottle. "Have another dollop of Napoleon . . . and try the *fromage de Brie*. It is quite delicious."

The luncheon had dragged on interminably for Charles as several of his father's friends had come to the table and joined in the birthday toasts. But at last it had ended and he had taken his leave.

The taxi arrived and he slumped onto the back seat. Anger and frustration made him mute and it took several seconds to compose himself enough to give the driver directions. God, he agonized, what was he going to do? He felt like a man tied to two horses pulling in opposite directions. It was obvious that his father would not be pinned down as to what specific action he might take. He couldn't actually stop him from marrying Lydia, wouldn't create a scene and bar the church door, but he might let them both know in no uncertain terms that as far as he was concerned the marriage did not exist. A marriage between two strangers, a union that he would neither witness nor acknowledge. Would Mother forbid him from taking such baleful measures? And if she did, would Father be swayed by any of her arguments in his behalf? He squeezed his hands tightly until the knuckles ached. Everything was in doubt and it was impossible to get solid, concrete answers. Evade the issue, play for time—that was his parents' game. And what of Lydia? What in the name of all that was holy would be her reaction if he couldn't assure her that she was marrying into the family? No woman would wish to marry a man ostracized by his own father. He didn't quite believe her assurances that he was all she wanted. Acceptance by society was important to Lydia, and she couldn't be blamed for that.

He stared gloomily out of the window as the taxi turned into the Mall. The park had never looked so beautiful, the trees a startling shade of green against the sky, a sky almost impossibly blue for England. An Italian sky, the kind one saw in Amalfi in August. The red brick towers of St. James's rose above the trees and the guardsmen stood in front of their sentry boxes at Buckingham Palace. The Scots Guard, he noticed as the taxi swung past the palace toward Lower Belgrave Street.

The Earl of Stanmore's daughter-in-law.

He could only speculate on the importance of that relationship to Lydia. What doors would it open for her socially that no amount of Archie's millions could ever have breached? Lydia *Greville*. That name carried an almost indefinable aura of prestige and privilege. It meant garden parties and balls at homes where Lydia *Foxe* would not have been welcome or, at best, merely tolerated. It meant a final and irrevocable acceptance in even the most rarefied levels of society—provided, of course, that the union had been publicly blessed.

"God," he whispered fiercely. What would she say if he had to tell her that it would not be blessed? That his father's presence at their wedding would be thunderously conspicuous by its absence? Would she smile, kiss him, tell him that it didn't matter in the slightest? He knew in his heart what her reaction would be and the thought turned his blood to ice. Lydia loved him—he had no doubt of that—but her love was based, at least in some measure, on his position in life. But what if he were wrong? What if she didn't give a tinker's damn about it and wanted a marriage, blessed or not? What then? Could he defy his father and run off with her? Toss away so casually every vestige of his sense of duty and obligation?

He felt that he was in the grip of a nightmare. His emotions were in such a whirl that when he arrived at his destination he handed the driver a five-pound note and told him to keep the change. The man drove off in a hurry before this madman could regain his senses.

Fenton Wood-Lacy's batman opened the door to the captain's tastefully furnished flat, which Roger was sharing while in London. Roger was seated on the drawing room floor, surrounded by printed proofs of his poems. Sprawled next to him was Rupert Brooke, shoes and stockings off, a white tennis shirt open down the front revealing an expanse of brawny, tanned chest.

Brooke's friend, Lascelles Abercrombie, sat in a chair, puffing on a pipe and reading the afternoon edition of the *Globe*.

"Hello, Rupert," Charles said. It was good to see the man again. The poet had left King's College when he and Roger had gone up to Cambridge, but his influence had been strong, had put a stamp on all literary societies that had flourished there. And Brooke had lived for a time near the college, at the Old Vicarage in Grantchester, and he and Roger, and many others, had spent hours there talking endlessly about books and poetry or swimming in the dam above Byron's Pool. . . . *"Yet stands the church clock at ten to three?/And is there honey still for tea?"*

"Hello, Charles," Brooke said with a lazy smile. "Happy birthday."

"Yes, Greville," Abercrombie muttered. "Many happy returns of the day."

"I gather Roger's been advertising the fact," Charles said.

Brooke nodded. "In the hope we can all pressure you into throwing a party for the occasion . . . or at least a bang-up feed at some small but epicurean restaurant."

"Be my guests," he said thickly.

Roger looked up for the first time and noticed the sickly pallor of his friend's face.

"I say, Charles, do you feel all right?"

"I'm fine . . . thanks."

"Well, you don't look fine. Webber!"

The batman darted into the room. "Yes, sir?"

"Fix Mr. Greville a large whiskey. And Mr. Brooke and Mr. Abercombie could go for a Guinness, if there's any left."

"There's one bottle, sir."

"Divvy it up, that's the good chap." He watched the soldier-servant scurry off. "My dear brother runs a niggardly house. No, Charles, you look pale as a ghost."

Charles sat on the edge of a sofa. He really didn't feel well at all. "It's just the heat and the petrol fumes.

God," he blurted, "I'd like to get away for a month or two. Can't you postpone that blasted book? Let's go to Greece. Train to Trieste and than shanks' mare to Epirus."

Abercrombie lowered his newspaper. "I'd stay away from that section of the world for a few months. Austria just sent a perfectly shocking demand to Serbia—a veritable slap in the face with an iron glove. There's bound to be another war in the Balkans. We were just discussing it before you arrived. Care to read the dispatch from Belgrade?"

"Oh, bugger Belgrade!" His tone had a bitterness that surprised even him.

"Oh, I say," Roger said. "We like little Serbia, don't we?"

It was all correct and proper, Fenton Wood-Lacy was thinking as he walked slowly toward number 24 Cadogan Square. It was the day after Winifred Sutton's debut ball, and it was socially correct to return, leave one's calling card, or thank the hostess for a grand time. He had come to do more than that. He had had only one dance with Winifred, but it had been the final one, a waltz, and after it was over he had overheard a woman mention to Lady Mary that her daughter looked beautiful, ". . . and they make such a lovely couple." Lady Mary had beamed radiantly. He had then brought Winifred a final cup of punch and had asked her if he might call the next day and perhaps, if she wasn't too tired from the exertions of the ball, go for a walk.

"I am so glad you asked," she had said. "And I shall let you in on a secret. *Mama will be pleased as well.*"

And so now he stood on the front steps of the Suttons' London house, feeling, he thought ruefully, very "suitorish" with a box of sweets from Fortnum and Mason under his left arm. A butler anticipated his ringing the bell and opened the door.

"Good afternoon, sir."

He was ushered, almost reverently, into the drawing

room, where Winifred and her parents were waiting. They all seemed immensely relieved when he walked in.

"Ah, Fenton," the Marquess of Dexford cried. He was a stout, balding man with the slightly bowed legs of a lifetime horseman. "Jolly nice of you to drop by, what? Care for a glass of sherry? Did I tell you I saw your uncle t'other day? At the Army-Navy. Looked fit. His division did damn well at Sal'sbury in the old maneuvers, what?"

The one-sided conversation became increasingly more fatuous, and then, blessedly, goodbyes were said, and he and Winifred were outside the house in the golden sunshine.

"Shall we walk up to Kensington Gardens?" he asked.

She put a hand on his arm. "Let's walk slowly to the river. I love Chelsea, don't you?"

He admitted that he did. He also told her that she looked lovely.

She blushed and her hand tightened on his arm. "Thank you. Is it wrong for me to say that you look lovely, too? That's not the proper thing to say to a man, I know, but it happens to be true. I feel very proud walking beside you."

Her usual reticence vanished once they were away from the house. She was candid about herself, aware of her shortcomings.

"But I *am* trying to better myself. Take this frock. I think it's very becoming, but Mother said no at first. She thought it was too daring in the bodice, but I don't think a woman should feel ashamed that she has a— well, a female chest, do you?"

"Certainly not."

"One of my problems has always been a sweet tooth. I used to be mad for cream buns, but one can achieve slenderness by being firm in one's resolve to avoid such treats. I shall treasure your box of chocolates, but I shan't eat them."

"I'm sorry. My next present to you will not be edible."

She slipped her arm through his. Her intimacy was childlike. He felt like a favorite uncle. Lord, he thought, how terribly young she is.

The Thames was sluggish in the afternoon heat, and their conversation about Chelsea began to wear thin. A public house in Cheyne Walk looked inviting, but he couldn't take her there. She seemed content just to be with him, walking decorously by his side, arm in arm, not caring whether they spoke or not. A tug plowed upriver, pulling a string of empty coal barges. Some gray birds rose from the mud flats in the shadow of Albert Bridge and flew off across the river toward Battersea. They walked on, leaving the embankment and walking slowly up King's Road in the direction of Sloane Square. A sentry standing by the iron gates of the Duke of York's barracks tapped the butt of his rifle twice against the pavement as they walked past him.

"Why did he do that?"

"Because he recognized me as an officer," Fenton said after acknowledging the salute with a slight nod of his head.

"Is he in your regiment?"

"He's in the Royal Sussex, but I've been to the barracks a few times. Perhaps he remembered my face."

"No. You just look like a captain in the Coldstream Guards. I think it's the way you wear your skimmer. It's the way I imagine Kitchener would wear his."

He leaned toward her and whispered loudly in her ear, "Don't tell anyone, but Lord Kitchener doesn't own a straw hat. Nothing but uniforms. Even his pajamas . . . scarlet with rows and rows of medals."

Her laugh was throaty and rich. "Oh, dear, poor Mrs. K., how she must suffer!"

He was enjoying her company. Was, in fact, beginning to like the girl. And that mildy bawdy allusion to old K. and his missus proved that she wasn't a prude. Yes, he liked her. She was on the dowdy side, no ques-

tion about that. Even the new frock was of no great
help. It showed her figure, to be sure, but it wasn't exactly a figure that would set a man's blood on fire. Her
hair was pretty in the sun and her complexion clear and
rosy. Good teeth. Lips that would be described in a
novel as kissable. He liked her. She was easy to be with,
and one could, in a sense, relax.

"Are you feeling a bit peckish?" he asked. "A cup of
tea, some sandwiches?"

"I'm always peckish. It shall be the death of me. On
my tombstone they will write: 'Here lies Winifred Sutton, fasting at last.' "

His laugh was a gunshot that turned heads. He took
hold of her hand and steered her across the busy street,
dodging cars and lorries, and into an Italian restaurant
that he remembered with favor. He had taken Lydia
there once. She had enjoyed the Milanese food, but had
been bored by the Chelsea "types"—the actors, writers,
and painters who haunted the place from morning to
night. Winifred, on the other hand, was delighted by the
revelation of a side of Chelsea she had never seen, nor
even knew existed. The dimness of the shuttered room,
the candles stuck into wine bottles on each table, the
Bohemian crowd fascinated her. A burly man with a
ragged red beard, a shabby velvet cloak draped across
his shoulders, paused in front of their table and eyed
Fenton up and down.

"You look like the Prince of Wales."

"Only when I'm sitting down," Fenton said, then rose
to his full six feet two inches.

Red beard nodded. "So I can see, mate. You and
your lady want your portraits done? Half a crown
each."

"And a liter of Chianti, of course."

"Of course."

The man sketched while they ate, using charcoal and
pastels. The results were very good.

"May I have yours?" Winifred asked. "I shall treasure it always."

She felt slightly tipsy from a glass of wine, and so he ordered a taxi and asked the driver to take a long way back to Cadogan Square. Her head cleared as they drove around the park, but she remained euphoric.

"This has been the most wonderful afternoon of my life."

"I'm glad you enjoyed yourself, Winifred."

She clutched the two portraits and turned on the seat to look at him.

"Can we do it again sometime?"

She was his for the asking. Hooked, netted, and placed in the creel. He felt a nagging sense of shame for being so cold-blooded about it, but, damn it all, he *did* like her.

"As often as you like. Although I suppose you'll be leaving London soon."

"Yes," she said quietly. "We go back to Dorset on the first of August." Her eyes had an almost haunted look of appeal.

"May I ask your father for formal permission to call on you, Winifred? Here in London—and—as often as possible at Lulworth Manor?"

She seemed to stop breathing for a moment, then she let out a tiny cry and leaned against him, her lips brushing the side of his face.

"Oh, yes, yes. Oh, my dearest, *dearest* Fenton . . . may God bless you and keep you always . . . *always*. . . ."

Martin Rilke tried to keep his mind on what he was typing, but the chatter of the Teletype machines intruded on his thoughts. He had been given the courtesy of a glass-enclosed cubicle, sharing the space with the theater reviewer, but the top of the cubicle was open and the sounds of the enormous room rolled over it like great waves over a dike. The banner of the morning edition had been made up, and he could see it as a copy boy hurried the proofs to one of the editors.

* * *

SERBIAN CRISIS GROWS

That was a feather in Jacob's hat, he was thinking. They had pulled him off murder trials and sent him hurrying off to Belgrade. He envied him. The page in his typewriter mocked the severity of the European situation:

> There is something about Lord's cricket ground that is humbling to even the most uninitiated of spectators. Standing in the Long Room, amid the almost holy relics of the game's past, looking up at the severe visage of W. G. Grace, whose bust dominates the pavilion, even this Yankee was struck by

Struck by what? The absurdity of the game? Men in white clothing standing about in the sun? The lack of passion? The elderly men seated in the shade, murmuring, "Good play . . . Oh, well done, sir"? Where was the explosive snap of the ball from home to second to catch the runner? And where was the runner himself, sliding in with his spikes high, trailing dust?

But the piece must be laudatory, with just the gentlest of digs at the more stuffy types of clubmen with their "haw haw" fatuity—a few thorn pricks amid the roses.

"Are you finished, Mr. Rilke, sir?" a copy boy asked, poking his head around the doorway. The accent was strong East End, but no longer incomprehensible to Martin's ear. He was becoming Anglicized.

"Another fifteen minutes, Jimmy."

"Right you are, sir."

Twenty minutes to the midnight deadline. He'd make it with ease, even with the rambling of his thoughts. When he was done, he raised his hand and the boy darted into the cubicle and raced away with the copy. Martin took off his glasses, wiped them with a handkerchief, and placed them in his pocket. The theater reviewer, a cadaverous man who had never been seen by anyone on the paper dressed in anything but evening clothes and white tie, rose stretching and yawning from behind his desk, where he had been sound asleep for the past two hours.

"All done, Rilke?"

"Yes. Put to bed."

"That's where I should be."

The reviewer yawned and drew a cigarette from a silver case.

"You could have been there for the past two hours."

"I know, but I feel restless. I rather miss Jacob. He's the only one I know who might conceivably understand what's going on. The other chaps around here are no bloody use at all." He smiled thinly. "They know only what they read in the papers. I tell you, Rilke, I'm most apprehensive about the Balkan situation. I can't see how it can possibly ease off or where it will end. Oh, well, worrying about it won't make it change, will it? Can I buy you a drink at Romano's?"

"No, thanks, I think I'll go straight home."

"I'll share your taxi, if you don't mind. I have this absolute horror of being alone lately. Can't explain it. Damnedest feeling."

It seemed to be a feeling that many people shared. It appeared to Martin that the streets of the city never emptied. The cafés in Soho weren't open twenty-four hours a day, but if they had been they would have done good business. Perhaps it was no more than the unusually hot weather that drove people, mainly young men, from their rooms and set them to wandering in restless bands through the West End. The groups were orderly—excessively polite, as a matter of fact—and the police were not concerned. It was almost Bank Holiday time and a certain anticipatory excitement was normal. And yet, somehow, this behavior could not be explained that easily. One of the *Post* editors had just returned from Berlin and had observed the same thing occurring in Germany but on a vaster scale—masses of young men hiking across the country to the Black Forest or to the mountains of Bavaria, singing *Brüderschaft*

songs, drawn by some deep urge that no one could ade-
quately express. It had struck the editor as being quite
odd, but then the Germans had always been a mystical
people. An atmosphere of impending climax seemed to
hang in the air like heat haze. Lord Crewe, stalking
through the city room on his daily tour of inspection,
had remarked that what Europe needed right at this moment was a bloody good thunderstorm with plenty of
rain to cool the blood. But there was no rain. The skies
were a savage blue. Jacob wrote from Belgrade: "One
can see the Austrian gunboats prowling the Danube,
which has never looked more beautiful, more conducive to song."

The flat in Soho smelled of furniture polish and am-
monia. The cleaning woman had been in during the
day; not that she could have found much to do since her
last visit. With Jacob away, the spacious apartment in
Beak Street remained clean and orderly—and empty.
The girls who used to taxi over to the place from their
theaters on Shaftesbury Avenue between performances,
many of them still in costume, for champagne and cold
lobster stayed away when Jacob was gone. Martin
wasn't sure whether Jacob had told everyone that he
was leaving London or if they simply knew he was
gone. Some sort of seventh sense. The theatrical grapevine, more likely. He missed the ribald gaiety, the perfume, feather boas, and expansive flesh of the chorus
girls. He also missed Jacob's untidy presence, the litter
of papers and books on floors and furniture, the blue
haze of his strong Turkish cigarettes, the torrent of his
conversation, which was mordant, exasperating, sedi-
tious, and profane—but always worth listening to.
There was nothing much to eat in the kitchen except
for canned Strasbourg pâté, water biscuits, thick glass
jars of Russian caviar, and a closet stacked with champagne. More substantial meals were eaten out or
brought up on trays from the Hungarian restaurant below, Jacob doing the ordering by shouting out the back

window into the alley, where the cooks and waiters lounged during their breaks, playing cards on an up-turned milk crate. The restaurant closed at eleven, and so he was stuck with appetizers. He put a bottle of champagne in the ice chest to cool, then got into his pajamas and carried his attaché case into Jacob's study, the only room in the flat that had decent lighting.

The notebooks had lain untouched since June. He hadn't had the time, not with five articles a week to turn out for the paper and the traveling involved in getting material for them. Also, he just hadn't felt like writing down his thoughts. He had hoped that his novel would take shape out of those random jottings—current observations drifting into thoughts of the past. That hadn't happened. His perspective of Chicago and the Rilkes had not been freshened in any way whatsoever. And Jacob had cast a pall of doubt over the project.

"Every first novelist feels that the story of *his* life and *his* family is a world-shaking event that simply screams for print. I went through that stage myself, Martin. I was twelve at the time, and I suddenly noticed something that perhaps you have noticed yourself—that I simply do not look at all like my father. Well, I began to ponder on that and reached the febrile conclusion that I was the result of a liaison between my mother and the King of Spain. Then, filled with plans for an epic saga of my first twelve years on earth, about the little English Jew who was in reality bastard claimant to a Catholic throne, I went browsing in the attic and found a trunk. In that trunk were tintypes of my father and his long-dead sister, Rose. I was exactly like her, a carbon copy of the poor departed dear. Not a royal bastard at all, simply a throwback to certain Whitechapel physical types, the influx of Sephardim into London in the eighteenth century. Ah, well, the world lost a great popular novelist and gained an unpopular newspaperman. My dear fellow, the times spin on at a dizzy pace. Do your utmost to at least keep abreast of them. You have a talent for keen observation of the pathetic, sometimes endearing, sometimes mundane foibles of mankind. Put it to use. Bang out copy with the fury of the anchorites shrieking their predictions to the stones. Hone your pen to a knife. Cut . . . cut . . . cut! And save your memoirs for venerable old age."

The champagne cork made a satisfactory pop and flew over the leather sofa. Jacob was as easy to live with as a mad wasp, but he made a certain amount of sense sometimes. The epic novel of the Rilkes would join his saga of the striking Chicago motormen in oblivion.

He poured a glass of champagne, spread a thick layer of pâté on a water biscuit, and then leafed through the stack of mail which the cleaning woman had placed on the desk. Dunning letters for Jacob mostly, but one envelope addressed to him. It was on Marlborough Club stationery.

Dear Rilke:

I have the unfortunate honor to be assigned Captain of the Guard over Bank Holiday. Promised you a look at the inner workings of Buck duty. Might make an item for the penny press. If you are not otherwise engaged, I look forward to your joining me and a few friends for dinner in Guards quarters, St. James's, Tuesday evening, August 4th, 7P.M. Black tie. RSVP if possible.

Sincerely,
Fenton Wood-Lacy

He made a mental note to reply in the morning. It should be interesting. He could probably squeeze two articles out of it.

The notebooks lay piled in the attaché case. The last entry had been at Abingdon Pryory before he had left on the tour. He had a hundred comments and reflections to write down, but he could do no more than enter the date and time on the top of a blank page: July 24th, 1914. Early morning. He toyed with the pen and sipped champagne. He felt too weary to write and too keyed up to sleep. One singular event stuck in his mind, lingering with a peculiar poignancy. Why should that be so? It had only been a couple of weeks before—a picnic beside the Thames at Henley with the Grevilles and a party of their guests—and yet the scene seemed to belong to another age, suspended in time and misted by a golden light. The Royal Regatta held on the smooth green water of the river; gleaming, highly varnished rowboats gliding as noiselessly as the royal swans, great bowers of willow trailing leafy tendrils in the stream, women in white dresses and large hats strolling along the banks, a band playing in a gingerbread pavilion.

Jacob's dispatch from Serbia had triggered the remembrance of that day. "One can see Austrian gunboats prowling the Danube. . . ." The squat iron hulls became superimposed on the delicate pageant on the Thames. There had been no talk of crisis that day as they sat on the grass and ate strawberries and cream. The archduke was two weeks in his grave and long forgotten. Now Austria-Hungary prepared for war as Serbia held firm. What would Russia do? France? England? Treaties and alliances bound country to country like bands of steel. Now lights burned all night in the chancellories of Europe.

With the strawberries and cream they'd had a white wine, the wine served by the Greville butler (for, of course, there were servants even at a picnic in a meadow) from a silver bucket filled with ice. He met Lydia Foxe that day. What had they talked about? He couldn't remember. Nothing of any consequence. A stunningly beautiful woman. Easy to understand Charles's infatuation, but he had detected a shrewd toughness behind the lovely face and the gracious manners. Charles leaped at her every request, clung to her every word. She was bright, charming—and yet, once he had happened to glance at her while she was watching the earl and Hanna eat their strawberries. The woman's eyes had been pure steel.

He put the pen down and closed the notebook. There was no point in even trying to write. He felt a sense of waiting, as though the entire world was holding its breath. Outside in the street he could hear the sound of footsteps ringing on the cobblestones. A group of young men heading up Carnaby Street toward Oxford Circus. He didn't even have to get up and look to know that there would be a dozen or more of them, arms linked, cloth caps perched on the back of their heads, cigarettes dangling from their mouths. Out on the town on a hot July night. Several of them were singing a popular music hall song, their voices loud and beery, but the sound faded rapidly as they moved up the short, narrow street: "It's a long way 'ome, so don't wait up for me. . . . I'll give you a kiss an' a thrup'ny bit, but don't wait up for me. . . ."

They all seemed to be watching the clock, although Roger Wood-Lacy tried to keep the conversation going by telling a few jokes. Uniformed mess attendants removed the dinner plates. There was, Martin noted, a good deal of uneaten food. But not on his plate. The rack of lamb with Cumberland sauce had been delicious.

"You have good cooking in the army," he said.

Fenton sat at the head of the long table in his scarlet jacket, brass buttons reflecting the candlelight.

"The palace chefs actually, but our own chaps don't do too badly in the mess. Do you know who provides this dinner, Martin?"

Martin raised his wineglass. "You, I suppose, so I offer a toast to the host."

Roger clapped his hands, the sound echoing in the vast room, with its black-oak Tudor beams and dark brick walls.

" 'A toast to the host!' I say, we're all rhymesters tonight."

"I suppose we'll be telling puns or reciting limericks next," Charles said gloomily.

A pink-faced lieutenant looked blank. "Rhyme? What rhyme?"

"Never mind, Ashcroft," Fenton said. "Getting back to what I was saying, the answer is no, I don't provide the dinner. The meal comes from the generosity of King George the Fourth, the great Prinny, better known to history as Beau Brummel's friend. Anyway, he was a lover of fine food and blowsy women. Unfortunately, he only willed the captain of King's Guards provision for the former. The meal is his legacy, for which generations of hungry captains and their guests have been truly thankful."

"Hear, hear," Lieutenant Ashcroft murmured.

Charles checked the time again. "Ten-thirty."

"That makes it two minutes later than when you last looked," Fenton remarked dryly.

One of Fenton's mountaineering friends, a ruddy-faced barrister named Galesby, frowned and shook his head slowly.

"You're taking all this very lightly, I must say. After all, what happens or does not happen in the next hour and a half concerns you a good deal more than it concerns any of us—Lieutenant Ashcroft excepted, of course."

"Of course," Ashcroft said stiffly.

One of the messmen brought around a box of cigars. Fenton selected one and passed it slowly under his nose.

"We have a rule in the Guards quarters against talking shop. War, my dear Galesby, is shop."

"To you. I never took the king's shilling, so I'm legally entitled to speak my mind. I ask you straight out, Fenton. Do you believe Germany will back down by midnight and refrain from marching into Belgium?"

Fenton lit his cigar. It was so silent in the room that they could all hear the hissing of the match. The messmen walked as though treading on clouds.

"We are long past the moment when anyone can back down. The Germans are in front of Liège, and God himself couldn't turn their troop trains around.

The politicians, the statesmen, the kings and emperors have done their jobs, and now the soldiers take over. It's simply come down to that. If we could whisk old Golden back from Serbia, he could probably explain it better than I can—although, on second thought, I doubt it. It's rather like explaining the color blue to a blind man."

The barrister accepted the port decanter as it made the rounds of the table.

"Lord, what a bloody awful week this has turned out to be."

The clock was ancient, a triumph of rococo design, a small face nearly lost in a welter of ormolu. A grenadier officer had found it in the baggage of a Russian general after a battle in the Crimea. The room was filled with the souvenirs of old glories. Silver candlesticks brought back from Portugal after the Peninsular campaign, silver salvers given to the Brigade of Guards by the Duchess of Richmond a year after Waterloo. What would they add this time, Martin wondered? He looked at the clock. The minute hand made a tiny jump. He could visualize trains, hundreds upon hundreds of them, rolling west across Germany in the night, rolling east across France. Along the Danube, there had been war for six days. By all rights, it should have stayed there, toe to toe between Austria and Serbia. Jacob had written that Serbia was small but tough and the Austro-Hungarian empire rotten from the core out. The Serbs would maul the Austrian invasion, and if no one rushed to the aid of either side the war would be over in three weeks, with a treaty of mutual compromise. A grudging, bitter peace perhaps, but still a peace. Jacob had added to his dispatch: "But does the world want peace?" One of the editors had scratched the question out.

"With your permission, sir, I would like to propose a toast," Lieutenant Ashcroft said, his face becoming pinker by the minute.

"By all means," Fenton said, scowling at the tip of his cigar. "It's a night for toasts."

The lieutenant shot to his feet. "To England!"

The minute hand jumped. In the silence, after the toast had been echoed around the room, they could hear the soft whirring of the clock's gears. The port was passed along. Glasses were refilled.

"Odd," Galesby said. "Incredible, really, if one stops to think about it. Just last week I was making plans to go to Lanersbach and stretch my legs with some good alpine rock climbing."

Fenton puffed a lazy plume of smoke. "Well, you can always go to Wales."

Fenton and Lieutenant Ashcroft had to inspect the guard at Buckingham Palace at midnight, and so the guests left at eleven-thirty. The parting in the austere treeless courtyard of St. James's had been gravely formal.

"Shall we share a taxi?" Galesby said as they walked into Cleveland Row.

Charles took a deep breath of the clean night air. "No, thanks. Can't speak for the others, but I could do with a walk."

The barrister hesitated. "Jolly good idea. I think I'll join you. Heading down to Whitehall, I suppose."

"We might as well be among the first to know," Charles said.

They all walked in silence to the Mall. St. James's Park was shadowed and gloomy across the wide tree-lined road. A night heron glided across the still surface of the lake.

"Yes," Galesby said, almost to himself, "quite odd. One would have thought that intelligent men could have settled issues across a conference table."

"That would be contrary to fate," Roger said, his tone strangely fervid. "War is a form of rebirth. A rite as old as time. I was talking to Rupert this morning on the telephone, and I've never heard him so enthusiastic, so revitalized. To go shining to war in defense of little Belgium has all the nobility and purity of Arthurian quests, Rupert said. I think it's more Grecian myself. A sailing for Ilium."

"I don't know about that," the barrister said, tossing his half-smoked cigar into the gutter. "All I know for sure is that everything is going to bloody well change."

"That might be a blessing," Charles said quietly.

They stopped at the end of the Mall. The Duke of York's statue loomed up against the sky, and the lights in Admiralty House twinkled through the trees at the edge of the park. Big Ben tolled the hour: twelve hollow iron peals. They could hear distant cheering and then the sound of a rushing crowd, hundreds of feet ringing on the pavements. Shadows raced past the pools of light cast by the windows of the Foreign Office. Other shadows streamed across the wide expanse of Horse Guards Parade. The streams converged, split apart, some moving rapidly along Birdcage Walk, others coming into the Mall. Men, mostly young, running with a wild exuberance.

"War!" they were yelling. "It's war!"

Martin and Galesby stepped back to keep from being bowled over by the frantic rush toward Buckingham Palace, which was now blazing with lights. Roger grabbed Charles excitedly by the arm.

"Come on, Charles! Come on!"

And then the crowd swallowed them. They were one with it, borne along.

A middle-aged man, red-faced and puffing, ran out of the shadows of Waterloo Place.

"Is it war?" he shouted. "Is it war?"

"Yes, you damn fool," Galesby said. "It is."

BOOK TWO

On marching men, on
To the gates of death with song.
Sow your gladness for earth's reaping,
So you may be glad, though sleeping.
Strew your gladness on earth's bed.
So be merry, so be dead.
     —CHARLES HAMILTON SORLEY
      (1895–1915)

VIII

Major-General Sir Julian Wood-Lacy, VC, CVO, stood beside his staff car on a low hill in the shadow of a derelict windmill. The road to Maubeuge lay below, the poplars lining it standing motionless in the heat, their leaves white with dust. The army had been moving up the road from Le Cateau since dawn and had ground the surface to a chalky powder. The general's division was coming along, the first battalion of the Lancashire Regiment almost abreast of him now, the Royal West Kent behind them, followed by three batteries of field artillery. The rest of the division was far down the road, a crawling line of khaki barely discernible through the dust. Two squadrons of the 19th Hussars, the troopers dismounted to spare the horses, moved across the skyline of a distant hill. By God, the general thought, rendered dumb from emotion that choked him, what a wonder!

The division had been on the move for three days, dawn to dusk, across the rolling plains of northern France. Three days of grueling route march from the port of Boulogne under a pitiless August sun, and now here they were at last, a mere ten miles from the Belgian frontier. The general removed his cap from his balding head and waved it vigorously. The colonel of the Lancs, riding in front of his leading company on a sorrel horse, waved back, then turned to shout something at the men striding along behind him.

The infantry, by Harry! The general replaced his cap and stiffened, as though about to salute his king. God, how he loved the infantry. And there they were, the battalions of his division, marching at ease, rifles slung, dust streaked, uniforms black with sweat, whistling, some playing mouth organs or Jew's harps, but every man jack of them keeping in step and in an unwavering column of fours. The general was sixty-one years old and had been an infantryman since his seventeenth year, when he had joined the old 24th Foot as a subaltern. God! How many roads had he marched along in Zululand, Egypt, the Sudan, India? Uncounted miles. He could remember the hardships of those stony ways, the poor food and the stinking roadside water, the ranks drooping like flies that terrible September on the road from Jalalabad. All that was changed. Now, behind every company in each battalion came the horse-drawn transport wagons loaded with supplies, an ambulance wagon, and the field cookers, comforting plumes of smoke drifting from the stovepipes.

The passing men looked toward the low hill and burst into a shout: "Are we downhearted? NO-O-O!" The sound of the company's voices rocketed up to the general like a burst of cannon fire. And then the men broke into song, the music hall ditty that the British Expeditionary Force had taken as its own: "It's a long way to Tipperary . . . It's a long way to go. . . ."

Succeeding units kept the verses going, rank after rank—the Wiltshires and the Royal Irish, the Highland Light Infantry and the Middlesex Regiment—sweated, sunburned faces turning toward the hill where "Old Woody" stood saluting them, yes, by God, until the last of his nineteen thousand men had passed by, or at least come into view.

"Goodbye, Piccadilly, farewell, Leicester Square . . . It's a long, long way to Tipperary, but my heart's right there."

The château at Longueville shone silvery white under the moon, fairyland castle with conical towers and pointed spires. It was the temporary headquarters of the

3rd Division, II Corps of the BEF, and the cobblestoned courtyard was crowded with staff cars, tethered
horses, and the motorcycles and bicycles of dispatch riders and battalion runners. Captain Fenton Wood-Lacy
rode his tired horse under the graceful wrought-iron
arch that spanned the stone columns of the gateway,
showing his identity papers to the sergeant of the guard,
and then dismounted and led his mount to the horse
lines, where a cheerful farrier corporal offered to wipe
the beast down and give him a good feed. Fenton
handed him some cigarettes for his trouble and then
walked stiffly toward the terraced stone steps of the
château.

The entrance hall was a place of bedlam. Signalers
were struggling to set up their telephone equipment in
one corner, and staff officers hurried up and down a
baroque marble staircase while clusters of company and
battalion commanders stood about in glowering impatience. Fenton felt conspicuous among so many majors,
colonels, and brigadiers—even more so when Colonel
Archibald Blythe, General Wood-Lacy's ADC, spotted
him and cut through the crowd of expostulating brass
with a deaf ear.

"Ah, Captain," the colonel said, pumping Fenton's
hand, "glad you received the message. The general's
most anxious to talk to you. Come along upstairs."

Fenton ignored the glares of his superiors as the elderly colonel, who looked more like a professor of
Greek than soldier, led him up the winding staircase to
the second floor and ushered him into a large room.

"How about a whiskey?"

Fenton made a futile dab at his dust-streaked khakis.
"I'd like that *and* a clothes brush."

"Good Lord, no," the colonel said. "Dusty uniforms
and dirty boots are strictly *de rigueur* in this division. I
believe your uncle would court-martial any officer who
showed up in clean kit." He gave Fenton a pat on the
arm. "Damn good to see you again, lad. Just stroll

about and I'll send for a bottle and some Vichy. His nibs'll be along in time."

"How is the old boy?"

"Happy as a lark in spring. He was planning his retirement two months ago, and now he's leading a full-strength division against Fritz. Rather makes one ponder."

Fenton walked slowly around the room, a gallery filled with paintings of bucolic subjects and objects d'art. The château of a cultured man. A soldier brought whiskey, Vichy water, and glasses, and Fenton made himself a stiff drink and sat down on an impossibly delicate Louis XIV chair to enjoy it. He was several degrees past weariness, having been in the saddle since dawn. Having been foot-slogging for the same amount of time, the men of his company were even wearier, but at least they were asleep by now in and around the haystacks of Neuf-Mesnils.

He had just finished the drink and was contemplating having another when the general came striding into the room. His uniform, Fenton noted, was suitably dust ridden. He jumped to his feet, shifted the empty glass from right to left hand, and made a proper, if hasty, salute.

"At ease, boy . . . at ease." Sir Julian faced his nephew and smiled broadly. "By thunder, but you're a sight to behold. Dirty as a collier. Glad to see the Guards doing honest soldiering for a change."

"Well, sir, it's good to be out of a red coat, I'll say that."

"Yes, by God, I bet it is." He clapped Fenton on the shoulders with both hands. "Damn, but it's nice to see you, boy. How's young Roger?"

"Hurrying to enlist, last I saw of him."

The general tugged at his bristly walrus mustache. "Jolly good for him, but this flap'll be over by the time he gets his uniforms tailored. Our Teutonic friends bit off a bit more than they can chew. They'll be scurrying back across the Rhine before the leaves fall."

"Do you think so, sir?"

He leaned forward and lowered his voice a notch. "I *know* so. They've been taking fearful losses at Liège, and they'll be taking worse if they try to storm the forts at Namur. Those Belgians are fighting like terriers. By God, I hope we get a crack at 'em, but I'm afraid they'll pull in their horns and rush back to cover their center. The Frogs have been on the attack since this morning . . . toward Morhange and Sarrebourg. They should be deep into Lorraine by this time tomorrow, and Fritz will be in bloody hot water. Never did think much of this tactic of theirs, thinning the center and throwing all their power on their right wing. Bloody damn silly, if you ask me. The Frog First and Second armies will cut through Fritz's belly like hot knives through wax. How about another whiskey?"

"Only if you'll join me, sir."

"Sorry, lad. Can't take the time. Got a devil's amount of work to do." He folded his arms and rocked slowly back and forth on his heels. "I shall be brief, Fenton, and to the point. I've just arranged your transfer to my staff."

Fenton glanced away from his uncle's bright, piercing eyes. "That smacks a bit of nepotism, wouldn't you say?"

"Smacks? Why, good Lord, it positively reeks of it. But let lesser tongues wag if they will. My senior staff are all for it. We move north into Belgium tomorrow, the entire army. I suppose you can visualize what that means . . . ninety thousand men on the move and hardly one decent map among all of 'em. Your brigade is supposed to stay in close contact with my right flank. That might be a bit tricky because of the roads and the terrain. I need a trustworthy liaison officer—someone who won't rub the Guards' brigadier the wrong way, if you get my drift."

"I do, yes, sir."

"You're just the chap for the job. Blythe will give you a map showing our intended position by the evening of the twenty-second and indicating where the

Guards Brigade should be at that time. Your job is to make bloody sure they're in that position. If they're not, then I must know exactly where they are so I don't leave my flank dangling in the blue. The signalers aren't laying wire except along the line of march. I can pick up the telephone and ring through to Calais or even Paris, but I can't bloody well speak to anyone five miles to my right or left. I hope you don't resent my turning you into a messenger boy."

"No, sir, not at all."

"Good. It's settled then. Fortify yourself with another whiskey and then go over the details with Blythe." His hard brown hand shot out and squeezed Fenton's arm. "By gad, it's good to have you with me. I made you my second-in-command when you were eight years old. Do you remember?"

"Yes, sir," Fenton said, grinning. "And Roger was adjutant."

"Wood sword, paper hat, and all."

Colonel Blythe appeared in the doorway and coughed discreetly for attention.

"The battalion commanders are assembled, sir—"

"Right," the general said, snapping out of his sudden reverie. "Take our new young thruster in hand, that's the good chap." He turned abruptly and strode out of the room, his spurred boots pounding a brisk tattoo on the landing.

Colonel Blythe smiled faintly. "Comforting sound."

"He certainly exudes confidence."

"Yes, and we should be grateful for that. The troops are cheery enough . . . and cocky as hell, but, except for Old Woody, the high command is as nervous as a maiden aunt at a men's smoker." He poured himself a whiskey and downed it neat. "The French Fifth Army is off to our right somewhere, but there's no communication between them and us—no cooperation of any kind. They may be massed along the Sambre, and then again they may not. They may be about to attack Fritz, and then again they may be planning to fall back. No one knows for sure—nor do we have the foggiest idea what Fritz is up to. There may be two German corps ahead of us or two field armies, but I dare say we'll find out soon enough." He drew a map from a leather case fastened to his belt and handed it to Fenton. "We start north at dawn tomorrow. Our corps area will go along the canal from Conde to Mons. Third Division HQ will be a couple of miles south of Mons . . . at Frameries. We want you up there with the advance party. When battalion areas have been established and you can place them on the map, you're to scurry over to First Corps and make certain the Guards Brigade has reached Villers-St. Ghislain and that they have at least two batteries of eighteen-pounders covering the road from Thieu—if there *is* a road. The maps are bloody useless when it comes to minor details like that." He ran a hand through his thinning gray hair. "Lord, what a way to go to war."

D Company was in bivouac in a field, most of the men rolled up in their blankets beside the hay mounds, but a few sprawled on the ground smoking and talking. The company had been brought up to full strength with reservists—two hundred and forty men in four platoons—and Fenton had hoped to lead it. But strict adherence to custom had prevailed: only majors to command companies. The majors would have preferred the captains had the job. Most of them were well into their thirties, and some, like Major Horace Middlebanks, who was now in active command of D Company, had been on extended leave for months—Middlebanks on his estate in Ireland, where he raised steeplechase horses and distilled whiskey. Too much sampling of the latter had played havoc with his liver, and he was far from joyous to see his second-in-command pack up to move out.

"Hell's bells, Fenton," he grumbled, pacing the tiny farmhouse room they shared as a billet. "I really feel rotten."

Fenton shoved his gear into a canvas kit bag and tried to ignore the major stalking back and forth in his underwear.

"Go see the MO."

The major snorted in disgust. "All he'll do is give me one of those blue pills . . . or yellow pills. Anyway, whatever the bloody color, they'll keep me chained to a latrine for a week. It just isn't fair for me to lose you now. What if I ruddy well collapse in the saddle tomorrow and have to be sent back to Boulogne to see a real doctor?"

"Then Ashcroft will take over. He's a good man."

"He doesn't have the experience," the major said with a snort.

"None of us have the experience, do we? I mean, this isn't maneuvers. Have you ever heard a gun fired in anger? No . . . Neither have I. . . . Neither has Ashcroft. What difference does it make? Go back to sleep, Horace, and stop worrying about everything."

The major tossed and turned in restless slumber, grunting and groaning. It didn't matter to Fenton. He found it impossible to sleep anyway; his brain wouldn't allow it. Thoughts swirled around in a hodgepodge of vivid images. It seemed unbelievable that he had been in France for less than a week. Six days ago he had been in Southampton waiting to board the transport. The Marquess of Dexford had been permitted to come dockside and had brought gifts for his son Andrew, embarking with the 4th Cavalry Brigade, and for "my future son-in-law."

He sat up in the hard, narrow bed and looked through a hazy mica window at a distorted image of the moon. Lord Sutton's gifts had been appreciated—a box of tinned delicacies from Harrod's, Abdullah cigarettes, a bottle of whiskey, and a beautifully made, but totally impractical, pocket pistol. He had traded it to a captain in A Company for some extra socks. Among the gifts had been a letter from Winifred.

My dearest Fenton: God protect you in this hour of trial. I know you will be brave and daring and help achieve a quick and glorious victory. I am most vexed at Germany for starting this war, but they shall soon rue it. All of the newspapers predict that it will be over by Christmas. I pray they are correct in that assumption and that we will be tangoing at a victory ball on New Year's Eve. Ever, Your Winifred.

He groaned as loudly as the liverish major. *Your* Winifred! It was a struggle to recall her face.

He was dressed and out before dawn, walking across the stubble field toward the crossroads, where a staff car was waiting. Private Webber, his batman, trailed along behind him, carrying the bags and whistling softly to himself. Happy to be leaving, Fenton was thinking. The idea of his officer being attached to staff was pleasing to Webber. No more thirty-mile-a-day marches, no more sleeping on the hard ground. No wonder he was whistling. The tune was certainly appropriate to their change in station, and Fenton mouthed the words: "I'm Burlington Bertie, I rise at ten-thirty . . . and go for a stroll like a toff. . . ."

"What's that, sir?" Webber stood still, head cocked to one side. There was nothing to be heard other than the thin, distant call of a nightingale from the dark woods that bordered the field, but something had moved against them, a pulse of air that was not wind, that could be sensed rather than felt. Then sound came—dull, persistent thuds far off to the northeast, a rumble of thunder bumping the horizon. Sheet lightning flickered against a sky that was beginning to pale.

"Blimey," Webber said, sniffing the air. "Don't smell like rain."

Fenton walked slowly on, watching the sky—the dim, shimmering orange and red glow that was, after six years of being a soldier, his first glimpse of war. Not his war, not yet. The heavy guns were miles east, at Charle-

roi or even Namur. It could be French or Belgian fire
and the German Army might be reeling back from
those withering blasts, but doubt gnawed at him. His
palms became wet, and he stuck his hands into his
pockets and strolled to the car with studied noncha-
lance.

The boat train from Cherbourg was seven hours late
arriving in Paris, having been shunted off the main
track half a dozen times to allow troop trains to speed
by. When it finally reached the Gare St. Lazare, there
were no porters available and the passengers were
obliged to carry their own baggage into the station. Soldiers thronged the platforms, while harried sergeants
and corporals struggled to sort the men into their respective companies and battalions. Bugles blew. Regimental colors were unfurled to serve as rallying points,
and gradually the soldiers moved out of the station in
orderly lines before more troop trains arrived to add to
the confusion. A band standing in the square in front of
the church of St. Augustin played the "Marseillaise"
and the "Sambre et Meuse" on bugle, drum, and fife as
the troops marched down the rue de la Pépinière into
the boulevard Haussmann. Thousands of Parisians
thronged the pavements, cheering the long columns of
men in their blue coats, red trousers, and red kepis.

To Martin Rilke it was a vision out of childhood. He
was seven years old again, standing with his mother and
her cousin Bette on the Champs-Elysées. The fourteenth of July. Bands and marching soldiers passed.
And the giant horses of the cuirassiers, tall men riding
them, steel breastplates and crested helmets gleaming in
the sun. There were troops of cuirassiers now, turning
out of the rue Pasquier to trail the infantry. They
looked the same as they did then, except for a covering
of brown cloth over their horse-plume helmets. A con-
cession to *la guerre*.

Tom Ramsey, an artist for *Leslie's Weekly*, murmured in appreciation, "Colorful . . . and Old World.

They look like they're ready to fight the battle of Sedan all over again."

"The *pantalon rouge* is sacred to the French Army," Martin said. "Although you'd think khaki would be more practical these days. Those red pants and hats are going to be easy to aim at."

Ramsey removed a curved briar pipe from his mouth and dug ash from the bowl with his finger.

"I was just thinking the same thing, but it's none of my business how they want to dress for war. Anyway, it's sure going to make my pictures a damn sight prettier." He stretched his arms in an expansive gesture, embracing the scene. "Paris! City of light and beauty. Red trousers and blue coats against chestnut trees. I'll do watercolors of regiments of cuirassiers and battalions of *pantalons rouges* in the gardens of the Tuileries."

Martin laughed. "What if they aren't there?"

The artist shrugged. "So what? Artistic license. Anyway, if they're not there, they should be." He breathed deeply. "Paris. Like coming home for me."

"Hey, you said you'd never been here."

"I haven't. Took my training in Philadelphia, but, boy, have I ever dreamed of this town. I guess I've looked at a million pictures of the place. I know it by heart. I can't tell you how much I envy you, Rilke. *Born* here. My God."

That fact had impressed all of the eleven American newspapermen who had been on the train. Most of them spoke French with varying degrees of ineptness. They could ask for simple things—a cup of coffee, a glass of wine, the direction to the lavatory—but more complex thoughts had been beyond their abilities to express. Their papers had arranged for interpreters to meet them in Paris, and Martin had been their spokesman during the interminable train journey, as not one porter, conductor, or waiter in the dining car could, or would, speak English.

"Why?" Jasper King of the New York *Herald* had wanted to know. "This is a boat train, for cryin' out loud. They must be used to English-speaking passengers."

"They all understand English," Martin had explained after conversing with a conductor in faultless French. "They're just irked at Americans. There was an editorial in one of the Paris papers about America's decision to maintain an impartial neutrality and to honor trade commitments with Germany. They're just giving us the needle."

Martin had been pumped for information about Paris—the best restaurants, the location of various hotels, the Métro system. There was nothing he could tell them. Paris was an alien city to him. All he could remember with any clarity were a few streets near the Luxembourg and the small park off the rue Campagne where he used to fly kites with his friend Claude. Paris was not his hometown. He would have traded the Champs-Elysées for one block of State Street.

But here he was, seated in one of the taxis provided by the French Minister of Information; an army officer rode in the leading taxi, and the little cavalcade was wending its way through the twisting streets of Paris to the Quai d'Orsay, to the grim stone building housing the ministry. His reason for being there was contained in his attaché case, in a letter that he had been asked to present to the third deputy assistant to the Minister of Information along with his passport. The letter was from Harrington Comstock Briggs, authorizing Martin Rilke to serve as sole European correspondent for the Chicago *Express*.

The deputy assistant solemnly checked before him on his desk a list of those newspapers in the United States which had revealed pro-German attitudes. There were quite a few of them in Milwaukee, Chicago, St. Louis, Philadelphia, and New York. The *Express* was not on the blacklist.

"You may go in and see the minister, Monsieur Rilke."

They were all acceptable to the deputy, as the deputy

knew they would be since their credentials had been checked in London before visas had been issued. It was a formality, and the deputy assistant was a stickler for formality.

"We are at war, monsieur," he had said icily to the war correspondent of the New York *Times*, who had had the temerity to lose his patience when the deputy had taken ten minutes to study his papers.

"Damn it, sir," the *Times* man had blustered, "I know it. Why do you think I came to France?"

"You did not come at our request, monsieur. I can assure you of that."

The chill deepened when the Minister of Information himself, a man of great girth and regal bearing, entered his chambers nearly an hour after the last newspaperman had been ushered into the room and told to wait. He offered no apologies for the delay.

"Gentlemen," he said, speaking English with barely a trace of an accent, "let me welcome you to Paris. I hope your stay here will be pleasant. This ministry will do everything in its power to provide you with up-to-date information on the progress of the war. Let me caution you on the use of the telegraph service and the postal service. Censorship has been imposed. Nothing pertaining to the war may be sent out of the country unless it has been approved by this office and stamped accordingly. No foreign journalist may venture into the Zone of the Armies without the written permission of Marshal Joffre. Such permission is not likely to be granted in the foreseeable future."

The silence was total. Finally, the war correspondent of the New York *Times,* a man with an international reputation for his coverage of every war since 1890, cleared his throat and got to his feet.

"Your Excellency, do you mean to say that none of us can visit the front? That we are forbidden to view with our own eyes the current battles in Lorraine?"

The minister's tone was bland. "There is no necessity for it, sir. We shall provide you with those data. Captain de Lange, who traveled with you from the station, will keep you abreast of all developments. The official communiqués will be at your disposal every afternoon at four o'clock in the Military Information Center on the second floor. Room number two hundred and twenty-five. Captain de Lange will give you today's communiqué, which you are free to transmit to your journals. If there is any way I can be of further service to you, do not hesitate to call upon me. Good day, gentlemen."

And then he was gone, striding out of the room as regally as he had entered it. A solid oak door closed noiselessly behind him. Captain de Lange, a tall, thin, gray-haired man who wore pince-nez glasses on the very tip of his nose, walked stiffly from the back of the room and occupied the spot vacated by the minister. He removed a single sheet of paper from the breast pocket of his uniform jacket and unfolded it.

"The following communiqué has been received from General Castelnau in Nancy. The Second Army, in close coordination with the First Army under General Dubail, has everywhere been successful in its drive toward Morhange. Our infantry has inflicted grievous losses on the enemy and has recaptured many towns on the sacred soil of the lost province, the flag of France flying above the town halls of the following places for the first time since 1870: Burthecourt, Moyenvic, Lezey, Donnelay, Marsal, Salival, St. Medard. Château Salins is expected to fall by dawn tomorrow. Our losses have been insignificant, and reports from field commanders indicate that the German Sixth Army is in a disorderly retreat. On the Alsace front, General Pau is in firm possession of Mulhausen and expects to reach the Rhine within three days." He folded the paper and placed it back in his pocket. "That is the termination of today's communiqué. Copies will be available. Are there any questions?"

Baker of the *Journal-American* stood up. "We heard a rumor in Calais that the Germans are well past Liège in force. That they crushed the forts there with some exceptionally powerful, highly mobile siege guns and are approaching Namur in strength, bringing these guns with them. It seems to me that if the Belgian forts at Namur should fall—"

"Let me advise you not to pay heed to defeatist rumors," Captain de Lange interrupted with a tight little smile. "There are a great many German spies on the loose. We are discovering them daily and putting a speedy end to their intrigues. The truth will be found in Room two hundred and twenty-five every day at four P.M. Are there any more questions? No? Then let me bid you a good afternoon."

The captain had been mistaken. It was evening when they left the ministry and walked across the broad courtyard toward the waiting taxis. Martin shared a taxi with Tom Ramsey and three other men, one of whom was struggling to unfold a large map of France which he had bought in Cherbourg. The taxi crossed the Seine on the Pont Alexandre III and plunged into the brilliantly lit boulevards beyond the Petit Palais. Sidewalk cafés were jammed with people. Soldiers and pretty girls strolled arm in arm under the streetlamps, and the traffic along the boulevard des Capucines was at a standstill. The city was in a fever of holiday.

"Got it!" the newspaperman said grimly. "Here they are, those towns he told us about: Burthecourt . . . Moyenvic . . . Salival. . . . Why, they aren't *towns* . . . just dots on the map. There may be a pigpen or two, but there sure as hell is no *town hall* in any of 'em."

"I think we made a mistake in coming to Paris," another man said. "We should have gone straight into Belgium by way of Holland. They're just going to feed us a daily dose of pap."

"That's all *Leslie's* is after," Ramsay said. "Pretty pictures of marching soldiers and cheering crowds. They think this war is going to be nothing but a lot of saber rattling and martial posturing. What does your paper expect from you, Rilke?"

Martin shrugged. "General background stuff . . . as objective as possible. We have a lot of German-American readers."

The letter from Briggs had come as a surprise to Martin, but the editor had been candid.

> . . . as long as you are already in England, there doesn't seem to be any point in sending another man from here, although Jack Pierson expressed a desire for the job. You speak French and German, which was another point in your favor. Martin, just keep your eyes open and write what you see. Don't slant your reports one way or the other. Most people I've talked to here believe this war is based on an economic struggle between Germany, France, and England, and there is a good deal of sympathy for Germany's position. I had a long talk with a brigadier general in the Illinois National Guard, and it is his opinion that the war will last only four to five weeks and that the French Army, being, in his view, seriously antiquated, will fold and that the token English force will go back across the channel without ever firing a shot at the Prussians. He does not believe the Germans will occupy any part of France, but will withdraw their armies in a hurry. If they don't, they'll be overrun by the Russians in the east. The way he sees it—and you can take this for what it is worth—is that the Germans' only intent is to eliminate France as a military threat to them. To be frank, I don't think the general knows any more about this war than the guy on the street—who knows nothing. I sure as hell don't understand it.
>
> You're a sensible young fellow with no ax to grind, so just remain objective and write down what you see. Don't fall prey to rumors, which always abound in a war, and take all official communiqués with a grain of salt. I discovered that when I was covering the Boer War for the old *Ga-*

zette. I will arrange monetary matters, salary and expenses, through American Express. I would suggest that you spend no more than ten days in France and then go to Berlin via Switzerland and get the German viewpoint. I want your articles to be as balanced as possible.

P.S. I saw your uncle at the Union Club and he wishes you well. He picks Cleveland to win the pennant.

There seemed to be little point in staying in Paris. He spent the night, wandered about the city the next day with Ramsey, who was delighted with every stone and made innumerable sketches, then went to the ministry at four o'clock along with a score of other reporters and listened to Captain de Lange read a communiqué.

". . . Château Salins and the town of Dieuze were captured this morning by General Castelnau's Second Army. However, a strategic withdrawal was advised by Marshal Joffre in order to consolidate the efforts of the First Army's drive on Sarrebourg—"

An English journalist was foolish enough to ask a question.

"Was this withdrawal in the face of German counterattacks?"

Captain de Lange looked piqued. "If there had been an enemy counterattack, it would have been mentioned in the communiqué."

The line to Basel passed through the French Zone of the Armies, and only a few civilians had been issued travel permits. Even with papers properly stamped and signed, Martin was given no guarantee that he would be allowed on any of the trains rumbling out of the Gare de l'Est; trains that left every fifteen minutes filled with troops, horses, and supplies. It was five o'clock in the morning before he and twenty somber Swiss nationals were given reluctant permission to board a small passenger car that had been attached to the rear of a freight train loaded with field guns and caissons. The train groaned slowly eastward along the Marne, stopping every few miles on sidings to allow faster trains filled with soldiers to go by. Late that afternoon they had reached Epernay, and the flatcars of 75mm guns were uncoupled and hitched to another train heading north for Reims. No one at the station seemed to care what happened to the detached passenger car, although a railway official made a vague reference to another train due that night from Paris and bound for the Swiss frontier.

The carriage was hot, the Swiss were sullen, there was nothing to eat and only lukewarm water to drink, and so Martin decided to leave. Judging by the heavy rail traffic going north, the war lay in that direction and he just might be able to see something of it. He was so deep inside the Zone of the Armies that no one he encountered in the crowded station questioned his right to be there, even though he looked like a commercial traveler, a lone civilian in a sea of uniforms. While he was having a meal of sausage, bread, cheese, and wine in an *estaminet* near the depot, an artillery major pulled a chair up to his table and sat down.

"Are you in the Chamber of Deputies?" the man asked.

"No," Martin said, "the Ministry of Information."

The major toyed with his mustache, which was heavily waxed.

"Information, eh? Well, I'll tell you something that you can pass on to your superiors. It is cannon and only cannon that the Boche will have any respect for. The Minister of War has given us a good field gun, but we must have bigger and better ones."

"I'll make a note of that."

The major twirled the points of his mustache into firm needles.

"They say it is the infantry who will drive the Boche into the Rhine, but I say it is the cannon."

"I agree with you wholeheartedly. Have some wine."

"Thank you," the major said, reaching for the bottle. "You seem like a fine fellow. Civilians don't understand the first thing about war. You mention cannon to them and they stare at you blankly. I can tell that you are different."

"I understand the need for cannon. Absolutely."

The major drank carefully from the bottle and then wiped a drop of wine from his lower lip.

"I admire a civil servant who understands the needs of the military. However, I do not believe that you are a civil servant. A man from the ministry would not wear a brown jacket and checkered trousers. He would wear a black suit and a shirt with a stiff collar. Also, you speak with a slight accent that is not familiar to me. Are you Swiss?"

"American—of a French mother."

"And you are . . . ?"

"A journalist."

"Ah." He took another drink of wine and then leaned forward across the table and lowered his voice. "Papa Joffre does not like journalists. No one in the high command likes them one bit. Are you trying to get up to the war?"

"That was my hope."

"Then I will take you. And in payment for my generosity, you will, please, inform the world that it is cannon that win battles. I will give you an artilleryman's cloak to cover yourself with . . . and a kepi. My battery is entrained and we leave for the Ardennes in an hour. We're the Twenty-seventh Regiment of Artillery in the Third Colonial Corps. Veterans, I can tell you. We've used our beauties more than once in Morocco. Fifteen rounds of shrapnel a minute. Bang . . . bang . . . bang."

Trains moved like snails along the line north of Reims. On the second day after leaving Epernay, they crossed the River Aisne and the major's battery was taken off the train, hooked up to the horse teams, and

put on the long tree-lined road to Mézières. Martin
rode in one of the transport wagons that creaked along
behind the clattering gun teams, nestled down among
the men's packs and a jumble of other gear. He wished
he had brought his camera to France, but the French
consulate in London had advised him against it. His
eyes must be the camera lens, the notebook on his knee
the photographic film. He jotted down impressions to
be fleshed out later.

Montigny-sur-Vence, August 22

A small village of whitewashed stone houses,
thatched roofs. Orchards beyond the village. Vineyards covering the low hills. Peasants in smocks
working trees and vines and not turning their
heads as the endless columns of troops pass
through the village and ford the sluggish, weedy
little river. Dragoons on black horses, cuirassiers
on grays. Infantry in great, untidy masses, like a
crowd pouring out of a baseball stadium. They
wear blue wool greatcoats despite the heat, the
tails of the coats pinned back. Their red trousers
are chalky with dust. The officers carry swords,
and many of them wear white gloves. French officers, after all, *très chic*.

Fontaine-Gery is a few miles up the road. Rolling hills, heavily wooded. The Ardennes is a dark-
green cloud mass along the horizon. A dispatch rider on a bicycle catches up with the battery, and
the major has ordered the guns pulled off the road
next to an ancient church and a crumbling ceme-
tery wall. A Zouave band stands in the sun patches
and shadows of an orchard. They wear yellow
Turkish trousers, vivid blue jackets, and red
fezzes. Like parrots among the trees. They play the
"Sambre et Meuse" march on drums and fifes.
Troops cheer and weep. We are not far from Sedan. Germany ground the face of France into this

road in 1870, and now her sons are coming back to make them pay for it.

There is a sound like rolling thunder ahead of us. We have heard it since dawn, but intermittent, extremely far away. Now, it is closer, a continuous bumping and thumping, as though hundreds of empty freight cars were rolling back and forth inside a long tunnel.

Congestion on the road. Peasants from the north, driven from their farms by the fighting that must be raging ten or fifteen miles away, push against the oncoming troops. They pull carts and wagons loaded with their belongings. Children sit crying on top of bundles of goods. The refugees are oblivious to the soldiers, who yell at them and try to make them leave the roads. Mixed in with the refugees are wounded soldiers. Some are in horse-drawn ambulance wagons. Others walk as though in a daze, clutching bloody bandages. The troops seem embarrassed by the sight of them. A colonel lying in the back of a wagon with a blood-caked bandage wrapped clumsily around his chest mutters over and over, "*C'est une castastrophe.*"

Hannogne-St. Martin

The battery has been moved at the gallop along dirt lanes and across fields to this village, which is seven miles closer to the front. It is late afternoon and the beech trees and poplars are pale gold in the waning sun. The guns are drawn up on a low hill screened by thick clumps of grapevines. 75mm guns. An ammunition limber is beside each cannon. A seven-foot metal ladder has been bolted to one of the limbers, and the major stands on the top rung behind a narrow metal shield, powerful binoculars in his hands. He scans the woods and fields ahead of the battery and then shouts, "*Fantastique! Magnifique! C'est incroyable!*"

Martin put aside his notebook and climbed out of the transport wagon. The major was coming down the ladder, shouting directions to the gunners for range, elevation, and type of shell. He tossed the binoculars to Martin.

"Have a look! Oh, my God, the poor bastards of infantry!"

Martin climbed up the ladder and focused the binoculars. He could see French infantry advancing out of a valley and up the grassy slope of a hill toward a dark line of woods. They were in long lines, shoulder to shoulder and walking slowly, rifles held at the hips, the long bayonets catching the sun. Officers with drawn swords walked in front of them. The red and blue of their uniforms and the white gloves of the officers created a living flag—the tricolor rippling across the green hills of France. On they moved, a thousand or more in three waves. A hundred yards from the trees the first wave began to falter—to stumble and fall—to wither away as some unseen, unheard force scythed through them. They fell over in heaps, and the second wave moved on over their bodies.

"Guns ready!" a sergeant cried out.

"Fire for range on command," the major shouted. He clambered up on top of the limber and stood on the ladder, holding on to Martin's waist and grabbing the binoculars from him. "Fire!"

A gun barked, and a few seconds later the shell burst above the treetops. Leaves and small branches disappeared in a froth of debris. The infantry was still advancing—tumbling forward, sinking to its knees, turning and twisting in a slow, silent dance of death.

"Machine guns," the major yelled. "The damn Boche! Down a hundred . . . fourteen degrees . . . fire! Fire! Fire!"

Every gun in the battery began to slam shrapnel shells toward the tree line four miles away; black bursts of smoke blossomed violently in the shadowed wood. Breech blocks clanged, and empty shell cases rattled against the iron tailpieces of the guns. The artillery fire was accurate and devastating, but it was too late to save the soldiers. The Napoleonic formations had disappeared. There was nothing on the slope but windrows of corpses, wounded struggling to crawl back down the hill, and a few men running for cover, the tall grass rippling around them as machine-gun bullets mowed through it.

The major tugged at Martin's clothes. "Get down before you lose your head. The Germans have cannons too."

A Renault whined up from the village in low gear. A colonel of artillery stood in front beside the driver, clutching the windshield.

"Drag your battery out, Duchamp," he shouted over the cracking reports of the guns. "The whole front's caving in. Pull back to Omicourt, and be quick about it." He spotted Martin climbing down from the observation ladder, the civilian clothes showing under the artilleryman's cloak. "Who in God's name is that?"

The major shrugged. "An American . . . from Chicago."

The colonel tugged at his Vandyke beard. "I won't ask you how he got here, Duchamp. I'm in no mood to listen to your tall tales. Get him into the car before someone shoots the bastard as a spy. I tell you it is all falling apart. A debacle!"

There was a roaring sound above their heads, a short, sharp whistle, and then a shell exploded in a patch of woods behind the village. The shock wave sent Martin stumbling off his feet. The noise cracked against the skull. Trees and soil rocketed upward in a cascade of smoke and flame.

"Howitzer!" Major Duchamp yelled. "Two hundred ten millimeter! Those damn Boches!" He grabbed Martin and propelled him toward the car. "Write about *that*. Tell them we can't fight against two-hundred-ten-millimeter howitzers with our seventy-fives. Tell them—"

But what else the major wished him to tell was lost in the shriek of heavy shells, one following the other, the explosions rocking the hill. Geysers of earth and shattered trees blew upward in a whirlwind of blinding flashes. A field gun lurched brokenly into a yawning, steaming hole. An ammunition limber began to explode, the hot rounds whirling off across the vineyard like giant pinwheels. Martin half fell, half dove into the back of the Renault. He felt the car turn and twist crazily as the driver gave it full throttle and spun the steering wheel. Martin lay on the floorboards, his face pressed against the bottom of the seat. Clods of dirt and bits of wood showered down on his back. Oh, God, he thought wildly, I wish I was on Maxwell Street. . . . I wish I was on Maxwell Street.

IX

"I'm afraid I'm lost, sir," the driver said.

"It's not your fault," Fenton said, scowling at his map. "That *was* Givry we passed through, wasn't it?"

"Yes, sir."

"It's the map then. Bloody work of fiction. This road doesn't go to Villers-St. Ghislain or anywhere near it."

The driver tapped his gloved hand against the steering wheel and whistled softly between his teeth.

"Stop that bloody whistling," Fenton snapped irritably.

He was immediately sorry that he had lost his temper and thought of offering an apology. That wouldn't do, of course. One didn't apologize to a man in the ranks under any circumstances. Poor chap was only whistling in the dark. It was an eerie feeling being alone in the middle of God knows where. The road they were on might lead them straight into the German Army for all they knew. Ninety thousand British troops in France, the French Fifth Army off to their right somewhere, and not a man to be seen. It was damn discomforting. He settled back in the seat and glared at the map. Why would a cartographer mark a road that didn't exist? Perhaps one had been planned and the map maker had simply jumped the gun in marking it down. That was a possibility. They weren't on a road, not a proper *pavé*, but rather a cow path that wouldn't have warranted inclusion on a map. He tried to figure out its eventual destination. Bray? Spiennes? A score of place names were clustered east of Mons. The path could lead to any one of them—or to none. He removed his cap and wiped his forehead with a handkerchief. Lord, it was hot, the noonday sun beating down from a cloudless, brazen sky. His batman was groggy from the heat, slumped sideways in a listless, soggy bundle. Poor old Webber, far past his prime. The driver, Lance Corporal Ackroyd, was a thin, wiry Londoner of the Middlesex Regiment. He'd hold up all right. Fenton reached into his pocket and took out a tin of cigarettes.

"Care for a fag, Corporal?"

"Thank you, sir," the driver said, perking up noticeably. "Been 'alf dyin' for a smoke, sir."

"Take a handful of them."

The driver did as he was told. "Blimey. Abdullahs."

"Might just spoil your taste for Woodbines."

"Might at that, sir."

Fenton smiled and the man grinned back. A certain amount of familiarity was unavoidable. They were, in a manner of speaking, in the same boat. He lit the corporal's cigarette and then his own.

"Bloody dismal country."

"Yes, sir. Mucked up a bit."

It was an ominous landscape, chilling even in the brightness of an August day: dank, overgrown patches of woodland, untilled fields, the sour smell of neglect. Weed-dotted slag heaps and conical structures of rotting timbers marked the sites of abandoned coal shafts. This was the edge of the Borinage—coal, slate, and darkly polluted streams.

Fenton folded the map and slipped it into its case. "Drive on another couple of miles. We're bound to reach some sort of village that'll give us a fix."

Lance Corporal Ackroyd put the car into gear, and they rolled bumpingly along the narrow, deeply rutted road, past eroded hills of slag, the edge of a gloomy wood, and then into more open country; flat fields of unharvested oats stretched away on both sides of them. Ackroyd suddenly braked and pointed ahead.

"Look at that, sir! Comin' straight for us."

The airplane had sideslipped over a line of poplars and was flying toward them no more than thirty feet off the ground. It banked sharply, and the pilot leaned far out of the cockpit and pointed toward the field.

"One of ours, sir?"

"Yes," Fenton said, studying the slow-moving machine carefully. "An Avro, I think. What the hell keeps them in the air?"

"Thinkin' the same thing, sir. Looks like a Chinese laundry cart, don't it?"

The plane's tiny engine popped and fumed, and the ungainly contraption of canvas, wood, and wire made a sickening lurch, straightened up scant feet from the surface of the field, and then glided to a perfect landing, nosing over slightly against the bamboo skids fastened in front of the wheels.

Fenton and the corporal got out of the car and ran across the field. The pilot was climbing carefully out of the cockpit, threading his way through the maze of wires connecting the bottom wing with the top.

"Hello, chaps," the pilot called out. "Any idea where I am exactly?"

"Only roughly," Fenton said. "You're somewhere between Givry and Villers-St. Ghislain. About eight miles east of Mons."

The pilot removed his leather helmet and scratched his head vigorously. He looked no more than eighteen years old to Fenton.

"Oh, I say. I thought I was *west* of Mons. No wonder I couldn't find the ruddy place. Been circlin' for hours, it seems. Can you spare some petrol? I'm down to my last few drops."

"There's a five-gallon tin in the boot," the corporal said.

"Thank the Lord. I can get to Le Cateau on that."

"Is it all right, sir?"

"Yes, of course," Fenton said. "Go fetch it."

The corporal ran back toward the car, and the pilot

leaned wearily against the edge of the plane's lower wing.

"F.A.M. Weedlock here . . . Lieutenant Weedlock actually." He held out a grimy oil-smeared hand. "And you are?"

"Fenton Wood-Lacy."

The pilot glanced at the pips on Fenton's sleeve. "Nice of you to help me, Captain. I shall do you a good service. Turn your car around. There's absolutely nothing ahead of you but Huns. Bloody hordes of 'em."

"How far away?"

"Ten miles or so. I've been as far as Nivelles and Charleroi this morning. Germans on every road . . . crossing every field. Bloody bunch of locusts. Never seen anything like it. Flew very low over 'em and the silly bastards waved at me. Thought it was quite a lark, they did."

Fenton drew out his map. "Where are they exactly?"

"Oh, Lord, *everywhere*." He drew his finger across the map, leaving a faint smear of oil. "From Charleroi all across to just north of Mons. There must be two hundred thousand of 'em. Looks like a gray river from the air. And artillery . . . miles and miles of horse-drawn gun transport. I've got to get my report to HQ . . . if I can ruddy well find it."

"Yes," Fenton said dryly. "I think they might be interested. See any French troops on our right?"

"Well, some of their cavalry—tossing plumes . . . breastplates shining in the sun. All that fancy-dress rot. A few infantry . . . all going south. If our chaps are at Mons, then their flank is in the air. I went up to ten thousand feet over Charleroi, and I could see nothing but battle smoke from the Meuse. Poor old Frenchy must be catching hell. Looked as though their whole line of battle was caving in."

The pilot ate some cheese and bread from the hamper in the car while Ackroyd refueled his plane. He then instructed the corporal on how to spin the propeller without decapitating himself and flew off, the plane rising as effortlessly as a swallow from the field. He made one stuttering turn around the car at a hundred feet and then headed south. They stood in the road and watched until the little plane was lost to view.

"Rather a pleasant way to travel," Fenton said quietly.

They reached the brick schoolhouse in the village of Frameries that was now 3rd Division HQ shortly after nightfall. The road to Mons was jammed with horse-drawn artillery and supply wagons, pipers of the Gordon Highlanders skirling away to help ease the tempers of the cursing drivers. Fenton dismissed Lance Corporal Ackroyd and Webber for the night and then made his way through the building, which was crowded with staff and line officers. There was an atmosphere of frenzied confusion, but Colonel Blythe assured Fenton that everything was firmly in hand.

"I suppose you know by now what's ahead of us," Fenton said.

The colonel nodded. "We've been getting reports in all day. It's the bulk of a German army . . . von Kluck's, we believe. The field marshal ran up from Le Cateau to tell us there's no more than two corps facing us, but we know better. The cavalry wallahs have been out all day and doing damn well too. They even brought in some prisoners. We're horribly outnumbered, but the old boy convinced the corps commander that we can stop them along the canal. I hope to God he's right. How are the Guards settling in at Villers-St. Ghislain? Do they have enough artillery in support?"

"They may . . . wherever they are. We finally found that damn village after driving around in circles for bloody hours, but there are no troops there. Not one. Your flank is, if you'll pardon the expression, naked."

"Good God," the colonel muttered. "Old Woody won't be happy to hear that, although I imagine he won't be terribly surprised either. High command is trying to run this show from thirty miles back: abysmal roads, faulty telephone wires, wretched maps. . . . It's a bloody ball-up is what it is. Well, I'll go tell him the good news. We have a mess of sorts down that hall. Get yourself a hot meal and a whiskey. It may be your last of both for some time to come."

Cooks were opening five-pound tins of stew and heating the contents over a kerosene fire. Foxe's Fancy Old Irish Stew, Fenton noted wryly. He wondered what Archie would be dining on at his London club. Not his own stew, surely, although it was certainly tasty enough. He ate two helpings and washed it down with a large whiskey and soda. One of the other officers who sat squeezed at the long table which had been designed for children's legs eyed him sourly.

"Where the hell is the First Corps? Should be in position on our right flank by now, shouldn't it?"

"Should be. But it's not . . . and it won't. There's nothing on *their* right flank. The French are falling back all along the line."

The glum officer toyed with his stew. "Could have told 'em that. Knew it would happen. We should have landed at Antwerp and let the bloody Frogs fight their own war."

So much for allied cooperation and friendship, Fenton thought as he sipped his whiskey. But why should officers of the II Corps of the British Expeditionary Force have a feeling of comradeship for the French Army when they didn't have it for their own I Corps? A major in the Manchester Regiment was glaring at his Coldstream Guards badges with open hostility. Fenton downed his whiskey and left the room without bothering to thank anyone for the hospitality of the mess.

The HQ was cleared by 2:00 A.M. as battalion commanders and their aides returned to their units. General Wood-Lacy, slurping away at a mug of steaming tea, continued to pace slowly back and forth in front of a wall map—a pathetically inadequate map but the best one available. Fenton sat behind a child's desk in the schoolroom and watched his uncle in silence. After ten minutes, the general turned away from the map and sat on the edge of a desk, tapping a wooden pointer idly against his booted leg.

"Well, Fenton, tomorrow will be all battle, and Second Corps will go it alone. No matter. We can cut it. We're blessed with Smith-Dorrien as corps commander. A good infantryman. Knew him well in Africa. Zulus almost scuppered him when he was a subaltern as they almost scuppered me. By God, this division won't let him down."

"What do I do, sir? Seems to me I'm a bit of a fifth wheel around here now."

"Oh, I dare say I shall keep you busy scurrying about. I can't send you back, can I? Lord knows where your brigade is right now . . . stuck along the road someplace well out of it. No, no, you'll stay attached to my staff for a few more days and earn your keep. You may also learn something about soldiering—that it isn't all walking Buck guard, seducing women, and playing cards."

Church bells tolled for early mass, but that was the last peaceful sound to be heard that Sunday morning. Fenton slept fitfully in the schoolroom, hunkered down at a desk. He woke to the sound of the bells and the distant clatter of rifle fire. Mess orderlies brought dixies of tea into the rooms for the sleepy-eyed staff officers. The field telephones began to ring.

"The Fourth Middlesex reports contact with the enemy at Obourg bridge."

A map pin was placed on the spot. Other reports came in, and the sound of distant small-arms fire became more rapid and intense.

"The West Kents and the Royal Fusiliers are heavily engaged. . . . Two Fritz battalions attacking Le Bois Haut . . ."

By ten in the morning German artillery began to

open up, and the telephone network to the line battalions started to break down as shellfire cut the wires. Messengers and battalion runners came and went. More dixies of hot tea were brought in along with bully beef and bread. Fenton sat in a corner of the operations room, drinking tea and smoking cigarettes. He felt out of things, a useless mouth to feed. He walked out onto the school play yard in the afternoon and watched the pall of smoke which lay heavily along the northern skyline. The towering slag heaps of the area chopped off visibility to a few hundred yards in any direction. A drab and miserable landscape, but people lived there, built homes, married, raised children, and sent them off each morning to this little dark brick school. Now shells were screaming out of the hot sky and thundering into the earth a mile from the village. The little houses stood waiting for the storm to reach them. Their occupants were gone or leaving; bundles of belongings were piled onto carts, into ancient, wheezing motorcars, in perambulators and two-wheeled dog carts. The shells inched closer to the village, and a haze of red dust from blasted houses obscured the sun. Chunks of debris splattered the yard, and the schoolhouse windows were starting to shatter under the heavy concussions.

It seemed foolish to stand in the open with a good part of Frameries falling about him, so Fenton walked casually back toward the school, aware that a platoon of Highlanders at the far end of the play yard, and prudently under cover, were watching him. It would not do, he thought grimly, for a captain in the Coldstream Guards to run. A piper with a sense of humor blew a few notes of "Johnnie Cope": "Hey, Johnnie Cope, are ye wauking yet?" The platoon laughed in appreciation, and Fenton doffed his cap to the piper when he reached the school building, a gesture that brought a burst of cheers—followed by a German howitzer shell which turned the center of the play yard into a volcano. The platoon of Royal Scots ducked, a swing and a teeter-totter were blown into lethal fragments, and Fenton dove headfirst through a door.

The headquarters staff was still working efficiently despite the broken glass and fallen plaster that littered the rooms. A medical orderly wrapped a bandage around Fenton's cut head, handed him a tot of rum, and then hurried off to aid the more desperately wounded, who were being brought into the schoolhouse in increasing numbers. Colonel Blythe, hollow eyed and grim faced, spotted Fenton nursing his head in a corner and came quickly over to him.

"Are you all right, lad?"

"Fine," he said thickly. "Just a knock on the head."

"Because we've got a job for you. We've received orders to disengage and pull back five miles . . . set up a new line by nightfall. This bloody artillery is getting to be too bloody accurate."

"What does the general feel about that?"

"Woody wants to stay and fight. He sent a message to GHQ asking for ten machine-gun teams. They won't send them, of course. I doubt if there are ten Vickers guns to spare in the entire army. Anyway, machine guns won't stop cannon, and the Huns are moving batteries of 'em onto our flank. We've got to pull back, but Woody's afraid that once we start retreating there'll be no end to it. He's sure we'll just keep sliding back to the coast."

"What do you want me to do?"

"We've lost all contact with Fifth Division HQ at Elouges. Get in your car and hurry over there, make certain they know we're pulling back to Sars-la-Bruyère. I'll give you the timetables for the withdrawal. We must coordinate our movements or there'll be frightful gaps in the line." He shoved a packet of papers into Fenton's hand. "Hurry along. That's the good chap."

*   *   *

Fenton gave Webber the choice of staying or going along with him. Like any devoted batman, Webber elected to stay "with my officer." He sat in the front with Lance Corporal Ackroyd, a loaded Lee-Enfield between his knees, convinced by rumors he had heard that hordes of Germans were on the roads disguised as Belgian nuns.

The pattern of the roads forced them due south for a mile before they could hope to turn west toward Elouges. It was a slow mile. The road was choked with artillery and transport turning to go back. Some artillery officers were refusing to turn their teams around, cursing the fact that they had yet to fire their pieces at the enemy. Squads of Tommies from the Wiltshire Regiment were acting as military police, and soon the jam of horses, wagons, and guns was broken and the retreat became an orderly and steady flow to the south.

The road to the west was narrow and twisting, meandering through fields, woods, nameless little villages, and past slag heaps and coal dumps. Streams of infantry crossed the road at a dozen places, moving away from the battle, which still cracked and thundered along the horizon. They were tired men, their uniforms torn and filthy, their faces black with coal dust, but they all appeared cheerful and full of optimism. A lieutenant in the Royal Irish, who flagged the car down to ask directions, told Fenton that they had stopped the Germans in their tracks at the canal.

"Shot them down in droves . . . five rounds rapid all along the line. . . . Didn't have to aim. . . . Came on in masses, shoulder to shoulder. I hear the Kaiser called our army contemptible. Wonder what he thinks now?" The lieutenant felt they were on the verge of a major victory even though they were, in his words, giving up a bit of ground. It seemed to Fenton that more than just a "bit of ground" was being given up. The army was turning its back on an advancing enemy, and it would be a logistic nightmare to get it turned around again. The lieutenant had assumed that the hundred yards or so of his platoon's front was the entire conflict, and he had seen the German attacks on that front wither away under the murderous rifle fire of his marksmen. He had not seen the big map at HQ that revealed the action at Mons as being only a tiny part of a huge battle raging from the Swiss border to Brussels. A battle is more than the sum of its parts. Even a stupendous victory at Mons would mean little or nothing if the French armies were falling back from the frontier, which they seemed to be doing. The tiny British Expeditionary Force was way out on a limb, and if it didn't pull back in a hurry, that limb was going to be chopped off. There was no point in trying to explain any of that to a euphoric young Irishman who felt he had just won the war. Fenton gave him some cigarettes, the directions to Sars-la-Bruyère, and told Lance Corporal Ackroyd to drive on.

No one at 5th Division HQ gave a damn about the withdrawal timetable of the 3rd Division. The pressure on 5th Division's front—and that pressure was severe—made it necessary for the officers to devise their own timetable for retreat. Shells were thudding closer and closer to Elouges and turning the roads into interlocking craters. German troops were across the canal in force and the rear-guard action was becoming desperate. Most of the bridges across the canal had been blown, but large formations of German cavalry supported by infantry were sweeping around the canal east of Conde and taking the division in flank. Coordinated withdrawal was impossible. Each battalion had to pull back when it could.

"Tell Sir Julian that we'll try not to leave any gaps, but we can't possibly guarantee it," the division commander's ADC said a bit testily. "After all, this isn't Salisbury maneuvers."

Lance Corporal Ackroyd was pacing restlessly beside the car as Fenton left the HQ building in the town square. A battery of eighteen-pounders in a seedy little park was firing shrapnel at a not-too-distant hill, and firing as rapidly as the crews could load the shells. Webber sat rigidly in the front seat clutching his rifle, head turned, watching the shells splatter the skyline with bursts of black smoke.

"Where to now, sir?" Ackroyd said as he opened the car's rear door. He had to shout to be heard.

Fenton looked at his watch. Four twenty-five. It would be dark by the time they got back to Frameries, and the chances were that the division would have pulled out by then. They would have to catch up with it on the road to Sars-la-Bruyère. He sat on the running board with Ackroyd and went over the map with him. The main road south was starting to clog up badly; transport wagons, gun teams, and troops were already backing up into the town square. To drive into that crush would be folly.

"We can easily go around, sir," the corporal said. "This is a big, powerful car and the fields are dry as stone. We could cut across country and be at this Sarla-brewer in two hours."

It sounded reasonable to Fenton, and he made a mental note to recommend Ackroyd for another chevron.

The car plowed through fields of oat and barley, leaving a wake of bent grain, but after a few miles the landscape changed from flat fields to a thickly wooded country interspersed with slate quarries and coal works. A labyrinth of narrow dirt roads, none of which could be found on the map, headed in all directions. They took one that looked promising, but, after two miles of steady travel to the south, the road ended abruptly at a coal mine and they had to turn back and try another. The new road wandered haphazardly south, then west, then south again, going through dense woods, the branches of trees forming a gloomy canopy. At one point Ackroyd had to brake in a hurry to keep from slamming into a troop of French dragoons who suddenly emerged from the shadowed woods at a trot, the horses lathered, the riders gaunt-faced with fatigue, moving across the road in a flood of foam-flecked horsehide and glittering accouterments. They were part of General Sordet's corps screening the BEF's left flank, clattering past in the fading sunlight like ghost cavalry on the way to Waterloo. The woods on the other side of the road swallowed them up.

"Blimey," an awed Ackroyd murmured. "They don't 'arf look a sight."

There were more cavalry further down the road— British hussars, a hundred or more walking their tired horses. The khaki-clad troopers looked less splendid than their French counterparts, but more warlike with their Lee-Enfield rifles jutting up from the saddle sheaths. Fenton recognized the major in command, one of the better whist players at the Marlborough Club, and called out to him. The man walked slowly up to the car, leading his horse.

"Hello, Fenton," he said. "What are you doing out here all on your lonesome?"

"Trying to reach Sars-la-Bruyère."

"Well, this road will take you there—eventually. But the place is an unholy mess . . . jam-packed with transport, and all of it moving back into France. What's happening up north?"

"Damned if I know exactly. Big fight this morning all along the canal from Mons to Conde. We did well, I think, but the corps's in full retirement nonetheless."

The major's smile was thin. "Talk about the fog of war. The right hand hasn't a clue to what the left hand's doing. I don't like this groping around in the dark one bloody bit, I can tell you. Got any whiskey?"

"Afraid I don't."

"Pity."

There was a crackle of rifle fire in the distance, the sound distorted by the wall of trees. The major cocked his head to one side like a hound. The rifle fire slacked off to be replaced by the unmistakable chatter of a machine gun.

"Trumpeter!" the major shouted as he swung up into the saddle. "Mount! At the canter! . . . Forward!"

A bugle blared, and the troop mounted and followed the major across the road and into the trees. They were soon out of sight, swallowed by shadows as the French dragoons had been. There was something foreboding about the woods that brought a shiver up Fenton's spine. They might not have seemed so ominous at noon, but the sun was almost down now, and the sky, or what could be seen of it, was a blood red. The faint light that filtered through the beech trees had the same sanguinary hue.

"Drive on," he said. "Fast."

The road curved east, then due west, and the woods began to thin out. The sun was a grossly enlarged scarlet ball that seemed to touch the road ahead of them. Shadows flickered across it.

"More bleedin' horses," Ackroyd muttered as he stepped on the brakes.

"Lancers," Webber said, squinting into the glare from the windshield.

Fenton caught a glimpse of the riders' headgear silhouetted against the sun. Not English cloth caps nor French brass casques, but small helmets with a flat projection on top, like a miniature center-post table upended.

"Uhlans," he said with remarkable sangfroid, considering the chilling quality of that name. "Back up."

Private Webber was only a batman, but even the lowliest guardsman went through the regimental training depot and its extensive musketry course. He stood up, braced his body against the windshield, raised the Lee-Enfield to his shoulder, and squeezed off a shot. One of the shadowy figures toppled to the road and a riderless horse careened wildly past the car. His second shot went wide as Ackroyd threw the gears into reverse and floored the accelerator, the car roaring back down the road, weaving from side to side. There was a burst of machine-gun fire from the fringe of the woods ahead of them, and bullets splattered the car, shrieking through metal, rubber, and glass. The front tires blew and the car lurched violently off the road into a ditch. Fenton caught a glimpse of Webber toppling backward with blood sheeting his face, and then he was flying out of the back of the car, crashing through branches and landing heavily in a drift of summer-dried leaves.

He blacked out from the fall, and when he opened his eyes he could see nothing but dancing red lights. He struggled to breathe, but something seemed to be pressing against his face, holding his mouth and nose with a suffocating grip. He began to struggle, and then a mouth pressed against his ear and the barely audible voice of Lance Corporal Ackroyd said, "Don't move, sir . . . don't move."

The grip on his nose slackened, but Ackroyd's hand was still over his mouth. His eyes came into proper focus, and he could see that the red lights that had been darting and flipping about had turned into billows of flame shooting up from the car. He was lying a good thirty yards from it, well into the woods, his view of the fire fragmented by slender black trunks. Surely, he thought, he had not been thrown thirty yards through a beech forest. Lance Corporal Ackroyd must have dragged him. By Harry, he'd see that the man made sergeant, and was awarded a DCM to boot. He nodded slowly, an assuring signal to Ackroyd that his restraint was no longer necessary.

"Where are they?" he whispered.

"Fuckin' everywhere . . . *sir*."

He could hear them now: the soft thud of horses' hooves, the crack and splinter of young trees and underbrush, the cursing of men—guttural German curses. There was a clatter of hobnailed jackboots on the road—the Jäger unit of infantry who followed along behind the Germany cavalry to support them with expert rifle and machine-gun fire. Someone shouted, "*Achtung! Die Engländer kommen!*"

A bugle call from far down the road, and then the

distant thunder of galloping horses. The uhlans who had been searching the wood crashed back toward the road. A machine gun began to clatter from a position near the still-blazing car. Rifles joined it, and the firing was sustained and intense. Fenton could see nothing of the action, but he could visualize it all too clearly—the hussars coming back at the gallop, drawn by the fire, or pyre, more than likely, because poor old Webber was probably being consumed by it. Horses and men would be going down in a heap.

"Oh, God."

"Shh . . . quiet, sir . . . quiet. Can you walk, sir?"

"I . . . don't know."

"Try, sir . . . *try*." There was an edge of desperation in Ackroyd's voice. Fenton got slowly to his feet. There was a dull pain in the small of his back, but nothing seemed to be broken.

"Keep low, sir . . . and run like hell."

The direction seemed unimportant at the moment, the only factor being to get as far away as possible from the German lancers and the Jägers; the latter, as Fenton knew, were born hunters and foresters. Bending nearly double, they began to run, Ackroyd in the lead, racing through the closely grouped trees, stumbling and plunging through the thick underbrush. The firing continued behind them, but no shots came their way until they broke out of the woods into a small clearing. Dark shapes moved, and rifles barked. Ackroyd dove for the tall grass with Fenton right behind him. They lay flat and crawled as bullets hissed through the grass around them. Once among the trees again, they stood up and kept running, dodging from trunk to trunk, not stopping until total exhaustion brought them panting and sobbing to the ground. Fenton vomited and rolled onto his back under a hawthorn bush. Ackroyd lay on his face as though dead. They were deep in the forest, and there was no sound but the gentle rustling of leaves, a nightingale's lilting notes, and their own tortured breaths.

*   *   *

They hid by day and moved by night, working their way slowly southward. The German Army was all around them, but not in a solid mass. There would be hours during the day when they would not see even one enemy soldier, and they would debate whether to leave their hiding place—be it copse or haystack, abandoned mine shaft or reeking pigpen—and walk on more quickly than they could at night, but invariably Germans would appear sometime during the day: a solitary squad scouting a road, or an entire battalion swarming across a field. And then there was always the lurking menace of uhlans, death's-head hussars, or less exotic-looking cavalry to worry about. So they walked south by night, traveling by the map, using kilometer road markers as points of reference, and avoiding the villages. They ate apples and wild berries and what little food they could find in the many abandoned cottages. The weather was good, hot by day and balmy at night, with cloudless skies and enough moon- and starlight to make walking cross-country easy. A sudden, violent thunderstorm struck during the second night of their journey and forced them to seek shelter in a barn. The rain stopped at dawn, but a different thunder continued—the thump-thump-thump of heavy shellfire. The artillery bombardment was nearly due east, ten miles or so away, at or near Le Cateau, as far as Fenton could judge. It continued from dawn to dusk and was obviously a major battle, but when the firing ceased there was no way of knowing who had won.

"I suppose we could walk to Le Cateau tonight and see who's in possession of the place," Fenton said, studying his map and eating an apple.

"We could, sir," Ackroyd said dubiously. "If we're awful ruddy careful about it."

It was impossible to maintain a strict officer-to-man relationship with Lance Corporal Ackroyd, considering the circumstances. Men who had spent hours together half submerged in the stinking wallow of a pigsty while uhlans foraged their horses nearby learned a great deal about each other's qualities as human creatures. Fenton had only the greatest respect for Ackroyd. He was uncomplaining, resourceful, cautious, and brave. The type of indomitable soldier any officer would want at his side when a situation became rather sticky.

"You don't think it's a good idea, Ackroyd?"

"Beggin' the captain's pardon, but no, sir, I don't. If there was a battle over there, it would seem to me that both sides'll be a bit touchy and we could get crumped by either of 'em if we got spotted blunderin' about in the dark. Fritz or Tommy . . . we'd still be feedin' the crows."

"A sensible deduction." He squinted at the map in the fading light. "Well, then, what say we keep going south until we reach the railroad line from Cambrai . . . then follow the track toward St. Quentin? If the Hun is that far south, then we know it's all up and we might just as well toss in the towel."

That met with Ackroyd's approval, and they set out as soon as it got dark. The moon rose early, and they made swift progress through fields and woods, reaching the railroad tracks before midnight. They rested in a culvert for an hour, eating the last of their apples, then walked along the edge of the tracks in a southeasterly direction. Fires ringing the northern horizon created a dull glow, as though some strange dawn were about to break. They could only speculate as to the source of the fires. Villages and fields going up in flames? The bivouac fires of some uncountable host? Either thought was chilling and drove them on without further rest. At four in the morning they reached the first scattered houses of a small town, a railroad sign beside the tracks revealing the name—St. Petit Cambresis. A narrow road leading to the town came into view, a white, ribbon under the dying moon snaking over a low hill and through vineyards. Transport wagons were parked along it, the draft horses grazing in a field.

"Ours, by God," Fenton said as he spotted the distinctive field cookers.

The two men paused to dab at their mud-caked, bramble-torn uniforms, then marched on smartly, Ackroyd whistling "Tipperary" to alert any sentries. They were not challenged when they walked along the station platform, nor when they went through the deserted station house onto the street beyond.

"A bit queer," Fenton said. "There should have been a sentry posted."

"Ruddy town seems to be empty, sir."

"Impossible."

They walked on, their boots ringing loudly on the cobblestones. The street curved and led to the town square, which was dominated by a stone fountain in its center. Around the fountain and spread out across virtually every inch of the paved square were the sprawled figures of soldiers, three hundred or more, lying like dead men. They were not from one unit. Fenton noticed the badges of half a dozen regiments. A sergeant in the Gordon Highlanders lay on his back in the gutter with his head resting on his pack. His left hand was swathed in a dirty blood-caked bandage. Fenton nudged him gently in the side with his foot.

"On your feet, Sergeant."

The man stared stupidly at Fenton for a moment and then stood up with a groan.

"What the hell is going on?" Fenton said sharply. "It looks like beggars' army."

The sergeant's red-rimmed eyes moved from Fenton's face to his regimental cap badge and then down to the pips on his stained, muddy sleeves. He pulled himself to rigid attention.

"All the lads just worn down, sir."

"I can understand that, Sergeant. But why are there no pickets out? Good Lord, man, Fritz'll be here by dawn."

"Yes, sir . . . colonel told us to stack arms and get some sleep, sir. Told us we were out of the war, sir."

"*Your* colonel, Sergeant?"

"No, sir . . . from the Winchesters, sir."

"How many Gordons are here?"

"Twelve of us, sir."

"Wake them up. Send six out along the railroad tracks and six down the road. Find the transport drivers and wake them up, too. I want those horses in the traces. Where is the colonel?"

"Town hall, sir . . . just across the square."

"Do you believe you're out of the war, Sergeant?"

The muscles in the tall sergeant's jaw tightened. "I can no' argue with a colonel, sir—even a colonel in the bluidy foukin' Winchesters, *sir*."

The foyer of the town hall and the central corridor were crowded with badly wounded men, who were being attended to by a couple of medical orderlies and a French civilian. The wounded were well bandaged and all of them appeared heavily anesthetized. Fenton was impressed by the efficiency.

"You men are doing a good job here."

"Thank you, sir," one of the orderlies said, then nodded toward the Frenchman. "Thanks to 'im. He's the local vet. Brung over bundles of 'orse bandage and plenty of morphine."

"Can any of the men be moved?"

The man rubbed the side of his face and looked thoughtful. His eyes were sunken and there were deep shadows under the sockets.

"A dozen maybe . . . if they're kept flat. Most are in rum shape, sir. Them bloody shells tear 'ell out of a man."

"Sort out the men you can move . . . you and your mate decide which one of you will stay behind with the rest. Toss a coin if you have to, but one of you must stay, I'm afraid. It won't do for the Germans to say we abandon our wounded."

The man nodded gravely. "Right you are, sir . . . only Colonel Hampton's been sayin' we're all chuckin' it in."

"Not so. Where can I find Colonel Hampton?"

The orderly pointed vaguely down the corridor. "One of them rooms, sir."

"Any other officers present?"

"Yes, sir, two lieutenants and a major. The major's over there on a stretcher. Fractured leg, sir. The lieutenants are with the colonel." He lowered his voice and looked earnestly into Fenton's face. "There's something a bit odd about the colonel, sir. I been in the RAMC for twenty years, sir, an' I've seen it happen before, more than once I can tell you."

"Seen what happen, Sergeant?"

"Why, sir, a man losin' control of himself. I think the colonel's half 'round the bend."

Oh, God, Fenton thought, what a bloody awful situation. The sight of the stuporous men in the square, the drug-deepened sleep of the wounded, made him realize how deathly tired he was himself. It would have been the simplest and most natural act in the world to lie down on the floor and close his eyes—and if a German boot woke him in a few hours, so be it. And there was a colonel down the hall, a regimental commander—most probably an elderly man who had seen long, honorable service—who was just as tired but was unable to cope with it, who had let exhaustion dictate his decisions. He must, somehow, relieve that man, assume command as senior officer capable of duty, and lead the ragtag and bobtail conglomeration of troops out of the town by dawn. It seemed like an impossible undertaking at the moment, like being asked to scale an insurmountable cliff stark naked.

"I respect your comments, Sergeant, but kindly keep them to yourself from now on. Is there anything you can give me that will keep me awake?"

"Sorry, sir. We don't have even a coffee bean or a palmful of tea." He smiled wryly. "I can put you to sleep quick enough."

"Thank you, Sergeant, but I can do that quite well on my own."

He found the three officers in the mayor's office, the

two lieutenants lying on the floor and the colonel stretched out on a leather couch. There was an oil lamp on the desk glowing feebly. Fenton turned up the wick, but no one moved a muscle as the sudden light fell upon them. He kicked the two younger officers until they stirred, groaning and mumbling, then shook the colonel vigorously. The colonel was white-haired, with a long cadaverous face. Sixty at least, with a faded ribbon from the South African war stitched to his tunic. Off the reserve list, yanked from his London club to lead a regiment to France and into battle. He could almost feel sorry for the man.

"Wake up, sir. Wake up."

Slack-jawed and glassy-eyed, the colonel stared at Fenton.

"What? What's that you say?"

"Wake up. Time to move out."

The colonel struggled feebly to sit up, and Fenton helped him by pulling on his tunic.

"Move out?" the old man said bewilderedly. "Move out, you say? What the deuce you talkin' about, sir? What the devil do you mean?"

Fenton glanced at the lieutenants, who were now on their feet, rocking slightly from fatigue. They were both Ninth Brigade men, one from the Winchesters and the other a Royal Fusilier.

"Had enough beauty sleep?" he said icily.

The Fusilier lieutenant rubbed his face vigorously. "God, what time is it?"

"Time to move along," Fenton said. "Go out on the square and start getting the men on their feet."

"What the devil you think you're doin'?" the colonel muttered thickly. "Get the men on their feet? By Harry, they've earned their rest, sir . . . earned their rest . . . fifty-two hours without sleep . . . two battles . . . they've done all they can do."

"Not quite, sir," Fenton said quietly. "Not quite enough yet."

The lieutenants seemed unsure of what to do, tensely aware that some sort of clash was developing between two superior officers.

"Stay for a moment," Fenton told them. "I'll need you as witnesses. I am about to request that the colonel place himself on the sick list."

The colonel's face turned a mottled shade of purple.

"Sick list? What the deuce you talkin' about?"

"There must be something the matter with you, sir, to permit your command to fall asleep and be captured by the enemy."

The elderly officer opened his mouth several times, spittle drooling from a corner of his lips. He was staring up at Fenton with the pop-eyed fixity of someone on the verge of apoplexy.

"What's that you say, sir? What? Good God . . . jetsam . . . not *my* command . . . flotsam . . . found 'em here . . . tired to the bone. . . . Can't expect 'em to go on . . . too bloody much to ask of any man. Not fair . . . not—"

Fenton interrupted coldly. "No colonel of the Winchesters would give up without a struggle unless he was an ill man. I needn't remind the colonel of his regiment's history."

The man's face became darker, the eyes more protuberant.

"Coldstream," he said thickly. "You bloody Guards are all alike . . . arrogant bastards, every man jack of you. Who the hell you think you are talkin' to me like that . . . tellin' me what to do? Ill? I'm not *ill*, sir!"

"You are either ill or a coward, sir. If you refuse to place yourself on the sick list, then I have no other recourse but to leave this room, come back with a rifle, and blow your head off."

The colonel seemed to stop breathing. His mouth worked soundlessly, then the staring eyes rolled back and he slumped forward. Fenton put his hands out to keep him from pitching to the floor.

"Poor old duffer," the Fusilier scoffed.

"Watch your tongue," Fenton said sharply. "Fetch the medical orderly and be damn quick about it."

The young officer darted from the room while the other lieutenant lurched almost drunkenly toward the couch.

"Is he all right?"

"Yes. Get out on the square. Rouse the men. Blow bugles . . . ring bells . . . kick posteriors . . . but get 'em on their feet."

"I'll try, sir."

Fenton glared at him. "Not *try*. I didn't ask you to *try*."

The colonel's wrist was clammy, but there was a faint, steady pulse. He would be all right. Or would he? No, how could he ever be "all right" again? The man might live to be a hundred, but he had died in France just as surely as poor old Webber had died. He let go of the wrist and eased the colonel onto his back. The orange-yellow-and-black South African ribbon looked a bit frivolous on his chest.

When he returned to the square, he saw that some progress was being made. Roughly one-quarter of the men were standing up, but there was nothing martial in their attitudes. They had ceased to be soldiers. They looked like tramps crawling out from under bridges in a cold dawn. Lance Corporal Ackroyd was helping the two lieutenants get men up, swearing and pleading with them, tugging at their belts and straps, kicking them. Some men rose, others lay half stupefied, muttering curses and threats. It looked to Fenton like a hopeless task, and time was running out. The Germans would be stirring smartly at dawn and moving on toward St. Petit Cambresis in a gray-green tide. He spotted three Cameronian privates buckling on their equipment near the fountain. One of them had a canvas sack slung over one shoulder, bagpipes jutting up from it.

"You there!" Fenton shouted at the man. "Blow us a tune."

"He dinna 'ave the breath, sir," one of his mates called back.

"He'd better bloody well find some!"

The piper grinned sheepishly and took his pipes from the bag. There was a slow howl like a dying cat, and then the skirling of "Blue Bonnets over the Border" issued forth, clear and stirring, with just that hint of sadness which all pipe music seemed to contain, summoning a vision of gallant men doomed on bleak moors in lost causes. The bonnie prince had listened to those same notes before Culloden.

"Walk around, man . . . walk around."

The piper moved slowly among the exhausted men, picking his way carefully to avoid stepping on anyone's face. Soldiers began to stand up. A few cheered feebly. A Royal Fusilier corporal cupped his hands to his mouth and shouted, "Bugger the Jocks!"

There was some laughter here and there. More men got up and began to buckle on their equipment.

"If you don't like Jock tunes," Fenton called out, "let's hear it from the Londoners!"

A mouth organ appeared from one man's pocket, a small concertina from a pack. "Who's Your Lady Fair?" and "The Old Kent Road" competed with "Blue Bonnets." Singing began, and the troops started to form fours and move slowly out of the square. There was a distant neighing of horses and the clatter and creak of the transport wagons. The men knew which way to go—south across the railway and a small bridge; slim poplars marked the road.

Fenton remained in the square until the last man, wagon, and horse had left the town. It was dawn, the dark stone of the church steeple turning to a pale rose. Swallows dove from the sun-tinged belfry into the dark folds of a chestnut tree. It reminded Fenton of Abingdon on any summer morning.

He turned to go, pausing for a moment to look at the medical orderly who was staying behind with the wounded. The man stood on the steps of the town hall, smoking his pipe, seemingly unconcerned. Perhaps he was relieved that he wasn't marching out with the others, that the war was over for him.

"Good luck, sir," the orderly called out.

Fenton raised his arm in a pointless gesture of farewell and walked away, limping slightly, the cobblestones painful to his feet, following the droning bagpipe out of the little town.

"Over by Christmas"—that was what everyone had been saying. "Home before the leaves fall." He pondered the truth of it as the first shells howled out of the dawn, the German gunners searching for the St. Quentin road and the troops they knew would be on it. The shells were fifty yards off target, air-bursting black and crimson, ripping shrapnel paths through a vineyard.

"Home before the leaves fall." A damn good joke, that.

X

The morning crackled with frost, the grass snapping under Jupiter's hooves as Lord Stanmore cantered out of a leafless copse and headed back across the fields toward Abingdon Pryory. A black February day with slate-gray clouds lowering against the frozen earth. The earl could feel the chill penetrate to his bones, and he was grateful when the stables came in sight. An elderly groom, well scarfed and sweatered against the cold, waited to take the horse.

The earl left the stable area in a hurry. It pained him more than anyone knew to see the rows of empty stalls, the shuttered cottage where George Banks had lived, the deserted bunkhouse that had once been noisy with the shouts and laughter of grooms and stableboys. All of the horses, with the exception of Jupiter and a twelve-year-old brood mare, had been given to the army in October. Cavalry losses had been heavy at the Marne and during the many clashes following the epic German retreat. The call had gone out for remounts, and the earl had been generous. He did not regret his gesture of patriotism—it was, after all, the least he could do—and yet, seeing the empty stalls brought a lump to his throat. The call to the colors had not stopped there. Banks had taken a commission in the veterinary corps, and the grooms and stableboys had joined the yeomanry or the regulars. No one left at Abingdon Pryory but the middle-aged and the elderly, the halt and the blind. And not just men either, the earl reflected bitterly. The last of the young maids had departed after Christmas, answering their country's call for women to take over the jobs that men were leaving. Men and more men. Kitchener had asked for one hundred thousand volunteers to form the nucleus of his New Army. Over a million responded.

YOUR COUNTRY NEEDS YOU

On posters one saw Kitchener's likeness, grim, steely-eyed, pointing his finger directly at one's face. Advertising the war, selling it like Pears' soap or White Manor Tea Shops. And of course the men would go, hurrying to the flag for a bit of excitement and adventure. The girls, too . . .

WOMEN OF BRITAIN ANSWER THE CALL

. . . to train as nurses in Queen Alexandra's Imperial Military Nursing Service, the QA's, or the Red Cross, or to learn the tricky business of stuffing lyddite into shell cases. Much jollier than waiting on tables or polishing the staircase banisters. The result of this exodus being that fully two-thirds of Abingdon Pryory was closed off, the furnishings covered with white sheeting. A house embalmed and awaiting resurrection. Dust settling gently in deserted corridors. Weeds peeking up through the flagstones on the terrace. He complained of neglect, the lack of help.

"It's the war, Tony," was Hanna's only reply. As if he had to be told! Charles in uniform, Roger Wood-Lacy as well. Not in France—yet. "In France." What an ugly sound—ominous as the sounds he had heard in late October and during the first weeks in November, early in the mornings when the air was still, the rumble of artillery bombardments across the channel in Flanders. And then the casualty lists on the first page of the *Times* to be scanned over breakfast. Fifty-eight thousand names of the dead, wounded, and missing after Ypres alone. So many names that he recognized, could put faces to, the names of men he had hunted with, played cards with, but mainly the names of their sons. No, he didn't need Hanna to remind him that there was a war going on.

The chill lingered even after two cups of strong tea, the final cup laced with a dollop of Jamaica. There was a permanent frost on his spirits, and he felt incapable of dispelling it. God knows the paper was of no help. Nothing in the *Times* but the war, the lengthening number of names in the Roll of Honor. Not too many wounded and missing listed. The fighting had bogged down in the snow and freezing sleet. Many of the dead would be those poor devils who had finally, perhaps even mercifully, succumbed to wounds received in the summer and autumn at Mons, Le Cateau, the Marne, Messines, and Ypres. He glanced at the list with a heavy heart. Two names stood out. Gilsworth, R. T., Col. I/Hampshire. Sutton, A., Capt. Royal Horse Guards.

He remembered Andrew Sutton as a boisterous fifteen-year-old taking every jump with a wild, blood-chilling yell, like a red Indian. Damn fine horseman. He must send the marquess and Lady Mary a letter of condolence. The eldest son. Christ, what a terrible blow. And poor old Ronnie Gilsworth. How many times had they tramped through the fields above Pately Bridge after snipe? Some good news from the Dardanelles. Admiral Carden's ships had successfully bombarded the Turkish forts on the Gallipoli Peninsular. Royal Marines had landed and poked about in the rubble without being fired on. The Turk had fled from the power of British naval gunnery. What they hoped to achieve in that remote corner of the world was not clear, but something was afoot. Strictly a navy show. Give the poor bloody devils of infantry a rest for a change, and yet the military seemed divided. The army very much against it. There was an article by Repington on page four:

Defeat of the Central Powers in 1915 can only come by a decisive victory in France . . . in the spring . . . combined French and British offensive in Artois and Champagne . . . overwhelm German trench structure . . . power of the British cavalry to exploit infantry gains . . . the First Lord of the Admiralty is misguided in believing that sea power alone can bring the Turks to their knees . . . vast numbers of troops needed . . . consolidate peninsula and Asiatic shore . . . troop deployment to the east would seriously undermine the plans of Sir John French and Marshal Joffre.

Dash it all! So much bickering back and forth between the services—not that he cared very much if young Winston Churchill was raked over the coals. Too bloody big for his britches, that fellow. Father died a lunatic.

Coatsworth shuffled in with scrambled eggs and veal kidneys. He set the dish before the earl and removed the silver cover.

"Ross is leaving us, m'lord," he said, looking vaguely pleased.

"What? Ross? Oh, I say."

"Yes, sir, just told us in the servants' hall."

"Send the chap in after I've had my breakfast. Ross leaving . . . what a bloody bore."

The earl lit his first cigar of the day after first offering the humidor to his chauffeur, who preferred one of the earl's Abdullah cigarettes from the tin of fifty on the table.

"Well, Ross, I hear you're rushing off to take the king's shilling."

Jaimie Ross looked pained. "I wanted to join the army, sir. Nothing would have given me greater pleasure than to wear a khaki uniform, but the fact of the matter is I received a letter this morning by special post. From the Rolls-Royce company."

"The Rolls-Royce company?" Lord Stanmore's incredulity showed on his face.

"Yes, sir. In regard to a patent I took out on a carburetion system. The Rolls-Royce company had been interested, but felt it wasn't necessary for their cars. But now they're going to make aeroplane engines, sir, up at Enfield, sir, and they think that my system will make their engines run much more efficiently."

Lord Stanmore drew the cigar slowly from his mouth and allowed the smoke to bubble out. He was quite mystified.

"*Aeroplane* engines?"

"Yes, sir," Ross said with great patience. He felt as though he were talking to a slow-witted child. "The army has ordered a great many aeroplanes, sir—for observation purposes and artillery spotting. What they have now are terribly slow, and the engine conks out if the machine turns upside down . . . drains all the petrol from the carburetor, sir. Same basic sort of trouble we used to have driving up Box Hill, tendency for the engine to stutter or even stall on steep grades."

"Upside down? Why on earth would they want to fly upside down, Ross?"

"I suppose they can't help it sometimes, sir. Strong winds . . . or evasive action." The ash was growing on his cigarette, but he couldn't quite muster the nerve to lean across the table and deposit it in the earl's silver ashtray. He placed his hand behind his right leg and dropped the ash on the carpet, smoothing it into the nap with his foot. "Well, sir, I received this letter and the Rolls-Royce people want me to come up to Enfield to work with their engineers. They say I can do more to crush the Hun there than by enlisting in the ranks."

The earl studied him through plumes of gray-blue smoke. Curious. *Ross*, of all people—*his* Ross—getting a letter from Rolls-Royce. Quite incredible. Of course, he had known that the lad was mechanically clever, always tinkering with the cars and making them run better than when the factories had delivered them. Still, it was curious. The chap probably had little education, and yet he was considered too valuable to go to France. Charles had left Cambridge with first-class honors, and yet no one could find a greater use for his services than a second lieutenancy in the Royal Windsor Fusiliers.

"I suppose these engines are quite important, Ross."

"Oh, yes, sir. I was reading just the other day in *Mechanics and Journeymen*—"

"In what?"

"*Mechanics and Journeymen*, sir, a periodical I subscribe to, very popular in the machinists and mechanics trade, sir. . . . Well, there was an article that caught my eye. . . . The editor of the journal wrote that it was going to be machines that would win the war, sir— better weapons, faster and more reliable aeroplanes— and that the men who produced them were more valuable . . . or, anyway, *as* valuable, sir, as Tommy in the line."

"Yes," the earl mused, eyes half closed, "yes, I dare say."

"In fact, sir, they're weeding out machinists from the army and sending them back to their lathes."

"Quite so. It was in the *Times*. When are you leaving us, Ross?"

"They want me as soon as possible. Within a few days at the outside."

"Dashed inconvenient for me, I must say. Where on earth shall I find another driver?"

Jaimie Ross shifted his feet uncomfortably. The cigarette had burned down to his fingers, and he was forced to crush it out in the earl's gleaming tray.

"There's always Maddox in the village, sir."

The earl made a scoffing sound deep in his throat. "Man must be eighty if he's a day."

"Or young Fishcombe, sir. He's only sixteen, but he drives his father's van."

"Yes, I suppose I could hire him."

"Or, begging your lordship's pardon, why don't you do your own driving? I could teach you in just a few hours. It's really quite simple."

"I'm sure it is, Ross," he said stiffly, "but I prefer to be driven."

He was struggling to prevent the patterns of his life from being irrevocably washed away. *It's the war, Tony.* It explained the giving up of his stable, the shutting down of most of his house, the gradual turning of his gardens into an unpruned wilderness. It explained the departure of his chauffeur and the difficulty of finding a suitable replacement. One had simply to accept it all as a fact, an idea against which there was no possible argument. It was childish not to consider Ross's proposal, but, surely, the war would be over by spring, and everything would return to normal.

He took a glass of rum neat and felt better for it. Sleet seethed against the library windows. Hanna had been on the telephone to Lady Mary for an hour. When she finally hung up, she was dabbing at her eyes with a lace handkerchief.

"She's taking it so wonderfully. Andrew wounds but was in no pain. Mary read me th colonel sent. The boy was terribly brave . . . troop against a machine gun that was holding vance. Terrible . . . terrible . . . and yet Mary seemed so resigned . . . so fatalistic about it. And she has no fears for her other sons. John and Timothy are in France, and Bramwell is in an officer-training corps at Oxford. She told me that she senses an aura of invincibility around them. A holy shield."

"I never thought of Mary as being a religious person," the earl said moodily, staring at the windows, the icy sheen across the leaded glass.

"She isn't. She believes there is a greater force than our modern conception of God . . . an ancient spirit that the Druids knew well. She told me once that she had felt that spirit surround her when she stood in the center of Stonehenge long ago."

"Utter rot," the earl muttered.

"Perhaps, but it comforts her."

"The 'holy shield' did damn little good for Andrew."

"She said only his body died. I'm not certain what she meant by that." She twisted the handkerchief into a lace string. "Alex told me this morning that she has a surprise for us. The child sounded quite excited."

"Alexandra is always excited."

"Quite bubbly, in fact."

"Did you tell her that Winifred's brother is dead?"

"No . . . not yet."

"Ronnie Gilsworth was killed also. You remember him . . . Colonel Gilsworth . . . we used to go hunting together."

"Yes," she said vacantly. "So many are gone in such a short time. Ours and theirs. I wonder if any of the Rilkes . . ."

She could not complete the thought. She could expect no words of sympathy from her husband over the fate of her relatives in Germany. Anti-German feeling ran like a virulent fever throughout the entire country. even talk in Parliament of suggesting firmly own that the name of the royal house be om Saxe-Coburg to something more English. ke, the baker who had sold his bread and cakes in Guildford for the past twenty years, had been interned, taken away without a moment's notice. Poor Adolph Koepke, who had always kept a small barrel of broken biscuits and jam tarts by the door for passing children to take free of charge, hauled off in a police van like a common criminal. The same children who had filled their pockets with old Koepke's generosity had stood in the street and jeered, then scrawled DIRTY GERMAN across the windows of his shop with paint. Mrs. Kenilworth, sister of the bishop of Stoke, lived in Abingdon and had the misfortune of owning a dachshund bitch. A boy hurled a stone at it, and she no longer dared take the poor little beast out of the house except at night. Madness.

She pulled and twisted the handkerchief abstractedly. There was a twelve-page letter from her great-aunt Louise, Baroness Seebach, locked in her sitting room desk. Martin had delivered it to her after visiting Germany in September. He had spent two weeks with the Rilkes and the Seebachs, the Grunewalds and the Hoffman-Schusters in Lübeck, Koblenz, Hanover, and Berlin. The baroness, ninety years old and, in Martin's words, "sharp as a tack," had entrusted the letter to him. It contained an up-to-the-second family tree painstakingly compiled by the old woman, showing the Rilkes and all their Germanic branches. So many names listed, so many young men—tiny asterisks beside the names of those in uniform. Cousin Frederick Ernst von Rilke's two sons, Werner and Otto—Werner the same age as Charles, Otto two years older. They had been in the reserve officer corps at the university of Lübeck. Martin had met them and liked them. They were in active service now, the infantry. Were they alive or dead? The cold rain hissed against the glass and gave no answer.

"Quite a remarkable country, Aunt Hanna," Martin had told her. He had been impressed by the efficiency of the modern German state, impressed by the things that had always impressed her when she used to visit Germany every spring: the absence of extreme poverty, the slumless cities, the school system and the working conditions in the factories—a nursery school for the children of women workers at the Rilke chemical plant in Koblenz—the sunny, well-ventilated electric motors plant at Potsdam, so unlike English factories, which were like dark airless caves.

"Werner and Otto showed me around. Very nice guys," Martin had said.

She glanced at her husband, who was staring into nothingness, brooding at the bleakness of the day, thinking no doubt of Andrew Sutton and Colonel Gilsworth. Tony had been fond of Werner and Otto. Otto had stayed at the Park Lane house for seven months in

1912 while studying chemical engineering at the University of London. He would not be fond of them now.

She had always been proud of her German blood and proud of what Germany had accomplished in less than half a century. The Germany that her father had known had been a land of peasants and artisans, a plodding, early-rising, thoughtful, God-fearing folk who spawned out of their lean soil great thinkers—Goethe, Kant, Heine, Schiller—and then, under Bismarck, great doers. "Aus dem lern-folk soll ein That-folk werden," Bismarck had promised, and now German industry was second to none in the world. Germany's steel production dwarfed that of England's. Its merchant ships challenged the British flag on the sea lanes. The roots of the war lay there—British fear of German expansion and German arrogance. Yes, German arrogance. It was not a perfect society by any means. Not Utopia. A rigid caste system dominated by Prussian militarism. No, not perfect by any means, but not a nation of red-eyed monsters either. German soldiers did not rape Belgian nuns on altar steps, did not spit Belgian babies on swords and bayonets and tie Belgian virgins by their hair to the clappers of church bells. All of that talk was propaganda nonsense, but it was believed as gospel truth, the ugly rumors spawned by the factual brutality of the German Army's march through Belgium. Martin had witnessed some of that brutality. Werner had been posted to a regiment in occupied Brussels, and Martin had traveled with him as far as Louvain. Soldiers there, infuriated by snipers, seeing *francs-tireurs* hiding in every alley, kneeling behind every wall, had lost their heads and run amok, shooting a few innocent civilians and torching a few buildings. The fires had spread out of control until large sections of the old town, including the medieval library, had burned to the ground. An appalling incident, but that was war. One terrible incident after another. Martin had explained it all very well, seated at the dining table the night of his return to England, the center of everyone's attention.

"Some troops went berserk. I suppose you could say that the burning of Louvain is similar to the burning of Columbia, South Carolina, by Sherman's troops during the Civil War. But, gosh, it was a shocking sight. Werner was horrified. We were all horrified. A colonel who traveled with us from Berlin wept at the sight of the—"

"A Hun colonel?" one of the guests had asked incredulously.

"A German, yes," Martin had replied quietly. "The man had visited Louvain long before the war when he had been a student at Heidelberg."

"A student of what? Butchery?"

There was no point in trying to speak rationally or objectively about the war, or about the Germans. Any chance of that had fled during the terrible weeks in November, buried forever with the British dead at Ypres.

"Mama . . . Papa . . . close your eyes!" Alexandra's voice from beyond the library door. It was easy for Hanna to comply. Her eyes were already closed, her lips moving slightly in a soundless prayer, "*Ach du lieber Gott . . .*"

The door opened. "You can look now!"

Alexandra in a nurse's uniform, pirouetting so that the long white skirt swirled, the white veil floating from beneath a white headband, red crosses on the sides of it.

"How . . . *summery* you look," Hanna said slowly, not trusting her voice.

The earl looked bemused. "What on earth . . . ?"

"I joined the Voluntary Aid Detachment of the Red Cross," Alexandra blurted happily. "Jennifer Wiggins, Cecily, Jane Hargreaves, Sheila, and I all joined up together." She made another dress model's turn. "Do you like it? Summery, yes, Mama, because this is the summer uniform. The winter one is a pale blue serge with accents of red . . . but it doesn't fit properly in the bodice. I shall have to return it to Ferris for refitting before they make the others."

"Others?" the earl muttered.

"Three of each—three summer, white . . . three winter, blue. And a couple of heavy wool cloaks for cold weather. And I must get the proper type of shoes. We shall be doing so much walking, you know."

"What on earth do you know about nursing?" the earl asked.

"Oh, we shan't be doing that awful bedpan and dressing type of thing. They have proper nurses for that . . . elderly women. Our jobs will be to look after men who are convalescing. Push them in their rolling chairs . . . write letters for them if their hands are bandaged or their arms are in casts . . . read to them if the poor dears have been blinded. That sort of thing. There will be ever so much to do."

"Will you be leaving home?" Hanna asked.

"Yes, in a way. We shall be living in a dorm. But I shan't be far off. The Hargreaves gave their house at Roehampton to the Red Cross . . . as a convalescent hospital for officers. They're jolly glad to be rid of it . . . such an awful barn of a place. They moved into a perfectly darling house in Portman Square." She made a final pirouette. "Do you like me in it? Isn't it chic?"

"Dashed smart," the earl said without conviction. "Are you sure you can do that sort of work? Some of those poor fellows will be quite badly off, you know."

Alexandra checked her image in a mirror and couldn't help but smile at what she saw. An angel of mercy. The headband and veil suited her. Made her look like an especially pretty young nun. Not too concealing, though. One could still see her blonde hair.

"I shall do quite well, Papa. I can feel it in my heart." She drew herself up proudly. A Nightingale figure in the glass. "It might be difficult at first, but this is war and one must be prepared for some degree of travail and self-sacrifice."

The rain seethed on the drill ground, turning the churned turf into a morass. The platoon moved across it, ankle deep in mud. Barely half of the men were in

uniform, the rest struggled along in cheap mackintoshes.
A bowler hat or two was to be seen, but mostly there
were cloth caps. The working poor were working at soldiering for a shilling a day. Only ten men had rifles.

"Platoon . . . halt! Dismissed!"

They streamed toward the barracks in a sodden mass.
Second Lieutenant Charles Greville watched them
go. He was properly dressed for a soldier of King and
Country in a well-fitting uniform, decent boots, a British Warm coat. The uniform was not provided by the
government; they merely gave him a token amount of
money toward its purchase. The uniform came from
Hanesbury & Peeke, Military and Clerical Tailors, the
Haymarket, London. It had cost a great deal of money
and was worth every farthing.

Strangely enough, the men did not resent his martial
magnificence in the least. When he stuck his head
through the barracks' doorway, they all grinned at him.

"You chaps all right?"

"Right as bloody rain, sir!" a gangly young man
said, warming his backside by the potbelly stove. "Are
we downhearted?"

The platoon answered with fervor, "NOOOO!"

So much for that. First Platoon, D Company, Second
Battalion of the Royal Windsor Fusiliers was right as
rain. Charles walked on to the mess, hurrying in antici-
pation of a whiskey and hot water—a double whiskey,
come to think of it.

The mess was crowded, the barman hard pressed to
keep up with the demand. The Royal Windsors shared
the mess with a new battalion of the London Rifles.
"Quite unthinkable before the war," the Royal Windsors' adjutant had remarked sourly when the London's
officers had first entered the mess. The breaking of tradition didn't faze the younger officers of either regiment. They were all civilians in uniform, a few short
months removed from Oxford, Cambridge, Eton, the
Inns of Court, or budding business careers. Sharing the
mess gave them the opportunity to share their uncer-

tainties at what they were doing—or trying to do. They were all candidly aware of their shortcomings.

"I wish to hell I had just one NCO who knew the ropes," a London Rifles lieutenant remarked moodily. "I feel such a bloody fool drilling the men with a book in my hand."

Second Lieutenant Roger Wood-Lacy, the Royal Windsors, took a sip of his ginger beer.

"The men don't mind. I told my chaps straight out that I didn't know the first thing about drilling, and we muddled through together. I must say, in all modesty, that we're first rate now."

"When are they going to instruct us on trenches?" a downy-cheeked subaltern asked.

"When we get to France," Charles said as he joined the group at the bar. "I understand they're building a training base at Harfleur, and they'll run us through it for a week or two before sending us up to the line."

"With half our lads in macks, bowlers, and brollies," Roger scoffed. "Fritz'll die from laughing."

"All of the men will be in uniform by the middle of next week . . . and they'll have Lee-Enfields and bayonets by then, too. Colonel told me this morning. That goes for the Londons as well."

"I hope you're right," a London Rifles officer said. "The lads find it difficult to feel like soldiers when they don't look like soldiers. I marched my platoon over to Datchet Common the other day, and some horrid chap standing outside a public house wanted to know where I was going with 'a mob of bleedin' navvies'! If there'd been a man among us with a working rifle, I'd have ordered the blighter shot."

"He'd only have missed," Roger said. "I doubt if there are ten men in your battalion or ours who know which end of the rifle does what."

Charles smiled sardonically and ordered his hot whiskey. He recalled Fenton telling him that the Guards never talked shop in the mess. That might well have been a tradition in the Royal Windsor Fusiliers too, but before the war, before the First Battalion, the regulars, had been destroyed at Ypres. New traditions were being formed at the depot in the shadow of Windsor Castle that were no doubt shocking to those who had known the regiment in peacetime. It was said that Queen Victoria used to watch the men drill from her sitting room window. She would have been dismayed if she had watched them now. But there was no point in reflecting on the past. There wasn't an enlistee in his platoon who could have told him what the regiment had done at Blenheim, Oudinarde, Badajoz, Vittoria, Quatre Bras, Inkerman, or Tel-el-Kebir. Those battles meant nothing to them—mere faded lettering on the regimental colors, half-remembered names from dimly recalled school lessons. They were eager to make their own history, singing "Tipperary" as they marched in the rain in their wretched clothes.

"What are you up to this afternoon?" Roger asked.

Charles looked at his wristwatch. "Meeting Lydia at Charing Cross—if I don't miss the train. I've got noon to midnight off."

"Lucky devil! Where are you taking her?"

"Lunch at the Piccadilly . . . perhaps the theater. I don't much care what we do. Lounging around on a sofa with a brandy and soda would suit me fine."

"Typical thinking of the active-service officer." Roger scowled at the bubbles in his glass. "I suppose you heard the news about poor Winnie's brother."

"Yes. Bad luck. Barely knew the chap . . . yet . . . well, it's rotten. I'll send her a letter."

"Got a note from Fenton this morning. They upped him to major."

"Still on staff?"

"No, back with the Guards. In trenches near Béthune. He says they're quite snug and enjoying the winter sports. Only a hangman would appreciate Fenton's humor."

"Well," he said lamely, glancing at his watch again, "you know your brother."

* * *

Did Roger? He wondered, seated in the train as it skirted the freezing Thames, if they would ever know Fenton again. Not the old Fenton, surely. "In trenches." Those two words separated Fenton from the majority of mankind as completely as though he were on the far side of the moon. Being "in trenches" was an experience that only those who had been in them could possibly imagine. Those few survivors of the First Battalion who had drifted back to the Fusiliers depot at Windsor never talked about their experiences at Wytschaete in November. Never in fact even talked to each other, although they all shared the same memories of that hellish place. They kept what they had seen and done on White Sheet Ridge to themselves. There was a veil drawn about each man that was totally impenetrable. They had glimpsed purgatory and were not whispering its secrets to Dante or anyone else. Fenton would be the same, withdrawing behind his gift for sardonic understatement to blot out the horrors. The official communiqués from France told of heavy artillery exchanges from Aubers Ridge to the La Bassée canal. Fenton would be somewhere in that area, "quite snug and enjoying the winter sports." He tried to imagine what it must be like to huddle in an icy trench while shells slammed into iron-hard ground. He could not bring any vision into focus. It was a mystery that must await his own initiation.

"How grand you look," Lydia said as he pushed his way through the crowded station to meet her.

"You look rather grand yourself," he said with a grin of pure joy. She looked so beautiful in a Russian sable coat that he felt like sweeping her into his arms and kissing her right there in front of a thousand people— not that anyone would have cared or even noticed. There were soldiers kissing girls everywhere one looked among the battalion waiting to board a train for Folkestone, their packs and rifles stacked in momentarily neglected rows down the platform, and yet he pecked at her cheek almost furtively.

"How demonstrative you are, Charles." Her smile was cryptic. "Have you missed me terribly?"

He took hold of her gloved hands. "You know I have."

"I would never know by your letters."

"Sorry." He squeezed her hands as though to prove his sincerity. "It was almost impossible to write. We've been on the go eighteen hours a day trying to learn soldiering and teach it to the men. It's been the blind leading the blind, but we're starting to form into shape now and I'll be able to come up to London more often." He was about to add, "Before they ship us to France," but thought better of it. There was no point in putting an immediate damper on the afternoon.

She kissed him squarely on the mouth. "There! That's a proper welcome. Kindly make a note of it, Lieutenant Greville." He hugged her to him, but it was awkward—so much fur and wool khaki between them. Her perfume made him giddy. How exquisitely marvelous was the smell of woman! He thought of the dankly rancid odor of his platoon in the tar-paper and wood barracks, the haze from sodden cloth as they ringed the stove.

"It's so marvelous to be with you again," he murmured, brushing his lips against her neck. "It seems like an age."

It seemed that way to her, too. This tall, uniformed, lean-faced man seemed almost a stranger in some ways. Not that he had changed that much in a physical sense—a bit thinner perhaps—but so much else had changed. The span of time between October 1914 and February 1915 could not be measured in months. It seemed like the gap between one century and another. She clung tightly to his arm as they walked out of the station. Ambulances were drawn up along the Strand for blocks, waiting for the hospital train from Southampton. They hurried past them in silence into Buckingham Street, where she had parked her car.

"I thought we might have lunch at the Piccadilly grill," he said as she handed him the car keys.

"It's terribly dull there. Nothing but grim-faced matrons and retired brigadiers. I took the liberty of reserving a table at the Cafe Royal . . . far from the orchestra, so we can talk, talk, talk."

Talking was out of the question except at a level near shouting that Charles found irritating. The Cafe Royal was jammed with men in uniform (most of them with the red tabs of staff officers on their lapels), businessmen, high government officials, and droves of elegant women (most of them considerably younger than their escorts). An orchestra played ragtime, and the dance floor was so densely crowded that couples could barely go through the gyrations of the "Grizzly Bear" or the "Temptation Rag." The menu was extensive and the prices outrageous. It was not a place where second lieutenants took their girls on a second lieutenant's pay. But he had left those modest trappings back at Windsor along with his muddy boots. In the Cafe Royal, he was the Right Honorable Charles Greville, heir to an earldom, and to hell with expense.

The food was ambrosial after regimental boiled beef and greens, the Pouilly-Fumé pure nectar, but the orchestral thumpings and wailings, the squeal of the female dancers doing the maxixe, became too much to bear. He smiled ruefully and raised his voice above the din.

"Rather difficult to talk here."

"Yes," Lydia agreed. "Shall we go?"

"Please."

It was raining again, an arctic drizzle from a black sullen sky. They drove to a house her father owned in Grosvenor Square, twenty rooms of Regency elegance, one of Archie's many London residences.

"Don't you feel cramped?" Charles asked, eyeing the domed ceiling in the foyer with its skylight of stained glass, the long marble corridors, doorways framed in the Ionic order.

"We do a great deal of entertaining lately," she said, handing her coat to a maid. "This place is really more for Daddy's friends at the ministry than it is for us."

"Archie in the government! I couldn't believe it when I saw the announcement in the *Times*."

"Yes, on a war committee, and enjoying every minute of it. He and the minister are very much alike."

"Langham, is it?"

"Yes. David Selkirk Langham . . . whirring like a dynamo . . . the Lancashire bantam cock . . . sharp of spur and tongue . . . soothing half of Parliament and irritating the rest."

"What exactly is your father doing?"

"Applying the Foxe Ltd. method to the war effort. The three pillars of the company—advertising, efficiency, and quality. He started by criticizing the recruiting posters. Kitchener sticking his fat finger in one's face will be replaced by more subtle inducements. And then there's the problem of army rations . . . the system is quite inadequate for the million or so men Kitchener wants. Food distribution is Daddy's game, you know. The whole purpose of Langham's ministry is to get experts to handle the logistical problems of the war. He believes that war is far too complex a matter to be left to the military. He just recruited Lord whatever-his-name-is—you know, the London omnibus tycoon—to help solve the army's transportation problems."

A fire burned in the drawing room, reflecting off highly polished wood, silver, and glass. It was an eighteenth-century room, large but warmly intimate. The maid drew the velvet drapes to shut out the bleakness of the afternoon while a butler in livery brought brandy in a cut-crystal decanter.

"And yourself?" Charles asked. "What are you doing to keep busy?"

"Oh, a rather ambiguous role in the war effort. I'm serving as Daddy's social secretary . . . Langham's

too, in a way. I arrange small dinners here . . . dining
room politics . . . Whig and Tory . . . capital and
labor breaking bread and resolving to pull together for a
change. I suppose it sounds rather silly and frivolous to
you, but more things are accomplished over a good dinner and a fine port than one could possibly realize"

"What do you think can be accomplished after a fine
lunch and a bottle of Pouilly-Fumé? Not to mention a
rare old brandy."

"That's really up to you, isn't it?" she said, sitting on
a divan and patting the cushion beside her.

Charles waited until the maid and butler had left the
room and then sat next to her.

"I know what I'd like to accomplish . . . and will."

She looked at him intently and placed a cool hand
against the side of his face.

"Please, Charles. Don't spoil a perfectly wonderful
day by making promises that you're in no position to
keep. It isn't fair to me . . . or you."

He drained his brandy in one swallow and set the
bulbous glass on a side table.

"That's all in the past, Lydia. I know it is . . . I can
sense it. Don't you feel a great change in the air? A
fresh wind? Oh, I don't know how to put it exactly. A
paradox. I mean to say, I rather dread the thought of
going to France and having shells tossed at my head,
and yet I'm glad we're at war and happy to be a part of
it. Something new and marvelously exciting is taking
place in our lives. A clean start for a tired old world.
The ranks are aware of it too—all those ex-clerks, delivery boys, apprentices. . . . They know that the war
will change their lives utterly—break the molds, the
ruts. That's why they're so cheerful and uncomplaining.
Their uniforms, when they have them, are shoddy, the
food is dull, the barracks damp and drafty . . . and
yet they act like schoolboys on holiday." He took hold
of her hand and kissed the palm of it. "We'll be going
across soon, at least that's the talk in the mess. . . .
Drive the Boche to the Rhine this spring and summer.

When I get back, I shall marry you . . . and if my father doesn't like it, he can lump it . . . and if he threaten to disavow me, I shall shame him in front of the peers. I shall go to the House of Lords and condemn him for his actions."

"Oh, Charles!" she laughed, "that's nonsense."

"I mean it," he said fiercely. "I mean every word. Or, anyway, I'd threaten such action and he'd back down in a hurry. By God, it's young men who are fighting this war and it's young men who must benefit from the victory. *I* shall not back off on *my* rights. *That* I promise you, Lydia."

He made an attempt to get down on one knee in front of her, but stumbled in doing so. The rich food of the Cafe Royal, the wine, the brandy, the glow of the fire, the fact that he had been up before dawn conspired to rob him of grace. His head spun and he sat at her feet and rested his brow against her knees.

"Lord," he muttered. "I feel like I've been drugged."

"Poor darling." She bent forward and kissed the top of his head. "You must be exhausted. Would you like to take a nap?"

"Yes . . . I think so . . . for an hour or two."

She stroked his hair, idly, unconsciously sensual. "We don't have to go to the theater. You can rest . . . and then we'll have supper here."

"I have to be back by midnight."

"I know. I arranged with Daddy to have Simmons drive you. The car will be here at ten-thirty. The night train is so horrid."

He nested his head in her lap and sighed with contentment.

"Oh, Lydia . . . I feel such peace with you."

"And I with you, my darling. But come on . . . don't go to sleep on the floor. You can stretch out in a perfectly luxurious bed."

"I haven't been in a perfectly luxurious bed in months. I'll never get up again. No . . . I'll just take an hour on the couch."

She helped him out of his jacket, laughing at the complexities of the Sam Browne belt, which resisted both their efforts to detach it. Finally, he was lying down, jacket and shoes off, head resting on a cushion. She covered him with a lap robe and kissed him on the brow.

"I feel such a fool," he muttered drowsily. "With the prettiest girl in England and I . . . take a nap on her couch."

She kissed him again. "I shan't breathe a word to your brother officers. It would ruin your reputation."

He fell asleep almost instantly, and she stood for a moment looking down at him, so blissful in sleep, so boyishly vulnerable. She felt a purely maternal emotion and tucked the robe gently around him, brushed a lock of hair from his eyes, and tiptoed from the room, closing the door quietly behind her.

Would he do it? She thought about it, seated in the morning room, staring through the tall windows at the green oval of the square. How dark and forbidding the iron railings looked, how bleak the sodden, leafless trees. A man crossed the road toward South Audley Street, clutching a wind-whipped umbrella with both hands. *Would he?* She lit a cigarette and puffed on it, drawing the smoke into her mouth and then blowing it out again rapidly. Yes. She had the feeling that he would. That *this* time he would. It was the uniform, being part of something that his father was not part of. *In the war.* His father might be Lord Stanmore, ninth earl, but he was Charles Greville, second lieutenant, the Royal Windsor Fusiliers. The importance of their respective statures had flip-flopped, at least for the time being.

> Oh, we do love the soldier boy,
> The lads in khaki proud.
> And Jolly Jack Tar and the bold marine,
> Who guard the empire 'round.

A silly music-hall ditty, but one that captured the public mood. Nothing was too good for the men who served King and Country. She half-closed her eyes against the caustic smoke of the cigarette and envisioned Charles standing in the House of Lords, his right arm neatly bound in a sling, a bandage about his Shakespearean brow, pleading his case with passion.

"My father is an honorable man, but I am not without honor of my own, the honor of shedding my blood for England. . . . And to have the woman I love denied my father's blessing . . . Shame, I say . . . Shame."

She almost laughed at the vision. It was so impossibly romantic, like a scene out of one of Alexandra's trashy novels.

There was a rumble of voices in the corridor, and then the door opened and her father stepped into the room, followed by a short, slender, dark-haired man of forty-five.

"Good weather for ducks," Archie Foxe growled, peeling furlined leather gloves from his pudgy hands. "Is that Charles sleepin' in the drawing room?"

"Yes," Lydia said, snuffing out her cigarette. Archie did not approve of women smoking.

"Anything the matter with the lad?"

"No, just tired."

"The rigors of army life, eh?"

"Something like that," she said.

"I have some telephone calls to make. Will you see to it that Mr. Langham gets a double brandy and soda to ward off the chill?"

"Of course. How are you, Mr. Langham?"

"Wet, Miss Foxe. Quite damp to the bone."

He was not, of course, wet at all, having stepped from a limousine to the front door under a large umbrella. His dark wool overcoat with astrakhan collar was unblemished by rain. Archie Foxe went off down the corridor toward the stairs and his office-bedroom on the second floor, the minister's overcoat was taken by the butler, and a large brandy and soda brought in on a silver tray. David Selkirk Langham, neat as a pin in striped trousers and cutaway coat, walked slowly about the room, his dark, piercing eyes taking in every detail.

"Sumptuous. There is no finer combination than a great deal of money and faultless taste. Did you choose the furnishings?"

"Yes," Lydia said.

"In all of your father's numerous abodes?"

She smiled faintly. "Those that I know of."

"Ah, yes," he chuckled. "I dare say the sly fox has his secret den or two."

"Complete with vixen."

"I detect a note of disapproval in your tone, Miss Foxe. One should not begrudge a man his amusements."

There was something devilish about his face, Lydia decided. The Tory papers often caricatured him as the Prince of Darkness whispering into Asquith's ear, or Lloyd George's. He had a narrow spade-shaped face with a long, sharp nose, thin eyebrows like pencil lines, and a trim Vandyke beard. The devil's countenance, but there was no hint of evil about him, only a quality of restrained amusement, as though he were always on the verge of breaking into peals of mocking laughter. David Selkirk Langham, born in a Liverpool slum, self-educated solicitor, advocate for the Mersey dockworkers, Member of Parliament, cabinet minister. A married man with five children, but there had been salacious stories whispered about him since the day he had entered Parliament in 1908. Women, it was said, were hypnotized by his eyes and his air of blunt, forceful virility. Tory lies, her father had said, but she wasn't so sure. She had heard too many stories to dismiss every one of them as false, and she had merely to look into his eyes to read the challenge there.

"The young man on the couch . . . is that Charles Greville?"

"Yes."

"The earl referred to me as a blackguard once during a speech in the House. Of course, there was nothing personal in the remark. He was merely angry at the way the election had turned out. Is the son as Tory as the father?"

"No. He has no political feelings one way or the other."

Langham raised one eyebrow in a sharply quizzical arch. "Is that so? Doesn't he know it's politics that makes the world go round? That it's politics that has him in uniform and politics that's likely to keep him in it for a long time?"

"He doesn't look upon the war quite that way."

"Foolish of him. It pays to be realistic in this day and age. The way some of these soldier lads talk, you'd think they were going off in suits of armor for to fight the King of France. It's going to be a long war and a bitter one . . . a war of political ideologies, a war of—"

Her laugh interrupted him. "Mr. Langham, you're not in the Commons making a speech."

He bowed slightly. "My apologies. It used to be my fame that I would make a speech on any street corner or in any public house for no better reason than to hear the sound of my own voice. Those are days long gone. There are more enjoyable things to talk about with a young, beautiful woman than the turmoil of European politics."

"Such as?"

"Why, the pure pleasure of your company . . . as just one example." He eyed her boldly, a smile lurking behind his dark eyes. He reminded her of a ferret toying with a rabbit. She could understand why many women would find him intriguing. There was nothing subtle or circumspect about him. Totally sure of himself and his power over the weaker sex. And he was such a little man. So trim and dapper one would have taken him for a tailor if he weren't so obviously a cabinet minister whose star was on the rise. She felt a vague excitement, a small knot of tension in the pit of her stomach. How many women, she wondered, had experienced that sense of excitement and succumbed to it? Her hand went idly to her throat and she looked away from him. Rain drummed against the windows.

"Where are you and Father off to this afternoon?"

Langham smiled at the huskiness of her voice and took a sip of his drink. "A meeting with the Prime Minister at number ten. Kitchener will be there to discuss this Dardanelles business."

"What do you think about it?"

"Brilliant in concept . . . just what one would expect from young Mr. Churchill's fertile mind. My own mind is not made up about it. Should the enterprise fail, the political repercussions could be disastrous."

"You don't strike me as a man who would be afraid of risk."

There was a sound in his throat, like muffled laughter or the purring of a cat. His hand brushed her arm, gentle as silk.

"Some games are always worth the candle and some are not. Don't you think that's true, Lydia Foxe?"

She ignored his touch, her eyes fixed on the cold glass windowpanes.

"I'm not certain, Mr. Langham. It's not candles I care about in games, only prizes."

XI

Martin Rilke sat in Regent's Park tossing pellets of bread to a flotilla of ducks. It had been a long, hard winter, and the ducks were celebrating the approach of spring by eating everything that was cast upon the waters. Martin sprinkled what remained of four slices of bread among the reeds and then stood up and walked slowly along a broad gravel path toward Clarence Gate. His hands were in the pockets of his overcoat, one hand curled around a crumpled letter from Chicago. The letter had arrived in the morning post and had contained a check from the *Express* for eighty-five dollars and some words of advice from Harrington Comstock Briggs.

> Dear Rilke:
>
> The enclosed check does not reflect your worth but does measure pretty accurately the extent of your usefulness to us at this time. The good folk in the Midwest are getting a bit irritated at old Europe and her wars. Sympathy along the lakefront from Milwaukee to Gary is pretty evenly divided. Many German-Americans are becoming vocal in their condemnation of England, France, and Russia—especially England—for conducting what they feel is a crush-German-trade war. The British naval blockade is certainly playing havoc with the grain merchants and the iron-ore shippers. Folks in these parts can't understand why they should be prevented from selling to the Central Powers. Even Washington is irked at the blockade, so you can

well imagine how feelings run in certain sections of Chicago and everywhere in Milwaukee.

Your Belgium sketches were good and fair, but your current things on wartime Britain are becoming too overtly Anglophilic to suit our readers. Never lose sight of the fact that the redcoats burned the White House—although I can think of a Republican or two who would gladly burn it down today as long as Mr. Wilson was inside. No, Rilke, I can't think of any good reason for you to stay in London any longer. Joe Finley had one bottle of rye too many, so there is now an opening on the police beat. The job is yours if you'll send me a cable. A simple yes or no will suffice. If you're short of the fare, say so.

P.S. I have to go with the Phillies this year for the pennant. Cliff Cravath and Grover Cleveland Alexander—too tough a combination to beat.

He removed the letter from his pocket, wadded it into a tight ball, and sent a hard fast one curving out and away from Cliff Cravath's knees. The paper hit the water and brought a flurry of ducks to the scene.

Jacob Golden was stretched out on the living room couch, staring at the ceiling. It was a position he had been in, almost without interruption, since returning from Serbia in January. He had said little and written less about his experiences there with General Putnik's armies. Some rift had developed between Jacob and his father, but until now Martin had not tried to nose out the cause of it.

"Enjoy the April sunshine?" Jacob drawled as Martin hung up his coat in the tiny hall.

"Yes . . . went up to the park and fed the ducks."

"Reach any firm decision?"

Martin shrugged and slumped into a chair. "Go back to Chicago, I guess."

"Turning your back on the war, eh?"

"It's being turned for me."

Jacob yawned and sat up. He had lost a good deal of weight and looked skeletal; the skin stretched across his face like parchment over a bone frame.

"Why don't you join the *Daily Post*? The guv'nor likes your writing, and he's sending me to Egypt to cover the Dardanelles expedition. You could take my spot. I plan to quit the old paper."

Martin mulled that information over for a few seconds. There was a clatter of dishes from the restaurant below. The Hungarians were gone, innocent victims of the war, replaced by a large Italian family, verbose and operatic.

"When did you decide that?"

"Been considering it for months."

"What happened in Serbia, Jacob?"

Golden ran his hands through his hair. "Christ! Nothing that I hadn't expected to happen. I told you that there was an unholy amount of hate in that part of the world. The war gave it an impetus and an outlet. Rape, torture, and butchery are simply words until one has seen the victims. I saw what the Austrians did to Serbian villagers, and I saw what Serbians did to Austrians after Putnik counterattacked across the Sava River. My dispatches detailed the atrocities on both sides, but only the Austrian outrages were printed."

"That shouldn't have come as a surprise."

"No, of course it didn't. I hardly expected gallant little Serbia to be vilified in the press." He smiled sardonically. "War and truth do not blend very well. I suppose I have an obligation as a journalist to bear witness to events even if the new censorship regulations prevent me from publishing all the facts, but I can't do it. There's something hideously wrong about this war. It's going to be a mindless, pointless, chaotic slaughter, and I don't wish to be involved in it."

"It's going to be difficult not to be involved, isn't it? Where will you go?"

"Why, into the army, of course. Best place in the

world to avoid emotional involvements of any kind. Chap I knew at Oxford is in the Royal Corps of Signals. Gave him a ring the other day and he offered me a commission. Back-room job in Whitehall . . . thinking up codes and ciphers. Cryptography has always been a passion of mine since I was six years old. How do you think I'll look in a uniform?"

"Gaunt."

He winced and ran a hand across his jaw. "Quite right. A bit on the lean and hungry side. I miss all that sour cream and paprika from downstairs. I suppose I'd better develop a taste for pasta and put some flesh on my bones."

"You seem to be a bit more cheerful all of a sudden."

"It's getting it off my chest, old boy. You're a marvelous chap, Martin. You let people speak without clucking your tongue or acting pontifically. I truly think you'd have lent a sympathetic ear to Attila the Hun."

"I suppose that's a compliment," Martin said with a dubious air, "but I'm not without some strong views."

"Of course you're not. It's just that you're far more objective about things than I am . . . and more truly tolerant of mankind's insanities than I could ever hope to be. This war is going to need a few unbiased witnesses, and you should definitely be one of them. Would you like to go to the Dardanelles?"

"If I can . . . sure."

"Right! I'll get on the blower and fix it up. Pop a cork of bubbly while I mend a fence or two with the guv'nor."

Jacob was on the telephone to his father when Martin came back from the kitchen with a bottle of champagne and two glasses.

"It just seemed the decent thing to do," Jacob was saying, his tone unctuously patriotic. "No reasonably healthy Englishman should be out of uniform, and so . . . Yes, Royal Corps of Signals . . . a full lieutenancy . . . their need for me is rather desperate . . . codes, ciphers, decoding—that sort of thing. Yes . . .

posted here in London . . . top-hole sort of job in
Whitehall . . . Yes, should make Mother happy. . . .
Quite right . . . they don't use code experts in the
trenches. Glad you understand, Father . . . that's why
I've been so moody and out of sorts lately . . . trying
to make up my mind as to the best thing to do. . . .
Thank you, Father . . . I appreciate your saying that,
. . . Now then, as for the Mediterranean business, I
can't think of anyone more suited to take my place than
Martin Rilke. . . ."

An outsider, he stayed apart from the other newspaper correspondents. He was "*that American chap*," tolerated but resented. The number of press representatives allowed to join the Mediterranean Expeditionary
Force was limited to a scant half-dozen. Kitchener
would have preferred none, but General Sir Ian Hamilton, commanding the expedition, had permitted a few
select men to come along as observers. Most of them
were elderly men who had covered military affairs since
the Boer War and even before. They were on a first-
name basis with all the staff officers and fitted neatly
into the social order of the mess. They could, in fact,
have been colonels or majors in mufti, so complete was
their grasp of military procedures and ethics. Martin's
very presence had been subject to doubt almost up to
the hour of sailing from Southampton. The advisability
of a neutral coming along had been questioned by the
War Office, but Lord Crewe's arguments had prevailed
in the end. It was his contention that Martin Rilke
should be allowed to accompany the expedition precisely *because* he was a neutral. America, he had stated
in a strongly worded note to the War Office, must be
made aware of the scope and grandeur of the British
adventure to the east. American sentiment about the
British war effort was at a low ebb, and British newspaper accounts of it were looked on as biased reporting.
"Let the truth come out in American papers, documented by an American whose sympathy and under-

standing for the English people in this war is beyond question," Lord Crewe had said.

And so he was part of the host gathering in Egypt for an assault on the Gallipoli Peninsula, a lone American strolling the gritty, crowded streets of Alexandria in an open-necked shirt, Kodak slung over one shoulder, notebook and pencil in hand. Little of what he wrote was passed uncensored by GHQ, and none of his photographs had been stamped with the censor's seal. It seemed curious to Martin that the British would be so touchy about what could or could not be sent back to London. The smallest, most ragged Egyptian shoeshine boy knew that the English were preparing to sail for Gallipoli by the last week in April. Fishing boats from Greece drifted with impunity through the vast armada of ships anchored in the roadstead. It was common knowledge that at least half of the Greek fishermen were either Turkish sympathizers or Turkish spies, and yet the censors sliced out the most innocuous comments from the newsmen's copy, as though a remark such as "The Australian and New Zealand soldiers appear to be very much at home amid the rock-strewn desolation of the Egyptian desert" were of prime military importance.

"Oh, can't have that, sir. Might tip off to the enemy where the troops are to be sent. Gallipoli is desolate and rock strewn, you know."

Martin wondered whether Jacob, in the brilliance of his mind, had not foreseen all this official fantasia and therefore had neatly euchred him into taking his place. He could imagine him laughing himself silly as he lolled about the flat in his silk pajamas, drinking champagne and renewing his friendships with Shaftesbury Avenue chorus girls. Still, he didn't care. It was Jacob's loss. London was fine, but it was only a city, not unlike Chicago or New York. Alexandria was the threshold of the East. Alexandria was time caught in mellow limestone. The city of Alexander. Al-Iskandarîyah. A city that was ancient when Euclid studied in its library. A city where Cleopatra dozed in the arms of Antony. He strolled along the broad avenue flanking the crescent-shaped bay, the Mediterranean blue-green to the west, yellowish brown to the east, stained by the soil of Africa in the Nile flood. There was a café near the docks which officers of the Royal Navy and the French Armée de Mer had taken as their own, hooting away any khaki-clad officer who dared to enter but tolerating the unobtrusive presence of a solitary newspaperman from Chicago, who took the furthest table on the terrace and spent his time over a beer or two writing in a journal and not bothering a soul.

Alexandria, April 10, 1915

Observations and Reflections. It is curious here. An air of almost unbearable excitement permeates every aspect of the expedition, as though nothing but laurel leaves and great honors wait over the horizon for every man bound to go there. What the Turks are thinking at this moment no one can say, but I doubt if they are filled with the same euphoria. I have tried without success to find out more about this peninsula where the armada is soon to head. It is waterless and desolate, I know that much, a spit of land dividing Europe from Asia, rock-strewn, mountainous, scrub-covered, bleak and inhospitable. Are there many beaches? No one seems to know or, rather, to say. Maps of the place are impossible to find. What few existed here in Alexandria and in Cairo have been bought up by the British and are securely in the hands of the top brass. Will it be heavily defended by the Turks? A month or so ago, marines and sailors from the fleet walked among the ruins of Turkish forts and gun emplacements after Admiral Carden bombarded the place. The British and French fleets attempted to force a passage through the Dardanelles into the Sea of Marmara, sail to Constantinople, and knock Turkey out of the war. A bold stroke. The Turks are uneasy about casting

their lot with Germany and Austria. The sight of
battleships like the *Queen Elizabeth* with her
fifteen-inch guns steaming through the Golden
Horn would no doubt have been the final straw to
break their nerve. But the battleships never
reached the Sea of Marmara. Admiral Carden—or
so the rumor goes—suffered a mental and physical
collapse. Admiral de Robeck, who replaced him,
tried to force the Narrows, lost three or four battleships in one day, and gave up the attempt. It
was decided that the navy would not try again until
the peninsula was in British hands so that the
Turks could no longer enfilade the warships from
batteries onshore or float mines out against them. I
know nothing of military strategy, but that seems
to make sense. I had a few drinks with an English
colonel and a colonel in the French contingent, the
commander of a regiment in la Légion Etrangère.
They were both of them quite glum. We sat on the
balcony of a fine French restaurant in El Fuwa
overlooking the Nile, and they explained their anxiety by pointing out that the Turks and their German military advisers have had a month of unin-
terrupted time for fortifying every possible landing
site. Barbed wire on the beaches and machine guns
on the bluffs will play hell with soldiers trying to
wade ashore. They don't like one thing about this
upcoming operation—a feeling not shared by the
rank and file.

Charles Greville is here! We met by accident in
the lobby of Shepheard's Hotel in Cairo, and I
spent a day with him and Roger Wood-Lacy, Rupert Brooke, and some other officers. Drove over
to Gezira and watched a cricket match, and then
out to Giza in late afternoon to see the pyramids in
the sunset. Brooke is a fine fellow with the ability
to talk for hours without boring anyone. The most
mundane, even shabby, things fill him with poetic
delight—the narrow, crowded, dirty streets of

Cairo, the tents of the army stretching for miles along the Nile, flags stirring lazily against the white sky, a frieze of palms along the horizon, the fellaheen working their fields, drawing water from the river, oblivious to the distant boom of guns as the artillery send practice rounds howling across the desert. The troops—French legionnaires, Senegalese, Sikhs, Gurkhas, British in khaki and pith sun helmets, Australians and New Zealanders in their broad slouch hats . . . "Now, God be thanked Who has matched us with His hour, / And caught our youth, and wakened us from sleeping . . ." Everyone in Egypt seems to know that poem of his. Don't care for it myself. Too romantic in concept. I can't look on war as being a blessing. Keep thinking of those poor bastards of infantry dying on that hillside near Hannogne-St. Martin.

Brooke is in the Naval Division, a marine unit that saw a little service at Antwerp last September. Roger Wood-Lacy was disappointed that he had not been able to enlist with Brooke, for some reason, but he's happy now that they are together in Egypt . . . a happy band of brothers—his words. *Everybody*, with the exception of my two glum colonels, is happy, all caught up in the magic of three words—Dardanelles, Constantinople, and Hellespont. Literary allusions abound. Keats and Byron are constantly being quoted, as is Homer, and the legends of Helle and the golden ram, Hero and Leander, are constantly being invoked. Men who a few months ago read nothing but the *Sporting News* and *Punch* now speak of "wine-dark seas" and say, "The winds are high on Helle's wave." Brooke is writing a poem about the expedition; so is Roger Wood-Lacy and, I assume, ten or twenty thousand other men. Even the commander of this invasion force is a poet and writer of note. The sole occasion when General Hamilton condescended to meet with the press corp en masse turned out to be rather like a literary tea. There is something professorial about Hamilton anyway, and when he opened his remarks by saying, "Gentlemen, we shall shortly be embarking for the peninsula of Gallipoli or, as I prefer to call it, the Thracian Chersonese," I had the uncanny feeling that I was back at the university. The poor Turks are about to be bombarded not only by fifteen-inch shells and field howitzers but by storms of anapests, dactyls, Alexandrines, and couplets as well.

April 12, 1915

Rupert Brooke is ill. A touch of the sun. Charles came up here and told me about it. Brooke assures everyone that sunstroke is not as terrible as it sounds, but his commanding officer thinks otherwise and he's being taken aboard one of the many hospital ships that have assembled at Alexandria. He will miss the Gallipoli landings, which must be a blow to him. I then went with Charles and the second-in-command of his battalion, a Major Thursby, to the Royal Navy dockyard to see a ship that three companies of the Royal Windsor Fusiliers will board next week. We took a venerable victoria drawn by four white mules, and a pleasant and quaint trip it was. On the way, Major Thursby told me a good deal more about the history of the Royal Windsors than I cared to know—this battle and that campaign and what "the ever glorious Captain Pikestaff" did at the storming of Badajoz. At one point in the narrative, Charles leaned close to me and whispered, "He's really a dreadful old bore of a man," and I quite agreed with him.

The ship that the Windsors will board for the Gallipoli landing muted even the garrulous Thursby. It's a rusty old collier called the *River Clyde*, the type of ship that chugs about the sea lanes of the world carrying coal in her bunkers to feed other ships. A sad-looking scow, paint-flecked and forlorn amid a cluster of new destroyers. Two square openings are being cut in her hull on both sides, and wooden ramps are being built that will be swung out on the cargo booms over these sally-ports when the ship is run close to shore. Two thousand men will be aboard her for the assault—the Windsors, Dublin Fusiliers, Munster Fusiliers, and two companies of the Hampshire Regiment. Officers from those units were on the dock, and they seemed no happier at the prospect than Thursby and Charles.

"Rather a seamy way to go to war," Major Thursby said.

S.S. Lahore, *April 18, 1915*

Received a cable from Lord Crewe, informing me that not one dispatch of mine has reached London. Discussed this with Ellis Ashmead-Bartlett, a morose and faintly eccentric London newspaperman, who was not in the least surprised. He plied a censor with a few drinks one night in Alexandria and discovered that all civilian accounts of the military preparations for the Dardanelles expedition were being held back. He also expressed grave doubt that any press representatives would be allowed to go in with the assault forces. We are all being encouraged to stay in Egypt, but he is determined to go; so am I and a myopic guy from Reuters. That's it, the entire press corps. The others are on the beach. One elderly war correspondent told me that he was staying behind "so as not to interfere with the army in any way," implying that I was simply being American and "pushy" for wanting to go along.

The S.S. *Lahore* is a P&O liner commandeered a few weeks ago to serve as a headquarters ship. Accommodations and service are the finest—

Lascar servants abound, all dressed in sparkling white mess jackets with brass buttons. I sit on a deck chair sipping a planter's punch and watch the armada steam out of Alexandria. Horns blow, steam whistles toot, signal flags whip up the halyards, lights flicker back and forth among the two hundred or more ships sailing from Egypt. We are heading for the Aegean, to the island of Lemnos fifty miles off the southwestern tip of Gallipoli. A ship's officer tells me that Mudros Bay on Lemnos is large enough and deep enough to contain every vessel in sight, with a good deal of room left to spare. I assume the final sorting out for the assault will be done there. Everything appears to be so smoothly handled, so efficiently worked out, that success must be assured.

Charles Greville stood in the bow of the *River Clyde* and watched the men of his platoon fill and stack sandbags to form a loopholed wall four feet high and many layers thick, thus turning the fo'c'sle into a small fort where twelve machine guns could be emplaced. The collier drifted slowly at anchor in the dead-calm waters of Mudros Bay, the sun hammering down on the deck plates.

"Like old Vulcan's forge," Roger Wood-Lacy remarked, wiping sweat from the back of his neck with a soiled handkerchief. He leaned against the rail and squinted toward the harsh treeless hills of the island. "Vulcan lived here, you know. His little paradise. One wonders what he saw in the place. Still, I rather like old Vulcan, solid type of chap. Never could understand why Jupiter kicked him out of heaven. Remember your Milton?

> . . . From morn
> To noon he fell, from noon to dewy eve,
> A summer's day; and with the setting sun

Dropped from the zenith, like a falling star,
On Lemnos, the Aegean isle.

"Makes one think, doesn't it? The proximity of the past. Vulcan up there in the hills looking down on us all. Wonder what *he* thinks."

"That we're a bunch of damn fools, I expect," Charles muttered. "Don't you have anything better to do than hang about quoting *Paradise Lost*?"

Roger tipped his sun helmet to the back of his head and then pointed off across the bay.

"Not till A Company arrives. That's them now . . . just crossing *Swiftsure*'s stern."

Troops had been coming out all morning from the transport ships. There were twelve hundred men aboard the collier now, fretting in the stifling hold. Eight hundred more were due—B and C Companies of the Windsors and two companies from the Munsters.

"You don't seem very happy about things," Roger said. "Anything the matter?"

"No, just tired. Talbot's supposed to be battalion machine-gun officer, but he's done fucking-all nothing since we came aboard."

Roger put his hands to his ears in mock horror. "My, my . . . what dreadful language. Haven't heard such speech since Aunt Mary caught her tits in the wringer!"

Charles laughed. "Hop to it and get your chaps stowed away."

He watched his friend go off down the deck toward the boarding ladders at midship. Not walking with languid grace any longer, the poet's stroll, but moving with a cocky swagger, a seasoned subaltern more than capable of keeping his platoon of tough South Londoners in line. He looked away and scrutinized the sandbag revetment.

"Pack 'em down hard with the flat of a spade, Corporal."

"Right you are, sir."

"Then start setting up the guns . . . and place bags on the tripod feet."

"Very good, sir."

He watched the Fusiliers and some Royal Marines clamp the Vickers guns to their mounts and uncrate the boxes of belt ammunition. The men knew what they were doing and needed no further direction. He leaned against one of the sandbag walls and gazed out at the host of ships in the vast harbor. Lemnos in the Aegean! The phrase rang through his head like poetry. Looking at the warships and the myraid transport ships floating so serenely on the bluest of waters under the bluest of skies, he thanked God for His mercy in not sending him to France. He could have conjured up a hundred images to dwell upon—Xerxes and his fleet sailing toward Salamis, Jason and the Argonauts seeking the Golden Fleece, Ulysses and Achilles tarrying here on their reluctant journey to Troy. And Bryon, of course, seeking Hero's tower overlooking Homer's wine-dark sea. Well, the blind bard had been wrong about that. An ocean like any other, blue or gray depending on the sky. But it *was* the sunlit Aegean and not the muddy wastes of Picardy that he looked at over the sandbag rampart. He whispered a silent prayer.

"Mr. Greville, sir." The megaphoned voice of Lieutenant Colonel Askins. "Kindly come up to the bridge."

The colonel stood timber-straight on the bridge wing, one large brown hand toying with his sun-streaked mustache. Charles faced his commanding officer with a clear conscience.

"Yes, sir?"

"Ah . . . Greville . . . Damn fine job of sandbagging there."

"Thank you, sir."

"What the deuce is wrong with Captain Talbot? That's his bloody job, y'know. Told me he had the cramps. Don't believe a word of it. Shirking, I call it. That's the trouble with the special reserve . . . too much time on civvy street and they go soft on you. I'm putting him ashore and making you acting captain and battalion chatter gunner."

"Thank you, sir."

The colonel's eyes became distant, and he looked away toward the nude brown hills of the island.

"You're a friend of that poet chap, Rupert Brooke. You and Wood-Lacy."

Charles felt his stomach contract. "Yes, sir."

"Wood-Lacy more than you."

"He knows him better, yes, sir."

"Chap died yesterday. Sorry to be so blunt about it, but the message from General Hamilton was as brief as that. It was directed to Wood-Lacy, but I thought I'd better tell you about it. We up anchor at midnight and draw into V beach at six in the morning as planned. Young W-L has a damned important job to do tomorrow, and I don't want his thoughts to be wandering about. You can break the news to him after we're safely ashore at Sedd el Bahr. I'm sorry about this, Greville. I know what it is to lose a friend."

The sun seemed to lose its heat, as though a great deal of the light had gone from the sky. The sea had turned sullen and oily. Charles stood at the bridge rail and looked down at the lighters coming alongside with their dense cargoes of men. Two thousand troops for V beach. Only the Lord and General Hamilton knew how many for W, X, S, Y, and the Anzac landing at Gaba Tepe. There seemed little point in grieving for one dead poet.

It lay ahead of him in the darkness, unseen except in the mind's eye, the sharp semicircle curve of Sedd el Bahr bay. Charles had memorized the map statistics: four hundred yards of narrow sand just west of the ruins of a medieval castle, the land rising gently behind the beach in a series of terraced slopes, a village of stone huts beyond the old fort. He peered through a narrow embrasure, his cheek resting against the cold metal of a Vickers gun. Nothing to be seen but the dark bulk of the land, nothing to be heard but the throb of the *River Clyde*'s engines and the rush of water past the prow. He straightened up and glanced toward the stern. The two empty lighters that would form a causeway to the shore were trailing in tow, dark shapes in the phosphorescent wake. Behind them, only dimly seen, were twenty cutters manned by naval crews and filled with Dublin Fusiliers. They would secure the beach while the *River Clyde* grounded herself in the bay and the lighters were warped around from the stern to make the bridge. Fifteen minutes after grounding, the whistles would blow, and the two thousand men in the collier's hold would pour out of the sally-ports, race down the wood platforms suspended against the hull, jump onto the lighters, and run onto the beach without getting their feet wet.

One hour to morning. A bell clanged and the ship slowed. From out of the dawn behind them came thunderclaps and chain lightning, stabs of intense orange and red light along the horizon. Then the heavy shells of the fleet roared overhead and screamed in their plunge to the land. The half-moon coast from Sedd el Bahr to the tip of Cape Helles exploded in flame.

"Stuff it to 'em!" someone called out in the gloom. "Bugger the Turk!"

The pale sky was sullied by sheets of dun-colored cloud. Grit settled on the deck, the dust of Gallipoli borne on the wind, the soil uprooted by the hammering shells. Explosions blinked and twinkled, sharp points of fire beneath fountains of yellow earth. Squinting over the sandbags, Charles could see the village on the high point of the cove disappear under the shock-wave blasts of the navy guns. He held his wrist close to his face and looked at his watch. Six o'clock. The guns of the fleet had been firing steadily for nearly an hour. Nothing— not a mouse, not a bird—could be alive in that boiling, churning, cordite-reeking stretch of land.

"God pity them," he murmured.

CLANG CLANG . . . CLANG CLANG

Bullets clanged against the steel plates of the *River Clyde* and thudded ceaselessly against the sandbags. The sailors trying to drag the lighters around from the stern were shot off the decks and catwalks. Other men took their places to haul on the two ropes for a few seconds before the shrieking bullet storm dropped them where they stood or sent them flopping over the side. A few bullets were coming through the embrasures in the bags and two machine gunners fell backward. Other men instantly took their places, and the guns kept firing, belt after belt uncoiling from the ammunition boxes, the water starting to boil in the jackets.

Charles slammed a fist against a bag and cursed under his breath. Why the hell didn't they back off and signal the fleet to start shooting again? "Fucking goddamn madness!" He tapped the broad back of a Windsor Fusilier sergeant and shouted loudly to be heard, "Going to the bridge. . . . Take charge."

He dropped down the fo'c'sle hatchway into a fetid gloom, skinning one knee badly on the iron ladder. Bullets slapping the hull made the interior of the ship ring like a bell. He stumbled through the fo'c'sle, which was stacked high with wooden boxes of cartridges and the belted rounds for the machine guns, brushed past the sweating ammunition handlers, and half-ran, half-stumbled out onto the well deck. A platoon of the Hampshires was kneeling in tight masses against the high iron sides as bullets passed over them, cracking like steel whips.

"What the bloody hell's going on?" a white-faced subaltern said.

There was no point in answering him. He'd find out soon enough for himself. The wooden ramps were being lowered over the sides; the operation was directed by Lieutenant Colonel Askins and a navy commander standing on the bridge, both men exposed to the fire storm and totally oblivious to it.

"What the hell you doin' here?" Colonel Askins said

as Charles reached the bridge. The colonel was staring at the shore, lips compressed to bloodless slits.

"We . . . can't . . . dampen that fire with the machine guns, sir. Can't . . . make a dent in it."

"I know. I can see that."

"Need . . . artillery . . . the fleet . . ."

"Too late for that . . . committed now . . . bloody ship's fast on the sands. Second wave coming in . . . now." He moved his right arm in a jerky fashion, pointing over his left shoulder.

Charles glanced aft. A string of launches and cutters packed with men were fanning into the bay.

"Signaling them to bloody well stop," the colonel said in a flat, tired voice. "General Napier's leading 'em in. Thinks he's Admiral bloody Nelson and turning a blind eye. Every son of a bitch wants the VC today."

The navy commander suddenly leaned over the totally inadequate barricade of boilerplate and sandbags that lined the bridge, roared orders to the sailors on the steam winches, then darted for the ladder.

"Have to do it myself, damn it!"

"That Unwin," the colonel remarked dryly. "He'll get his cross today . . . or a pine box . . . or both." He looked at Charles with distant eyes. "It's a bloody ball-up, Greville, but we have to stick it . . . get the men ashore . . . bayonet the Turk up the beach. No other bloody way to do it now. Understood?"

"Yes, sir."

"Good lad. Get back to your guns and keep—"

And then he was dead, the top half of his skull spinning away toward the ship's funnel, hair and cap neatly together, brains splattering the wheelhouse with a pinkish gray slime. Charles dropped to his knees and pressed his hands to his eyes to shut out the horror. There was no point to it. He knew that. Anyone seeing him would only mistake his cringing attitude for cowardice. He wasn't afraid. He was far beyond fear. Terror created its own unique form of courage. It was just that the colonel's death had come with such explosive suddenness, he hadn't been prepared for it. The death itself was meaningless. What of it? He could have died at Tugela or Spion Kop during the South African war. Boer bullets had missed him. Turk bullets had not. He glanced at the long, sprawled, blood-draining body and stood up. A navy signaler crouched with his back against a slab of boilerplate and stared at him with hollow eyes.

"Keep signaling the boats to stop," Charles yelled.

The man's stare was fixed, like an epileptic's. There was no point in telling him to do anything. He ran humpbacked from the bridge to search for the adjutant and tell him that the colonel was dead. He found the man at the bottom of the starboard bridge ladder, flat on the deck with Mauser holes across his chest.

The broad, flat lighters had been lashed together in front of the bow; the debarking platforms sloped down along the ship's sides from the sally-ports cut in the hull. Whistles blew, and men of the first platoon, A Company, the Royal Windsor Fusiliers, started down for the beach, running hard, the starboard platform rattling at their pounding feet.

"Stick it, the Windsors!"

Charles caught a flashing glimpse of Roger, revolver in hand, whistle in his mouth, leading his men down. Bullets slapped against the ship or ricocheted off with a whirring howl. It was like standing in a blizzard of lead, the ferocity of the storm increasing as the troops ran down to the lighters. Charles flung himself to the deck and lay flat behind the slim protection of a lifeboat davit, the boat long gone, rifled to dangling shards. He looked over the side under the bottom rail and saw to his horror that the ramp was empty, the platoon gone. A few men lay in the lighter in a bloody heap, the others in the water, motionless clumps of dark brown, sinking slowly, trailing plumes of scarlet. A whistle blew— the second platoon of A Company ran the gauntlet and withered away to six lone men before they reached the lighter. A platoon of the Munsters followed instantly and died as they ran, tumbling head over heels into the sea.

Dead. Roger was dead. The realization materialized slowly. Dead and gone. One of the corpses in the lighter . . . or one of the bobbing sacks of khaki in the water. Gone. Vanished without a goodbye, a parting word. The insanity numbed him. He became oblivious to the fire and stood up, made his way slowly back to the fo'c'sle, and took his position again amid the steaming, clattering Vickers guns.

"Blimey," the Fusilier sergeant said, "I didn't give you a snowball's chance in bloody 'ell of makin' it."

They were snug and safe here, Charles thought dully. The wider embrasures had been plugged with bags. The gunners were no longer bothering to aim their weapons because there was simply nothing to aim at. They lay on the deck and pressed the triggers while Turkish bullets cracked and hummed or thudded into the heavy sacks of white Egyptian sand.

A major in the Hampshires crawled up from the well deck and shouted to Charles over the stuttering roar of the machine guns, "No more . . . chaps . . . going in. . . . Waiting . . . till . . . nightfall. Keep . . . the guns . . . firing."

Charles nodded and rested his head against the sun-heated bags. Through a peephole he could see the bay—the drifting boats of the second wave, filled with dead, countless bodies rolling in the surf, blood staining the water a rose pink . . . a Burgundy red. God, he thought, old Homer had been right after all. It *was* a wine-dark sea.

Guv'nor—had been right, of course. The war had to go on, even if it shambled forward at the moment overburdened with inept and unimaginative commanders. Things would change in time, he supposed. Fresh minds rising to the top. Doubt about that gnawed at him. He had had the chance to observe the command structure of the army at first hand on Lemnos—the tight clique of brother officers above the rank of colonel, an esoteric fraternity that resented and feared outsiders. They had refused—politely, for politeness was inherent in their bones—war correspondents the permission to visit the battlefront until three weeks after the landings, and then only for limited times. He and Ashmead-Bartlett had ignored those restrictions when they finally reached the peninsula by the simple method of going directly to the front-line trenches, a spot where staff officers were loath to follow. A kind of vacuum existed between the men at the front and the men at headquarters. Operations were planned on maps at Lemnos without the staff officers having any clear idea of what those operations entailed for the men ordered to carry them out. Fifty yards looked a tiny distance on a map, a distance easily covered if one ignored the fact that every inch of those yards was barren of cover and under the sights of zeroed-in Turkish artillery and machine guns. The staff never talked of "the men"—that is, the tired, dirty, lice-infested, fly-plagued soldiers, weak from diarrhea—but always in terms of "the regiment." "The Royal Windsors can do it. . . . One can always rely on the Lancashire Fusiliers. . . ." As though those dun-colored ranks living like moles were scarlet-clad phalanxes of immortals.

He tapped the briefcase and stared sourly at the crowded pavements. The holiday atmosphere irked him. Why? It was Friday afternoon, and people who had worked hard all week had a right to look forward to the weekend. Many of them probably had sons, fathers, brothers, husbands, or lovers at the front and felt the presence of the war keenly. That didn't mean that they should walk around in mourning or not walk around at all. He was annoyed at them because he felt a pang of guilt for sitting in perfect safety on top of a London bus holding on his lap journals of anguish and fear. The men he had written about—the English, Indians, Frenchmen, Australians, and New Zealanders, the sun-scorched, thirst-plagued infantrymen clinging to their toehold in the Aegean—might at this moment be corpses turning black on the dead ground below Achi Baba or Chunuk Bair. Charles among them. That thought made his palms sweat. He had sought out Charles on his first trip over to Gallipoli from Lemnos, not knowing whether he was alive or dead, knowing only that his cousin's battalion had been badly cut up leaving the *River Clyde.* "By gad, we can all be proud of the Windsors," an elderly staff officer seated on the terrace of a café in Mudros, drinking Greek wine, had said the day after the landings. "Those chaps know how to die!"

The face of a woman in the crowd as the bus turned off the Strand toward Charing Cross Road. A slim, ivory-pale face. Thin, delicate features, slender nose, black hair. She had been in a uniform when he had seen her last; she was in a uniform now—the blue and red uniform of an army nurse. The bus slowed as a torrent of pedestrians crossed the street, heading for Trafalgar Square. He spotted her again, walking slowly, drifting along with the crowd. There was no point in yelling. She wouldn't hear him, and quite possibly it wasn't her at all. Clutching the briefcase to his side, he dashed down the aisle and half-ran, half-fell down the narrow curving steps to the bottom deck and then leaped past an astonished conductor into the street.

"Get killed that way, mate," the man yelled after him.

Hemmed in by a crowd watching a recruiting drive of the London Scottish, kilted pipers parading under Nelson's column, he lost sight of her in Trafalgar Square.

He climbed onto the petal of the monument in order to
see better and spotted a blue and red figure at the far
edge of the square walking slowly toward the Haymarket. A recruiting sergeant made a grab for his arm.

"That's the lad! There's nothing to beat the London
Scots!"

"Sorry," Martin said, pulling away. "Thought you
were the Black Watch."

She was standing in front of a dress shop, gazing reflectively at the display in the window. He studied her
profile for a second and then walked up to her.

"Ivy Thaxton?"

She looked at him curiously and then smiled. "Why,
if it isn't Mister Rilke . . . from Chicago, Illinois."

"That's right," he said, grinning broadly. "Railroads
and stockyards. I spotted you from the top of a bus
. . . knew it was you. . . . Or, anyway, hoped it was.
How are you?"

"Fine. And yourself?"

"Swell . . . just swell."

"You certainly look fit. Been at the seaside?" Her
violet eyes were innocent enough, but he felt disquieted
by their steady gaze.

"Say," he said nervously, "you're not going to hand
me a white feather or something, are you?"

"Why, whatever for?"

"Well, it happened once today. I guess I looked too
healthy to be out of uniform."

"You should have told her who you were," she said
heatedly. "The silly twit." She touched his hand and
smiled again. "I'm sorry if I gave you a turn. I was just
being facetious. We've all read your articles in the *Post*.
The men in the ward say you're the only one who
knows what the soldier goes through. I'm terribly proud
of you, Mr. Rilke, and I do brag a bit about knowing
you. Fancy! I used to make your bed!"

"Golly, that was a long time ago."

She scowled. "Oh, the more I think about it, the an-grier I get. All those feather girls are frumps. Nothing better to do with their time than hang about street corners and shame young men."

He touched the soft fabric of her uniform sleeve. "You've sure found something better to do with your time."

"Yes. Joined the QA's last September. Her ladyship helped me get in by writing a letter of recommendation. I'm not a sister yet, of course. It takes ever so much training to become that. I'm a probationer, training at All Souls Hospital in Holborn."

"You'll make it."

"Yes," she said thoughtfully, "I will. I know how to work. And, oh, Lord, do they work us hard. This is my first afternoon off in weeks and I doubt if I'll get another one for months."

"When do you have to be back?"

"Eight o'clock."

"It's only four-thirty. Had tea yet?"

"No."

"Neither have I. Will you join me? I have great respect for the QA's. I met a dozen of your Sisters on Lemnos, and I owe every one of them a good cup of tea. There's a White Manor in Charing Cross."

"I understand it's awfully posh," she said doubtfully. "An orchestra and everything like that. I wouldn't want you to go to any expense. I believe there's an ordinary White Manor on Shaftesbury Avenue."

"Ordinary places are for ordinary people. You're special, Ivy. And anyway, I've got three months' pay burning holes in my pocket."

He talked about Gallipoli as they walked slowly toward Charing Cross and told her how he had met Charles Greville there, in the trenches at Cape Helles. She listened gravely, keenly aware of death and wounds.

"I hope that Master Charles is all right. That must be a hellish place. We haven't received any of the Gallipoli wounded. They send most of them to Egypt and Malta.

It's just as well—we have so many coming in from Flanders."

"Will they be sending you to France?"

"Not until I'm qualified to work on a surgical team. That might be nine months to a year from now. I hope the war will be over by then. Do you think it will?"

"No, I'm afraid I don't."

"Oh, dear," she sighed. "Neither do most of the chaps I talk to in the wards. But one lad placed a little sign behind his bed. He lettered it himself very cleverly with a colored pencil. It reads, 'Peace be with us in nineteen sixteen.' Not that it will make much difference to him. He lost both legs and an arm at Festubert."

Her somber, reflective mood changed as they walked into the plush elegance of the Grand Tea Salon on the second floor of the White Manor. An orchestra was playing a tango and many couples were dancing.

"Oh, my, isn't it the grandest place!"

The tea was lavish—petits fours and éclairs, slices of Madeira cake and ices—too rich for Martin. He toyed with a piece of cake and watched Ivy eat.

"A welcome change from hospital food, I bet."

She nodded and bit into a petit four. "Yes, they boil everything. I missed Abingdon Pryory at first. They had such good cooks there, didn't they? I'm very fond of food, in case you haven't noticed, but I never gain an ounce. Must be glandular."

"Just youthful energy burning it off. How old are you, Ivy?"

"I turned eighteen in March. Getting on in life. Oh, dear, there are so many things I'd like to do . . . places I'd like to see. Do you know, this is the first time I've ever been out to tea with a man. Think of that!"

"Make the most of it then. Would you care to dance?"

"I never learned how. I'd hate to make a fool of myself in front of all these people."

"Watch the dancers. None of them are very good . . . just having a good time. Come on, they're playing fox-trots now. That's easy to do . . . just walk back-ward while I hold you."

"It doesn't sound easy," she said dubiously, "but I'll give it a whirl."

The first touch of her slender body made his legs feel weak. It seemed incredible how neatly she fitted against him. He marveled at that revelation and held her tightly.

"Am I doing it correctly?" she asked.

"Oh, yes," he said, brushing his cheek against hers, "you're doing just swell."

They danced until the tea dansant ended at six-thirty and the orchestra played its final number. It had been the most enjoyable couple of hours Martin had spent in a long time, and the most enjoyable she had ever spent, a fact that she made a point of telling him as they walked toward St. James's Park.

"Oh, I did like that! I can't wait to tell the other girls. And, oh, how beautiful some of those women looked in their gowns!"

"None as beautiful as you, Ivy."

She stared ahead as though she hadn't heard the compliment.

"Do you go dancing with lots of girls, Mr. Rilke?"

"Martin . . . please call me Martin. And no, I've been too busy to go dancing."

"Did you go dancing in Chicago?"

"Sometimes. There were frat house dances occasionally."

"I never went to a dance. Da didn't approve of them. My da is a bit straitlaced."

"Your father, you mean?"

"That's right."

"What does he do for a living?"

"Works in a shoe factory. He's doing very well now. His establishment is making boots for the army. Queer, isn't it? Times were so hard for him before the war and now he's making ever so much money. Quite odd, if you stop to think about it."

It would be light until nearly ten o'clock and this hour was the loveliest of the day, the sun catching the tops of the trees and all the buildings along Whitehall, the air cooling after the heat of the long day. The park was crowded with soldiers and their girls.

"I feel kind of silly carrying this briefcase, like some sort of door-to-door drummer."

"I think it makes you look distinguished. I'm sure people think you just left Parliament and are on your way to see the king."

"Taking my nurse with me, I suppose."

"Yes. You're subject to seizures and fits . . . like my Uncle Arthur, only Da says he only has fits when he suspects the publican of watering the beer." She suddenly spread her arms wide. "Oh, I do love green parks! London would be such a lovely town if they'd only allow grass to grow in the streets."

He took her hand and led her away from the path toward a grotto of trees.

"You're such a happy soul, Ivy."

"Do you think so? I'm not really. I'm a bit on the glum side most of the time. It's being around so much pain. Oh, you have to keep cheery, Matron insists on that, but inside—around the heart—there's always a dull ache."

"Do you feel it now?"

"A little, yes. I mean to say, I'm enjoying myself and I'm awfully glad to be with you, but I have to be on duty in an hour and part of my mind is back in the ward. I'm in the amputee ward, you see—have been for the past nine weeks—and there's such a terrible amount of sadness there."

He dropped the briefcase and took her impulsively into his arms, pressing her to him, his hands strong against her back. There were couples all around them, seated or lying on the grass, under the trees, strolling by the dark green lake. No one paid the slightest attention as he kissed her firmly on the lips, as she kissed him. All the horrors of Gallipoli lay in the leather case at his feet, but all thought of them vanished for a moment in the sweetness of her mouth.

Hanna Rilke Greville lingered over her tea on the terrace of Abingdon Pryory; it was a high tea, with watercress sandwiches and thinly sliced ham and smoke Scotch salmon. She avoided large, heavy meals in the summertime, believing them conducive to gout in later years. Across the stone balustrade she could see William and four of his friends making a mockery of a tennis game, slamming balls into the well-rolled, clipped grass to see how high they could bounce or using their rackets as cricket bats and slapping the white balls into the trees. High-spirited lads, happy to be down from Eton for the holidays. Seventeen. A difficult age—not quite boys, not yet men. She knew that her son and his houseguests smoked cigarettes behind the stables and sampled the sherry; Coatsworth turned a blind eye to the latter while keeping the better casks firmly under lock and key.

The heat lingered, rising from the terrace stones. She fanned herself with a silk Japanese fan and watched the boys, leaping over the net now, back and forth, back and forth, like sheep over a fence. William was growing so tall. He would be taller than Charles. A fine, strapping boy and the apple of his father's eye. So much like Tony—fine rider, good shot.

She felt a sense of dread the moment she saw the footman walk onto the terrace from the conservatory. His very age was disquieting. He moved so slowly and painfully on his old feet that it was really high farce to dress septuagenarians like him in livery. The poor man's leaden countenance foretold doom. The pale blue envelope on the small silver tray he carried confirmed it.

"By special post, your ladyship," the footman said.

"Thank you, Crawshay."

She held the envelope in her hand until the man had gone. War Office stationery. Addressed to her, but then they always addressed the letter to the mothers. She slit the envelope with a knife, her hand calm and sure, only her heart racing, a throbbing pain behind the eyes.

17th July, 1915

Dear Countess Stanmore:

It is with regret that I have received word today that your son, Capt. Charles Greville, 2/RWF, has sustained wounds during the recent fighting at Cape Helles. Accounts of the extent and severity of his injuries are necessarily sketchy at this time, but it is known to us that he has been evacuated from the peninsula and taken aboard a hospital ship.

We wish him well.

Yours sincerely,
T. Pike, Brig. Gen.

There had been a great many men wounded or taken sick during the July battles at Cape Helles and Anzac Cove. Finding the exact particulars about one man was next to impossible. Lord Stanmore haunted the War Office, and Martin sent messages through the press channels to Alexandria and Lemnos. Nothing. Captain Charles Greville was simply one of a multitude evacuated from the Aegean on hospital ships. No one was quite sure which ship had received him, and there was no way on earth of finding out until the ship docked somewhere and disgorged its sick. At that point, hospital orderlies would write down the particulars on each man and forward that information to London. It took two weeks, fourteen days and nights that moved in a timeless vacuum of nightmare for Hanna. Her husband's assurances that Charles was bound to be all right ("probably no more than a flesh wound") sounded hollow and forced. She spent the days working on needlepoint to try to keep her mind occupied, but there was nothing she could do at night except lie in bed in a cold sweat and imagine her son lying on an antiseptically white bed, his body shattered and mutilated—limbless, faceless, a hollow-mouthed creature that could no longer even scream. She felt on the verge of madness. And then the afternoon came when William ran whooping into her sewing room, yelling, "Old Charlie's all right! Fractured hip and pelvis is all. They took him to Toulon on a French ship. . . . That chap from the army just rang up Father and told him!"

She burst into tears and was weeping uncontrollably when her husband came into the room. The sight of his mother's hysteria embarrassed William and he was moody for the rest of the day.

9th August, '15

My dearest Mother, Father, William, and Alex:

This short letter is for you all. I was almost literally hit by a Turk shell. The great ugly thing landed right next to where I was lying but failed to explode. Broke my right hip and pelvis in several places, but the bones are mending well. I am quite wasted from dysentery, but that condition is on the mend, so I should be back to passing normal in a few weeks and fit for active duty within three to four months.

I am in the French naval hospital in Toulon, a great stone barn of a place built by Napoleon with a magnificent view of the docks from the windows in my room. Long, cool passageways, very pretty French nurses, first-rate food, and a doctor who believes that half a liter of good red wine a day never hurt any man. Bless the chap in your prayers! I could not ask for better or more sympathetic care and will be evacuated to a hospital in England in about three weeks' time. It will seem odd coming home. I don't quite know how to put it, but I am not the same man who left just a few short months ago. So much has changed. So much more

will be changed. But we shall talk about that when
I arrive.

My warmest regards to Coatsworth, Mrs.
Broome, and all the staff. Also, please convey to
the vicar that God has been kind to me and I
much regret filching pears from the vicarage garden when I was eleven. All my love.

                                        Charles

The earl scowled at the broken top of his soft-boiled
egg.

"What do you think he means about change? Of
course he's changed. Can't get hit by a shell and not be
affected by it somewhat."

"I suppose he means . . . many things," Hanna said
quietly. She read the letter through again silently and
then placed it on the polished surface of the breakfast
table. "I could weep."

"Oh, Mother, *please*," William muttered, then
glanced quickly toward his father. The earl did not admonish him. They both shared a horror of emotional
outbursts.

"Sounds cheerful enough, my dear, considering the
circumstances."

"I was thinking of poor Roger," she said. "If only
God had showed a little kindness to him as well."

She was not being entirely honest. She grieved for
Roger Wood-Lacy, but what truly distressed her was
Charles's assurance that he would be "fit for active duty
within three to four months." An unexploded shell.
Would God grant any man two miracles in a lifetime?

"I would like us to go to France, Tony."

The earl dabbed at his mouth with a napkin. "That
might be quite difficult. Restrictions on civilian travel
to the Continent are severe. I might possibly be able to
arrange it, but it could easily take a few weeks and
Charles could well be on his way here by then. There's
really nothing we can do for the lad by going—in fact,
I think it would only distress him, knowing we were

crossing the channel on a passenger ship with all those
blasted U-boats skulking about. He must, surely, have
heard about the Lusitania going down."

"I suppose you're right," she sighed. "Yes, it would
worry him, I'm sure." '

Her instinct to protect and cherish her firstborn was
being thwarted by the dictates of the war. Civilian travel
to France was not encouraged in the least. Visas would
be required, skeins of red tape to cut through. Tony was
right, it would be an unnecessary gesture at best.
Charles would be in England in a matter of weeks to
convalesce. She had read that soldiers were often sent
as close to their homes as possible, and there were several war hospitals within half an hour's drive from
Abingdon.

"Patience, my dear," the earl said gently. "You must
have patience."

She reflected on her husband's attitude, and that of
William, as she sat in the music room working on a tap-
estry. She worked swiftly with the needles and the many
strands of colored thread, shading and highlighting the
spire of Salisbury cathedral in petit point. William she
dismissed with a sad smile. He was at an age that ignored tragedy utterly. His brother had suffered an accident, no worse than that, like a crash in a motorcar or a
fall from a horse. Fear, death, and mourning were not
words in his vocabulary. As for Tony, she felt a grudging respect. She knew how he had suffered for the past
two weeks, had noticed what no other eyes but her own
would have seen—the hint of pain in his eyes, the paleness at the corners of his mouth. Once, unable to sleep,
she had opened the door to his room and had seen him
standing in front of a window in the darkness, his head
pressed against the glass. He had been weeping, very
quietly—an insular sadness that she had not dared to
intrude upon.

Men did not cry, except in their hearts or in the
aloneness of midnight rooms, away from prying eyes or
the unmanly comfort of a woman's arms. She under-

of new equipment for the army. Major General Sir Thomas Haldane will head it and he's looking for bright men to staff it, preference going to officers who have seen the war at first hand and understand the army's needs. I thought of Charles right away."

"Yes," Hanna said, speaking slowly so as to keep any tremor of emotion from her voice, "he would certainly qualify, wouldn't he?"

"Of course. Not quite as much scientific background as General Haldane might like, but that obstacle can be overcome easily enough. Charles has a quick mind. He can learn anything if he has to."

"Would he take such a job? Leave his regiment?"

"He would have no choice. Mr. Langham has given General Haldane top priority on this. He can order the transfer of any line officer he wishes to have."

"It sounds like a satisfying and worthwhile task."

"Very. The Prime Minister and Lord Kitchener are terribly enthusiastic about it. So much of the army's equipment and weapons is antiquated. Charles would be doing far more for his country in Whitehall than he could ever do in the trenches."

Hanna felt faint as weeks of unending tension suddenly left her body. She was grateful for the brandy when it arrived and inhaled the heady fumes before taking a sip.

"To Charles," she said. "And to you."

Lydia smiled and reached across the table to touch Hanna lightly on the arm.

"Thank you, Lady Stanmore. I know everything will work out for the best. I shall make Charles a very good wife."

"I'm sure you will, my dear," Hanna said with the barest trace of a smile. "He's a fortunate young man."

And she meant that from the very bottom of her heart.

XIII

Number 7 Red Cross Hospital at Chartres occupied a limestone château overlooking the River Eure. It had been conceived as a center for the convalescence and rehabilitation of severe fracture cases, but the heavy casualties in Artois during the spring offensives had flooded it with every imaginable type of injury. Wooden barracks had been erected in the once lovely gardens, and the stables and coach house had been turned into wards and living quarters for nurses. The expansion barely kept pace with the flow. Fortunately, there had been minimal activity on the Western Front during the summer, but the *médecin-chef*, Dr. Gilles Jary, had just received notice from Paris that he could expect a marked increase of patients by the third week in September. The notice had arrived by ordinary post and the contents infuriated him.

"Such stupidity!" he stormed, pacing his small, crowded, untidy office in what had once been a garret room for lackeys. "*Merde!* That is all I can say . . . *merde!*" He held the offending message between two fingers and then let it drift to the floor. His matron of nurses, a stout, middle-aged Englishwoman, watched him impassively.

"May I read it, Doctor?"

"Why not? Why should you be an exception?" He kicked at the paper. "But I shall save you the bother. We are to prepare for many casualties by the third week in September. Identical messages have no doubt been sent to every other hospital. Perhaps they also sent the message to Boche headquarters! 'My dear Fritz, as you can see by the enclosed notice, we are preparing to attack you on or about the twenty-second day of next month. Cordially, Maréchal Joffre.'"

The doctor lit a cigarette from the butt of another one smoldering between his lips.

"You shall set your beard alight one day," the nurse said.

"Perhaps. It does not matter in the least."

"Where do we put more wounded?"

"A question for which there is no answer, Matron—no answer at all. Clear beds, I suppose. Any *blessés* capable of standing must·be moved out . . . sent down to Moulins . . . Lyons . . . Valence. I don't know. I will have to make inquiries as to available beds. Then there is the Hôtel Marcel in town. We could requisition it for the ambulatory."

The nurse smiled faintly. "You see, Doctor, there are answers to everything."

"I suppose." he growled, running a hand through his shaggy hair. "Now then, what problems do *you* have for me this morning?"

"None . . . a small pleasure. Three VAD's have arrived from England, very eager to serve, anxiously awaiting their first meeting with the *médecin-chef.*"

"All of them blonde and willowy?"

"Only one is blonde . . . and rather more *voluptueuse* than willowy, I would say."

"Ah," he sighed, "English girls. As aromatic as their tea. They stir the dead ashes of my youthful lechery."

"How Gallic you are today, Doctor. Shall I send them up?"

"No . . . I shall meet them in Ward D. They can follow me on rounds."

Alexandra Greville walked gravely behind Dr. Jary, the English matron, and a French nurse. The other two VAD's stood as close to the doctor as they could, both of them jotting down what he said in notebooks. Their eagerness pleased the doctor, and he complimented them extravagantly after the rounds of wards D and F had been completed. He then turned to face Alexandra.

"You do not keep notes, Miss . . . Miss . . . ?"

"Greville. No, I have a very retentive memory."

"You seem, if you will pardon me, abstracted. Is anything the matter?"

"No, just a bit disappointed."

Yes, Dr. Jary was thinking, *voluptueuse* was certainly the word to describe this blonde beauty. Most English girls he had known were virtually breastless and hipless. This one was superbly endowed in both respects. She reminded him of the opulent nudes of Ingres. It was quite easy to visualize her naked, and he felt a momentary regret at not being thirty years younger.

"Disappointed? With our little hospital?"

"Oh, no, Doctor," she said quickly. "Not at all. It's just that I had hoped to be sent to Toulon . . . to the naval hospital there."

He squinted at her through plumes of tobacco smoke. "Ah, you perhaps have a lover who is a wounded sailor. Is that it?"

"No," she said, blushing hotly. "My brother—he was wounded at Gallipoli. The moment I found out where he was I volunteered for duty in France. I requested the Red Cross to send me to Toulon, but I ended up here."

"Well, one must make the best of it, no? *C'est la guerre.* Come with me, child. We shall walk through Ward C together."

Ward C was a fracture ward. Fifty men lay in rows of beds, their limbs in plaster casts, suspended by weights and wires.

"Half a hundred *blessés.* All of them, as you can see, gravely injured. All far from their loved ones." He stopped by a bed. "Young Rialland here . . . nineteen years of age . . . wounded at Lens. He is a long way from his home in Bordeaux. Think of *him* as your brother."

The young man on the bed was staring at Alexandra as though a vision had appeared before him.

"*Un bel ange*," he whispered.

"*Merci*," she murmured shyly.

"You see!" The doctor patted her affectionately on the shoulder. "You are an angel to him, and a pretty French nurse will be an angel to your brother. You will be happy here and we will certainly be happy to have you."

She looked older. Only two weeks in France and yet, studying her face in the dressing-table mirror, she could discern subtle changes in her appearance. She had seen true suffering—that was reflected. And she had worked hard, harder than she had ever worked in her life. And done disagreeable, even repugnant tasks. That was reflected also.

"Yes," she whispered, bending closer to the glass and running her fingers across her cheekbones. "The war is changing you."

She felt a sense of pride in herself. She had stuck it out and had come through with flying colors. The hospital in Chartres was quite unlike the convalescent hospital for officers in England. Her duties there had been, looking back on it, quite laughable. A companion, no more than that. A sympathetic female. Someone to joke with the recuperating men, play cards with them, lead them into the garden for walks, perhaps push them in a wheelchair. The staff at Chartres expected a great deal more from their VAD girls. They were understaffed, and the trained nurses had enough to do without having to bathe the bedridden or cater to their bodily functions. Her first bedpan had made her retch. The second had made her gag. The third, fourth, and fifth had done no more than make her wrinkle her nose in disgust. Now the duty was commonplace and automatic. And she could bathe men now without feeling squeamish about touching their naked flesh with a soapy rag.

"I am altered," she murmured. "I've become . . . a woman."

It was as though she had suddenly walked through a door, crossing from one room to another, with no possibility of ever going back. She doubted if her mother and father would understand the change in her, and her letters to them were filled with the type of formal observations that had characterized her letters from boarding school:

> . . . Chartres is a beautiful old town and the cathedral is quite magnificent, a purity of Gothic art. I have not been to visit it yet as we are quite busy, but hope to do so soon. However, one can see its towers rising above the trees. I am allowed one afternoon off a week—rather like being a housemaid!—and may request, and probably be refused, three days "leave" a month. I am quite happy and the food is plentiful, although lentil soup can become quite tiresome.

She reserved her innermost thoughts for Lydia Foxe, filling page after page with a hasty scrawl, a tumultuous outpouring of intimate reflections. These letters were written in the room that she shared with four other girls, in the golden light between daylight and dusk, the sun sinking late in early September . . . sleep measured from sundown to dawn.

> Dearest L.
>
> The *blessés* never talk about their experiences. Why this is I do not know, but the fact remains that they are quite mute regarding the circumstances which brought about their injuries. Places may be mentioned, which draw nods of understanding from their fellows in adjacent beds, the names of villages, woods, crossroads, trenches, but never a word about the actual event that crippled them. They keep that awful moment secret, fearing

"Damn."

"Jenny's talking to him in Nepali, but not making much headway, I'm afraid. Oh, well, can't be helped, can it? Have to chop-chop quick-quick or the poor fella's done for."

Robin stood up with obvious reluctance. "I suppose you want a formal introduction, Vale?"

"Yes," he said, grinning at Alexandra. "If you don't mind, old chap."

"Miss Greville, Captain Vale. Captain Vale, Miss Greville." He tapped out his pipe in a shell-case ashtray. "I'll be an hour. Show Miss Greville around the place, will you, Vale?"

"Be delighted, dear man . . . positively delighted." He took a sip of the major's tea and then lit a cigarette. "Curious chaps, these Gurkhas. Damn good fighters. Give Fritz cold sweats, but we have no end of trouble with them. Rather die than have an amputation. Believe in reincarnation, you see. Won't tolerate the idea of going into the next life missing a limb. I say, you're a smashing-looking girl. Don't mind my saying so, do you?"

"No." He reminded her of Carveth Saunders, Bart., only she assumed his Mayfair tone to be nothing but a pose.

"Care to see our little carnival?"

"Yes, I would, thank you."

"A bit on the empty side at the moment. We cleared shop by six this morning . . . ready for the next batch. Rather like old Waterloo Station. Chappies come and go."

"Go where?"

"Oh, by hospital train to Saint-Omar . . . Calais . . . Rouen . . . or down the road to the graveyard. We do more than our best, but we lose quite a few."

Her nagging sense of trepidation returned when Captain Vale showed her through the wards. They were coldly functional. No white-sheeted beds—simply row upon row of canvas cots with brown army blankets folded neatly at the foot of each. Rolling carts piled high with dressings, bottles of antitetanus serum, hypodermic needles, and morphine capsules were next to every fifth bed. The sisters and RAMC orderlies looked at her with frank curiosity.

"It's your uniform," Captain Vale said. "Obviously not a regulation issue. Leave it to the sisters to note *that*. As for the orderlies, it's what's *in* the uniform that they're gaping at." He opened a door and led the way across a duckboard past a fieldstone structure that might once have been a stable. "That's where we operate . . . move the chappies in, move 'em out . . . cut cut cut. Tommy calls this place Mendinghem. . . . Number fifteen CCS over at Neuve-Eglise they call Bandagehem. The French hospital at Hazebrouck is Endinghem. Tommy has a droll sense of humor."

"Is Major Mackendric in charge here?"

"Oh, my, yes, the top doctor wallah. It's a colonel's job actually, but surgeons are spread thin these days. Even have some Yank chaps coming over to us from Harvard medical school. Should be here any day now, God bless their Colonial socks."

A bell rang: four loud clangs . . . pause . . . four more.

"What's that?"

Captain Vale's expression hardened slightly, a tense thinning of the lips.

"Staff call. Get the news of what we're in for today. Nasty bit of firing since dawn. Won't be a pleasant afternoon, I'm afraid. Oh, well, can't have sunshine and flowers every day, can we?"

Alexandra stood at the far end of the mess tent, out of everyone's way. Doctors, surgical and ward nurses, orderlies, and the various technicians stood about in silent groups. Finally, Mackendric, a surgical gown over his uniform, came into the tent.

"All right," he said. "Brigade just rang through. The Bedfords and Suffolks were in it this morning up at

White Sheet and got scuppered. Half their wounded are on the way down to us now, three to four hundred of them . . . sitters and stretchers. . . . Stretchers predominate, I gather. They were badly shelled, so prepare for extreme multiples. The bearers found thirty or so Cameronians who had been lying out in the wire since Wednesday. We know what to expect there, so be sure to have chloroform handy." He glanced at his watch. "Should be arriving by sixteen hundred hours, so get your suppers out of the way and prepare for a long night. I want as many as possible on the train by dawn."

She had hoped he would find time to talk to her again, perhaps even have supper with her, but although she wandered about the hospital she never caught so much as a glimpse of him. Then the elderly sister she had met that morning came up to her as she sat dejectedly in the mess tent.

"Feel a bit lost, do you?"

"Yes, a bit."

"Well, can't have that, can we? Have you been taught anything useful?"

"Yes," she said bridling, "of course."

"Can you insert a catheter?"

"No . . ." she said hesitantly.

"If I told you to inject a man with five hundred units of ATS, would you know how to go about it? Or how much morphine to give without killing him? Or how to set up a Carrel drip?"

"No . . . I . . ." She could feel her face burning. The woman's gray eyes seemed to bore right through her.

"I'm Matron here," she went on, not unkindly. "Major Mackendric asked me if there was any possibility of my using you. I'm afraid there isn't. You'll have to go back to Saint-Omer tomorrow. But you look like a strong, healthy girl, and I can certainly find something useful for you to do this afternoon. We'll be receiving casualties shortly and you can give the orderlies a hand. Find a smock to put over your uniform, so you don't get it messy. You can report to Corporal Hyde in number five admitting . . . that's the building over there with the *green* cross on the tenting. We had a very nice soldier do a bit of painting for us and he turned out to be quite color-blind."

The orderlies were tense but friendly, offering her sweet, milky tea and some practical advice.

"Speed's the ticket," Corporal Hyde said, a cigarette pasted to his lower lip. "It's like a ruddy factory when we get movin'."

"What exactly do we do?"

"Turn the lads over to the sisters as unmucky as possible, so's they can get to work on 'em. They'll have all kinds of rags and tatters about their wounds. Cut the old dressin's off and toss 'em in a bucket. If there's lots of mud, we wash it off with green soap and antiseptic solution. There'll be three sisters with us givin' ATS shots and morphine, an' they don't take kindly to holdups. Fast but thorough is the bloomin' motto around here."

At three forty-five the first ambulances and army lorries came rocking and swaying up the deeply rutted road that led to Wytschaete and the front. Gears ground and the vehicles lumbered into the compound and drew up in front of the admitting tent. Orderlies and stretcher bearers ran to open the ambulance doors and to get the wounded from the back of the lorries even as more ambulances, some of them horse drawn, came up the road.

There was a sound that Alexandra could not associate with anything she had ever heard before—a muttering, moaning, muted howl of a noise coming from the mud-encrusted conveyances parked in front. She glanced at the sisters standing by two dressing carts. Their faces were impassive, their eyes devoid of any expression at all. "Stretchers" and "sitters." The words were self-explanatory. Stretchers were the men who had to be carried in by the bearers. Sitters were men capable of stumbling into the tent with minimal aid. All brought the sound with them: a continuous groaning . . . a stifled shriek . . . deep, body-convulsing sobs. All had been hastily bandaged at their regimental aid posts, given morphine pellets, but the effects of the drugs were wearing off. Pain beyond comprehension gripped many of them, and they threshed about on their stretchers or clung kneeling to the wooden benches along one wall of the tent.

"Hop to it, girl," one of the sisters said in a taut voice.

She had been among the wounded before. All the *blessés* at Chartres had been hit—but that had been weeks before they had arrived at number seven Hôpital Croix Rouge. She had seen them only as clean, well-bandaged men, aware, many of them, that further operations might be necessary. But "further operations" held no terror for them. Body casts and bandages might be uncomfortable, but their beds were clean, the food was wholesome, there were flowers in the wards.

"Arterial hemorrhage, Sister!" an orderly shouted out.

Alexandra saw a stream of blood pump upward from a sodden khaki bundle lying on a stretcher. The sister knelt quickly beside the groaning man and clamped off the flow. Alexandra could only stare as more and more men were brought into the large tent. Horror piled on horror. A man with his eyeballs blown out, dirty cotton stuffed into the sockets. Sheared-off legs and arms, the stumps wound with blood-caked bandage or soiled puttees. A man screaming and twisting like an animal in a trap, hands pressed against a bulge of intestines that were slipping through his fingers. Her legs shook and an icy chill clutched her head and made her scalp crawl. Corporal Hyde thrust a pair of scissors into her limp hand and whispered fiercely, "Come on, miss, don't stand about."

She sank to her knees beside a stretcher, not from choice, her legs giving way beneath her. She stared down at a blackened muddy bandage covering the man's upper thigh and hip . . . dirty gray flesh beneath the slit trouser leg. As she cut hesitantly at the bandage, the man screamed and cursed and tried to sit up. Corporal Hyde held him down.

"Cut them bloody rags off, miss!"

She cut, her hand shaking so violently she almost dropped the scissors. Beneath the bandage lay a bloody puddle with bits of hipbone jutting up from the ooze. Vomit rose in her throat and she clamped her teeth to hold it back. The vomit scorched and choked her as she swallowed.

"Keep them moving along, for God's sake," a sister called out in exasperation. "They're beginning to pile up outside."

Nausea came in wave after wave. Her jaws ached and her throat was on fire. Sweat clung in cold beads to her pallid face. There seemed to be no end to the writhing, grunting, animal-like creatures who were laid in front of her by the stretcher bearers. The bucket of filthy bandages she had snipped away overflowed and another was quickly brought, then another and another. She did not become numb to the ghastliness revealed when each rag of a dressing was removed: splintered ends of bone, loops of gut, the red hollow where a lower jaw had been. Each revelation seemed worse than the last. The nightmare only deepened.

"Cameronian," an orderly muttered to her as a mud-encrusted form was set down in front of her by the bearers. The orderly placed a dark brown bottle of chloroform and some cotton batting on the floor beside her. "Just douse the little bastards."

It was a Cameronian sergeant, four days in a shell hole between the wire—four days of sun and rain. The letter T had been painted on his forehead with iodine. They had done that much for him at the aid post: anti-tetanus serum, no more than that. A self-applied dressing under his right armpit bulged over the festering wound beneath. She cut the dressing away with difficulty, dried blood holding the edges like tar. Pus flowed yellow green, and then, boiling up out of the suppurating depths of the shell-chewed cavity, a mass of living things, a churning, undulating ball of fat white maggots, creeping into her fingers along the blades of the scissors, up her fingers, squirming blindly along the back of her hand.

She screamed and could not stop screaming. She screamed as she stumbled to her feet, kicking the bottle of chloroform. She screamed as she staggered, retching, toward the door. A sister grabbed her arms and then slapped her hard across the face, once, twice—stiff-fingered blows. She felt nothing, saw nothing as she slipped down into a misty, comforting darkness.

It was peaceful in the back of the ambulance. Around her in the blackness were silent forms, drugged, still as death. She pulled her warm cloak up to her chin. Someone out there in the inky night was calling her name. She could hear it softly . . . softly: *Alex* . . . *Alex* . . . She stared fixedly at the bottom of a stretcher laid on the brackets above her.

Alex . . . Alex . . .

The ambulance began to move, creaking and lurching slowly across the compound. Taking away the wounded. Yes, she thought dully. Taking them away. And she was one of them, just one of the wounded. Perhaps even one of the dead.

BOOK THREE

God knows 'twere better to be deep
Pillowed in silk and scented down,
Where love throbs out in blissful sleep,
Pulse nigh to pulse, and breath to breath,
Where hushed awakenings are dear . . .
But I've a rendezvous with Death
At midnight in some flaming town,
When spring trips north again this year
ALAN SEEGER (1888–1916)

places at the same times—rue du Bois and Festubert, Auchy and the dismal approaches to Loos. Their words nagged at old pains and still raw nerves.

"Must be off," he said, draining a whiskey and soda after glancing at his watch. He walked briskly out of the club and along Pall Mall toward the taxi stand in St. James's Square. Tattered sheets of gray cloud scudded overhead. The streaming fragments reminded him of shrapnel bursts and he could see his last command in the wind: B Company, struggling through cratered ground, whizz-bangs and machine guns catching them. The first platoon lurching toward the ridge, stopped by the German wire, dozens of them hanging in the rusty thickets for days. Ragged husks, blackened clods against the skyline. . . .

The taxicab door closed with a comforting chunky sound. Although sealed from the counterbarrage by solid Austin walls, he sat stiffly on the edge of the seat all the way to Cadogan Square.

The war had touched half a million English homes, an avalanche of letters or telegrams pushed through letter slots telling of dead or wounded men, missing men, captured men. Number 24 Cadogan Square was such a home. Two dead sons. Two living sons anxious to get over to France and . . .

"Scupper Boche," Lord Sutton remarked heatedly as he poured whiskey into two glasses. "By gad, Fenton, that's all young John and Bramwell think about . . . getting up to the line and killing the blighters."

He had never met them, but they were probably like Andrew and Timothy had been—recklessly brave. Their father's sons. He glanced past the portly red-faced man. A full-length portrait of him hung on one wall of the library. The young marquess in hussar uniform. The painter had captured that look of zeal and arrogance that had sent Victorians galloping heedlessly toward the guns: "Into the jaws of Death, Into the mouth of Hell. . . ."

"It pays to be cautious in France," Fenton said quietly.

If Lord Sutton heard him, he paid no attention to the remark.

"A mere dollop of soda water. Too fine a whiskey to spoil. Pure malt, sir. From my own distillery in Kinlochewe. No contaminating neutral spirits, which I wouldn't rub on a horse." He handed Fenton a glass and raised his own. "To your decoration and your rise in rank. I suppose this means you'll be commanding a battalion now, eh?"

"Yes, sir . . .. one of the New Army mobs. I'm to train it and have it in France by next spring."

"As part of which regiment?"

"The Green Howards."

"I was with the Eleventh Hussars . . . Prince Albert's own . . . the Cherry Pickers, sir!"

Lord Sutton was not really looking at him, Fenton realized as he sipped his drink. The eyes were glazed and fixed on some point in the distant past. They were the eyes of a man who was fortunate to have his own distillery. He talked ceaselessly, leaping from one disconnected subject to the next until Lady Mary entered the room, and then he sat down and lapsed into a moody silence.

"Ah, my dear Fenton! Most noble heart!" She came toward him like some gaunt predatory bird. Her hands never stopped moving, and long ropes of jade and jet beads swung from around her throat. "Dear little Winifred will be ready shortly . . . fussing with her hair, poor child. I am quite vexed with her today . . . quite vexed, really I am. Her own brothers crying out from that awful void, anxious to come home, and she won't lift a finger to help them. But of course you understand, I'm sure."

He listened with growing apprehension to Lady Mary's talk of the spirit world, of Ouija boards and Ram the Nubian. He pitied Winifred living amid such irrationality. She'd always been under her mother's thumb, and her refusal to take part in this nonsense was bound to have its repercussions. He expected to see a mousy, half-beaten creature, so he barely recognized the tall, beautiful woman who entered the library.

In the back of the taxi, as they drove to Mayfair, he couldn't keep from staring at her. The change in her was dramatic. He had remembered her, with twinges of shame, as a schoolgirl of touching eagerness, whose gratitude for his attentions had been almost embarrassing. And yet there had been a quality about her even then that had intrigued him. He had truly enjoyed being with her and he felt that same sense of ease now.

"Why are you staring at me?"

"I'm sorry," he said. "I was trying to recall the Winifred I knew."

"Have I changed that much?"

"Well, you're older, of course."

"So are you, for that matter."

"Yes, about a century older." He didn't want to appear rude, and so he deliberately looked away from her and stared at the back of the driver's neck. "You're a very lovely young woman, Winifred."

"Thank you . . . and you're still a very . . ." A smile barely teased her lips. "I was going to say 'lovely-looking' man. But that's hardly the correct word, is it? The word to describe a colonel would be 'distinguished.' Yes, you're very distinguished." She glanced out the side window. It was getting dark and crowds streamed across Hyde Park Corner toward the Underground station in Piccadilly. "Must we go to tea?"

"Don't you feel like having tea?"

"Not especially."

"What would you like to do?"

"Oh . . . go to Madame Tussaud's. I've always wanted to see the chamber of horrors . . . Sweeney Todd cutting throats and Jack the Ripper. Father would never take me to see that section of the waxworks, but I had a friend in school, Rose Collins. She's seen it several times. Her uncle used to take her."

His hearing was not so numbed by shellfire that he couldn't detect sarcasm when he heard it. He leaned forward and tapped on the glass.

"Stop here, driver."

They walked along Piccadilly in silence, not because they had nothing to say to each other, but because the wind had picked up and was driving grains of ice into their faces. He took hold of her arm and led her into Half Moon Street and into the warm, spacious lobby of the Torrington Hotel.

"Did your friend's uncle ever buy the child a pink gin?"

"He may have," she said thoughtfully. "But I doubt it."

"May I buy you one, or will it alter your growth?"

"You're angry, aren't you?"

"Don't you think I have a right to be?"

"Yes . . . and no. Let's just say, for the sake of fairness, that we both have a right."

The saloon-bar was crowded with officers and well-dressed women. There was a tiny dance floor—every hotel saloon-bar had a dance floor now—and a four-piece ragtime band was playing the Castle walk. Winifred cast a stony glance at the women and a wildly cavorting Canadian second lieutenant.

"Could you find someplace quieter?"

He escorted her upstairs to the main salon, where more sedate couples sat taking tea or cocktails. An elderly waiter in livery showed them to a table on the glassed-in balcony that had a fine view of Green Park. Fenton ordered a pink gin and a whiskey-soda and the drinks were quickly brought out on a silver tray.

"You feel that I'm being patronizing, don't you?" he asked.

"No," she said. "I think you're just being noble . . . the honorable thing to do. A less considerate man would have simply ignored the situation entirely and not called on me at all." She took a sip of her gin. "Quite tasty. Odd. Us having a drink together in a public place.

Quite unthinkable a year and a half ago, but '*tempora mutantur*' and all that."

"Yes, times change, but human emotions do not. If I've hurt you, Winifred, I'm deeply sorry."

"You have nothing to apologize for. The war has changed everyone's plans. I suppose we'd be married by now if Germany hadn't marched into Belgium. I wonder if we'd be happy. Probably. I would have a handsome husband you would have . . . what? Why did you choose me, Fenton? It wasn't love. I wasn't under that illusion even then. Fundamentally monetary, I suppose. Or is that an uncalled-for remark?"

"No. You deserve to know why. It's true I needed money to stay in the regiment. It was either marry well or resign my commission. Your father understood my motive, so did Andrew. Their feelings were that I'd make you a good husband. That was my rationale as well. And I would have. But it wasn't just money—I wasn't that cold-blooded about it. I would have sought out some simpering daughter of a Sheffield millionaire if I had been. God knows there were enough of that sort fluttering about Mayfair ballrooms. I liked you . . . enjoyed your company. I enjoy it now."

She toyed absently with her drink, turning the slender glass between her fingers.

"What would you do if I held you to your obligation to at least ask me to marry you?"

"I would propose, of course."

"Of course. I hardly needed to ask the question, did I?" She set her drink on the table and looked at him, her face expressionless. "I have difficulty sometimes in remembering what I was like that summer . . . or what you were like. We're different people now, aren't we? Not just in a physical sense. I mean to say, too much has happened in our lives for us not to have been altered quite drastically. But I recall how infatuated I was . . . how utterly giddy I felt. I knew in my heart that you couldn't possibly be in love with me, but I was desperate to be engaged by the end of July. I felt I owed it to my mother for all of her efforts to see me wed. She made me feel that it was all my fault Charles hadn't dropped on one knee . . . that, somehow, I'd made a mess of it. But then she never had to walk in the garden with Charles as I did, knowing that every time he looked at me he was comparing me with Lydia Foxe. That was cruel. I couldn't possibly compete. I felt like such a frump. And then, out of the blue, you strolled into my life with a box of sweets under your arm. No man's timing could have been more perfect . . . or more deliberately planned."

He took a hefty pull at his drink and then dug into his jacket for a tin of cigarettes.

"I hope you don't mind if I smoke."

"Not at all."

"This is rather like hearing a story about two unattractive strangers. You're an exceedingly beautiful woman. You don't need to feel grateful if a man looks at you."

"And you don't need a rich wife in order to stay in the army. The slate has been wiped clean, Fenton. It's like meeting for the first time."

"My feelings exactly. What say we make a proper evening of it—dinner at Romano's or upstairs at the Cafe Royal . . ."

Her smile went unnoticed as she took a sip of her drink.

"Sounds like fun, but I really don't feel up to celebrating. Will you be in London long?"

He felt a twinge of disappointment and a sense of having been deliberately cut by her. How deeply did she resent him? he wondered. He blew a thin stream of cigarette smoke from the corner of his mouth.

"On and off for the next two weeks. I'm going down to Abingdon for the weekend. May I telephone you next week?"

She looked at him without a flicker of emotion—a cautious, deliberating gaze. "Yes," she said with a slight nod. "If you really want to."

* * *

There was a bleakness to the countryside that Fenton had never seen before during all the many winters he had spent in the North Downs and the Weald. A shabbiness and neglect that was not solely attributable to the weather. The lack of able-bodied men, he supposed, as the train lumbered slowly past one neglected-looking village after another: Effingham and Horsely . . . Clandon and Merrow. Roofs needed repair, walls thirsted for whitewashing, orchards were unpruned. The train was delayed at Abbotswood Junction to permit a battalion of New Army troops to double-time across the tracks. The West Surreys, he noticed, catching sight of the flag-bearing lamb badge on an officer's cap. The officer was gray-haired and rode his horse with taut-bodied fury, probably mentally cursing the shambling mob of soldiers, who were obviously in the first stages of their training and could not run across a railway track without stumbling into each other or tripping over the rails. The West Surrey officer saw only a thousand green troops foisted on his ancient, noble regiment to meet the needs of the war. Fenton saw one thousand bricklayers, house painters, carpenters, well diggers, tree pruners, butchers and butchers' boys, and God knew what else. The heart's blood of the shire running across the embankment and on into the misted, sleet-covered fields beyond.

Charles had warned him that there might not be a taxi for hire in Godalming and to telephone the house when his train got in. There was a taxi, if he cared to wait an hour for it, but Mr. Pearson, the brewer, was driving his lorry into Abington with six barrels of ale and offered Fenton a lift.

"Like when you was a young 'un," Mr. Pearson said jovially. "You and young Mr. Charles and your brother, God bless him, 'opping on the wagon when I'd slow them old Percherons o' mine on Burgate Hill."

Summer fields and dray horses. Fresh in old Pearson's memory, but beyond recall to Fenton. He got out

at the iron gates that marked the mile-long road to the
house and walked the rest of the way, his kit bag slung
over one shoulder. The Pryory looked as weathered and
bleak as everything else he had seen, the house stretching away in the afternoon gloom like some abandoned
relic. The once-manicured quadrangle of the Italian
garden seen beyond the weed-dotted terrace was a tan-
gle of unpruned cypress. The stables, he knew without
seeing, would be empty, the horses given to the cavalry.
They might just as well have stayed in their warm, comfortable stalls for all the good they were doing in
France.

But the house only looked abandoned. There were a
number of cars parked at the end of the driveway, and
when Coatsworth opened the door, Fenton saw he was
in full livery.

"Why, Mr. Fenton, sir, good to see you."

"Thank you, Coatsworth. Did I walk in on a party?"

"Just a few of his lordship's friends. Last gathering
for some time, sir." He took Fenton's trench coat and
kit bag and whispered, "They're closing the Pryory after
Christmas, sir. We all move to the Park Lane house.
Only forty rooms there . . . much easier to keep up."

Only forty rooms, Fenton thought wryly as he walked
down the corridor toward the library. Well, everyone
had to make sacrifices in wartime.

The candles in their silver holders were reflected in
the highly polished surface of the long table. But for the
lack of footmen—there were only three, who were old,
older even than Coatsworth—it could have been any
gathering for dinner at Abingdon Pryory at any time.
The war was snugly tucked away as Lord Stanmore
sliced the roast mutton and Coatsworth uncorked the
hock. It seemed to Fenton that he had but to close his
eyes for a second, and when he opened them again
Roger would be arguing with Charles about current
trends in modern poetry and Alexandra would be chat-
tering away about Paris frocks or what was playing at

the cinema in Guildford. But time did not come back, no matter how familiar the surroundings. Roger was dead. Charles was a married man, and Alexandra hadn't opened her mouth all evening except to say hello. Some things never changed, however. Mr. Cavendish, squire of Dilton Hall and the second largest landowner in the district, still bore his grudge against the Liberal party, although Lydia Foxe Greville's presence at the table caused him to keep his comments to a near-inaudible mumble.

Lydia Foxe Greville. Fenton was seated opposite her and it was impossible for their eyes not to meet. What did he see there? A hint of triumph? A veiled smugness? Perhaps. It had always been difficult to tell what Lydia was thinking. When toasts were offered, he raised his glass to her and she smiled at him, as though saying, "You see, I told you I would do it." The future Countess of Stanmore. It seemed incredible, but there she sat, looking to the manor born—and almost excessively lovely.

"So the fighting has wound down for the winter and I would like to know what we've got to show for it." Brigadier General Sir Bertram Sturdee, long retired, tapped his wineglass with a spoon. "Nineteen fifteen is not a year I would ever like to see again."

"Must we talk of the war, Bertram?" Hanna said.

"It's on everyone's mind, Hanna. *Non*war conversation always seems to flounder somewhat. And with Fenton's DSO ribbon staring me in the face, I can't quite keep my thoughts on local matters."

Hanna rose majestically. "You may talk of the war all you wish over the port. We ladies would prefer to be spared."

Alexandra stood up with the other women and then walked to the head of the table and kissed her father on the temple.

"Good night, Papa. I'm going to bed."

"Still feeling under the weather?" he asked.

"Yes," she said, "a bit." She turned to Fenton and

placed a hand on his shoulder. "Good night, Fenton. It's so good to see you again."

He touched her hand. It was cold and her face had a waxen appearance.

"Alexandra not well?" he asked after the women had left the room.

"One bout of flu after another," the earl said, passing a box of cigars to his right. "Caught a chill of some sort in France and can't shake it."

"Alex was in France?"

"Thought you knew. Yes. Went over with the Red Cross . . . came back in October quite ill."

"Mustard and vinegar," Mr. Cavendish said. "Rub it thickly on the child's chest, wrap it in flannel, and keep her in bed. Works wonders."

Brigadier General Sturdee lit a cigar and waited for Coatsworth to pour the port.

"So Sir John French is out and Sir Douglas Haig is in. So much for the politics of the high command. You're in Whitehall these days, Charles. What sort of wild tales filter through the War Office halls?"

"Not too many filter down to my office," Charles replied, scowling at his glass of port. "I'm rather a new boy and not on the grapevine. But I understand that Haig would like to end the war next year with one huge blow in late summer . . . up at Ypres. Joffre would prefer having our offensive launched closer to the French buildup in Champagne . . . perhaps along the Somme. Either way, it's going to be a big push and nineteen sixteen might just be the victory year."

"Don't bet a quid on it," Fenton said. "They're just getting light-headed up at GHQ seeing all these New Army battalions come into being. A million men under arms. They're mesmerized by the figures, but it doesn't change the formula. *Ten* million men could have gone over the top at Loos, and they still would have been stopped by the wire and the Boche machine gunners. The Hun formula for defense is basic, simple, and works like a bloody charm. We have to make a radical

happened when she was in France, but I can't get a word out of her. Very curious. She used to overwhelm me with confidences."

She concentrated on the road. There was very little civilian traffic but a good deal of army transport, most of it horse drawn. She passed the long columns slowly so as not to spook the animals.

"I find you a bit curious as well," she said. "You haven't said anything. Not one word."

"About what?"

"Charles and me."

"You seem like a happy couple. What am I supposed to say?"

"You never thought it would happen, so you must have some degree of inquisitiveness."

"I gave up being inquisitive about anything that happens these days. I wouldn't have raised an eyebrow had you married the Prince of Wales."

"Please don't play the bastard with me, Fenton. We've known each other too long for that."

"Very well, I'll be suitably brotherly. Are you happy?"

She hesitated slightly. "Yes."

"Do you love him at all?"

"He loves me. That's all that matters."

"Did you get him his job with NS Five?"

She stiffened. "What makes you ask that?"

"Because I know how the army works. General Haldane's a Royal Engineer. There must have been any number of RE officers he could have picked with more technical training than Charles. I suspect a bit of string pulling by you or Archie."

"All right. I talked to a few people. Is there anything wrong in that?"

"No. I would gladly have done the same. He probably realizes it, but he thinks he's only doing this until he's fit for duty in the line. Is that how it works, or is there something he doesn't know yet?"

"He's locked in for the duration of the war," she said flatly.

"He'll hate you for it when he finds out."

"How regimental you sound. He might just be grateful for being spared the trenches."

"Most men would be, but not the Right Honorable Charles G. As long as you're married to him, you might take the trouble to understand his class."

"God! The peerage have their little ways, don't they? Duty . . . self-sacrifice . . . stalwart resistance to change. One wonders sometimes if they'll emerge from this war with their coronets intact."

"I assume they'll survive," he said quietly. "They always have."

"Charles will survive. That's all I care about."

"With coronet in place?"

She brushed a loose strand of hair from her forehead and smiled.

"England will always be England. The power may rest one day in the hands of an ex–Liverpool solicitor, but the people will bow at the sight of a coronet, be it tarnished or not."

Bristol Mews was a short brick-paved street near Berkeley Square. Lydia parked the car in front of a narrow three-story house that had been built during the reign of George II. The windowsills had been freshly painted white, the shutters and front door a gleaming black.

"Handsome-looking place," Fenton said.

"It's quite charming on the inside, too. Care for a drink?"

"I could go for a whiskey, yes."

There were painters' ladders in the foyer and a strong smell of turpentine, wallpaper paste, and wood shavings throughout the first floor.

"It takes forever," Lydia said. "It's so difficult finding good workers, and those you do find are unbearably independent. It's more ordered on the upper floors."

She led the way up a gently curving stairway to the second-floor landing and into a large room furnished in the Oriental manner, with black- and red-lacquered cabinets and tables, a huge Chinese screen, and low divans covered in pale green silk.

"Like it?"

"Yes," he said, after giving it some thought. "A change from Burgate House."

"Daddy told me to take furniture from there, but there was nothing in the old place except Sheraton and Hepplewhite. I wanted something different."

"Very exotic. I feel out of place in khaki."

"There's whiskey and soda in the teak cabinet. Help yourself while I change."

An elderly maid came in to light the fire while Fenton was pouring himself a whiskey. No neutral spirits—which made him think of Winifred. He was still thinking of her when Lydia came back into the room, her traveling suit of heavy tweed replaced by a flowing silk hostess gown in shades of blue and dark green. Yes, he thought, it had been cruel of Charles to compare Winifred to Lydia. The difference between them was not as marked now as it had been then, but there was certainly an air of chic about Lydia that Winifred would never acquire.

Lydia closed the doors and walked over to the fire, the glow of the flames turning her loose hair a shimmering copper. Fenton fixed her a brandy and then sat beside her on a divan facing the fire.

"How long will you be in England?" she asked.

"Four or five months. I go up to Leeds after New Year's and start training a battalion. One of those chums-and-pals conglomerations . . . all the lads enlisting together. I'll feel a rank outsider."

"I'm sure they'll be proud having a Guards officer commanding them. I know I'd be."

"I can just see myself ordering *you* about."

"I don't know," she said tautly. "That would depend on what you ordered me to do."

She set her drink on a low table and turned to him. He moved his arms around her, feeling the warmth of her body beneath the silk gown.

"I want you, Fenton."

"You *have* Charles."

She undid the middle buttons of his shirt and slipped a hand through the gap.

"His love is ethereal. Passion shocks him."

"You'll have to teach him. One doesn't learn much about women at Eton and Cambridge. Be patient."

She kissed him on the mouth, her tongue gliding against his teeth.

"I don't feel very patient at the moment," she whispered. "Please, Fenton . . ."

He could take her to bed. Or he could take her on the divan. A pleasant afternoon's rutting in Bristol Mews—the first step to becoming her lover. She might talk to a few people and he would find his orders mysteriously changed. Staff job in Whitehall. Nothing to be ashamed of. Brother officers would say that he jolly well deserved it after Mons, the Marne, Festubert, and Loos. Her tongue sought the deeper recesses of his mouth. Lingered, drew back.

"Please . . ."

She was warm . . . vibrant . . . passionate. Infinitely desirable. But there was a taste of brass in his mouth. The taste of tarnish.

"No." He pushed her gently away from him and stood up. "We're much too late for this, darling Lydia. We quite missed the boat."

She lay back against the cushions, staring at him, her eyes reflecting the fire.

"You're not serious."

"Yes, as a matter of fact I am."

"Why? Charles would never know. You wouldn't be hurting him or ruining his marriage in the slightest."

He buttoned his shirt and straightened his tie. "I wasn't thinking of Charles, actually. He never crossed my mind. I was thinking of myself. Everything is becoming so shabby these days. So lacking in worth. I just don't feel like joining the trend."

"You son of a bitch," she said quietly as he walked out of the room.

XV

Martin Rilke struggled along Oxford Street, the wind yanking at his umbrella and threatening to tear it from his hand. A middle-aged woman waiting at a bus stop stared at him without sympathy.

"Slacker," she said in a strong cockney accent. "Strong chap like you."

He was used to it, the insults and the white feathers. Quite a large number of men whose work was vital to the war effort or who had been judged medically unfit for service had taken to wearing armbands to avoid being harassed. He had considered the idea of wearing one with a small American flag stitched to it, but had thought better of it. It would only have led to other snide remarks: "Too bloody proud to fight, eh?"

He entered the White Manor at Marble Arch, removed his raincoat and hat, and handed them to a cloakroom attendant along with his battered umbrella. An orchestra in the second-floor dining salon was playing a waltz, the soft strains fragmented by the clatter of plates and teacups in the crowded, plebeian first floor. He looked around and finally spotted Ivy Thaxton seated at a small table next to a travertine column. He felt like shouting at the sight of her—he hadn't seen her for three and a half weeks—but suppressed the urge.

"Ivy!" He slid into the chair opposite her and reached across the table to touch her hand. "Gosh, it's good to see you. I hope you weren't waiting long."

"No, just a few minutes." She smiled warmly, her hand clenching his. "Have you been all right?"

"Of course."

"You look pale."

"I'm fine."

She frowned slightly. "I mean it. A bit wan under the eyes."

"I know you've been capped, but don't play nurse with me, Sister. . . . I'm just weak from hunger."

"So am I."

He looked around. There were tables almost on top of them—two hefty kilted highlanders within touching distance.

"Wouldn't you rather go upstairs? Maybe we could get a better table . . . and dance."

"It's horribly crowded up there, too. And besides, the food's the same up or down. Let's just have our tea and talk about dancing later."

She could eat, bless her. He felt almost paternal watching her devour what was placed before her—a hot pork pie, tea sandwiches of ham and cress, a slice of Dundee cake, and cup after cup of tea. And yet she was as thin as a waif. She amazed him.

"Stop staring at me."

"I like to watch you eat."

"It's rude."

"Sure, but you know how we Yanks are." He took a cigar from his pocket but didn't light it. She frowned on his smoking while they ate. "I have a little something for you. A Christmas present."

She looked at him sternly. "That's not fair. We made a promise not to exchange gitfs."

"Okay, I welshed on the deal. But I saw this certain item in Regent Street the other day and I knew you'd like it, so I bought it for you."

"You shouldn't have."

"Ah, but I did . . . and they won't take it back." He toyed with the cigar. "You'll be going to France, won't you?"

"Yes." She looked down at her plate and crumbled a bit of cake between her fingers. "My group leaves on the third of January . . . number nine Stationary Hospital in Boulogne."

He fished for a match and lit the cigar. "So soon?"

"Afraid so."

"Will I be able to see you before you leave?"

"I doubt it. We go down to Portsmouth for an orientation course right after Christmas . . . the twenty-seventh, I believe. Sorry, Martin, but this is our last get-together. . . ."

"Date," he said, forcing a grin.

"Yes . . . 'date.' I must remember that word."

"I could come over . . . write an article or two about number nine Stationary Hospital in Boulogne and Sister Ivy Thaxton of the QA's."

"Please don't. It's going to be a difficult time for me . . . adjusting to the type of cases we'll meet there. I would only be terribly distracted if you were hanging about."

His grin was genuine this time. "Would you really?"

"Don't look so pleased with yourself." She frowned at the demolished fragments of cake. "I shall miss you, Martin. Miss you very much."

"I'll sure as heck miss you. Funny, come to think of it. We hardly see each other—maybe once every month or so—and yet just knowing that you're in London is a comfort to me. When I got back from France last trip, my train got shunted around a lot coming up from Folkestone and we pulled into Euston Station instead of Waterloo. I took a taxi down Gower Street, past the university, and there was All Souls. A couple of guys from the *Journal-American* were with me and I pointed the place out. I said, 'There's the best training hospital for nurses and army doctors in England.' One of them said, 'Jesus, looks like the biggest and oldest brickyard in the world.' Well, it sure didn't look like that to me because somewhere in that maze of buildings was my best girl."

Ivy blushed and poured herself another cup of tea. "Is that what I am to you, Martin?"

"Why do you have to ask? I've told you enough times. Sure, you're my best girl. Heck, you're the only girl I know."

"You must meet so many girls in . . . well, Paris . . . places like that." ·

"I only meet generals in Paris, drinking port at the Hotel Crillon."

"And Cairo. They say that Egyptian women are the most exotic women in the world."

"Who told you that? You can't even see them. They wear black sheets over their heads." He stubbed out his cigar because the smoke was drifting into her face. "Look, you're a daisy and my heart jumps into my throat whenever I see you. Okay? Do you believe that?"

"If you say so, yes."

"You don't seem very pleased about it. Anything the matter?"

"No . . . I suppose not."

He reached across the table and touched her cheek. "You've got the blues because you're leaving soon. I feel the same way about it, but it won't be forever. After you're used to the hospital and sure of yourself, I'll come over. Maybe you'll be able to get a few days' leave and we could go to Paris and I'll show you the sights. And anyway, I'll be writing to you all the time, so we won't get out of touch . . . not for a minute."

"Perhaps it would be better if we did get out of touch . . . at least until the war's over."

"I don't see any reason for that, Ivy." He leaned back in his chair and lit his cigar again. "It seems to me that a war's the best time to hang on to friendships, not abandon them. Why don't you finish your tea and we'll go over to the flat and I'll give you your Christmas present. Okay?"

Something was troubling her and he wasn't sure what it was. Simple anxiety and depression, he hoped. That was to be expected. She had never been out of England before and the idea of going across the channel to France—to work as a regular nurse in a huge base hospital—must be unnerving to her. He held her hand tightly as they left the restaurant, but she seemed unresponsive to his touch and barely said a word in the taxi as they drove to Soho.

The flat was tidy for a change because Jacob rarely spent any time in it. The first time he had brought Ivy there, she had been appalled by its disorder and had spent half an hour, over his protests, picking things up.

"How about a glass of sherry?"

"No, thank you." She sat stiffly on the edge of the sofa. "Sherry makes me feel tipsy."

"Do you good. Make you relax a bit."

"I'm quite relaxed, thank you."

"Well," he said lamely, "have it your own way." He clapped his hands and said with a forced cheerfulness, "Santa Claus has come to town . . . so close your eyes and don't open them until I say so."

He ducked into the hall and brought out a large package from the hall closet. It had been wrapped in bright paper and tied with a red ribbon. He placed it on the cushion next to her.

"You can open your eyes now."

She had never received a present in her life, at least not one that came wrapped in a package. A rag doll and three pennyworth of rock candy in a Christmas stocking were the only presents she had ever been given. She looked at the parcel in awe and could do no more than touch the ribbons.

"Open it. Go on."

She undid it carefully so as not to tear the paper. A large white box with the name of the firm embossed on the lid was revealed.

"That's such a fine shop," she said. "What on earth did you buy me?"

"You'll never know until you lift the lid. It's practical, I'm sorry to say. I wanted to buy you a whole raft of things—you know, feminine things—but I figured there was no point in getting you stuff you couldn't use right now."

"No," she said, touching the crest on the lid, "that's true."

She opened the box gingerly and stared in awe at a large glove-leather carrying bag; IVY THAXTON was stamped in gold on one of the many flapped compartments. It was as sturdily constructed as a cavalry saddle, but amazingly light.

"Oh, my," she whispered, stroking the leather. "It must have cost a fortune."

"You bet it did. Nearly beggared me." He sat next to her and put one arm about her waist. "There are all kinds of things inside: brush and comb . . . nail kit. . . . You can carry all your gear in it."

"It's beautiful. Just beautiful."

He kissed the side of her neck. "So are you, Ivy."

She half-turned and seemed about to say something, but he stopped her with his lips. She resisted at first, her mouth hard, unyielding, and then she suddenly responded with a degree of passion that left them both a little shaken.

"Oh, Ivy . . . Ivy . . ." he whispered hoarsely, his lips against her cheek, one hand lightly stroking the curve of a breast through the winter serge of her uniform.

She moved his hand away with regret. "No . . . we mustn't. . . ."

"Marry me, Ivy."

She drew away from him, shaking her head firmly. "No. You shouldn't ask me."

"Why not? You know how I feel about you . . . and you knew I'd ask. I've done everything but advertise in the papers that I love you."

"And I love you, Martin . . . really I do . . . but it wouldn't be right. You'd only regret it after a while."

He tried to read the meaning of that remark in her violet eyes. Her eyes were usually so expressive, but they were fathomless now.

"I don't know what you mean. Why would I regret it? Is there galloping insanity in your family or something? That doesn't make any sense, Ivy. Only the world's biggest fool would regret marrying a girl like you."

"And what would your family think?"

He sensed a bitterness in her tone as she looked away from him and stared down at the leather bag.

"My family? Boy! I know what my Uncle Paul would say if he saw you. He'd say that I'd finally done something really smart for a change."

"And what would . . . Countess Stanmore say?"

So that was it. He understood clearly now. The upstairs maid. He put an arm about her shoulders and gave her a hug.

"Aunt Hanna would love you as much as I do. She's a fine woman. Don't let her English airs throw you. Underneath it all, she's Hanna Rilke from Prairie Avenue. She wouldn't bat an eye if I told her you were the girl for me."

"I saw her this morning," she said quietly. "The Duke and Duchess of Redford came to visit the convalescent ward in D wing . . . to hand out little Christmas presents to the men. There were several other people in their party . . . the baron this and the lady that . . . and Countess Stanmore. Miss Alexandra was with her. I tried to be as inconspicuous as possible, but her ladyship spotted me right off."

"And?"

"Oh, she was very gracious . . . held out her hand and asked me how I was . . . things like that . . . how was I getting along and all and how pleased she was to see me. I don't know what I said . . . just stammered a few words. I felt awkward, somehow. And Miss Alexandra just stood behind her mother, staring at me, not saying a word. I think perhaps she was a bit shocked to see me, Ivy Thaxton, shaking her mother's hand. She kept on staring at me even after they moved down the row of beds. There was something in her eyes, a coldness . . . I don't know how to explain it, Martin. You just wouldn't understand."

He attempted to draw her closer to him, but her body was rigid.

"Look here, Ivy. That's got nothing to do with us. If we got married, we wouldn't be moving into the same house with Alexandra."

"Perhaps not, but you'd still be marrying her maid. And think how awkward it would be if we were invited to dinner. Can't you just see Mr. Coatsworth's face if he had to serve me at the table?"

"The butler, you mean?"

"Yes. And all those stuck-up footmen. I know one of them would trip on purpose and dump soup on my head."

She smiled to herself and then turned to Martin and rested her head on his shoulder.

"Oh, I know I'm being silly. I really shouldn't care about that. We'd live in America, wouldn't we, Martin? In Chicago, Illinois . . . on Lake Michigan."

"Anywhere you wanted to live," he said, stroking her hair. "Anyplace in the world. The Associated Press wants me to leave the *Post* and work exclusively for them. They're dangling a lot of money in front of me and I'm seriously thinking it over. AP men go all over the world . . . China . . . Japan . . . the South Seas. And anyplace they sent me, you'd be right there with me."

She nestled closer to him and was silent for a time, content to lie against him while he stroked her hair. Then she said, "I'm going to France, Martin. I could never marry you until this horror is over."

"I know," he said quietly. "I know that."

"I've been nursing gas cases the past five weeks. I never told you. It's frightful working with them. There's so little you can do. They sit propped up in bed and cough themselves to death . . . and they're so terrified."

"Shush," he whispered, holding her tighter. "Don't talk about it."

"We lose sixty percent. And they're not the worst

ones. The really bad cases are left in Boulogne. They're the ones my team will be nursing. They need me more than you do at the moment, Martin."

"I understand," he said, thinking of the stumbling, retching men he had seen at Hulluch in late September. Chlorine gas . . . the brass buttons of their uniforms turned a vivid green . . . the stark terror of death in their eyes. He held her closer. "I understand."

She felt like walking even though it was dark and the wind was bitter. It wasn't that far and the rain had stopped and they enjoyed striding briskly side by side along Old Compton and Charing Cross Road and Great Russell Street, past the looming black hulk of the British Museum and then up Gower to the sprawling hospital. Lights glowed from the hospital's myriad windows—no blackouts tonight, no fear of Zep raids in this wind. The leather bag hung from Ivy's right shoulder on its broad sheepskin-padded strap, and, looking at her out of the corner of his eye, at the smartness of it and her obvious pride of ownership, he couldn't have felt more pleased if he had bought her a diamond ring—although he would have much preferred *that* expense.

"Well, here we are," she said, facing him. The brick structure of the main building rose behind her like a cliff. "I shall write you when I get settled and give you my address."

"Number nine Stationary . . . . Boulogne."

"Yes . . . but it might be number four in Salonika for all we know. Nothing can be relied on these days, can it?"

"No." He wanted to embrace her, but a great many people were walking past them in and out of All Souls. He bent forward and kissed the tip of her nose. "Take care of yourself."

He was gone. She stood for a moment watching him walk away, and then she turned and entered the building. A group of sisters passed her on their way out. A tall red-haired girl stopped and touched the bag.

"I say, Thaxton. Wherever did you get it?"

"It was a present. From my young man."

The redhead leaned closer, swaying forward like a sapling.

"The Yank chap?" she whispered.

"Yes. Isn't it grand?"

"Lovely! Mine gave me a rather smallish box of sweets—but that's a Welshman for you! Oh, by the way, Thaxton, your friend has been waiting for ages. I let her sit in the sisters' lounge in D wing."

"Friend? What friend?"

"Blonde lass . . . very pretty."

"Oh," Ivy said, momentarily stunned. "Thank you . . ."

It was the only blonde girl she could think of, but it couldn't be, could it? Why on earth . . . ? But when she reached D wing, after hurrying along what seemed miles of corridors, and peered through the glass panel in the door of the sisters' lounge, there she was, the Right Honorable Alexandra Greville, seated on a shabby leather couch in the empty room.

"Hello, Miss Alexandra," Ivy said, walking up to her. She did not curtsy. Was it a slight? Her face burned. Alexandra had been staring down at her lap. She looked up and Ivy noticed how blank her eyes were. Then she smiled slightly.

"Hello, Ivy. I suppose you're surprised to see me."

"Yes." She stood stiffly, not knowing what to say. "Have you been here long?"

"A couple of hours, I suppose."

"I was off duty."

"So I discovered."

"I go back on at nine."

Alexandra glanced at a wall clock. "That gives us about an hour. That is, if you can spare me the time."

"Time for what, Miss Alexandra?"

"To talk." She reached out and took Ivy gently by the hand. The well-manicured fingers were icy. "And please don't keep calling me *Miss* Alexandra; you're not my maid any longer."

No, not a maid any longer, and yet she suddenly felt awkward. She could almost hear Mrs. Broome whispering over her shoulder, "Stand up straight, Ivy, and for heaven's sake, don't fidget or stammer. A good maid is both at ease and respectful when talking to her betters." She felt vaguely sick to her stomach. How terribly wrong Martin was. But how could an American possibly understand?

"Do sit down, Ivy."

"Yes, ma'am." She sat stiffly on the very edge of the couch. Alexandra still held her hand, so she couldn't sit as far away as she would have wished.

"I was surprised to see you this morning, Ivy. I had quite forgotten that you had joined the QA's. How smart you look in your uniform. You're a nursing sister now, aren't you?"

"Yes."

"You must be very proud." She released her grip and folded her hands in her lap. "I haven't been very well and I didn't want to visit All Souls, but Mother insisted that I come with her."

"Not well?"

"A bit . . . under the weather."

"I see." She looked up at the clock. The second hand had never moved so slowly. "Are you living down at Abingdon?"

"No. We just moved to the Park Lane house."

"That's nice."

"I've always liked being in London."

It was not the same Alexandra Greville, Ivy was thinking, watching her. Certainly as pretty as ever, and as smartly dressed, but the manner had changed. The bubbling, talkative girl had turned into a somber, introspective woman. The eyes looked troubled. The hands were restive, fingers clenching and unclenching. Bloodless. Cold and white.

Ivy cleared her throat. "I was quite surprised to see you and her ladyship. Quite . . . happily surprised, I should say."

"Were you? That's nice. I was . . . happy to see you. So was Mother. She made a point of telling Mrs. Broome when we got home."

"How is Mrs. Broome?"

"Her nephew was killed at Loos in September, which upset her very much, but she's quite her old self again. An indomitable woman, Mrs. Broome."

"Yes, she is."

It felt horribly hot in the lounge, but Ivy resisted the urge to stand up and remove her heavy cape. Alexandra was wearing a coat with sable collar and cuffs. She looked cool as marble.

"Mother and the Duchess of Redford were quite upset after touring the wards. We had lunch at Claridge's and they cried all the way through it." She looked at Ivy and her eyes were bitter. "Odd they would be so moved. It was merely a nice ward, wasn't it?"

"A . . . nice ward?"

"I think you know what I mean, Ivy. A show ward. All the lads so cheerful despite their wounds. And all the wounds so trivial and so neatly bandaged."

"They . . . the chief of staff, that is, doesn't like to upset important visitors."

"I can understand the point. It would have upset Mother and the duchess dreadfully to have seen a man with his face blown off . . . especially before lunch."

Ivy's mouth went dry. "That takes getting used to," she said with difficulty.

"Does one ever get used to it? Is it possible to cope with a sight like that?"

The intensity of Alexandra's stare was disquieting. Ivy shifted slightly on the seat and rubbed the back of her hand across her lips.

"It takes . . . time."

A young doctor wearing a white jacket over an obviously new uniform stepped into the lounge.

"I say, are you on duty, Sister Thaxton?"

"No, sir. Not till nine."

"Have you seen Sister Jones?"

"Which Jones, sir?"

"Number sixteen Jones."

"She was assigned to Abdominals this afternoon by Captain Mason."

"Mason? Do I know him?"

"Regular, sir . . . Indian Army . . . purple nose."

"Ah, yes," he said, as though that took care of his immediate problem. "Thank you, Thaxton."

"They're becoming younger every day," Ivy said after the doctor walked off. "Barely qualified for surgery, but they do a very good job despite their lack of experience." She had been grateful for the slight interruption.

"One gains experience very quickly these days, I would imagine."

"There's no lack of patients here."

"Nor in France," Alexandra said quietly.

A dozen probationers carrying notebooks followed their nursing instructor down the corridor and into the lounge. The probationers were all young and gaunt with fatigue. They stared at Alexandra as though she were a creature from an alien world. The nursing instructor was a tall, jolly woman of forty who took everything in stride.

"Hello, Thaxton! Entertaining visitors, are we? Well, not in here, my girl. We were right in the middle of wet dressings and got kicked out of room fifty-six by the jaw and plastic lads."

The two women walked into the corridor.

"Is there anywhere private where we could talk?"

"No," Ivy said stiffly. "This is a very crowded place."

"You resent my coming here, don't you?"

Well, Ivy thought, an honest question deserves an honest answer.

"Yes. I don't wish to hurt your feelings, but I don't

have the time for small talk. And, after all, we really don't have that much to talk about, do we?"

"The reason I came, Ivy, was simply to ask you a few questions. You see, I want to join the QA's."

Ivy's stare was rude, frankly incredulous. "You?"

Alexandra flinched. "Why not me?"

"I don't know exactly. . . . I just can't see you going through the training. It's a lot of hard, dirty, exhausting work. The maids at Abingdon Pryory were never worked as hard. There's a Red Cross VAD unit here for ladies of good birth . . . mornings or afternoons . . . writing letters . . . reading to the men . . . rolling bandages. . . . Why don't you join that?"

"Oh, dear," Alexandra said, drawing in her breath sharply, "what an awful little snob you turned out to be."

And she was gone, half-running down the corridor. Ivy stared after her in bewilderment. Her hidden anger and resentment turned to cheek-burning shame.

"Wait!"

She ran swiftly, dodging nurses and orderlies. She caught up with Alexandra near the end of the corridor, grabbed her by one arm, and propelled her toward a narrow green door, which she opened and closed after them with the quickness of a conjurer. They were in a blanket-storage room, lit by a low-wattage bulb dangling from the ceiling. Ivy slid a bolt into place and leaned back against the door.

"I'm not a snob," she said in between deep breaths.

Alexandra stood stiffly, her face taut and pale. "Yes, you are. It would be like my saying that all *you're* suited for is making beds and carrying tea trays!"

"I was only speaking my mind. I just can't imagine you as a QA probationer, that's all. If it's a question of wanting to do your bit—"

"I joined the Red Cross at the beginning of the year. A convalescent home for officers in Wimbledon . . . writing letters . . . fluffing pillows. . . . All the things that ladies of 'good birth' do as volunteers."

"There can be more to it than that."

"I know. I went to France after my brother was wounded and mastered the art of emptying bedpans!"

They studied each other like two strangers. But there was a bond of sorts. The Rt. Hon. Alexandra Greville had always been kind.

"I'm sorry," Ivy said. "I'm sure you didn't wait hours just to tell me that you wanted to join up." She waved a hand at their cramped surroundings. "You asked for a quiet place to talk."

"Thank you, Ivy. Something happened to me in France . . . a kind of breakdown . . . more emotional then physical . . . and although I want very badly to become a military nurse, I have this fear, you see, this feeling of inner panic that . . . under similar circumstances . . . I might break down again. It's not a fear I can express to the director of recruitments."

It was so quiet in the closet that Ivy could hear the thumping of her heart.

"Tell me about it."

She kept her eyes on Alexandra's face, seeing pain and honesty and truth mirrored there. She could visualize the Alexandra she had known, romantic and vain, play-acting the role of a nurse in her elegant and expensive uniforms from the House of Ferris. "Alexandra Nightingale," "Saint Alexandra"—the girl mocked herself without indulging in self-pity. Ivy knew the inevitable outcome of her folly as Alexandra told of her trip in the ambulance from Saint-Omer to the casualty clearing station at Kemmel. Reaching out, she took Alexandra by the hand and pressed firmly.

"You don't have to tell me what happened there. I can guess."

"They needed help so badly," she whispered. "Hundreds of men, Ivy . . . men without arms . . . legs . . . faces. I could do so little for them . . . and what little I began to do . . ." She paused, running her tongue over her dry lips. "I failed them so completely. . . ."

"You didn't fail anyone," Ivy said sternly. "You can't fail at something that you weren't equipped to do in the first place. Don't be a twit!" She turned to the door and opened it. "For God's sake, let's get out of here before we suffocate."

They walked slowly down the corridor toward the main entrance. Nurses, orderlies, and doctors passed them, some nodding in recognition to Ivy, all eyeing Alexandra with varying degrees of curiosity.

"I look out of place," Alexandra said.

"Do you feel out of place? That's what's important, you know."

"I'm not sure I understand what you mean."

"I meant . . . will you be comfortable in the QA's? Is it what you *really* want to do? Or are you just trying to prove something to yourself?"

"I want to be useful," she said flatly.

"Fine. We can use all the help we can get. And as for your fears . . ." She stopped and faced Alexandra. "We all have a certain amount of fear every time we walk into a ward. Do you see those two girls standing by the dispensary window? One of them is the daughter of a parson in Ludlow . . . the other taught school in Wales. A cut finger or a broken ankle were the worst injuries they'd seen before coming here. Now they work ten hours or more a day with men who are coughing up their lungs bit by bit. They don't have some special kind of bravery that you lack. What they have is the assurance that twelve months of training has given them. The only courage you need is the courage to begin that training and the courage to stick it out."

The bells of University College chapel pealed the first stroke of nine.

"I must go," Ivy said. "Perhaps we can talk again tomorrow."

Alexandra bent quickly forward and kissed her on the cheek. "I'll be joining up tomorrow. Good night . . . *Sister* Thaxton."

"Well, I never," Ivy murmured, holding one hand to

her cheek. She stood in the corridor and watched Alexandra cross the vast entrance hall, crowded now with
departing visitors. The frescoes on the hall's walls de-
picted famous healers, and, stretched above the door, a
twenty-foot sign lettered by the ambulatory patients
said, PEACE ON EARTH, GOOD WILL TOWARD MEN.

> God rest ye merry, gentlemen:
> Let nothing you dismay.
> Remember Christ, our Savior,
> Was born on Christmas Day.

"The carolers are not quite what they used to be,"
Lady Margaret Wood-Lacy whispered. "Jim Penny,
Will Adams . . . oh, all the best baritones are in the
army."

They sounded harmonic enough to Fenton. He invited them in for hot whiskies or punch, but they grace-
fully declined and moved off down the lane toward the
Shaw house, where Mr. and Mrs. Shaw and their five
children waited expectantly.

> It came upon a midnight clear,
> That glorious song of old. . . .

Fenton closed the front door and followed his mother
down the hall and into the parlor. An aroma of roasting
goose filled the house.

"I'd better see how Jinny is coming along," Lady
Margaret said. "She gets forgetful sometimes."

Jinny was eighty years old and the only servant Sir
Harold and Lady Margaret had ever had, or needed,
having lived most of their married life in cottages at the
various job sites—Balmoral, Sandringham, Abingdon
Pryory. But the small exquisitely constructed house in
Suffolk—an architect's house, after all—had always
been waiting for them, with Jinny puttering about in the
kitchen.

Fenton poured a whiskey and stood by the bay window. The last glow of the pale winter sun glinted off the cold wind-stirred waters of the River Deben. Home for Christmas, but his thoughts were far from carol singers, holly, and roast goose. It was the second Christmas of the war and far different from the first one. He had celebrated that Christmas in France, quartered in a château near Béthune. All conversation in the mess had been of peace, perhaps not on earth, but surely in France. They had all believed that the war would be over within a month. Astonishing reports had come to them of British and German troops meeting in no-man's-land to exchange gifts and to sing carols.

"It means the end, you know," Captain Jarvis had remarked sagely. "Our lads have lost the fighting spirit and the Enemy is as exhausted as we are. It's up to their politicians to work out something with our striped-pants brigade. There'll be a general cease-fire within a week. You mark my words."

He had buried Captain Jarvis three months later at Neuve-Chapelle with one hundred sixty of his men.

One year.

Not just men had died. War destroyed more than human life. It nibbled away at the spirit, corroded the senses, mocked all the old values. It was what the French liaison officer at Laventie, in the wisdom of a Cognac haze, had called *le cafard*. It was empty stables and un-pruned trees at Abingdon. It was a thousand men in sodden khaki, who could have been better employed, stumbling across a railway track with rifles in their hands. It was Lydia Greville naked by a fire.

He looked in on Roger's old room before going to bed. It was exactly as Roger would have expected it to be, had he suddenly come bursting into the house. The bed made. A notebook and pencil on the nightstand. His books, well dusted, on the shelves.

"It's not a shrine," his mother said quietly, seeing him standing there in the hall. "And I have no illusions about him being a prisoner of the Turks. It's just that I hated to put away all the things that he had loved. He wouldn't have wanted his Wordsworth and Shelley sealed in a box."

There would be unfinished poems in the notebook, Fenton knew. Lines for an unfinished life.

Le cafard.

His mother was on a dozen committees of one kind or another in Woodbridge, and certainly did not lack for friends. She enjoyed being with her son, but did not need him for comfort.

"You seem restless, Fenton," she remarked on the Thursday before New Year's Eve. "Thinking about your new job?"

"And other things."

He took the train that afternoon, a slow train crowded with sailors from Harwich going to London on leave. It was dark when the train pulled into King's Cross. He shared a taxi with five naval officers who insisted on buying him a drink at the Army-Navy Club. Conversation in the bar ranged from the merits of oil-fired ships vis-à-vis coal to the bedroom antics of French women. He had one drink, excused himself, and left.

It was a familiar route that he walked—along the Mall, past Buckingham Palace, and into Lower Belgrave Street. He strode past his old flat without glancing at it and continued on to Sloane Street and across Pavillion Road into Cadogan Square. Number 24.

If the butler was surprised at the lateness of the call, he did not show it by so much as a blink of the eye.

"Miss Winifred, sir? I do believe she has retired for the night."

"Who the devil's at the door, Peterson?" A testy voice sounded from down the corridor, and then Lord Sutton emerged from the gloom in maroon smoking jacket and carpet slippers.

"Fenton, by gad! What the devil you doin' here at this hour?"

"I was . . . in the neighborhood," he said lamely. "Sorry if I woke up the household."

"Nonsense." The marquess dismissed the butler with a gesture. "It's good to have company. Close the door before you freeze us out."

"I didn't realize it was so late."

"It isn't. We retire early . . . except for me. Just goin' to have a nightcap or two."

A slender shaft of light fell on the dark stairwell from the upper floors, the light widening with the full opening of a door. Fenton looked up at the figure standing by the second-floor balustrade.

"Hello," he said.

"We still have a telephone," Winifred said.

"I'm sorry. . . . I intended to call . . . but . . . one thing and another came up . . . and then I went to Suffolk for Christmas—"

"There's nothing to explain, Fenton."

"I think that there is."

Lord Sutton scowled at Fenton and then glared up at his daughter.

"Either come down or go back to bed, Winnie. As for me, I'm goin' to the library and closin' the door."

"Well?" Fenton asked after the marquess had done just that.

She came down the stairs clad in a long, quilted-satin dressing gown, her hair loose about her shoulders. She did not descend to the foyer, but sat on the third step from the bottom.

"What an odd man you are, Fenton."

"Impulsive . . . also a bit reflective." He leaned against the banister post below her, hands shoved into the pockets of his trench coat. "I've been doing a lot of thinking the past few days. You said that we're different people now. I know I'm not the same, but I can't say that about you. You're older and wiser, but essentially the same. I don't think anything will ever change you radically, Winnie."

"Everyone changes."

"I suppose they do. It's a matter of degree, isn't it?

Some people tarnish more quickly than others. You will always have a polish . . . a certain luster."

She folded her arms about her knees. "You came to propose, didn't you?"

"Yes."

"That'll make Father very happy."

"It's not your father I care about pleasing."

"It'll make me happy, too. I love you, Fenton. I fell in love with you when I was sixteen and Andrew brought you down to Lulworth for my birthday party. Or was it your scarlet jacket I fell in love with then? Difficult to say. I don't love you for your jacket now. In fact, I love you in spite of it. I hate this war. If you marry me, you'll be in the odd position of having a pacifist for a wife."

"General Davenport's wife is a suffragette. She chained herself to a letter box once. It didn't ruin his career."

"I pray for the day when *your* career is unnecessary."

"So do I."

She looked at him in silence for a moment and then hugged her knees tighter to her body.

"One thing has been left unsaid. Father will be happy . . . I'll be happy. What of yourself? Do you love me?"

"If wanting to be with you is loving you . . . if feeling at peace is loving . . . then, yes . . . I love you."

She nodded somberly. "How blunt and honest you are. Shall we go in and tell Father?"

"I would like that, yes."

"Shall we be married in London? Or would you prefer Suffolk?"

He rubbed the side of his jaw. "The fact is, I have only five days' leave left. I thought we could . . . well, go up to Scotland tomorrow and get married in Gretna . . . stand in line with the other couples. That is, if you don't mind."

"Oh, Lord," she laughed. "Gretna Green! What will Mother say?"

"She won't have a chance to say anything." Lord Sutton stepped into the foyer, a bottle of champagne under each arm. "Knew how the wind was blowin' when you knocked on the door, Fenton. Put the bottles in your kit bag. Mumm's nineteen ten. The Royal Mail leaves Euston Station at midnight. You have plenty of time to make it if you can hurry your packin', Winnie."

She stood up slowly. "We can miss the train, Fenton, if you have any doubts at all . . . any second thoughts."

"Why would he have doubts?" her father blustered. "I'll ring 'round for the car."

"I mean it," she said.

He reached up and touched her hand, his eyes steady on her face. "No second thoughts, Winnie."

She turned quickly and hurried up the stairs.

The marquess gazed after her, then handed the bottles of champagne to Fenton.

"I'd crack one of these with you, but there ain't time for it. I'm glad to see her leave this house, Fenton, and I think you know why. She's a good girl. Clever. Strong in body and mind. And she's a Sutton . . . she'll bear sons."

The wind came in a flood off the Irish Sea to churn the waters of Luce Bay and rattle the windows of the inn. Putting one hand on the glass, Fenton could feel the chill power of it. The wind had chased the mist, and the hills of Cumberland were like banks of green cloud across the Solway Firth. He drew his robe tighter around him and then lit a cigarette, the draft through the windows spiraling the smoke behind him.

"What are you thinking?" she asked after a time.

"Oh, one thing and another. It's New Year's Day, and a bright, cold day it is, too."

"A good beginning."

"Yes. To see the sun in Wigtownshire on the first of January is cause for celebration."

"You've been here before, haven't you?"

"Port William, you mean?"

"This inn."

"Oh, yes, several times. A friend of mine kept a boat at Stranraer and we used to sail these waters—Islay, Mull, the Hebrides—and up and down the Solway, of course. Tricky seas and bloody dangerous at times."

"Ever bed a girl here?"

He puffed on the cigarette. "What a question. Downright Elizabethan phrasing. The answer is no. I never bedded a girl—*here.*"

"I do love you, Fenton. I think you're quite incapable of lying. Even your white ones have the ring of truth."

His feet were numb with cold. He ground the cigarette out in a saucer and got back into bed. Winifred opened his robe and pressed the warmth of her body against him.

"I'm not a disappointment, am I?"

"You're an astonishing revelation," he said.

"It's being a country girl," she said, stroking his hip. "I know all the natural acts."

He turned onto his side and kissed her forehead. "And a few naughty ones, too. A sweet doxy."

"Who's being Elizabethan now?" Her arms enfolded him. "May I ask you something that you don't have to answer?"

"Yes."

"Was there someone you would rather have brought here than me? Someone you couldn't have?"

"That was an age ago," he said quietly.

"Do you find yourself comparing us?"

"There's nothing to compare. You are . . . Winifred. Uniquely yourself."

"The colonel's lady."

"Yes. A lady to your fingertips."

Her hands glided up and down his back. "Not all the time."

He did not think of Lydia, nor had he while making love to her during the night. The act was beyond the objective comparing of one woman to another, one body to another. It was even beyond the seeking of pleasure. It was life that he sought in her, and creation. The war kept its hold on him even in bed. His thrusts into her warm living body—her gasps and cries— became the antithesis of death and pain to him. He sensed her understanding of that, her awareness of his need, and it set her uniquely apart from any other woman he had known. The wind, tugging at the windows, rattling them in their frames, howled and shrieked under the eaves, reminding him of the demented sound of shells. He pressed his face into the soft hollow between her breasts as she clasped him tightly, as if to shield him on this first day of the year from all the days to follow.

XVI

Charles left the War Office and walked briskly along Whitehall to Charing Cross. It was an almost too perfect April day, the type of day that would inspire a poet to rapture. The wind out of the west was gentle and carried with it a heady perfume of spring rain. Soft, impeccably white clouds drifted across a flag-blue sky, and a shaft of sun, as though arranged by the Almighty, fell directly on Admiral Nelson standing on his column. At the base of the monument, clustered like gray pigeons, old women were selling violets by the bunch.

He crossed Trafalgar Square and strode as though in a great hurry up St. Martin's Lane until he reached a four-story nondescript building on Shelton Street. There he paused to straighten his uniform, dust his shoes with a handkerchief, and allow his heartbeat to return to normal. He then entered the building and walked slowly up the stairs to the second floor. There were half a dozen officers ahead of him, standing in the corridor or seated on the two wood benches that flanked the door marked NO. 7 MEDICAL BOARD. One or two officers carried canes, but most of them looked fit and not altogether overjoyed at that fact.

"Don't I know you?" a major in the Rifle Brigade asked, puffing on a cigarette.

"I don't believe so," Charles said.

"Thought I did. Sorry. Name's Merton and I'm fit as a fiddle, worse luck. Bound to be sent back to the salient, and I won't be as bloody lucky next time, I can tell you."

Charles turned away from the man and slowly paced the corridor. At last his name was called.

A gray-haired lance corporal seated behind a desk checked his name off a typewritten list. "Major Greville? Colonel Beaumont would like to see you in his office . . . third door down that hall, sir."

Colonel Beaumont had been a prominent Harley Street surgeon before the war. Now, at seventy, he found himself a colonel in the RAMC, assigned to a medical board whose job it was to certify wounded officers fit for duty in the line.

"Ah, Greville," he said warmly as Charles entered his small cluttered office. "How's the pelvis?"

"Better than new."

"And the leg?"

"The same. One hundred percent. I walked very quickly all the way from Whitehall and don't feel a twinge."

"Good . . . good. And all the Asian bugs out of your system?"

"I hope so." He smiled to warn the old man that he was telling a joke. "Haven't seen one of the blighters in weeks."

"Quite so." The colonel looked down at his desk and shifted a few loose papers around. "Your coming here today is rather academic, Greville. I am personally delighted to know that you feel as good as new, but you are no longer the responsibility of this board."

"I'm not sure I understand you, Colonel."

"We received a directive from General Haldane yesterday informing us that your name is to be stricken from the list of wounded officers awaiting certification for active duty. It would appear that you are part and parcel of NS Five and something calling itself the Landship Committee. Just what a 'land' ship could be is quite beyond me, sir, but there it is." He leaned across his desk and extended his hand. "Good luck, Greville. I'm glad I'm not sending you back to the trenches."

He took a taxi to his office in Old Pye Street, to the

building that had been quarters for a variety of governmental functions since the days of Pepys. The marine sentry opened the front door without asking to see his credentials. He was well known now, he thought with a twinge of bitterness. One of the old hands in NS 5. He took the narrow stairs two at a time and went up to the room on the third floor which he shared with a group of other officers, two of them from the navy, and two civilian engineers. Only Lieutenant Commander Penhope, RANS, was at his desk, leaning back in his chair and reading the afternoon edition of the *Daily Post*. A headline screamed:

VERDUN COUNTERATTACK— LARGE FRENCH GAINS.

"Fisher's been looking for you, Greville," the naval officer said without glancing away from his newspaper.

Charles sat on the edge of his desk and lit a cigarette.

"Oh? What did he want?"

"The usual strafe. Big Willie failed to impress some brass again. Low on power. He wants you to go up to Yorkshire, or some other heathen place, and check out the specs on a new engine. You're to take Bigsby with you."

Charles blew a savage stream of smoke. "Why the hell doesn't he just send Bigsby on his own?"

"You know why," Penhope drawled.

Algernon Bigsby was a civilian, a consumptive-looking middle-aged man who dropped his *h*'s. He also chewed cigars and spat a good deal. Algernon Bigsby knew everything there was to know about engines, but staff officers detested him on sight. It would be Bigsby who would check out the specs on the engine in Yorkshire, and Major Greville who would pass on the information—"sell it," in the argot of NS 5—to the brass.

"Did he say where in Yorkshire?"

"His girl has all the information and the travel vouchers."

A messenger boy. No more than that. His contribution to the caterpillar-tread landship, now called "tank" MK 1, or Big Willie, as opposed to Little Willie, which had been a washout, was limited to his ability to be articulate—and, of course, to the assurance of his immediate acceptance in any mess. Algernon Bigsby might have the know-how, but he did not wear a smartly tailored uniform with the badges of the Royal Windsor Fusiliers on his jacket lapels.

There was a cocktail party in progress when he reached home. He had promised Lydia he would be there, but had completely forgotten about it. Archie found the warm yet elegant atmosphere of Bristol Mews conducive to business, to getting disparate elements together, and his daughter was the perfect hostess. Odd types conversed in the second-floor drawing room—a Manchester mill owner cheek to jowl with a labor MP, General Sir William Robertson nodding his head to whatever David Langham was telling him; scientists, engineers, red-tabbed Whitehall brass, politicians, business leaders, and beautifully dressed women blending harmoniously.

Archie met Charles as he came up the stairs and pressed a drink into his hand. Archie Foxe, the perfect host, treating every house he was in as his own.

"Langham is talking to Wully Robertson," he whispered. "The general would like to meet you. He's expanding his staff, and Langham's been telling him what a fine job you've been doing with NS Five."

"It's nice of Mr. Langham to look after my interests," Charles said tautly, "but I'm not suited for a staff job at such a high level."

Archie's gaze was dyspeptic. "You're too self-effacing, Charles. Thump your bloody chest once in a while and people will sit up and take notice."

There was no point in trying to explain to Archie that he didn't want to be noticed. Ambition was the banner under which Archie Foxe had always marched. He had carried it proudly out of a Shadwell workhouse to the marble halls of power, and there was no reason for him to think that all other men did not share his belief in it. Sir William "Wully" Robertson certainly did. He had come up from the ranks in Victoria's army to become chief of the Imperial General Staff, and he had not done so by being modest. Robertson liked ambitious people because they were more inclined to get the job done than the stick-in-the-muds.

A job on the general's staff. Red tabs on his lapels. Perhaps a lieutenant colonelcy, to boot. It was his for the asking—if he impressed the general with his zeal, his eagerness to get ahead:

"Yes, sir, I like NS Five, but I find it constricting. My job there is pretty much routine and I'd like to be involved in broader aspects of the war effort."

Langham would stand on the sidelines, smiling that faintly mocking smile of his, and General Sir William Robertson ("Wully" to his intimates) would smile knowingly, nod his head, and say in, effect, "Can I trust you? Will you do as you're told? Will you aid me in kicking Lord Horatio Herbert Kitchener of Khartoum into a cocked hat?"

The politics of the war were being fought in the drawing rooms of London. The unseating of Sir John French, the rise of Sir Douglas Haig, the battles between the Minister of War, Lord Kitchener, and the chief of the Imperial General Staff, "Wully"—it was all going on in this particular drawing room on this particular afternoon in Bristol Mews. Should Kitchener be dethroned—in a polite way, of course—there would be a vacancy in the cabinet, and David Langham might just be the man to fit the empty chair. He would get along well with Robertson and the high brass, but it wouldn't hurt to have a friend on the general's staff.

Good reasoning, Charles thought as he sipped his drink. The only thing wrong with it was that he didn't like David Langham and he had no intention of approaching General Robertson. He drifted to the opposite side of the room, turning his back to the crowd and gazing through the tall windows at the narrow brick-paved street below.

"You're not being very sociable," Lydia murmured, coming up beside him. "Don't you feel well?"

"I feel fine. Like new, in fact." He took another pull on his drink. "The medical board informed me that I'm not fit for duty in France . . . but not for physical reasons. Too bloody important for such crass pursuits as shooting Germans. I'm locked into NS Five."

"Oh, dear"—she kissed him lightly on the cheek—"I had a feeling that would happen. You proved to be too useful to them." She kissed him again and ran a hand across his back. "Don't fret, my darling. Did Daddy tell you about General Robertson?"

"He . . . mentioned something."

"A staff job . . . liaison between the General Staff and Haig's headquarters in France. You'd be in Montreuil as much as you'd be in London. And, knowing Wully, I'm sure he'd have you poking your nose into the divisional headquarters to get the type of information he requires. You'd be right in the thick of things and not spending your time with all those eccentrics in Old Pye Street."

"They're not such bad chaps."

"Of course they're not, darling, but you do feel a bit out of place. On staff is much more like being in the army. And being across the channel would be more satisfying to you than trudging about farms or visiting factories."

Her perfume was exquisite. Her silk gown caressed his hand as she pressed against his side. Her touch lingered on his back. He thought of Algernon Bigsby squirting tobacco juice at the oily base of a turret lathe.

"I suppose you're right."

Her fingers dug into him. "I know I am. Come on, talk to Wully . . . just for a moment . . . just a hello."

He went over to the general, but had to fight to keep

a straight face. General Sir William Robertson dropped his *h*'s just like Algernon Bigsby did.

They had separate bedrooms. Hers was frilly and feminine, in cream and gold; his, richly masculine, in mahogany and brass. He came to her room, as his father had gone to Hanna's.

He slumped beside her, feeling sweaty in his nightshirt. He had found it impossible to make love to her. He felt too keyed up, too pressured. He had done no more than move her satin nightgown up to her hips and touch the warm dampness of her thighs.

"Sorry," he said. "I should have left you in peace."

"It doesn't matter." She bent over him and kissed his brow. "Poor tired soldier."

"I feel such a fraud, Lydia. Too important to be sent to France, and yet anyone could do my job."

"Perhaps. But not anyone can be on Robertson's staff. He uses his own judgment on that. Did you know that he told the Duke of Hereford that his son wasn't fit to shoe cavalry mounts? It's true! Percy! You know him . . . captain in the Blues. His father could get him that commission, but not a staff job with Wully."

She stroked his chest, her palm light on the flannel nightshirt. No more than that. It distressed him if she became too bold. Men initiated acts. Women did not.

"I have to go to Yorkshire tomorrow," he said after a long silence. "To Huddersfield . . . to look at some engines. I take the seven-ten from Saint Pancras."

"I'll get up early and drive you to the station."

"No. A car will be here to pick me up." He turned away from her and sat on the edge of the bed. "I thought I might drop in and see Fenton. He's at Flockton Moor camp, just a short drive from where I'll be."

"Give him my best," she said, staring at the ceiling.

"Of course." He was standing now, ready to go back to his room. He leaned across the bed and kissed her. "When I get back, we'll take off a few days and go down to Lyme Regis. We can rent a cottage . . . bathe in the sea. Would you enjoy that?"

"Very much."

"And I'll seriously consider that staff appointment . . . if I get asked, that is."

"You'll get it. He was impressed with you."

"After a little nudge from Langham?"

"No," she said tonelessly. "You get everything on your own."

She parked her car and walked along the embankment, noting the Thames at low tide, birds pecking in the mud flats. She entered the ministry from the river side. The lone marine on guard there telephoned up to Langham's office before allowing her into the building. She did not get lost in the maze of corridors and stairwells and entered the inner chamber of Langham's suite through a side door. It was a dark, musty room lined with law books and great clothbound volumes on economics and vital statistics, coal output, railway tonnage, steel production, and all the other dry facts of national functions. She sat on a leather couch, and after ten minutes David Langham came into the room from the outer office and closed and locked the door.

"I'm glad you came," he said, barely glancing at her. He removed his coat and began to roll up his sleeves as he walked into the small lavatory to wash his hands. "The general called me this morning. He was impressed with Charles . . . well, why wouldn't he be? The archetype of young peers. Wully admires nobility, but then don't we all?"

"I doubt if you do."

"Quite wrong, my dear Mrs. Greville. I'm a firm believer in the preservation of relics and national treasures of all sorts." He came out of the lavatory wiping his hands on a towel. "So, a joyous morning for you. Young Charles will get red tabs on his collars and will no doubt become a brigadier before the war's over. And after the war? Well, who knows? Governor of some speck of the Empire . . . A firm but just hand on the native throat . . . the governor's lady by his side dressed in imperial white, a parasol shielding her lovely head."

"You do enjoy baiting people, don't you?"

"I enjoy foretelling futures. You would enjoy yourself immensely. And it would be a charming spot . . . Bermuda, perhaps, or Malta." He rolled the towel into a ball and tossed it through the open lavatory door. "I have spent all morning foretelling futures . . . none as pleasant as yours. The French are being bled white at Verdun and are demanding that we begin our offensive on the Somme immediately. The PM is quite upset at the demand, and Kitchener is in a dither. Sir Douglas Haig claims that he won't be ready to jump off before the end of August, but the French might cave in before then. We will attack by the end of June, a compromise that will please neither Haig nor the French. I sent a strong letter to Poincaré suggesting that the best way for them to cut their losses would be to withdraw across the Meuse and let the Germans have Verdun. It has no strategic importance whatever. Why treat it as a holy shrine? But of course it isn't up to poor Poincaré. After all, he's only the president. Joffre and the generals don't give a damn about losses. Men are mere digits to them. Eighty-nine thousand dead poilus so far, and God knows how many maimed for totally useless ground. A mere bagatelle when weighed against the glory of France. *Ils ne passeront pas! Vive la gloire! La voie sacrée!* Schoolboy rhetoric."

He stood facing her, hands on hips, his slim body taut as a bent bow. A fiery little man, his dark eyes burning.

"How spellbinding you are, Mr. Langham. I would hate to be a Frenchman debating you."

He waved a finger under her nose. "War is far too complex a matter for the military mind to grasp . . . but then you've heard that speech before, haven't you? Why must I always make speeches when you come here? Such a terrible waste of time." He sat beside her on the couch and cupped her chin in one hand, turning her face toward him. "You're much too beautiful, Mrs. Greville. If I had married a woman with your face, I would still be a Liverpool solicitor."

"Is that why successful politicians have plain wives?"

"It's vital on the hustings. Men will never vote for someone with a beautiful wife. They feel he has achieved enough. Why grace him with further rewards!"

"I could ask the same question."

He let his hand drop to the top of her dress and began to undo the buttons with nimble ease.

"One wonders who is being rewarded the most by these brief encounters. Your appetites for the pleasures of the flesh match my own, stroke for stroke." His hand was inside her chemise, pressed firmly against a naked breast. "You see? Your heart races . . . the breath catches in your throat."

"Please hurry."

"We shall make haste slowly, if you don't mind. Savor it as always."

"Hurry . . ."

"My, my . . . what a passionate little whore we are today."

"Please . . ."

It had been raining steadily in Yorkshire, and the factory on the outskirts of Huddersfield was surrounded by a lake of mud and standing water. A tall chain link fence topped with barbed wire enclosed the place, and there was no signboard to say what kind of factory it was or to whom it belonged. Only when the army car which had brought them from Leeds pulled up in front of the main building did Chrales see a small sign on one of the doors: ROLLS-ROYCE MOTOR WORKS —EXPERIMENTAL.

A gangly young man wearing a blue work smock stepped outside to meet them.

"Major Greville? Mr. Bigsby?"

"Aye," Bigsby grunted. He spat a stream of brown saliva into a puddle. "Bloody 'orrible bit o' country, Yorkshire."

"Dampish," the young man said. He directed his attention to Charles. "My name's Wilson. I'm plant manager here. Our Mr. Ross is over in shed number four . . . next to the railway siding."

"The package arrived, I hope," Charles said.

"Oh, yes. It was delivered early this morning. Ugly-looking thing, isn't it? We pulled the engine out already." He pointed off into the swirling drizzle. "Just keep to the duckboards. No point in driving there—your motor would only sink below the wheels."

Big Willie was inside the large corrugated iron building, electric lights shining off its steel-plated sides. It was a great rhomboid-shaped monster, with six-pounder naval cannons jutting from the sponsons on the sides. Men in coveralls were crawling all over it, and there was the dull boom of heavy hammers from inside the hull. Charles and Bigsby climbed onto the back of the tank and peered into the open engine hatch.

"Is Mr. Ross there?" Charles yelled.

The hammering ceased. An oily-faced workman looked up at them.

"Aye, he be that. Mr. Ross, sur . . . coomp'ny callin'."

A tousle-haired man in grease-stained coveralls emerged from the inner gloom of the hull. Charles stared at him in disbelief.

"But . . . you're *our* Ross!"

Jaimie Ross grinned and pulled himself out of the hatch.

"Not exactly *your* Ross any longer, sir." He wiped his fingers on a cloth and held out his right hand. "It's fair good to see you, Mr. Greville. Indeed it is."

"I'm quite flabbergasted, Ross. I knew you'd gone with the Rolls-Royce company, but to find you here. . . ."

"Oh, they've moved me back and forth a bit, sir. I've been at this factory the past three months." He folded his arms and looked Charles up and down. "Major Greville. My, my. You look right smart in the uniform, sir. You one of the chaps responsible for this clanking dragon of a thing?"

"Not really. Just sort of an overseer."

"I talked to one of your bunch in London . . . telephoned up here the other day. He said the machine was underpowered. That's a bit of a laugh, you know. This must weigh thirty ton and its got a one-hundred-five-HP engine in it. Doubt if you'd get more'n three miles to the hour on a dead-flat hard-paved road."

"That's about it," Bigsby said, spitting over the right side track.

Ross stepped down to the ground and gazed reflectively at the tank's engine, which hung in chains from a pully.

"Daimler. A good engine, but not for this . . . *thing.*"

"Do you have a better one?" Charles asked, stepping off the tank and standing beside him.

"Oh, yes . . . two-hundred-and-fifty-HP inline, ready for production. A proper beauty. We also have a three-hundred-and-fifty-HP in the testing stage. Aircraft engines. But as I tried to explain to that sod in London, we don't have them on the factory line. Won't have 'em either for at least four months. Now, these hundred-five-HP Daimlers must be bulging out of the warehouses."

"Right," Bigsby said. "That's the bloody rub."

"We can fit one of our prototype Falcons in this hull so you could see how it'd move with a hundred more horsepower inside, but if time's the problem I don't much see the point of it."

"Neither do I," Charles said. "They're prepared to build fifty hulls now and they can't wait four months for engines to go in them."

"If we could coax more bloody power from what we've got," Bigsby said.

Ross closed his eyes and clasped his hands behind his back. He rocked slowly on his heels for a minute and then said, "The gear ratios seem wrong to me somehow . . . and the carburetion and exhaust systems are inadequate for the amount of stress the engine's going to be put to. She's goin' to be fuel-starved . . . and she'll vapor-lock sure as hell takes sinners."

Bigsby squirted juice again. "The gear box is a bloody 'orror. I've been tellin' 'em that all along. I know what it needs."

"Yes," Ross said, "I think I do, too. If you could give my lads three days . . . around the clock. . . ."

"Of course," Charles said.

"Modifications with available parts. Shouldn't hold up your schedule by more than a week or two, and it would make a ruddy big difference in performance."

"Sounds good," Charles said.

"Fine. We'll get on with it then. Like a mug of tea?"

"Yes . . . I would at that."

"Mr. Bigsby?"

"I'm not much for tea." He chewed on his cigar and squinted at the dangling engine. "Bloody 'ot water's bad on the 'eart."

It seemed odd to be walking beside Jaimie Ross, odder still to be seated across from him in the tiny engineering office. Ross poured two mugs of sweet, milky tea from a tea urn and then sat behind a battered desk.

"Funny us meeting like this, isn't it?"

"Yes," Charles agreed. "It is rather."

"I read about Mr. Wood-Lacy dyin' at Gallipoli. Sorry. He was a nice chap. How's his lordship and ladyship?"

"They're fine, thank you."

"And Miss Alexandra?"

"She's training as a nurse . . . at All Souls Hospital in London . . . the army nursing service."

Ross shook his head. "Hard to believe. She was

tango-mad last time I saw her. The old world do change a bit, don't it?"

Charles stared into his tea. "Yes, it does."

"Been changin' a bit for me, too. I got seven patents on this new engine. It's really my idea and I'm responsible for its mass production. The company's sendin' me to America at the end of the month . . . to Cleveland and Detroit. The Yanks are going to build the bulk of 'em under license for us. Lor', think of it, me, Jaimie Ross, goin' to America." He sipped reflectively at his tea. "That Algy Bigsby's a wonder, he is. I used to read his articles all the time in *Mechanics and Journeymen*. Quite an inspiration to me when I was a nipper. I never knew you to be much intrested in mechanical things."

"No. I'm still not terribly interested."

Ross smiled. "I get the picture. I've had to deal with the army chaps on a few occasions. They turn deaf when a man with grease on his hands speaks to 'em. I suppose old 'spittin' ' Bigsby tells you and you tell the brass. Is that it?"

"Something like that." His face felt hotter than the tea.

"God, the bloody army. They think they're fightin' in the bleedin' Crimea or in India's sunny climes. Must be a strain on you. Still, as long as the job gets done . . . that's the main thing, isn't it? Get the better equipment out to the lads. Anything to that land fort?"

"Some people seem to think so, but most of the generals are dubious. One of them called it a pretty toy. I'm sure it's more than that."

"Looks like it could crush barbed wire and deflect bullets easily enough. That is, if it has enough power to move across no-man's land."

"That's your job now, isn't it?"

"Yes. And it can be done. It won't be perfect by any means. You can expect twenty percent breakdowns at least. The ratio of weight to power plant is ridiculous. It needs at least a three-hundred-horsepower engine to give it momentum. . . . Eight to ten miles per on the flat . . . five on shell-pitted ground. Tell 'em that."

"My job," he said hollowly.

"That's right," Ross said, slurping tea. "Your job, and you're bloody welcome to it."

He was too much the outsider. Bigsby and Ross, the grimy mechanics, they spoke an arcane language that set them totally apart from him. They all seemed relieved when he excused himself and went back to the car. He told the driver to take him to Flockton Moor. After a fifteen-minute drive over sodden hills, they came to a featureless moor, with rows of wooden barracks, corrugated iron huts, and bell tents. He saw a flagpole, the Union Jack whipping in the wind . . . a sentry box on the side road . . . men at drill . . . a skirmish line moving through the gorse. . . . He felt a sense of peace. His familiar element. He thought of Windsor and the Second Battalion . . . first platoon . . . D Company . . . "Right as bloody rain, sir!"

The officers' mess was in a tar-paper and wood shack that leaked in a few spots. There were no battalion trophies to be seen, simply because there were no battalion trophies to be displayed. No honors won but the honor of having been formed in the first place. Volunteers all—except for a sprinkling of regular officers and NCO's seconded to the battalion from other units. For the sake of administrative convenience, the War Office had attached this battalion of amateurs to the Princess of Wales's Own Yorkshire regiment, the Green Howards, but not one man in a hundred knew anything at all about that venerable concern.

"Nor cares less," Fenton said, nursing a whiskey. "Mill hands for the most part—the woolen trade—but they're tough birds and eager to kill Germans."

Fenton looked lean and fit, Charles was thinking, feeling a pang of envy.

"Are you up to strength?"

"Over strength as a matter of fact, except for officers and NCO's. I should have thirty-five officers but have only twenty-six. But it's the same everywhere, and they're eager chaps and not afraid to work hard. The senior NCO's are first-rate. Seduced a couple away from the Coldstreams, and one who had been with me during the retreat, Sergeant Major Ackroyd. I stole him from the Middlesex."

"Bit of a pack rat, aren't you?"

"Got to be, old fellow. There are just so many experienced men to go 'round and I want my battalion to have its fair share. It's trench experience that counts. Yorkshiremen love a good fight, but I need calm and steady hands to tell the lads when to shoot and when to keep their bloody heads down."

Charles sipped his whiskey and glanced across the room. Two pink-cheeked first lieutenants were playing darts. Their combined ages wouldn't have reached forty.

"They're getting horribly young."

"Yes," Fenton said. "Coming right out of public school. Make them full lieutenants if they've had any OTC." He drained his drink. "Winnie's with me, you know. We found a roomy old house up the road at Highbury. Stay the night with us. No point in your driving back to Huddersfield."

"No . . . I shan't be missed."

The Royal Windsor Fusiliers and the Green Howards had fought side by side at Inkerman in the Crimean War and had shared the same marching tune ever since, "The Bonnie English Rose." It was an apt description of Winifred, Charles decided as they walked on the moors after supper. The rain had stopped and the sky flamed with sunset. He stood beside Fenton and watched Winifred striding through the gorse in muddy boots, whistling for her Bedlington, which was off on a rabbit hunt.

"I'm glad for you and Winnie. You seem very happy together."

"She's a fine woman."

"And a downright lovely one."

Fenton lit a cigarette and blew smoke through his nose. "I detect a vague bitterness in your manner, Charles. Are you and Lydia getting along . . . or is it rude of me to ask?"

"Oh, we get along without strain . . . considering the circumstances."

"What circumstances?"

"My job. I hate what I'm doing, Fenton. And I feel manipulated . . . pulled onto an inside track by invisible wires. Well, not so invisible, come to think of it. I've just closed my eyes so far."

Fenton dropped his half-smoked cigarette at his feet and crushed it with the heel of his boot.

"If Lydia is pulling a few wires, it's only for your benefit. You came within an inch of being killed at Gallipoli, old boy. She wouldn't be human if she didn't think of that. And you're not skulking in an attic, you know. For every man at the front, there are a dozen serving usefully—no, *vitally*—behind the lines. Only amateurs feel compelled to charge the foe with drawn sword. Professionals take the billets as they come, fair or foul, good job or bad. Make the best of it."

"It's rather a question of my own self-respect, Fenton."

"Bugger that," Fenton said angrily. "You're one of the few men left in the army who went ashore from the *River Clyde*. That ranks with the Charge of the Light Brigade or the bloody stand at Albuera. There isn't a soldier alive who wouldn't touch his cap in respect. Stop sticking needles in your flesh."

"A man should do what he feels is the right thing for *him*," Charles said with a quiet intensity. "If he doesn't, he pays for it in some way. This may sound like an odd paradox, Fenton, but I never felt so alive, so needed, as I did at Gallipoli. My function was simple . . . to lead and inspire my men. I did that well. I was a damn good officer and . . ."—his voice trailed off until it was virtually inaudible—"I was happy."

* * *

Fenton found it impossible to sleep. Not that it mattered very much. He had told his batman to wake him at four, as always. Usually, he was in bed by ten-thirty, and after a quick shave, a spot of breakfast, he was off to the camp before reveille. But tonight he had sat up drinking with Charles until two in the morning. No more talk about Lydia or his problems, thank God, just jawing about old times at Abingdon Pryory. But the man's moodiness had still remained, like a dark shadow beneath the surface.

Winifred stirred and moved against him. Her hand created an opening in his pajamas and drifted slowly across his chest in a loving tracery.

"Thought you were asleep," he murmured.

"No. Just silently respectful. I could almost hear you thinking. Dull army matters, no doubt . . . How many cans of bully beef per man . . . boot laces . . . spare socks? I wonder if Napoleon thought about such things."

"Probably."

"But that's not on your mind, is it?"

"No. I was thinking of Charles. I have a feeling he's going to do something rash."

"Charles never does anything rash."

"He let you get away. But that was more foolish than rash, I suppose."

"Some people might say it was sensible."

"Some people still think the earth is flat."

She lay silently beside him, listening to the night wind moaning and whispering down the chimney. Then she said, "Does Charles know that Lydia was in love with you?"

He raised himself on one elbow. "Whatever gave you that idea?"

"Women can sense those things. I'll never forget the look in her eyes when you were teaching me how to tango. She was dancing with Charles, but watching us. I was just eighteen, but women are born with the instinct for understanding other women. Were you in love with her?"

"Does it matter?"

"No. Even if you were, you're not in love with her now. A woman can sense that, too."

He bent his head and kissed her. "You're the only woman I love . . . the only woman I shall ever love. I'm a disgustingly lucky man, Winnie."

"Like Napoleon?"

"His luck ran out. And besides, I'm taller than he was."

Charles stayed at the factory for the next two days—forty-eight hours with virtually no sleep, watching what Ross and Bigsby instructed the mechanics to do. He kept meticulous notes and drew diagrams of each procedure. When the job was completed to Bigsby's satisfaction, the men from the test center at Hatfield Park who had brought the tank drove it out of the building and onto a flatcar on the railroad siding. They then covered it with canvas, so not an inch of its metal body could be seen.

"And that's that," Ross said. "What do you do now?"

"Follow it down to the test ground and demonstrate it for some generals and war ministers. Rather like selling a terribly expensive motorcar to people who don't really want to buy one."

"You handle the test, do you?"

"Oh, no . . . just the selling part. I mingle with the brass . . . answer questions, tell a few jokes, and talk shop. Above all, I keep cheerful . . . even when the damn thing runs off its tracks or the engine explodes. Keep cheery about it . . . make light of the problems with a sort of 'Well, sir, we'll do jolly well better next time' attitude."

Ross shook his head in wonder. "Queer way to fight a war, ain't it?"

"Yes. I think it is." He held out his hand. "Good luck in America, Ross. It's been splendid seeing you again, and I mean that most sincerely. Truly splendid. You know what you can do and you do it to perfection. I admire that. You must be a very happy man."

Ross frowned slightly. "Well, sir, I don't know about that, but I'm satisfied. Is that what you mean?"

"Yes. I suppose it is, Ross. I suppose it is."

There were more people than Charles had expected. The ground was relatively dry except for the mud-filled hollow, which was one of the test obstacles. The absence of rain and the crisp April air had everyone in a good mood, and they strolled about in the sun outside the refreshment tent downing whiskey sodas or drinking tea and munching ham sandwiches. The usual type of crowd had come—army and navy officers, frock-coated civil servants, and ministers. General Haldane did not mingle with any of them. General Haldane, Royal Engineers, chief of NS 5, stayed as far away from them as possible, his pale eyes fixed on the tank as if he were examining every bolt, screw, and rivet. He was sixty-two and had spent forty years of his service life in India and Burma building railroads and steel bridges from Mysore to the Salween. He had no capacity for small talk of any kind. He was waiting for the driver of the machine to signal that his crew was ready. When he did so, he turned to Charles and growled, "Tell 'em all to watch. And keep bloody well cheery."

She was dressing for a dinner engagement when he came home, dried mud on his boots and badly in need of a shave. His entrance into her pristine dressing room was almost an obscenity.

"Charles! You could at least have telephoned."

He slumped into a small velvet chair and looked at her, groggy from fatigue.

"How fragile you look," he said.

She turned back to her dressing-table mirror and applied the slightest amount of rouge to her cheeks.

"Most naked people do."

"Half naked," he corrected. "What do you call those skimpy things?"

"Underclothes."

"Must be more to it than that. Hardly the army manner, is it? Chemise, mark one. Garter belt, model nineteen sixteen dash seven one two H."

She glanced over a white powdered shoulder. "Are you tipsy?"

"God, no. Just worn to the bone. Big Willie did himself proud for a change. Even knocked over a small tree. Went seven miles at four miles per hour and didn't break down once. No jammed gears . . . no stalls for lack of petrol. Everything clicked. General Haldane was so pleased he smiled—at least I think it was a smile. If an iceberg could smile, it would look like Haldane's smile. He thanked me . . . and I told him I was chucking it in . . . resigning from NS Five. He wasn't the least bit surprised."

"That's because he already received notice. Someone the General Staff informed him this morning."

I got the appointment," he said in a flat, weary

f course. You impressed General Robertson favorably, to say the least."

"I'm chucking that in, too. I don't want to be on *Wully's* staff."

She studied an eyebrow in the glass. "Oh? What do you want to do then?"

"Go to Windsor and rejoin my battalion."

She plucked a solitary hair with a pair of tweezers. "That's ridiculous. You don't have medical clearance and you're on staff. Don't make gestures, Charles."

"It's not a gesture. I want to be doing something that fits my abilities for a change . . . and my temperament. I just won't fit on Robertson's staff. There's too much politics involved . . . too much spying and skulking about expected. Haig is Robertson's creature, and any mutterings about Haig from divisional commanders must be quashed. That's where I would come in—and others like me—hanging about various HQ's in France and keeping our ears open. I don't want that kind of employment. I want something clean . . . manly. I want to be a company commander and take my chances in the line like everyone else."

"Not 'everyone' is in the line." She put the steel tweezers down very carefully, as though they would smash if she dropped them on the table, then turned in her chair and looked at him. "I fail to see anything *manly* in wanting to get killed."

"I don't expect to be killed. I expect to serve a few tours in trenches and then be rotated by the winter . . . given a battalion to train. The same kind of process Fenton went through."

"Fenton's a regular army officer," she said, measuring each word. "What he did in France . . . what he's doing now . . . is expected of him. You fulfilled your martial duties on Gallipoli. Nothing further is expected of you except the wearing of a uniform and the performance of some useful task. Being a staff officer such a task, Charles. There's more to it than 'sku about,' as you put it. It's a job that requires intel and tact—two qualities you possess in abundan. , why don't you take a bath and a shave, put on some clean clothes, and come with me. I'm meeting some people at Claridge's and then we're going on from there to the theater."

"No, I'm going to get some sleep. I want to be at Windsor first thing in the morning."

She stood up and leaned back against the edge of the dressing table.

"Manly," she said softly. "That's the crux of it, isn't it, Charles? Your periodic bouts of impotence distress you."

He looked away from her. She reminded him of an illustration he had seen once in an erotic novel someone had abandoned in a railway carriage, *La Passion de Marie*. The nearly transparent chemise . . . the lace belt supporting dark silk hose.

"I wonder if you'll appreciate it a week from now," Fenton said.

Mesnil-Martinsart, June 23, 1916

This village is approximately in dead center of the British assault line, which begins at the Gommecourt salient seven miles to the north and ends eight miles to the south, where the British link up with the French in the marshes of the River Somme. The objective of the British offensive is the town of Bapaume, nine miles to the northeast, straddling the straight-as-an-arrow Roman road that runs from Amiens. The timetable calls for a total rupture of the German trench system on day one and the taking of Bapaume by the cavalry on day two. Roads and railways radiate from Bapaume to Arras and Cambrai, and a breakthrough there would put the British to the rear of the German armies with a good chance of rolling them up and forcing a major retreat. The optimism of the troops—Fenton and the old sweats excepted—verges on the ecstatic.

"We're going to scupper 'em, old chum," a private in the 13th Yorks and Lancs (Barnsley Pals) told me. This is the New Army for the most part. Volunteers . . . men joining up together . . . battalions of friends and co-workers. Hull Tradesmen . . . Sheffield City Battalion . . . Grimsby Chums . . . Glasgow Tramways . . . Tyneside Irish . . . Liverpool Pals. Pals and chums and post office workers—even a group of footballers, cricketers, and Rugby players who formed a battalion. They have been tacked on to the traditional units of the army, but each group has its own particular and unique ties. A people's army if there ever was one—like the army Grant led down the Mississippi to Vicksburg—and they are here on the Somme determined to win the war. The enthusiasm is electric.

June 24

The barrage began today. Birds flutter in confusion above Aveluy Wood. There is simply no way to describe the power of it. The earth rocks and the air reeks (battle-reporting cliché number 346, but, dammit, the earth *does* rock and the air *does* reek). Birds fly erratic patterns across the Aveluy-Hamel road into Thiepval Wood. Not a shred of cloud and the heat is intense. One can see—I'm sure of it—a twinkle of brassy specks far off in the sky as the howitzer shells pause in their arcs before plunging to earth.

June 27

In a front-line observation post with Fenton and several other officers. They are checking the effect of the bombardment on the German wire. Fenton and the others grim. The belts of wire with their inch-long barbs are a hundred yards deep in some places. A jungle of steel brambles. Artillery using 18-pounder guns firing shrapnel to cut the thickets. Not too effective. There are gaps here and there, but Fenton explained that the Germans will deliberately leave gaps so as to channelize attacks. Men bunched up going through a gap become easy targets for machine gunners. To compound their concern, one of those freak summer storms has swept in, and the heavy rains will make the churned-up ground tough going for the infantry.

Château Querrieux, June 28

HQ of Sir Henry Rawlinson, commanding general of the Fourth Army. He has called a meeting of his corps commanders, and I have driven here with Sir Julian, who is in fine spirits. I tell him of Fenton's concern about the wire.

"Bugger the wire," Sir Julian says.

June 29

Fenton's battalion HQ. A comfortable old farm-house. Excellent meal. Plenty of whiskey. Fenton tells it straight to his company commanders. Attack will jump off on the morning of July first. Sir Julian's unconcern for the uncut wire is now obvious as Fenton reads a message sent down to all battalion commanders:

"There will be nothing ahead of you but dead or wounded Germans and a few crazed derelicts. Troops may slope arms if they wish while crossing no-man's-land. The bombardment will roll ahead of you and destroy any semblance of resistance."

"We will exercise full caution," Fenton says tightly. "And we will move at the ready and as quickly as possible."

The barrage grows in intensity. Candle flames sway in the shock blasts. Looking outside, one can see nothing but bolts of flame erupting from the German front lines. It seems inconceivable that so much as a rat could be alive over there.

"Colonel's a bit of a worrier, isn't he?" a young captain whispers in my ear.

Thiepval Wood, July 1

Men packed into the forward trenches five hundred yards from where I sit in what had once been a fine old wood. Most of the trees cut down, either by German shelling or by brigade artillery so as to give better fields of fire for their guns. Rain has stopped and the sky is clear, sun hot. Barrage has been continuous all night. Suddenly ceases at 7:30 A.M. Silence catches at the heart, and I can clearly hear the whistles blowing all up and down the line. One hundred fifty thousand Englishmen climb out of their trenches and start across. Twinkle of sunlight off bayonets for as far as the eye can see in both directions. Many men with rifles sloped. They are heavily laden and walk slowly, almost casually, in long lines . . . nearly shoulder to shoulder. I think of an illustration in a history book—8th grade?—the redcoats marching up Bunker Hill. A Highland battalion off to my right is being piped across.

Machine guns at a distance sound ineffectual—a metallic, rattling sound, like a marble shaken in a tin can. Nothing dramatic takes places as it does with artillery—no scream of shell . . . no bursting charge and fountain of earth. . . . Nothing to a machine gun but that clattering sound and the invisibility of death. The lines of walking men begin to melt away. Some begin to run toward the German wire. They do not get far. Others waver . . . turn in confusion and drop. The second wave plods on. . . . The third wave follows the second. There may not be many Germans left alive in the ruins of Thiepval or in the shell-pulverized trenches, but there are enough. Their machine guns scythe the middle ground and the Tommies die where they stand. Difficult to write . . . hands shaking badly. . . . Generals were quite wrong. . . . Battle of the Somme will not be won today—or tomorrow, or the day after that.

Alexandra Greville waited with her group on the deck of the small steamer that had brought them up the Seine to Rouen. There were eighty of them, and they stood silently together, wrapped in their wool capes, flurries of rain sweeping the river in the chill September wind.

"All right, ladies," a sergeant in the RAMC called out cheerfully as he came across the gangplank from the quay. "All off, an' a nice mug o' tea waitin' for you at the canteen."

The quay was jammed with men, mules, artillery pieces, great mounds of unfused shells, new ambulances, and an assortment of myriad other supplies. The nurses joined hands to keep from being separated and followed the sergeant past a maze of open-sided storage sheds and giant warehouses and then into the streets of the town.

"Not far now, girls!" the sergeant said gleefully, grinning at them as though they were all his personal possessions. "Don't wander off. This is France . . . and you know what they say about Frenchmen!"

France. Alexandra felt a tightness in the throat as memory stirred. It all seemed so long ago, almost a different war. The soldiers in their steel helmets and rain capes looked alien to her—medieval, like the men-at-arms who had burned Joan of Arc in Rouen in yet another war. Lorries filled with troops clogged the street leading away from the docks. Australians, veterans of Gallipoli. One of them leaned out over the tailgate and said, "You'll be washin' me bloody stumps in a month, Sister!"

The soldiers in the lorry laughed. The nurses stared fixedly ahead.

At the Red Cross canteen a short baldheaded captain addressed them.

"My name is Captain Jenkins, and I'm rather a long way from Harley Street. You are all a long way from other places . . . from your homes . . . your loving parents. We of the Royal Army Medical Corps greet you fine young women of Queen Alexandra's Imperial Military Nursing Service." He paused for effect. "My, my, takes as long to say *that* as it does to sail to France, doesn't it?"

The nurses, tense with fatigue and trepidation, laughed much too loudly.

Captain Jenkins waited patiently until the laughter subsided. "Well, now. Here you are. No longer probationers but qualified nursing sisters in the QA's. I realize that your training has been cut short due to the increased casualty rate on the Somme throughout the summer, but you will soon pick up any fine points you missed at All Souls. You are greatly needed here. . . .

We will work you hard, and I know you will do your very best. I salute you . . . and may God bless you."

She lay on a cot in the nurses' quarters of one of the base hospitals on the outskirts of Rouen, drifting in a vague half sleep. She was riding in the back of an ambulance, and Robbie was kneeling beside her, holding her hands. "Alex . . . Alex . . . Alex . . ."

"What? What?" A light was shining in her face. . . . Someone was kneeling beside the cot, touching her.

"It's me . . . Ivy."

She sat up and embraced Ivy fiercely. "Ivy! How on earth . . . ?"

Ivy Thaxton set her lighted torch on the floor and returned the hug.

"I got your letter last week, and I've been checking the draft lists ever since."

"Did you come down from Boulogne?"

"No. I'm based here now . . . in the hospital train unit. We're getting twenty of your group, so I made sure your name was included on our list." She drew back and took a folded sheet of paper from her carrying bag. "We leave at five-thirty . . . running empty to Amiens. Here's the list of girls. You can help me find them."

"I'm glad you did this, Ivy. Glad we're together."

"It helps to have a friend," Ivy said.

The runner from brigade HQ came along Ale trench, paused for a second at the corner of Bitter and Stout, and then turned into Stout, moving swiftly in a half crouch like a large and wily rat. A bullet cracked loudly as it passed over the narrow trench. Sniper's corner, but he had been this way many times before and knew all the bad spots. Stout was a horrible trench—tumbled in from shelling, full of deep muddy sumps and broken duckboards. It meandered along the edge of High Wood in the direction of Martinpuich, in and around the shattered stumps of blackened trees. Cadavers had been spaded into the parapet, and bony fingers and legs min-

gled with the snaky roots of the trees. The stench on a
hot day was enough to stifle a man, but it was raining
now, and cold, and the smell wasn't too bad. He passed
four New Zealanders squatting in an observation sap,
their faces smeared with mud, only the eyes bright, luminous as the eyes of ferrets.

"What's your bloody 'urry, mate?"

He didn't pause for conversation but hurried on, the
leather message pouch flopping against his hip. The
shriek of a 5.9 sent him headfirst to the trench bottom,
and he hugged the crumbling sides as the shell exploded
ten yards behind the trench. Four more shells followed
the first, each explosion further away. The salvo was
badly off range—creeping the wrong way. He got up
and ran on to Clapham Junction and turned sharply to
his right into Watling trench. There he rested and lit a
cigarette. Watling was deep and the sandbagging in
good repair. He could see men sleeping further down
the trench, in niches cut into the sides. A sentry kneeling against the parados above him was so caked with
mud he blended into the background. The runner didn't
see him until the man turned his head and looked down
at him.

"Can you spare a fag, chum?"

"Yes," the runner said. He handed up his cigarette
and lit another for himself. "This the Second Windsors?"

"You got it, chum. Which comp'ny you lookin' for?"

"Battalion commander."

"First communication trench and back fifty yards.
Can't bloody well miss it. Thanks for the smoke."

"Think nothin' of it, mate," the runner said as he
scurried on his way.

He was not surprised to find a major commanding
the battalion; he had seen captains handling the job,
and there was a rumor that a lance corporal had led the
Ninth Battalion of the West Yorks after the Delville
Wood attack. It meant nothing to the runner. He
handed over his message from brigade and waited.

Major Charles Greville slit the flimsy envelope with his thumb and read the contents, holding the paper under the hissing pressure lamp which dangled from the ceiling of the dugout.

"No reply," he said crisply. "Tell the storeman to give you a double tot of rum."

The adjutant stirred on his wire-mesh bunk. "What's up?"

Charles stared at the paper. "We're to attack Hanoverian redoubt at 0800 tomorrow with A, C, and D. No whimsy about taking the ruddy place. We're to draw fire, I suspect, while the New Zealanders go in on our left."

The adjutant lay back with a groan. "Bloody waste."

"See if you can ring through to brigade."

"No point to it. The wires must be cut in a hundred places after yesterday's strafe. They wouldn't have sent that poor sod of a runner if they could have got us on the blower."

Charles sat down at the table and sipped his tea. It was ice cold and tasted of kerosene. The stupidity of the order caused his hand to tremble with rage. The battalion had lost nine officers and two hundred sixty men in its last attack, half the casualties occurring as the men went through their own wire. One corporal had managed to get close enough to the German positions to hurl a Mills bomb, and he had died throwing it. Five officers and a hundred fifty men had come up from the reserves during the night, but the battalion was seriously under strength and now they wanted another attack on a totally impregnable position, carried out in broad daylight. He couldn't even inspire the men by telling them they were going to take Hanoverian and clean out that corner of the wood once and for all. No, they were simply to go over the top and give the Boche something to shoot at while the New Zealanders clawed their way up Guinness Ravine. No artillery support mentioned in the order. New theory at staff—artillery preps tip off at-

tacks. It was as good a theory as any other, he thought
bitterly. All the theories were bloody wrong.

The adjutant swung his legs off the bed and scratched
his chest.

"Do you realize something, Charles? We've pushed
the Germans four miles since the first of July. Young
Baker figured it out last night. By his calculations, we'll
have 'em over the Rhine by the summer of nineteen
thirty-eight. What do you think of that?"

"I think Baker's an idiot," Charles said savagely. "If
he had told me, I'd have put him on charge."

"He's a good lad. I knew his brother at Harrow. We
used to rag about a bit."

Charles stood up, took his helmet from a peg on one
of the support beams, and went up the dugout steps into
the trench. B Company was in reserve, the men squatting in their shallow funk holes, eating their dinner, rain
capes draped over their heads. At least the food was
hot; steam rose from the tinned stew in their mess
plates. The three companies in the forward line weren't
that lucky. It was bully beef and biscuits for them, with
perhaps some hot tea going up after sundown if there
was no night barrage.

"Stretcher comin' down!" someone shouted from
further along the trench.

"Mind the wire there! Watch your bloody heads!"

He walked toward the commotion. The bearers were
lugging a big groaning man along the communication
trench. The bearers were small men, and it was taking
four of them to carry the stretcher through the mud.

"Who is it?" Charles asked.

"Corporal Thomas, sir," one of the bearers grunted.
"Rifle grenade 'it the parados, bounced back an' blew
his 'and off."

"Damn." Corporal Thomas was one of the best
NCO's in D Company. He was going to be damn hard
to replace.

The stump of the corporal's right hand was heavily

bound with bloody bandgage. There was blood on his face as well, smeared by the rain.

"Is me face gone?" he whispered in terror, struggling to sit upright. "Is me face gone?"

The bearers set the stretcher down for a moment to rest. One of them knelt beside the corporal and patted his shoulder.

"No, Bert . . . just a few scratches. It's your right 'and. Sliced clean as a whistle. It's Blighty for you, Bert."

"Thank God for that," the corporal sobbed. "Thank God I'm out of it."

" 'Ave to diddle the old woman with your left 'and from now on, Bert. Make a nice change for 'er."

"Thank God for it," the corporal said, slumping back on the stretcher. "What's a . . . bleedin' . . . 'and?"

The bearer stood up and glanced at Charles with an apologetic smile. "It's the morphia, sir. Gave 'im two pellets and he's gone out of 'is 'ead. Don't pay no never-mind to 'im."

"Get him down to the aid post," Charles said stiffly. It wouldn't do to show sympathy for a man who felt blessed being wounded. He made a cursory inspection of the trench and went back into the dugout, pausing before he did so to glance down the slope behind him at the burned-out hull of an MK 1 tank, a Big Willie. The tank had come groaning and sputtering and backfiring up the road from Bazentin the week before, moving at about two miles per hour, lurching in and out of ditches and shell holes like some dying beast. Seeing it that day had made him think of Jaimie Ross, and how Ross would have shaken his head and muttered something about too little power—not enough bloody engine to crawl through mud. Brigade had rung through and told him to send two companies up the hill into High Wood behind the tank. The tank never came within five hundred yards of the wood. The Germans had shelled it with whizbangs and Big Willie had exploded. Not knowing what it was they had shelled and burned, the

German gunners had gone into a frenzy and laid down a blanket barrage for two hours, killing sixty men and wounding one hundred and seventy.

The company commanders and seconds-in-command came to the dugout that evening for a briefing and a share of the whiskey bottle. They listened in silence as Charles explained the order of attack: "D Company at 0800. A to follow at 0810. C to give covering fire with the Lewis guns and then to go across at 0825."

It was all meaningless and everyone in the dugout knew it. The Germans would see the first men pop up, and the barrage would start before they had found the taped paths through their own wire. D Company could be written off. If A Company were lucky, the Germans would spot the New Zealanders moving up Guinness and switch their battery fire to that spot. Then all they would have to contend with would be the machine guns firing from concrete revetments half buried in the earth, the intricate belts of wire, and half a dozen *Minenwerfers* lobbing high explosive on their heads. C Company had picked the right card. He could justify calling off its attack if the first two assault waves suffered more than fifty percent casualties—which was almost a certainty. Seventy percent was more like it. If the two New Zealand battalions got up Guinness from Stout trench and took the Hanoverian redoubt in flank, forcing a withdrawal, then it would be worth any sacrifice—a lofty, patriotic observation which he passed on to the captains and lieutenants. The words were greeted by half-concealed sardonic smiles. They would accept the sacrifice because they had no choice in the matter. They did not expect anything to come of the attack.

Dawn came in misty rain. The New Zealanders would have left Stout trench before dawn, using the mist as a cover to crawl as far as possible up Guinness Ravine through a splintered wilderness of trees. They would make their rush for the crest of High Wood when they heard the Royal Windsors drawing fire. Charles put a whistle between his teeth and looked at his wristwatch: 0757 . . . 58 . . . 59 . . . he knew that if he survived the war he would never be able to wear a wristwatch again. . . . 0800. He blew a shrill blast on the whistle, the captain and platoon leaders blew theirs, and two hundred men scrambled up the ladders, bunching up as they hurried through the precut gaps in their own wire. Ten yards . . . twenty—they were scrambling in and out of old craters, bayonets gleaming through the mist. Thirty yards now . . . forty—almost to the German wire, which was fifty yards deep. Signal rockets hissed upward from the enemy lines, bursting yellow and green against the low clouds.

"Damn . . . oh, damn," Charles whispered as he heard the drone of howitzer shells. The drones turned to shrieks, the shrieks to thunderbolts and vomiting geysers of earth and flame. The salvos walked the edge of the German wire. Clods of earth and truncated men hung motionless for a split second against the gray sky. What was left of D Company scattered away from the wire and dove for the steaming shell holes.

0810. Charles blew his whistle with a dry mouth. A Company was slow to leave the trench. Whistles were blowing furiously and the platoon leaders were cursing and shouting. A dozen men went up the ladders and through the wire, keeping low as the Lewis gun teams from C Company began firing over their heads. The heavy German machine guns started to hammer through slits in the thick concrete revetments; the fire interlocked, catching the men of A Company waist high and ripping along the top of the sandbagged parados. The platoon leaders kept shouting and more men went up the ladders, some only reaching the lip of the trench before tumbling back again. It was a clear washout, and Charles, calling for artillery, yelled at the signalers to send up Very lights. The trapped men of D Company might make it back under the covering fire of the counterbarrage. If they couldn't, then they'd hole up in the craters and wait for night.

"You rotten little coward!" Lieutenant Baker yelled,

his voice high-pitched with hysteria. "I should damn well shoot you!"

Charles hurried out of the observation sap into the front trench. A dead man hung head down, one foot caught in the rung of a ladder. He ran past the corpse to where young Baker was standing flourishing a revolver.

"What's the matter?" Charles shouted.

The lieutenant pointed his weapon at a private who sat slumped against the fire step, his rifle beside him, bayonet jammed in the mud. The soldier's face was the color of putty and blood poured from under his right boot. "Shot himself in the foot! Ordered him up the ladder, and he just turned and looked at me . . . reversed his rifle and gave himself a Blighty." He waved the revolver under the man's nose. "It's a firing squad for you now . . . sure as hell!"

"Get him back to the aid post," Charles ordered.

"Under guard?"

He looked at the soldier leaning against the trench wall. His eyes were dull, uncaring, oblivious even to the pain of his wound. He was no more than eighteen.

"Yes," Charles said dully. "Under guard, of course."

They would tie him to a post more than likely, shoot him by firing squad, or the Military Police would pistol him in the head without ceremony. Damn, he thought, clenching and unclenching his fists, why hadn't the man been clever enough not to shoot himself in front of his lieutenant! But what was one more corpse? What did it matter? Brigade artillery was firing shrapnel against the German revetment now and the Boche machine-gun fire had ceased. The shrapnel fire was desultory and dwindled to a final burst, the smoke drifting in the wind through a grove of skeleton trees. A Boche machine gunner fired a few rounds, a staccato thumb to the nose. There had been heavy German shelling in the direction of Guinness Ravine, and that, too, ceased. The men of A Company stood white-faced and tense on the fire step of the trench.

"Stand down," Charles ordered. Any further attack would be less than futile.

Out between the wire somewhere, in a shell hole or abandoned sap, a man was screaming—ragged shrieks and sobs. The sound went on and on, rising and falling, dwindling at times but never ending. 0830. When night came, he would send out the stretcher bearers. He prayed fervently that the shrieking man would be hours dead by then.

Colonel Robin Mackendric completed his first surgical shift of the day and went to the mess tent for a mug of tea and a late breakfast. He did not wear his colonel's crown and stars on his uniform because he was oblivious to rank. It was purely a by-the-book promotion, due to the army's obsession with having the proper rank in the proper job. Commanders of casualty clearing stations were supposed to be colonels, and so, finally, the War Office papers had caught up with him just as his team was shifted from Kemmel to the Somme. Being a colonel instead of a major had not affected his duties in any way, and so he hadn't bothered to remove the old badges and have new ones sewn onto his shoulder straps. Not so Captain Ronald David Vale, who had been upped to major. He wore the crown badges on his underwear—or so it was rumored.

"Had a funny one just now, Mac," Vale said as he joined Mackendric at the table. "Skull furrow . . . clear to the bone and all the way around. A perfect circle. Bullet penetrated the chap's helmet and just bucketed around inside of it like a buzz saw. He'll go through life with a nice groove to rest his hat on."

Mackendric eyed him sourly and sipped his tea. "You're collecting some marvelous tales for your dotage."

Vale grinned and reached for a plate of buns. "Well, to tell you the truth, it didn't go *all* the way around, but it was quite miraculous."

"We can use a few miracles."

"Yes," Vale said, suddenly subdued. "I had more than my share of horrors yesterday. You were lucky to be in Amiens."

"I heard all about it."

"Yes . . . well, the point is, Mac, I don't see how it can get better before it gets a damn sight worse. Are they going to keep on butting their heads against a wall here, or blow the bloody whistle and call time?"

"They're going to keep butting." Mackendric dunked a bun in his tea and munched on it slowly. "That was the gist of the meeting yesterday. The French medical services have gone to pot . . . just worn out by Verdun. Haig and Rawlinson are afraid the same sort of wear and tear will break us. We all told them that it wouldn't, and then they began to drop dark hints that we could expect even heavier casualties between now and November."

"Three hundred thousand isn't enough for Haig?"

"Don't be sarcastic, Vale. I pity the man in a way. He's got Joffre on his back like the old man of the sea. . . . Attack . . . attack . . . attack. It's a war of attrition now—that's obvious. We lose three hundred thousand and the Germans lose four hundred thousand. That spells victory to some minds."

Vale shoved the plate away as though the idea of eating a bun was repugnant.

"Last man on his feet wins the war, I suppose."

"Something on that order. Don't try to make any sense out of it. Just go on doing your job."

"Oh, I do, Mac, I do. I really love the army, that's the joke of it. I'd rather be a battalion MO than a Harley Street surgeon any day in the week. I think that's why I'm more bitter than you are about all this waste—or, anyway, more vocal about it. You hide everything behind that infuriating Scottish stoicism of yours. But if it keeps you sane, why should I care?"

Afternoons were worse than the mornings. The ambulances bearing the casualties of dawn attacks rolled into Corbie from the battalion aid posts and dressing stations in Albert, Ginchy, Mametz, and Bazentin. Number 85 CCS received its full share.

Mackendric was taking his turn as triage officer, examining, with three sisters to aid him, each stretcher case that was brought in, sorting out those men who needed immediate surgery and might live because of it; those who needed surgery but would die no matter what was done; and those who could be sent "as is" to the hospital trains and dealt with at one of the base hospitals in Rouen. The first group were carried to the surgical huts, the second to the moribund ward where they would be kept under heavy sedation in clean beds until they died without pain, and the last carried back to the ambulances for the short ride to Corbie Junction. It was not a job that anyone wanted, but none of the doctors shirked it. The number of men being sent to the moribund ward seemed to increase daily.

"The men are getting reckless," a battalion medical officer had told Mackendric one day. "They've lost all sense of caution. It's as if they didn't give a damn if they're hit or not."

He was checking his sixtieth case when Captain O'Fallon hurried up to him.

"I'll take over, Mac. Vale's in a bit of trouble. Better take a look-see . . . hut six."

"What sort of trouble?"

"Military Police."

Two sergeant MP's and an elderly captain stood in number 6 surgical hut. They were watching, grim-faced, as Major Vale worked to close a massive axillary wound. The two sergeants continued to stare intently at the procedure, but the captain turned angrily to face Mackendric when he strolled in.

"Are you in command here, Major?"

"Colonel, actually," Mackendric said, fingering his tunic flaps. "Haven't had time to add the pips. But I am in command, yes."

The provost marshal was slightly abashed. "Oh, I

see. . . . Well, *Colonel*, I shall be forced to register a complaint, sir. I brought in a prisoner for official confirmation of self-inflicted wound, and this man, this *doctor*—" His contempt and anger rendered him momentarily speechless.

"Major Vale, do you mean?"

"Yes . . . if that is his name."

"Bugger off," Vale muttered as he tied a ligature around the axillary artery and prepared to pluck shards of the smashed humerus from the cavity.

"What exactly seems to be the matter?" Mackendric asked politely.

The provost marshal turned his back on the operation and stepped out into the corridor of the tar-paper and wood building.

"I need hardly tell you, sir, that a self-inflicted wound is a most serious matter. The . . . *creature* on that table is suspected of shooting himself in the armpit with a revolver."

"Suspected?"

"No one actually saw him do it, but his platoon leader told us that the edges of the wound were scorched. Powder burns, sir."

Mackendric rubbed the side of his jaw. "Well, now, difficult to say . . . could have been dirt, you know."

The captain stiffened. "Precisely what your Major Vale said when he sliced the evidence away and tossed the flesh into a bucket! I have been in the service for twenty-three years, sir. I know the difference between dirt and powder burns."

"Major Vale is a first-rate surgeon. I can hardly question his judgment. If he claims it was dirt, then I must respect his opinion. I would suggest that you do not pursue this matter any further."

"Quite so," the captain said, eyeing Mackendric frigidly. "May I remind the colonel that it is the duty of the medical service to report all incidents of self-inflicted wounds to the provost marshal's office. This . . . *epidemic* of Blighty wounds done by one's own hand must be stopped. It is un-English, sir, and a disgrace to our heritage. I served in the South African war, and not once during that conflict did I hear of a soldier being so craven as to shoot himself."

The provost marshal strode off and the two MP sergeants followed him, still looking suitably grim-faced. Mackendric glanced into the operating room.

"Will he lose the arm, do you think?"

"Oh, hell no," Vale snapped irritably. "But it won't be worth a damn. Smack in the armpit with a Webley! Stupid sod."

"Take the afternoon off. Go into Corbie and have a brandy or two."

"I bloody well intended to do just that. I might even have three."

It was evening before Major Vale got back to the CCS. He was not drunk, but he was far from sober. His breath, Mackendric noted, smelled like a brewery floor.

"Gave up on the brandy, I take it," Mackendric said as the young surgeon came into his room and slumped happily into a canvas chair.

"Met some Australian chaps . . . marvelous fellows. . . . Knew of an *estaminet* near the junction that serves real English beer . . . none of that pallid French stuff. Sat . . . talked . . . watched the trains go by."

Mackendric sat on his cot in his pajamas, reading a book.

"I'm glad you enjoyed yourself."

"One of the Aussies—a colonel—used to be a barrister in Melbourne. . . . He said that he could prove, without a doubt, that the whole bloody war is illegal. Think of that."

"Fascinating. Why don't you go to bed?"

"Yes . . . might do that little thing . . . have a decent sleep for a change. Popped in here for some reason . . . had something in mind to say."

"The illegality of it all. In Australia, at least."

"More than that." He got clumsily to his feet, yawning, tugging at one ear. "Ah, yes . . . spotted an absolutely smashing QA in the junction off one of the hospital trains. . . . She was buying some apples at the canteen. Blonde stunner . . . seen her before."

Mackendric lowered his book and peered over the wire rims of his eyeglasses. "Oh?"

"Yes . . . Couldn't be two faces like hers . . . or two figures when it comes to that. Positive I'd seen her before—but I wasn't sure, you see, didn't want to make a fool of myself. But I'd swear it was the same girl who came up to Kemmel last year . . . the one who went bonkers on us. Remember?"

"Yes."

"Friend of yours or something, wasn't she?"

"Something like that."

He stayed awake far into the night, trying to read, but forgetting to turn the pages. There were sounds all about him—the rattle of the dressing carts in the wards down the corridor, the rumble of gunfire from the direction of Delville Wood—but he heard nothing. He was miles away, walking hand in hand with her along the rue Saint-Honoré, window shopping the afternoon after the first night. Had that really been him? He felt old and tired. There was a good deal of gray creeping into his hair. His eyes were giving him a few problems—too much straining in the inadequate light of the operating room—and his fingers ached constantly from clenching instruments for too many hours a day, too many days at a time. Burning himself out. Thirty-three and he felt like an old man. She would be what now? Twenty? She had taken his advice and undertaken the training to become a nurse. Perhaps she had taken the rest of his advice as well and had met a handsome man of her own age and forgotten all about him. A possibility. He would never know unless he talked to her. He could contrive a way to do that easily enough. Hospital Trains Detachment. A telephone call to Captain Frazier in Rouen. Frazier arranged the complex train schedules and would know to the lowliest orderly who was on

which train and when and at what time. His little corner
of the war.

"Greville, Alexandra, QA's. Train ninety-six. Rouen
to Corbie via Amiens . . . Tuesday, Thursday, and
Sunday runs. Know the woman, Mackendric?"

Yes. He knew her and needed her. But did she need
him?

Sister Pilbeam dipped ether onto the nose cone. Vale
clutched the rib spreaders while Mackendric excised a
shell-shredded lung. He kept glancing at the wall clock
as he finished off.

"You in a hurry to catch a train?" Vale quipped.

"Yes," he said quietly, "as a matter of fact, I am."

She was busy, as he knew she would be. After coming empty into Corbie, the trains had been shunted onto
a spur at the junction where the ambulances and the
walking wounded were waiting. He spotted her among a
score of other nurses as he walked along the platform
past two hundred New Zealanders lying patiently on
their stretchers. Bearers and orderlies moved among
them, lighting cigarettes, helping the wounded men fill
in Field Service postcards:

> *Strike out what does not apply:*
>   I am quite well
>   I have been admitted into hospital:
>   sick   and am getting on well
>   wounded   and hope to be discharged
soon

"How do I tell my mum I lost a foot?"

"You don't, mate. Save it as a surprise."

She was giving ATS shots with cool proficiency,
checking dressings, telling the bearers in which car to
place the men that she had checked and tagged. Rain
thudded off the corrugated iron roof of the long platform. The train glistened dark olive green, the red
crosses bright on a white field.

"Your efficiency is to be commended, Sister."

She paused in what she was doing but did not look up at him.

"Hello, Robbie."

"I shan't keep you from your work, Alex. Bit of a surprise seeing you again . . . a happy surprise."

She nodded, bending lower over a stretcher which rested on two sawhorses, her hands sure and knowing on a dirty scrap of bandage covering a mud-encrusted leg.

He leaned closer to the wounded man. "Calf wounds. Not serious."

"Hurt like ruddy fire," the wounded man said.

"Dare say, but you'll be kicking a football with that leg in three weeks' time."

He watched Alexandra wash an area of flesh around the jagged, blood-clotted holes with green soap solution and then wrap a clean bandage around the leg. She made a motion with one hand, and the bearers lifted the stretcher and carried it into the train.

"Next," she said, straightening up. Her eyes met Mackendric's for the first time. It was like an embrace. "You're good to see, Robbie."

"Do you mean that, Alex?" His voice was solemn.

She nodded fiercely. "Yes . . . yes, I do. Now please go away or I shan't be able to concentrate. If . . . if you can get away this Saturday . . ."

"I will," he said flatly.

"To Rouen . . . number fifty-two train. I could meet you at the station."

"I shall be there."

"And no lectures this time, Robbie. No telling me what's best for me."

"No. I've stopped giving advice."

"And there would be nights when we could be together . . . in some charming country inn."

He could remember her saying that on a Sunday morning in Paris. No country inn, charming or otherwise, in the Ypres salient. But this was Normandy. Apple trees and rich earth between the great loops of the Seine. Clusters of villages with stone houses. Inns with rooms facing the orchards and the banks of the river. Clean linens and feather beds. He held her tightly, watching the sunset through the windows, one hand drifting idly down her naked back. She turned slightly in his arms and moved her lips across his chest.

"I shall never give you up," she whispered.

"I won't talk you out of it . . . although I should at least try."

"It would only be a gesture. You want me, Robbie."

"Yes. I want you." He held her silently, gently stroking her back, the curve of a hip. Then he said: "I didn't tell you about Dennis. He's in Ottawa . . . flying instructor. Got shot down last April near Abbeville and walked away from the crash. He might not be so lucky next time. I'm glad he's in Canada."

"So am I," she murmured.

"He wrote me a long letter . . . about Canada . . . the people. . . . Quite a different world. You know, I'd already decided that I couldn't go back to England. If this war ever does end, I want a new sort of life. I'd go to Toronto . . . or west to Vancouver. I wrote my wife that and asked her for a divorce . . . Be the best thing for her, too. What she really wants is a respectable sort of chap who stays home, makes lots of money, and votes Conservative. We were never a good match."

She pulled back from him, her breasts resting lightly against his chest.

"Will she give you a divorce?"

"I don't know." He began to caress her nipples, tracing the rosy circles with his finger tips, the taut buds. "I hope to God she does, but Catherine could deny it out of pure spite."

"It won't matter," she said, her voice husky. "I don't care. I'll go with you, Robbie . . . live with you . . . married or not."

"You might regret that one day, Alex."

"Never . . ."

Never . . . never, she thought, moving her body in a slow rhythm with his. And not because of this, not the feel of him inside of her, the pleasure mounting in gentle spirals. It went beyond passion. Their lives had meshed and become one. She would go with him wherever he went and live with him without shame. And Mama and Papa? They would never understand why, never comprehend that her need for him was inextricably woven with his greater need for her.

"I love you, Alex. . . ."

"Yes," she said, "yes . . . yes."

Martin noticed a certain chill as he walked into the brigade headquarters in Bazentin village. One of the officers who had always been friendly and generous with information pretended to be too busy to say hello. The HQ, with its tunnels and rooms cut into the chalk hill behind the ruins of the village, was located in one of the deep German galleries captured in late August. Two brigades had their headquarters there, as well as a signaling company, a dressing station, and stored supplies of all kinds. It made for a crowded, noisy place, the tunnels and rooms lit by electric lights which burned day and night.

"Is the colonel too busy to see me?" Martin asked.

The officer who was usually so talkative began to shift papers around on his tiny desk.

"Afraid he is, yes."

"All I need from him is a pass to go up to the line."

"Out of the question. Sorry . . . Perhaps tomorrow."

"I'm sure you know how difficult it is for me to come this far. As long as I'm here . . ."

The officer half-turned his back and toyed with a field telephone. "Look, Mr. Rilke, I'm sorry, but—"

A heavy gas curtain serving as a room divider parted and Fenton peered through the opening.

"Oh, for God's sake," he said wearily, "you couldn't

shoo Mr. Rilke away with a broom. Come on in, Martin."

Fenton's section of the dugout contained a desk, maps pinned to the chalk walls, one chair, and one canvas cot. Fenton drew the curtain back into place and then sat on the edge of the cot and rubbed his eyes.

"I was trying to get some sleep."

"Sorry," Martin said, straddling the chair. "I didn't mean to wake you."

"I said I was *trying*. You didn't wake me. So you want to go back up to Delville Wood, do you?"

"If at all possible."

Fenton nodded slowly and groped for a tin of cigarettes among the disordered blankets.

"I'm afraid you are suddenly *persona non grata*. Received a crisp directive to that effect from Corps yesterday. If you are spotted in battle area, you are to be escorted to the rear. Anyplace beyond Albert is out of bounds to you, old boy."

Martin lit a cigar and then bent forward to light Fenton's cigarette.

"There's nothing in Albert for me to write about, Fenton. The Salvation Army runs canteens in Albert. I might as well be in Biloxi, Mississippi, as far as writing about the war is concerned."

"That might not be a bad idea . . . Biloxi, Mississippi, I mean. Some of your by-line stories in Yank papers came to the attention or our military mission in Washington. They cabled their shock to London. . . . Gruesome descriptions of British fighting in August—"

"They weren't gruesome descriptions."

"No, I'm sure they weren't. Just Martin Rilke being graphic about the attacks on Thiepval."

"That's right."

"How'd you get them past the censors?"

"Gave them to a fellow AP man going back to the States."

Fenton smiled ironically and flipped ashes at his feet. "Naughty boy. Not playing by the rules, are we? The articles were an embarrassment to the General Staff. Thiepval should have been captured on July first. Here it is damn near the end of September and the place is still a boil in our flanks. Downright humiliating to be reminded of their failures. You are not supposed to mention the names of places, either . . . just 'somewhere on the Somme.' Isn't that right?"

"I suppose so." Martin shrugged.

"And soldiers aren't 'blown up' . . . or 'torn apart by a shell' . . . they don't 'sit screaming in shell holes.' Soldiers simply 'fall.' "

"I take it you read the articles."

"No. I don't need to read them. I was there, remember? Sir Julian read me the juicier bits over the telephone. He was madder than a raped baboon. Well, can't blame the gaffer. Wully Robertson raised hell with Haig, Haig raised hell with Rawlinson, and Rawly jumped all over Uncle Julian."

"And now you're jumping on me."

"Right. I don't know who you can jump on."

Martin studied the ash on his cigar. A fifty-center. One of the few luxuries he permitted himself. He did not disturb the ash, but let it flake away on its own.

"Storm in a teacup, Fenton. I sent those articles out past the censors deliberately. For American consumption only. Tried to bring home to them the reality of this war over here. They may be drawn into it themselves one day, and they have a right to know what twentieth-century battle is all about. The fact is, American papers didn't give it much of a play. Everyone in the States is more concerned about Pancho Villa shooting up New Mexico again than they are about a few thousand Tommies dying for fifty yards of French real estate. I guess it just didn't make any sense to them."

There was heavy shelling going on. British eight-inch and French 105's hitting Delville and High Wood a mile away. The volcanic explosions could be felt rather than heard—a trembling in the walls, a fine haze of chalk dust.

"Doesn't make a whole lot of sense to me, either, Martin. Well, what the devil . . . I'll pretend I never saw you, but stay out of my area from now on. I'm acting brigade commander now. . . . Being brevetted to brigadier general until they dig up a real one from the reserve and ship him out here—kicking and screaming, no doubt. Anyway, I've got five battalions under my rather loose command—the Royal Windsors, Green Howards, and some throw-together battalions with everything in them but the Girl Guides. We're to go over at dawn to the west of High Wood with three other brigades and probe for Flers behind the tanks."

"I heard about it. That's why I'm here."

"Of course you heard about it," Fenton said bitterly. "No one can keep his mouth shut in this army. Every whore in Amiens knows more about high-command strategy than I do." He squashed his cigarette out on the chalk floor and drew another from the tin. "They have a few tanks left from the fifty they shipped over, so they're giving them another try. Rotten terrain. Steep and muddy and peppered with old shell holes. Fragile bloody things, these tanks. Break down if you give 'em a sour look. But I can see their potential. If they could move as fast as a man can run . . . and had the power to go up a hill . . . we'd be on the Rhine in two weeks."

"Americans are interested in tanks," Martin said lamely. "An American invented the caterpillar-tread tractor . . . Uncle Benjamin Holt."

"Bully for Uncle B.," Fenton said dryly.

On the Somme, Sept 21, 1916

Observations and Reflections. And a cold wet day it is. My observation point in a sap covered by a camouflaged tarpaulin is reasonably dry, although there is mud on the bottom of the sap up to my knees. Intense British and French artillery fire whacking High Wood, the shell bursts reflected by the rain causing a sheet-lightning effect across the crest of the stump-dotted hill. Same effect can be seen to the east at Delville Wood and Longueval. Appear to be more than four brigades committed to this assault. Have even seen cavalry along the Contalmaison-Bazentin road, troopers and horses black with rain. Cavalry suffer greatly from exposure. Theory behind having these English hussars and Indian lancers standing about in the rear must be tied in with morale factor, possibly to give infantry moving up to the line the feeling that a breakthrough is in the works—that they have only to chop a few holes through the German trench system and hordes of horsemen will burst through like rockets and ride "into the blue," as Haig so quaintly put it. No "blue" ahead of me, just dancing flames and muddy, pocketed ground. No German return fire. They will be, as always, deep in their bunkers with tons of ferroconcrete and sandbags blunting the blows. When the barrage lifts and the British infantry go forward, they will emerge, as they always do, and cut the attack to pieces. This has been the pattern since the first day, and no one has yet come up with a plan that alters that depressing scenario.

In trench—2nd Royal Windsor Fusiliers. Sangfroid not an expression that fits the American temperament—certainly not the American military temperament. Lee may have had sangfroid, but Grant didn't, nor any other general I can think of. American military men have always been hat slappers, sword benders, tobacco spitters, and high cussers. Charles Greville has sangfroid. He stands in exposed position on top of parados and scans High Wood with binoculars. Cool as ice. I feel like shouting, "Hey, that's my cousin standing up there." Brave but dumb. Lots of German stuff coming this way now. Machine-gun bullets crack as they pass over the trench. Charles has sangfroid.

He steps down into trench and scribbles notes for the runners. Sending two more companies across—as ordered by Brigade HQ. Timetable for attack must be met. He is writing out death notices for a few hundred men. His hand doesn't tremble, his face shows no expression at all. Must ask him one day what he was thinking.

German counterbarrage heavier than anyone expected. Trench rocks, bags of sand fly. . . . Bits of wire . . . bits of men trapped out between wire. Someone shouting, "Tanks are catching it good an' proper." Cockney voice, sounds almost pleased. . . . Shorthand becoming unreadable. No point in

PARIS (AP) *December 12, 1916.* Martin Rilke of the Paris bureau of the Associated Press has been released from the Hôpital St. Antoine after suffering severe wounds on the Somme front in September. He is recuperating satisfactorily at St. Germain en Laye outside Paris.

XVIII

Jacob Golden crossed the Champs-Elysées against a swarm of traffic, smiled affably at shouting taxi drivers, and ignored the blare of Klaxons. On reaching the sidewalk, he straightened his bowler hat, smoothed the moleskin lapels of his overcoat, and strolled into the glittering lobby of the Hôtel Monceau, swinging his cane with the jaunty air of the born *boulevardier*. He ordered a Dubonnet at the bar, speaking to the barman without the slightest trace of an English accent. A British colonel standing at the bar drinking whiskey asked him in halting pocket-dictionary French if he knew of a place in Montmartre where the "*jeunes filles dansent . . . à nu,* don't you know."

He replied in halting English, giving the man directions to a place on the boulevard de Clichy where the only things naked and female were the chickens dangling from hooks in the window. It was the finest poultry shop in Paris and he hoped the colonel enjoyed the visit.

He had nearly finished his aperitif when he saw the burly figure of Claude Lenard enter the bar and sit at a table in a dim corner. Picking up his glass, he strolled casually over to him and sat down.

"Good afternoon, Claude."

Claude Lenard, Socialist editor, had been a lifelong friend of Keir Hardie and Jean Juares. His cause in ruins, his very freedom in constant jeopardy, he looked slowly and suspiciously at every person in the bar before grunting a reply.

"Let me buy you a drink, Claude."

"It is not necessary, Golden."

"Perhaps it isn't, but it is normal. Men do not come into this bar just to sit."

The tiny eyes, almost lost in the massive face, the bush of beard and mustache, flickered. The great head nodded.

"I will take a beer."

"A brandy and soda. This is not a *syndicaliste* bar, Claude. When in Rome and all that."

The editor glanced bitterly at the cherry-wood-paneled walls and the elegantly carved rosewood bar, with its copper, not zinc, top.

"I do not belong in such a capitalist place."

"No," Jacob replied blandly, "and the special police wouldn't think to look for you here. This is the safest possible spot for us to talk. This may come as a shock to you, Claude, but you're the image of Ravenot, the munitions tycoon."

"So I have been told," the old man said dryly. "Very well, as long as I am Ravenot, order me a brandy and soda—an Armagnac and soda."

Jacob snapped his fingers for the waiter. The two men sat in silence until the drinks came.

"All right," Lenard said. "I have found a printer for you, willing, for a price, you understand, to undertake what you want. It is not only money. . . . He lost three sons at Verdun and is understandably bitter about it. The man can be trusted, but the price will be high."

"Money is not a factor. I want a quality paper."

"He is capable of it. A master printer."

Jacob removed a thick envelope from the inner pocket of his coat and placed it in front of Lenard.

"This should show my faith. Take whatever you need for yourself out of it."

Lenard tapped the envelope with his blunt fingers. "I hope you understand the risks in this, Golden. It is a bad climate for this sort of undertaking. They are sensitive about Verdun. They wish to keep the full truth of that abattoir buried with the corpses. The English, too, with their debacle on the Somme. Any criticism of the war is looked on as treason."

"I know it."

"However, there are writers here in Paris who worked for me in the old days. Impassioned, fearless men willing to go to prison for their beliefs."

"I don't want impassioned writing, Claude. This is not going to be a tract for the Second International."

"Not spoken as a good Socialist."

"I'm not a Socialist," Jacob drawled, "good or otherwise. Politics of all kinds bore me. No, Claude, I am just Jacob Golden, swimming against the tide."

Lugging a portmanteau from his apartment on the rue Pigalle, Jacob took the Métro as far as Pont de Neuilly and then hired a taxi to take him to St. Germain en Laye. The driver, grumbling because it was a long drive and gasoline was scarce, said he could make more money and use less fuel with short runs. Jacob dipped into his coat again and gave the man double the fare in advance. Money was not a problem—yet. It would be once the paper went into production, but he would contrive some way of getting money out of England. There was no point in worrying about it now, and so he leaned back in the taxi and watched the gaunt winter woods flash by. The third winter of the war. The very trees looked tired.

The house that Martin Rilke had rented was set in the middle of a well-cultivated garden surrounded by dense groves of beech and pine. It was a small two-story house of weathered limestone, built at the turn of the century for the mistress of a Parisian banker. It had stood empty since the Germans threatened Paris in the first weeks of the war.

A tall, forbidding-looking woman with iron-gray hair opened the door. She wore a slate-gray uniform with a tiny red cross stitched above her ample bosom.

"It is not a good idea for Monsieur Rilke to have

visitors," she said with a strong Breton accent. "I hope you will not stay long."

"Oh," Jacob replied airily, removing his hat and tossing it neatly onto a hatrack peg, "no more than a week or two."

Martin sat in a small, comfortably furnished room at the rear of the house, propped up on a couch, his canes resting beside him. He was both surprised and delighted to see Jacob stroll into the room, and tossed aside the book he was reading and fumbled for his canes.

"Jacob! I don't believe it."

"Ah, how fickle is memory. I sat by your bedside after your second—or was it your third operation? No matter. I was there in your moment of pain and suffering and I wager you can't recall it."

"That's right. I can't." He struggled to get to his feet, but Jacob made a gesture of restraint.

"Don't get up for me, for God's sake. Where do you keep the champagne?"

"In the pantry."

"Well, we shall crack a bottle or two later." He removed his coat and pulled a chair closer to the couch. "Damn fine little house. You own it?"

"No . . . but I might buy it. The price is cheap enough. The owner still expects hordes of uhlans to come crashing through the woods any day."

"Come into money, old lad?"

"Back pay and bonuses by the bucketful . . . and my Uncle Paul was so upset I was hurt, he cabled his import agency in Paris to put forty thousand francs in my account. It pays to get hit by a trench mortar."

"How do you feel?"

"Strong as an ox—until I stand up. But having Madame Lucille nursing me is an incentive to recovery, as rapid as possible."

"Yes, I met the lady. Pleasant as a prison warder."

Martin leaned back against the pillows and looked Jacob up and down.

"How come you're not in uniform?"

"Oh, I severed my relationship before coming to France. I've been here for six weeks, by the way. Rented some digs in Montmartre, but there are far too many distractions there. Haven't lost my penchant for chorus girls of low repute, I'm afraid to say. They take far too much of my money, not to mention creating a severe drain on my energies."

"Wait a second, Jacob . . . go back a bit in the narrative. What did you mean by 'severed' your relationship?"

"Just that, old fellow . . . I resigned my commission in the Royal Corps of Signals."

"You can do that in the middle of a war?"

"They're beginning to close the loopholes now that conscription is some sort of reality, but, oh, my, yes, one serves king and country on a strictly volunteer basis. Ranks might enlist for the duration, but officers, being gentlemen, are under no such obligation. Men of breeding simply do not resign, do they? But I did. I then fulfilled the requirements of the new law and registered with the conscription board. I informed them that I was a conscientious objector and skipped over here before I could be rounded up and put to hard, if worthwhile, labor on some sugar-beet farm in Suffolk."

"You sound awfully damn breezy about it. I never knew you to have strong religious beliefs."

"I don't, but I do have strong conscientious objections to this war. I consider it to be a foul joke played on mankind. A monstrous deceit. I used to read the battle reports sent in code from Haig's HQ. It amused me to see how the newspapers elevated the capture of a trench into a major victory. It did not amuse me to read how many lives were squandered for possession of the muddy ditch. I've decided to try and do something about it by publishing a newspaper which will print the unvarnished, unglamorized truth."

Martin whistled softly between his teeth and groped in the pocket of his robe for a cigar.

"You won't get away with it. They close down pacifist newspapers all the time . . . here and in England."

"I know that, but this won't be a shrill broadside crudely printed on a hand press and tossed around in the streets by young anarchists. This paper will be as sober as the *London Gazette* and as well written as the *Times*. No one who reads it will be able to either dismiss or ignore it. It will contain articles of such documented authenticity that readers will demand inquiries from Parliament or the Chamber of Deputies. It will be published in English and French, by the way. And as for being closed down, once the paper has reached a wide readership, doing so might cause more of a furor than permitting its existence." He scowled slightly and tugged at one ear. "Of course, reaching that readership might be difficult. The initial distribution will be a problem that I have to solve."

"You might solve yourself right into big trouble. . . . For sedition in France, for which you could be shot, and for violations of the Defense of the Realm Act in England. Which could land you in the pokey for the rest of the war . . . fifty years, the way things are going. I'd think twice about this if I were you, Jacob."

"I've thought a thousand times about it. My mind is made up . . . calm, cool, aware of all dangers, but also aware of the rewards. If I can cause just one person to stop singing 'Rule Britannia!' or the 'Marseillaise' every time they read an official communiqué from the front, and to begin thinking about this war—to truly ponder the cost of this insanity—then going to jail would be a pleasure."

"And you want some articles from me—is that what brought you here, Jacob?"

"Yes and no. Yes, I want some articles, unsigned of course, and, no, I didn't come just to mine your experiences. I need a quiet place to stay for a while and I value your company."

"I value yours, Jacob . . . and your friendship. I wouldn't be much of a friend if I encouraged you in this idea. You know, the cost of the Somme offensive has been pretty much tallied up. England lost four hundred thousand men there in four and a half months—nearly half a million dead, wounded, or missing for six miles of ground. People want something for that price, Jacob. That's why they believe the official reports that tell them it was worth it . . . that something great was accomplished there . . . that the sacrifice had meaning. They'll only reject the truth because it's too damn painful to swallow. No one can stop this war . . . certainly public opinion won't. It has a life of its own now, like some runaway locomotive. Only one side or the other caving in will stop it. Only victory with a fat capital V will stop it. You're just crying in the wind with this newspaper of yours."

Jacob stood up with a sigh and stretched his arms above his head.

"I surrender to your logic, Martin. I know you're right, but I enjoy crying in the wind on the off-chance that I might just be heard. No, I'll put out a paper and it'll be a damn good one."

"So Jacob the iconoclast has finally found a cause to believe in."

Jacob clenched his hands behind his back and walked over to one of the windows. He looked at the neatly trimmed hedges in the garden, which were white with frost.

"Only partially, Martin. There's a side of me that just enjoys running the wrong way in crowds . . . another side that wants passionately to do something in life that has lasting value. Perhaps I was born to lead an army of pacifists. Perhaps not. I shall soon find out. Now then, to more immediate concerns. Where is this pantry of yours and how good's the champagne?"

Madame Lucille of the Croix Rouge was a woman of many objections, and she was not afraid to voice any of them. She objected to visitors, let alone guests, and she objected to the consumption of spirits, the smoking of cigars and cigarettes, and the letting in of fresh air. She

also objected to Martin's objections to the food that was
served him. Martin had hired a cook-housekeeper who
had been recommended by the major of St. Germain for
her gastronomic skills, but he had yet to see any of her
cooking; all he got was gruel, a watery barley soup, and
plain boiled chicken. When he demanded that a couple
of ducks be roasted, along with potatoes, to celebrate
his guest's arrival, Madame Lucille declared that she
could no longer be responsible for the health of her patient.

"Good," Martin said, "that's fine with me. Goodbye." And that was that.

"What are you going to do for nursing care?" Jacob
asked as he carved the ducks.

"Hell, I don't really need nursing care. I get around
okay, and the wound on my hip may look ugly as sin,
but it's healed. What I need is strength—roast duck
. . . roast lamb . . . mutton chops . . . pork chops
. . . ham and eggs . . . a liter or two of Burgundy
and ten good cigars a day. Anyway, I've got a nurse
coming to see me in about a week when she gets her
leave. Army nurse. . . . You remember her—Ivy
Thaxton. You met her at the flat in London a couple
of times."

"Slender dark-haired girl with violet eyes?"

"That's the one."

"Not my type. Too fresh and virginal."

"That's because she is virginal . . . not like the
flappers you race after."

Jacob raised an eyebrow and carved the breast.
"Flappers? Right up to date with your slang, aren't
you?"

"I keep up with the language. It's my job."

"Is she going to spend her leave here?"

"I'm going to do my best to talk her into it."

"Ah."

"What the hell does 'ah' mean?"

"Ah means ah. In this case, it means I'll move into

that inn down the road while she's here. Three, old boy, is a crowd—although not always to the French."

She arrived four days before Christmas, on the morning train from Rouen to Paris, and walked the three kilometers from the station to the house, her leather carrying bag slung over one shoulder. Martin, watching for her through the drawing room windows, came out to meet her on the path, walking stiffly with two canes, concealing the pain in his hip with a gritted-teeth grimace. Jacob stood a step behind him, ready to catch his friend should he stumble.

"Why didn't you take a taxi?" Martin called out. "You shouldn't have walked."

"I love to walk!" Ivy shouted as she came down the long gravel path from the tree-lined road. "And it was only a mile or two." She stopped in front of him, smiling, brushing a strand of black hair from her forehead. "Oh, my, look at you, the wounded warrior."

"Just a shell-scratched scribe," Martin said. He looked her up and down, forgetting the pain in his hip at the sight of her. "Gosh, but you're a tonic, Ivy. Do you remember Jacob?"

"Oh, yes," she said, holding out her hand. "How are you, Mr. Golden?"

"Jacob," he corrected. "Only my enemies call me Mr. Golden. Let me take your bag while you help this Boswell of the Somme back to his sofa."

Ivy wandered about the house while the cook prepared lunch. She looked at everything in silent wonder and then sat in a chair next to the couch where Martin half-reclined, his legs propped up on a pillow.

"It's a beautiful house, Martin."

"I've never seen the upstairs. Not worth the pain of climbing up there."

"Don't tell me you sleep on the couch?"

"There's a small room off the hall with a bed in it and a kind of trapeze bar above it so I can lift myself in and out without any trouble."

"You didn't leave the hospital too soon, did you?"

"No. And, anyway, they needed the bed. They had cases in the hallways . . . on cots."

She stood up and held out her hands to him. "Come on, up you get. I want you on the bed with your trousers down."

"What?"

"You heard me. I want to take a look at your wound."

"It's okay," he protested. "Coming along just fine. A surgeon from Harvard—American volunteer group—did the operation. Good man."

"Well, he's not here to examine it, is he? Do as you're told, please."

He led the way into the bedroom, lay on the bed, and glowered at the ceiling as Ivy took down his pants. The red weal traversed the right hip and dipped down across the upper thigh so there was no question of trying to cover anything. He closed his eyes and clenched his jaw as her gentle fingers traced the scar.

"No inflammation," she said. "You're a lucky man, Martin. You missed emasculation by an inch."

"I know," he said thickly.

"Do you have any unguent? It looks puckered and must itch badly."

"I itch all over."

"You do?" She ran her hand with professional sureness across his belly. "Odd. Your skin doesn't feel dry."

"It's not my skin, Ivy. I sort of itch inside. A visceral burning. It's called 'yearning for Ivy Thaxton disease' and it's curable."

"Where's the unguent?" she asked crisply. He told her where to find it, and she rubbed the yellow ointment into the edges of the scar and then stepped back. "You can pull up your trousers now."

He did so gratefully, letting his breath out through his mouth.

"This is a hell of a time to propose, Ivy, but I wish you'd reconsider the whole thing . . . look at it from my point of view. I wouldn't expect you to quit the nurse corps any more than you'd expect me to give up reporting the war, but, I mean, you do have two weeks of leave, and two weeks of happiness isn't a bad deal in these times. Anyway, I only ask you to give it some thought . . . weigh it up . . . examine all the angles."

"I made up my mind when I wrote you last week. It wasn't an easy decision to reach."

"Oh," he said, his tone hollow, "I guess not."

"But if you really *want* to take on the obligation of having a wife—"

The trapeze bar clanged as his hands gripped it. "Oh, boy, do I!" He pulled himself upward, shouting for Jacob.

"What's the commotion?" Jacob asked, peering around the edge of the door. "The girl assaulting you?"

"Call for a taxi! Alert the mayor that he's got a wedding to perform!"

"Congratulations. And now you know what 'ah' means. I'll walk down to the inn and see if there's a car there. The telephone's on the fritz."

"We'll all go," Martin said, easing his legs off the bed. "There's a wheelchair in the hall closet and it's downhill all the way. Come on, Jacob, don't just stand there!"

"Impetuous rascal, aren't you?"

"Will it be legal?" Ivy asked, looking worried.

"Of course it's legal! What kind of a guy do you take me for? Monsieur le Maire can marry anyone . . . like a ship's captain. We can always have a church ceremony one day, Ivy, if you'd like that."

She leaned forward and kissed him on the cheek. "I don't care, Martin . . . just so long as I can write Mum and Da with a clear conscience."

There was no car in the inn, but there was also no lack of strong backs willing to push *le bon Américain* into St. Germain, especially for such a purpose. Bride and best man walked beside the chair as two stable hands pushed Martin at a brisk pace down the center of

the road and into town. After a brief ceremony in the
lobby of the city hall, the mayor drove them back to the
house in his wheezing Renault.

"I am happy." Martin sighed. "Drunk with joy."

"And champagne."

" 'Fill every glass, for wine inspires us . . . and
fires us with courage, love and joy. . . .' *The Beggar's
Opera*. There's more to it—something about women
being the most desirable things on earth. But only one
woman, Ivy."

Later, after they had all gone, she sat beside him on
the bed in her army-issue nightgown, plaiting her hair
into braids. He reached out, brushed her hands away,
and began to loosen the neat coils.

"I like your hair long and loose. You're very beautiful, Mrs. Rilke."

"And a bit drab-looking. I never imagined I'd spend
my wedding night in a flannel shift with the initials of
Queen Alexandra's Imperial Military Nursing Service
embroidered on the hem."

"I'll buy you a dozen silk gowns tomorrow. They say
there are some fine shops in Saint Germain. . . . Or
we'll go into Paris—shop, then spend the night in the
best suite at the Crillon."

"Hush now. We're in our own house. What could be
better than that?"

She stood up and blew out the lamps.

"Sorry about the electricity," he said, "but we get
none after eight at night. Power shortage."

"There was a permanent power shortage in my home.
I like lamps."

She moved around the bed in the darkness and after
a moment slipped in beside him. The flannel gown was
gone and her body was cool and fragrant beside him.
He attempted to turn toward her, but let out a groan
and lay back.

"Damn the Boche," he muttered.

"Shush," she whispered. "No bad thoughts. If you
hadn't been hit by a shell, you might be in China now,

or Mesopotamia, or some other far-off place, and not lying beside me." She undid his pajamas and rested her head against his chest. "Your heart's a trifle fast."

"A trifle? It's trying to hammer its way through my ribs."

"And your breath is shallow."

"It's a wonder I can breathe at all. If you only knew what I'm going through right now. I was a fool to marry you until I was capable of doing handstands . . . and jumping fences . . . and . . . Well . . . lots of other things."

She burrowed closer to him.

"You can hold me, Martin. Hold me very tightly."

"Sure," he said thickly. "Sure can." He folded his arms about her, his hands gliding up and down. "Velvet, pure velvet . . . the most wonderful body on earth."

"All Norfolk girls have good bodies."

"Gosh," he whispered, "what a place that must be if they're half as wonderful as yours."

"Oh," she said, "I didn't measure up, that's why they chucked me out. I shall never take you there to see the women they kept."

"God, but I love you, Ivy."

She sat up, her body slender and pale as ivory in the moonlight.

"Will you mind terribly if I discard maidenly modesty, but there's no point in our pining away if we don't have to. I mean to say, I *am* a nurse, so if you will just move your good leg—your left leg—as far to the side as you can. . . ."

"Is this going to hurt?"

"I'm supposed to ask that, Martin, not you. . . . No . . . it won't hurt a bit if you keep your right leg very, very still. . . . And I shall just . . . shift my left leg . . . like this . . . and . . . raise up a bit . . . and . . . and . . ."

"Oh, Ivy! God! You're a wonder. . . . You're—"

"No . . . ! Please, Martin . . . don't say anything. . . . Don't say a word."

Jacob cut a small pine tree and dragged it through
the snow. It had been the first real snowfall of the winter—soft, wet flakes drifting from the gray sky. Ivy
helped him to get the tree into the house and set the
sap-dripping trunk into a wood keg filled with sandy
soil. They decorated the branches with whatever bright
ornaments they could find—strips of red and yellow
cloth, tiny silver teaspoons tied on with thread, holly
berries from a bush in the garden, tin foil from cigarettes.

"A quite acceptable tree," Jacob said.

"I think it's beautiful. If we had some tiny candles to
place on the branches . . ."

"We could burn the house down."

"Yes," she sighed, "I suppose you're right." She
glanced at the mantel clock. "I'll wake Martin from his
nap. He'll be ever so surprised."

"Let him sleep a bit longer. He's a lucky man having
you to wake up to."

"Thank you, Jacob. That was a nice thing to say."

"I mean it sincerely. Tell me, Ivy, do you know
about me?"

"Your being a pacifist, you mean? Yes, Martin told
me."

"I hope you don't despise me for it."

"Despise you?" She smiled bitterly. "I've had two full
years of seeing what war does to men. There are no
saber rattlers in the medical services, Jacob . . . and
no enemies. We treat a German's pain the same as an
Englishman's. There hasn't been a night when I haven't
prayed that the war would be over when I woke in the
morning. I don't know very much about politics . . .
or the balance of power . . . or any of those things.
. . . But I do know the terror a man feels when he
comes out of the ether and realizes his legs are gone.
God in heaven, Jacob . . . how could I despise you?"

"Thank you." He bent down and kissed her on the forehead. "Merry Christmas, Ivy."

The House, January 2, 1917

Observations and Reflections. The House—*our* House. My present to Ivy. Gerard Dupont drove out from Paris in his limousine and we signed the papers in the drawing room. M. Dupont casting uneasy glances toward the windows, expecting to see German infantry emerge from the woods before he had my check in hand. The price for house and two acres of land is ridiculously low, but Dupont is more than happy at the deal. He views the Allied line from Arras to Reims as a sheet of glass about to be hit by an iron Teuton fist. Snow is thick on the ground, but M. Dupont remembers that the German hordes struck at Verdun in the dead of winter. "I shall be leaving for Geneva in a day or two," M. Dupont says. "For my health." I feel sure that, win or lose, M. Dupont will survive the war with all his assets intact.

January 3.

I was able today to mount the stairs with no problem—except spasms of intense pain, which I stoically ignored. Two fine bedrooms upstairs, one room empty, the other partially furnished. I sat down on the bed to ease my leg and Ivy sat beside me. We made love, she protesting at first that making love in the middle of the day is wicked. Pale sun through large windows. Is there anything more lovely than her body tinged with such a light? If there is, I'll take an option on it, as Uncle Paul would say. Silent, reflective exhaustion afterward. How fragile we are naked. Distant thunder growled and bumped along the horizon, making us both think of the Somme barrage. Had we been lying here between July and November, it might well have been the guns we heard, but the Somme

battles are bogged down in mud, snow, and freezing rain, the armies more exhausted than spent
lovers could ever hope to be. Still, the sound was
sobering. She goes back to Rouen tomorrow for
reassignment, most probably to All Souls in London—which is how my luck runs. Still, I'll be able
to wangle a trip to Blighty every month or so and
we can use Jacob's flat. I know now what Sherman
meant when he said war was hell.

Major Charles Greville studied the list placed on his
desk by the adjutant. The names of the living and the
names of the dead. Few of the names were familiar to
him—the battalion had received far too many replacements for that. Names without faces: Jenkins, A. P.;
Johns, D. R.; Johns, L.; Johnson, R.

Roster—2nd Royal Windsor Fusiliers
Duty strength: 18 July, 1916
    Officers 36   Other ranks 1005
Duty strength to date: 3 January, 1917
    Officers 8   Other ranks 325

He signed his name on the bottom of the typewritten
sheet: Maj. Chas. Greville (Acting Colonel).

"And that's that, I suppose."

"All correct and properly executed," the adjutant
said as he retrieved the lists.

"What happens now?"

"I send this to Brigade, who will send it to Corps,
who will pop it up to Fourth Army, who will in turn flip
it along to the War Office. Sometime between now and
spring we'll be fleshed out. Rather like ordering so
many links of sausage from the butcher shop."

The allusion seemed appropriate. Sausages to be fed
into some future sausage grinder. Charles stood up and
looked out the window. The village of Guyencourt-sur-
Noye lay beyond the ice-rimed glass, its narrow cobblestoned street meandering down to the frozen river and a

wooden bridge. What was left of the 2nd Battalion was billeted in the houses and barns. An exhausted unit licking its wounds and waiting for replacements before being sent back up the line. The barns where most of the men had their billets were far from warm, but they were infinitely cozier than the freezing mud of the Somme trenches. Food was good and plentiful, and there was an *estaminet* in the village that served wine and beer at a fair price. For the officers, Amiens, with its bars, restaurants, and brothels, was only ten miles up the road. Yes, life was sweet in Guyencourt-sur-Noye—not that it mattered to Charles. His leave papers were in his pocket. The signing of the roster was his last official act. The new battalion commander, a lieutenant colonel, would be arriving from Saint-Omer in a day or two.

"Well, Charles," the adjutant said, holding out his hand, "you did a bloody fine job."

And that was that. He took a train to Rouen, then a leave boat to Southampton, and finally a train to London. Twenty-four hours after shaking the adjutant's hand, he was walking through Victoria Station with a thousand other men, back in Blighty on leave, carrying his own kit bag, just one with the khaki mob.

"Charles . . . ! Charles . . . !"

Her voice was thin against the clatter of hobnail boots. He had almost forgotten that he had written to her, certainly hadn't expected her to meet him at the station, but there she was, beautiful in dark furs, waving to him from the far end of the platform.

"Hello, Lydia."

"Charles." She bent slightly toward him and kissed him on the cheek. He put down his kit bag, took her firmly in his arms, and kissed her on the mouth—a hard, lingering kiss.

"That's the way, ol' sport," a passing sergeant called out.

"Yes," Lydia murmured when he released her, "it is." She touched his face with a gloved hand. "It's good to have you back, Charles."

"And it's good to be here."

"I didn't tell Hanna and your father. Felt you wished to surprise them or you would have written to them."

"One letter was all I could manage. But, yes, it might be nice to just walk in."

She was looking at him oddly. "Are you all right?"

"I'm fine. Not a scratch."

He couldn't tell her how he felt because he couldn't explain how he felt. Disembodied, as though he were two people walking side by side. Flesh and shadow, and difficult to know which of the two was *him*.

"Do you want to go to Park Lane now and see them?"

"No," he said. "I'm horribly dirty. I'd like to go home, take a hot bath, and get to bed."

She gave his hand a squeeze. "Whatever you want, Charles."

The palest of light filtered through heavy silk curtains and glowed against the cream-colored walls of the bedroom. He was not there. He was floating off in some vast distance of time and space. Silent shell bursts crawled through a wasteland of pollarded trees. A man writhed against ripped sandbags, mouthing screams. The naked woman on the bed writhed as well, head twisting on the pillow. He was above it all. Serene. An impassive watcher. He felt nothing, neither pleasure nor pain. Beyond feelings of any sort. No room for frenzy. One must remain calm at all costs. The woman clutched at his back as the shadows of the second platoon slipped through curtains of rain. They became lost to view, then reemerged beyond the wire. Half a dozen bent figures.

Christ! Where's the rest of them?

Whose voice was that? he wondered. It hardly mattered. They were dead, of course. Foolish of the chap to have even asked.

"Lovely," Lydia whispered against his cheek. "Not the old Charles."

"No," he said stonily. "Not quite the same."

* * *

Watching his father made him think of the parable of the prodigal son, a roast sirloin of beef being a fitting substitute for a fatted calf. The earl carved the meat to perfection and Coatsworth served. It hadn't been his job in the old days, but the servant problem was acute—a condition that seemed to dominate the conversation.

"I really don't know what we'll do, Charles," Hanna said. "We're one of the last houses on the street that is still a private residence. The Prescotts donated their house to a branch of the war ministry, and Lord Doncannon gave up his place to the Red Cross. It's becoming quite impossible to maintain and I expect we'll have to move into a flat."

"Nonsense!" Lord Stanmore growled.

"I quite agree," Lydia said. "That is nonsense, Hanna. I know I can find you a perfect little house near Regent's Park that would suit you."

"Alex not home?" Charles asked, just to change the subject.

His father paused in his carving to swipe the knife against the steel.

"No. Decided to spend her leave in Paris. Can't for the life of me understand why."

"And William? Still at Eton?"

Hanna laughed nervously. "Good heavens, no, Charles."

"The lad's eighteen," the earl said. "Training with the Public Schools Battalion. He gets passed out as a second lieutenant next week."

"Difficult to believe," Charles said as Coatsworth bent forward to serve him. The slices of beef sent rivulets of scarlet juice across the white plate.

His mother seemed to be sending signals to him, and so when she excused herself right after dinner, complaining of a sudden headache, he dutifully escorted her up to her room.

"Headache better?" he asked as he closed the door behind him.

"Much." She faced him, her face pale and drawn. "May I be blunt, Charles?"

"By all means."

"William has become a terrible concern to me."

"Being in the army, you mean?"

"I can understand his anxiety to join up. He's big, strong, fiercely patriotic. He was in the Eton Boys' Brigade last term . . . and the term before that, I believe. All of his friends joined up as well . . . all with the same excessive zeal to serve their country. I can't fault that, can I?"

"No." He thought of young Baker waving his pistol. Second Lieutenant Owen Ralston Baker. In hospital now. Both eyes blown out by the same shell that had ripped poor Martin's hip. "It's becoming a boys' war now, Mother."

Her hand darted to her throat, fingers worrying a string of jet beads.

"William is such a superb horseman, as you know. It would please your father and me if he took a commission in the Queen's Bays—the Second Dragoon Guards. One was offered."

"Oh."

"That's all you can say?" she asked sharply. *"Oh?"*

"Oh is simply an interjection, Mother. It gives me time to think. Naturally he turned the offer down."

"Why *naturally?* It's one of the most prestigious regiments in the army."

"If this were the Boer War, he'd jump at it, but the cavalry is something of a joke in France. All dressed up and nowhere to go. His refusal to join the Bays is understandable. He's a true Greville."

"If . . . if he were *ordered* into the regiment . . ."

"As I was 'ordered' into NS Five?" He smiled and shook his head. "It won't work, Mother. You and Lydia should know better."

"What has Lydia got to do with it?" she asked cautiously.

"You know perfectly well what Lydia has to do with

it, Mother. Lydia has entree. Now more than ever with Lloyd George in Downing Street, Archie minister of war production, and David Langham as—what? The gray eminence? I'm sure Lydia could get Willie posted to the dragoons—'ordered,' if you will—but he'd only slip out of it."

"How could he slip out of a direct order?"

"By resigning his commission and then reenlisting as a private in an infantry regiment. He'd be commissioned by that regiment the same day. The infantry is starved for young subalterns after the Somme. Officers with fighting spirit are ducking out of the cavalry every day, using that dodge."

Hanna's laugh was like a wail. "Fighting spirit! I think William is too young to have 'fighting spirit.' He thinks the war is some sort of game . . . like a Rugby match!"

"Football," Charles said blandly. "Quite a few chaps kicked footballs toward the German lines when they went across. They were shot down, of course. Germans are such poor sports."

"Don't be so glib!" she hissed.

"Am I being glib, Mother? I'm sorry. But we must all take our chances. There's no room for cowardice in the British Army."

The fervidness of his tone surprised him.

The cocktail party had become firmly entrenched as a London social custom, replacing afternoon tea. There were those who claimed that the cocktail party had been invented by Lydia Foxe Greville. Not true, London's leading light-comedy actor remarked. It was simply that Lydia had raised the rather barbaric custom to a fine art. The house in Bristol Mews sparkled from sundown to early evening with bright, brittle conversation, or huddled, serious talk among huddled, serious men, the conversational gamut depending on which circle of Lydia's friends one happened to drift in upon. Charles found all of the talk boring. He stood apart from the

crowd, barely touching the contents of his cocktail glass
and letting the verbiage wash over him the way waves
wash over a rock in the sea. A woman with an ample
bosom only partially concealed by a gown in the latest
style came up to him and said: "I understand from Ivor
Novello that you've seen a good deal of the fighting in
Picardy."

And he said matter-of-factly: "You know, the first
thing that strikes one about the front is the almost over-
powering stench of human feces. It's the shells, you see.
Men tend to become terribly constipated—for a variety
of reasons—and then when they're hit by a shell all of
that *accumulation* simply bursts forth and is scattered
everywhere. It's more pronounced in summer, but that
stands to reason. Does it not?"

"What on earth did you say to Countess Bland-
hurst?" Lydia asked him soon after with a frown.

"Who? I haven't said a word to anyone all night."

"She feels insulted."

"Does she? How curious."

And there was David Langham, speaking to two admirals and the First Lord of the Admiralty.

"Haig is certainly aware of this U-boat problem. He
would like to break out of the Ypres salient and smash
for the channel ports . . . past Langemarck and Passchendaele to Bruges, cutting off Ostende and Zee-
brugge. He smells victory in that direction sometime
this summer."

"Only if the wind is in the proper direction," Charles
said.

He felt the sensation very strongly while walking
down Regent Street. It was morning, shopkeepers opening their shutters, the winter day bright and clear. Brisk,
cold wind. Patches of snow in the street, dirty gray piles
in the gutters. He walked slowly until he came to Conduit Street before daring to stop and look back. No one
was behind him, and yet he could have sworn that had
not been the case since he turned into Regent Street

from Hanover Square. Someone had been following him step for step, practically at his elbow. And yet that was clearly impossible. Odd. Shadow and substance. Which was which? He lit a cigarette and blew a stream of smoke into the wind, standing on the corner of Conduit until he had finished it, then crushing the butt under his foot. He continued walking, more quickly than before, and he was quite alone this time. Just Charles Greville in uniform, with his Burberry trench coat well buttoned up against the wind. He turned sharply—a drill turn, pivoting on the heel of the right foot—into Burlington Street and then into Savile Row. In the window of one shop he spotted a small, neatly printed sign which read: OFFICERS' TRENCH ACCESSORIES ALSO SOLD. He went in, the door ringing a copper bell as he opened it. It was a uniform shop primarily, and several young men were standing about in various stages of their fittings. One sat astride an elevated barrel which had been painted red and had a saddle fastened to it.

"Make sure the jacket doesn't blouse out."

"No fear of that, sir," the tailor said. "I can assure you."

He selected what he wanted from a display case, and the clerk nodded his approval.

"A fine choice, if I may say so, sir. Would you also be interested in a truly first-rate trench compass?"

"I don't think so," Charles said.

"Or a guaranteed water- and moisture-proof match-box."

"No. This will suffice. Thank you for your patience."

"No trouble at all, Major. We are here to serve."

"Quite so. As is everyone in these times."

He swung onto a bus leaving Piccadilly Circus for Southwark—Battersea—Clapham Junction—Wimbledon. He got out at the end of the line and walked to Wimbledon Common, toward neat rows of canvas-roofed clapboard and tar-paper huts. A wood draw-gate barred the path, a sentry from the Public Schools Battalion standing beside it with rifle and fixed bayonet. The man presented arms, and Charles walked around the gate, which was no more than a symbolic barrier to traffic, and on into the camp.

"Dashed nice of you to drop in, Major Greville," the second-in-command said, leaning back against his desk. "I believe we met at Albert last August."

"Perhaps. There was a Public Schools Battalion at High Wood."

"Yes, but we're primarily a training unit now. Our lads are being posted to any number of regiments."

Charles looked out the window of the hut. He could see the drill ground, squads of men marching in lines, a group of men far away at the old cricket grounds spearing straw dummies with bayonets.

"The training looks efficient."

"We turn out first-rate infantry subalterns . . . a credit to any regiment they join."

"Where will my brother be sent?"

The second-in-command, also a major, rubbed the side of his ear with his thumb.

"Well, a sticky situation, don't you know. Been ordered to the dragoons, but refuses to go. Wants to join the Fifth Bedfords in trenches near Arras." The man chuckled. "And he'll do it, too. Young Greville has a mind of his own."

"Yes, he does. I bought him something useful to have in trenches."

"Dashed good of you. He'll be along shortly. By the way, perhaps you'd like to give the lads a bit of a talk after mess. They've all heard my tales of the Somme any number of times. Another view of the show might be refreshing."

There was a crisp knock on the door and then William stepped into the hut, his boots and puttees covered with mud. He saluted his own major smartly and then grinned at Charles.

"Major Greville . . . sir!"

"Hello, Willie," Charles said. "There's something I want you to have."

The duty clerks and the OOD heard the quick splatter of shots and burst into the room from the outer office. Acrid blue smoke hung in spirals, drifting down toward the figure writhing on the floor, clutching a bullet-splintered knee. They hurled themselves on the trench-coated man holding a pocket pistol and bore him down across the top of a desk. He did not offer any resistance as he let the gun fall from his hand.

"What in God's name did you do?" the second-in-command shouted, coming out of his momentary paralysis.

"I gave him a Blighty," Charles said calmly. "He didn't shoot himself . . . he didn't shoot himself."

XIX

The rain had ceased, but ominous banks of cloud obscured the peaks of the Welsh mountains and slipped like dark smoke into the valleys. The crenelated façade of Llandinam War Hospital was shrouded in mist.

"Ugly-looking place," Fenton muttered as the driver of the car pulled up in front of the iron gates and called out to the gatekeeper.

Martin, seated beside Fenton in the back, leaned forward to peer through the windshield.

"An old castle?"

"No, just some Victorian coal baron's idea of a fitting house for himself. Wales is littered with such monstrosities. All of them," he added bitterly, "eminently suitable as lunatic asylums."

The sprawling house became less forbidding when they drove up to it. The dark brickwork was mellowed by a sheen of ivy that covered many of the walls, and the window frames had been freshly painted white. The grounds were neatly pruned and mowed and the gravel drive freshly raked. It could have been the clubhouse of some ancient, noble golf club if it hadn't been for the ambulances and drab-colored army cars parked in front of it.

"I shall wait for you, shall I?" the driver asked in a singsong voice.

"Yes," Fenton said. "We want to catch the London train at Llangollen at six-thirty."

"Oh, yes, sir, can be done, I think. If you have a mind to it."

"We do. I'm sure you can get a cup of tea if you can find the kitchens."

"Oh, yes, sir, I know my way about it, sir. I have been here before and that is the truth, sir."

"Nice little man," Martin said as he walked beside Fenton to the front door, slowly, leaning on his cane. He used only one cane now—a major advance in his recovery.

"All the Welsh are pleasant, but independent as hell. I hope he remembers to wait for us."

The once spacious foyer had been partitioned into cubicles for the use of the clerks and medical orderlies. A corporal in the RAMC took their names, asked them whom they had come to visit, and then led them out of the foyer, opened a thick locked security door, and told them to go along the passageway to the office of the resident doctor on duty. Once they stepped into the corridor, the oak-and-steel door closed behind them with a thud.

"I don't like one damn thing about this," Fenton muttered.

Neither did Martin, but he refrained from saying so.

The doctor was a jovial heavy-set man of fifty who introduced himself as Major Wainbearing: ". . . trained as a general surgeon. . . . Became a specialist in brain disease . . . and then into psychoanalytic science, a field of medical endeavor barely scratched. . . . Learning a great deal from this war . . . quite a gold mine of neurasthenic ailments. . . ."

"It must be very interesting," Martin said.

"Yes, it is." Major Wainbearing leaned back in his comfortable chair in his spacious, pleasant office and smiled affably at the two men seated across from his desk. "Now, then, you are Mr. Rilke, I take it—Major Greville's cousin."

"Yes, that's right."

"And you, of course, are Colonel Wood-Lacy."

No reply seemed necessary. Fenton fingered one of his shoulder tabs, tried to smile pleasantly, but found it impossible to do. The doctor folded his hands across his stomach and pursed his lips, a sudden frown appearing on his elderly cherub's face.

"Major Greville was brought here as a clearly diagnosed neurasthenic. He was passive—no restraint was needed—but he was hallucinating. . . . Deep in conversation with a certain Second Lieutenant Baker . . . a rambling monologue on Blighty wounds and firing squads. Are either of you familiar with a Lieutanant Baker?" They shook their heads. "No matter. He was soon out of that form of shock and quite normal within a week. He has remained so. We walked out of the grounds last Monday and played a round of golf at the links in Glyn-Ceiriog."

"How nice," Fenton murmured.

"He did damn well, considering the appalling state of the greens. On the way back we stopped at a place and had tea. I told him how pleased I was at his progress and that I was prepared to release him from here and to recommend a medical discharge from the army. Cured, you understand, but obviously too—*carefully* balanced to risk further military duties. I told him to go to some quiet spot and avoid stress of all sorts."

"Sound advice," Fenton said with thinly veiled sarcasm.

"He told me, in his gentle way, that if I did such a thing he would contrive, in some unspecified manner, to kill himself."

A wall clock chimed three dulcet tones.

"Do you think he was being serious?" Martin asked.

"Oh, no doubt in my mind at all. Quite a number of patients talk of suicide, but they are mostly impassioned threats, verging on the hysterical. It is the quiet, lucid statement of intent that we become concerned about."

"Perhaps if we talk to him . . ." Fenton said.

"Yes, by all means do. He's been looking forward to your visit. . . . The only two people he wishes to see. You know, his mother and his wife came here last month, but he stayed in his room and refused to come down to talk to them." He reached out and pushed a button on his desk. "One of the orderlies will take you to him. He'll be in the rec room, more than likely. And do stay for tea. We have a wizard pastry chef here."

Men in gray dressing gowns and pajamas stood staring out of windows or walking aimlessly in the corridors. A few of the patients were in uniform, but the badges of their rank and emblems of their regiment had been removed.

"All officers here, I presume," Martin said.

"Quite correct, sir," the orderly replied. "The men have their own shell-shock hospitals."

Martin noticed a tall gray-haired man who could easily have been a colonel or brigadier. He sat huddled in a corner with his hands firmly locked on top of his head. A younger man lay near him in a fetal position. Rank could mean nothing to those two, Martin thought, but class divisions had to be maintained no matter what the circumstances.

The rec room, with its banks of windows on three sides, was large and airy. It might have been a ballroom or music conservatory at one time, but now it was an untidy collection of sofas, chairs, card tables, and benches. A dozen men were in the room, the majority of them in uniform, reading or playing cards. One player's hands shook so violently that he could barely hold on to his cards.

"Major Greville's over there," the orderly said. "At the corner table."

Charles was in uniform, bent studiously over a writing tablet, and did not look up until they had walked up to the table and stood in front of him.

"Hello, chaps," he said quietly. "Good of you both to come."

"The least we could do, old boy," Fenton said with forced affability.

"You look good, Charles," Martin said.

"I feel very well," he said gravely. "They say that I'm cured."

"Yes," Martin said. "The doctor was telling us."

"Of course, they don't say exactly what one has been cured *of*, but I suppose they know what they're talking about. They do some quite remarkable things here in their quiet way. All through the gentle art of conversation. One simply talks. It supposedly clears the mind."

Fenton pulled two chairs up to the table. "And now you may talk to us, if you'll permit me to get right to the point."

Charles capped his pen and set it down beside the writing pad.

"I'm sure you feel uncomfortable being here, Fenton."

"Not in the least," he said a little too quickly. "If I can help you in any way—"

"You can both help me . . . if you will." Charles sorted through some neatly inscribed papers, folded two of the sheets, and placed them in envelopes. "I wrote a long letter to my father . . . and one to William at Charing Cross Hospital. Both were sent back to me unopened. There's not much point in writing to William again. I doubt if he will understand, or forgive, what I did. Perhaps he will one day, but not now. I've written a shorter, more concise, explanation to Father, which I would appreciate your handing to him, Martin. He might feel obligated to at least open it if he receives it from you. The other letter is for Lydia, which you can post. It's an apology—of sorts—for all manner of things. But I shan't bore you with that. As for you, Fenton, I ask a favor."

"Anything at all, old chap."

Charles picked up the pen and toyed with it, rolling it across the table from hand to hand.

"I was committed without a hearing. The medical officer of Willie's battalion judged me unsound of mind and I was sent here. Now, six weeks later, I am to be released as cured, handed a medical discharge from His Majesty's Forces, and put quietly out to pasture. I'm sure that will please the War Office. They're no more anxious to know why I shot Willie than my father is. The act of a temporary maniac. So be it."

Fenton leaned forward and folded his arms on the table. "I don't believe it was the act of a maniac and neither does anyone else . . . at least no one who has been in trenches. You snapped with the strain, Charles. Too many bloody weeks of having to stay calm in that hell. It took its toll. You didn't know what you were doing, and the very best course of action at the moment would be for you to accept a medical discharge and regain your full strength of mind."

"I have that now, Fenton. What I don't have is any *peace* of mind. I may not have been very lucid after I shot Willie, but I knew why I shot him. It was a deliberate, premeditated act, and I want the reasons for it to be made a matter of record—if not public, at least official."

"What sort of record are you talking about?"

"I've given this a lot of thought, Fenton . . . gone over it in my mind time and time again. I've been tracing my steps as it were, but backwards. The shooting of Willie in the knee . . . the buying of the pistol . . . the feeling that someone was walking just behind me . . . those weeks in trenches, in and out with the battalion. . . . The men who shot themselves . . . or killed themselves . . . or prayed they'd get shot so they could get out of that trap."

He paused and shook his head groggily. "So damn many thoughts whirling through my head that it's difficult to sort them all out in proper order, but I shall."

"Maybe you'd like to take a rest," Fenton suggested. "Lie down for a bit."

"No . . . not yet. I must settle this first. I'm sure that Martin understands the need to put experiences down on paper so others can read them and share them. That's the creed of a journalist, isn't it, Martin? Seeing to it that events are kept alive."

Martin exchanged puzzled glances with Fenton and
then said, "Are you asking me to write an article about
it?"

"No, not exactly. That wouldn't suffice, would it? I
mean to say, I doubt if many newspapers would want to
print it . . . too defeatist. And even if it were printed
in some anti-war paper, what would happen after it was
read? Yesterday's news . . . just an old scrap of newspaper blowing about in the gutters. What I want is a
record . . . a transcript . . . The kind of transcript
that you could provide, Fenton."

"Oh?" Fenton said. "And what sort of transcript is
that?"

"Why, the official transcript of my court-martial, of
course . . . for maiming, quite literally, a brother officer."

Fenton could merely stare at him. Martin gripped his
cane and tapped it gently against the floor. A tall
ruddy-faced man with Kitchener mustaches who had
been pacing restlessly from one end of the room to the
other suddenly strode up to the table, hands jammed
into the pockets of his dressing gown.

"Now look here, Randall," he shouted, staring hard
at Charles. "Get brigade artillery on the blower right
away. Tell the bastards that they're fifty yards short and
are hitting D Company . . . quite wasting the attack.
. . . Quite wasting it, sir!"

"I'll do it right away, Colonel," Charles said in a flat,
tired voice.

"See that you do!" the man said. "Bloody scrim-
shankers!"

"We get a lot of that here," Charles said after the
man had strolled away, apparently satisfied and at
peace. "There's a young chap in my room—a second
lieutenant I imagine, judging by his age. Spends most of
his time seated on his bed with the coverlet thrown over
his head. Still in his dugout at Delville Wood and won't
come out until the shelling stops. Not much older than
William. Only thing is, Fenton . . . Willie would never

have broken down. Too strong and brave for that. The best sort of man England can produce. Willie would have gone over the top like a shot, whistle in mouth and revolver in hand. He might have cleared our wire . . . gone ten, perhaps fifteen yards . . . and then died . . . for absolutely no purpose at all. Just like Roger."

Fenton licked dry lips, reached out, and gripped Charles by the wrist.

"Tell all that to Martin. Tell him everything that went through your mind before you pulled the trigger. Tell him everything that happened on the Somme . . . every damn horror that drove you to scuppering your own brother. He'll send it to America and a newspaper will print it. That's the only record you need. Don't ask for a court-martial, because you'll never get it."

Charles shook his head stubbornly. "I'd get a hearing, at least, wouldn't I? A hearing to see if a court-martial was justified. They would keep a transcript of it. . . . War Office document number whatever . . . inquiry into the shooting of Second Lieutenant William Greville by Major Charles Greville. One day, after the war, Willie could take it out of the archives and read it."

Fenton withdrew his hand and sat back stiffly in his chair. "I think you're bonkers, Charles. A man can't ask for his own court-martial."

"No," Charles said, "of course not, but you could demand that one be held. I told you I'd thought this out. It may be stretching a legal point, but you were technically my superior officer at the time. I was on leave and my new orders hadn't reached me yet. The Windsors were attached to your brigade."

A bell rang for tea and someone in the room cried out in terror, "Gas! Gas!" Someone else said soothingly, "It's all right, Smithy . . . all right, lad."

"It happens every time they ring that bloody bell," Charles sighed. "I do wish they'd install something less strident."

"Now look here, Charles," Fenton said firmly. "The

brass aren't fools. They'd know something was fishy if I put in such a request."

"Not request, Fenton . . . *demand*. You have that right and the Judge Advocate General's office would be forced to hold a hearing. I hate to sound like a barracks room lawyer, but there it is. King's regulations."

He looked pleased with himself, and Fenton's scowl deepened.

"You want a forum. That's it, isn't it, Charles? You just want to stand up before a panel and a stenographer and voice your outrage at what went on over there."

"At what's still going on," Charles said, so quietly they could barely hear him. "And will continue to go on . . . and on . . . and on. Yes. That is precisely what I want." He folded his hands, the fingers as white as the writing paper they rested on.

"Christ," Fenton said, pushing back his chair and standing up. "You're asking a lot of me."

"Yes."

"As a soldier I should turn you down flat, but I'm more than that, aren't I? I'm your friend. This won't change a damn thing. It's just a gesture that no one is going to appreciate, but if it will give you some kind of peace, then I'll do it."

"Thank you," Charles said, staring at his hands. "I knew you wouldn't let me down."

Fenton sat in brooding silence during the ride to the railway station at Llangollen. It had started raining again, and the dark hills and crags of north Wales looked sinister in the gloom. They barely caught the London-bound train as it stopped briefly on its run from Holyhead. The carriages were filled with Irish troops from County Down and Antrim, most of them sporting bits of orange cloth in their hatbands to show their contempt for the "wearin' o' the green." They were all in boisterous spirits. Out of training camp at last, heading for the war: "Look out, Kayzer Bill!"

"Bloody idiots," Fenton muttered as he slumped into a seat in a virtually empty first-class compartment. An Irish colonel and his adjutant were the only other occupants, and the colonel glanced up curiously from a newspaper.

"Did you address me, sir?"

"No, sir, I did not. I was discussing the weather with my friend."

"Yes. A man can drown in Wales when it rains. And the Taffies have the gall to say Belfast is wet!"

"I suppose you had no choice," Martin said quietly after the Irish colonel had turned back to his paper. "He obviously has a fixation about this court-martial thing and if you had turned him down—"

"He might have killed himself. That thought had some slight effect on my decision."

"What happens now?"

Fenton drummed his fingers on the window ledge and stared at his own reflection in the rain-streaked glass.

"I send in my—*demand* through the proper channels, and the Judge Advocate's office will set a hearing date. Before that happens there will be a few gentlemanly calls from various staff brigadiers in Whitehall, asking me to reconsider my action. I shall decline to do so on the grounds that I consider the shooting of one officer by another bad form. There will be a hearing, and Charles will be permitted to talk for as long as he wishes in order to explain, justify, or defend his act. The panel will then deliberate for a second or two and rule that no court-martial is warranted because of the mental condition of the accused. Charles will then be sent back to the hospital and quietly discharged from the service. Rather a waste of everyone's time, isn't it?"

"Reading about this frog general in the *Standard*," the Irish colonel said, looking up. "Nivelle . . . hero of Verdun, they call him. Claims to have a plan that'll crush Fritz in twenty-four hours. Twenty-four years is more like it. The poor sod." He turned pages and immersed himself in the sporting news.

"And the war goes on," Fenton said wearily. "I'm glad Charles is out of it."

"But he isn't out of it, is he? It's all spinning around in his brain. You were right in saying that he's seeking some kind of peace, and if his hearing will give it to him it won't be a waste of *everyone's* time."

"No, I suppose you're right."

"Would they allow me to be there? Not as a member of the press, but as Charles's cousin?"

"No. They wouldn't allow God himself to attend. There'll be a panel of two or three officers . . . a clerk stenographer . . . Charles, and myself. Charles could request counsel, what's known as a prisoner's friend, but that would have to be a fellow officer and he doesn't need one."

"Please write me how it turns out . . . care of AP, rue Chambord. Will you do that?"

"Of course. When are you going back to Paris?"

"Sometime tomorrow. As you said, the war goes on."

Wales had been corrosive to the spirit—so had writing up the request for court-martial. Both were behind Fenton now as he arrived at his mother's house in Suffolk, where Winifred was staying. He found solace lying on the bed with her, his hands moving gently over the great bulge of her womb.

"We're going to have a forty-pound baby. I swear it."

"Twins," she said. "At least I think so. I'm sure I can feel two distinct pairs of kicks."

"Clever girl," he murmured, kissing the taut skin. He could sense the life beating beneath the surface.

"Happy?"

"Yes."

"Do you want sons very badly?"

"I want children very badly . . . sons or daughters. I'll leave that up to you. Surprise me."

"Another few weeks."

"Must be pure hell for you."

"Not really . . . Just boring sitting around . . . and uncomfortable trying to walk. Your mother and Jinny wait on me hand and foot. I feel horribly pampered, like some grossly fecund queen bee. Do you think my body will ever get back into shape . . . or will I always be nothing but breasts and belly?"

"I like breasts and bellies," he said, kissing both. "And I love you."

They clung tightly to each other as the March winds moaned across the river and hammered at the casement window.

"You haven't said a word about Charles," she said softly.

"There isn't a great deal to say. A sad man in a sad place. Just one more casualty of the Somme—Charles Greville and four hundred thousand other men."

He didn't tell her about the request for the court-martial, or the fact that Charles had contemplated suicide. Winifred had enough to think about being with child and worrying about her brothers John and Bramwell, who had gone through the Thiepval attacks and were now back in trenches near Arras.

"Does Lydia see him often?"

"I gather he doesn't want to see her . . . or his mother. There's really nothing he wants to talk about except the war."

And nothing that Fenton wanted to talk about less, but there was no escaping it. On the third morning home the telephone rang; a Brigadier Tydman was ringing up from London:

"About this court-martial request of yours for Major Greville. Sticky business, don't you know. . . . Be much better all 'round if you reconsidered it."

"I can't do that, sir."

"Can't, eh? Rather delicate, to tell you the truth . . . peer's son and all that. Chap went 'round the bend and plunked his own brother. Medical wallah of the Public Schools Battalion did the proper thing . . . certified him mentally unsound and sent him right up to Llandinam Hospital. That kept the whole sad affair quiet, don't you know. No point in kicking sleeping dogs now, to use a figure of speech."

"I'm sorry, but I insist on a hearing."

"I see. . . . Well, won't interfere with your rights as the lad's superior officer, although I strongly disapprove of your insistence. Rather harsh, I must say. Very well then . . . Hearing set for Thursday next . . . at Llandinam . . . North Wales. Better than bringing the chap down to London for it."

"Make certain a shorthand stenographer is along."

"We're quite capable of conducting a proper hearing," the brigadier said stiffly. "Good day, sir."

Paris, March 12, 1917

Observations and Reflections. Trying to catch up on this. Too damn busy writing personality pieces on General Nivelle, Pétain, and all the other new luminaries of the French Army to pay much attention to this journal. Papa Joffre of the big belly is out. Nivelle with his good looks, good English, good manners, and boundless optimism is very firmly in. Every shoeshine boy in Paris knows what Nivelle has in mind, as, I imagine, does every shoeshine boy in Berlin. Keeping secrets is not an Allied military virtue. A million poilus along the Aisne preparing to lunge for the chemin des Dames and burst through the Hindenburg defenses like water through a dike of sand. British to aid the offensive by striking around Arras. God help all of them.

Difficult even after ten days to write about Charles without experiencing a sinking feeling in the pit of the stomach. Shell shock. No two doctors seem to agree on the cause. French medical officer I met at Maxim's one night says that shell shock is caused by a partial vacuum created by passing shells, affecting the brain cells. I believe that it

means being shocked, period. Shocked by too
many corpses, too much pain, too many hopeless
attacks. Too many days and nights of never-ending
fear. Shock after shock until the mind can no
longer take any more punishment and begins to
turn in upon itself. Charles is a shell shock case.
Too much sangfroid for his own good. I know now
what he was thinking when he stood on the parapet at High Wood and watched his men get slaugh-
tered in the wire and among those nightmare trees.
He was thinking the thoughts of the damned and
keeping them bottled up inside. Something had to
give in that noble head of his.

Lord Greville, ninth Earl of Stanmore. More
sangfroid in action. I went to the house directly
from the train, still damp from Wales.

"So, you saw Charles, did you?" he said when I
handed him the letter. He opened the envelope
and read the contents without blinking an eye.

"Thank you," he said, putting the letter in his
pocket as though it were a bill from his tailor. I
was invited to stay for a drink, but sensed it was
merely a gesture of politeness and so I declined.
Aunt Hanna is up in Derbyshire, where they have
a small estate, looking after William, who is recuperating there. And how is William? I ask. "He
will never ride a horse properly for the rest of his
life." Odd answer. Charles is in such a delicate
mental balance, he could end up not knowing a
horse from a steamroller. Does the earl's attitude
come with the blood? Cold and blue? Hard to say.
May be no more than a pose. Bad form to reveal
one's deepest emotions. The earl stands in his
magnificent study overlooking Park Lane very
much the way Charles stood on the top of his
trench.

About fifteen minutes with Ivy, in the main reception room of All Souls. Is it possible she's my
wife? Hard to believe. We held hands in a room

about the size of Victoria Station, filled with the relatives of wounded men. Simple-looking people. Londoners mostly. The "lower orders," as the earl would say. The Somme offensive has been over for four months, but the residue packs the wards. Eighteen-hour work shifts for the nurses, more for some of the surgeons. Over in Whitehall the lights burn as new offensives are planned. "Mum" and "Dad" wait patiently in the vaulted room to see their sons, bearing small gifts wrapped in newspaper.

"Assiduous diarist, aren't you, Martin?"

"Well," Martin said, glancing up at the bureau chief, "I like to scribble away. I find it relaxing."

"Care for a drink at the Café Bombe?"

"No. My hip's giving me hell. Must be the weather. I'll be able to predict rain till the day I die."

"Take a week off. Go up to that house of yours in Saint Germain and forget your troubles. I just got a cable from Atkinson. That piece you did on Pétain . . . the 'Warrior Monk' thing. First-rate reception. The *Atlantic* gobbled up the magazine rights. Congratulations. Your telephone work out there?"

"Sometimes."

"Well, if anything comes up, I'll send the kid out to fetch you."

And so this was a break, Martin thought as he took the Métro at Parc Monceau. He had had it up to the neck with interviewing generals and listening to all the theories on how the war could be won *'rapidement.'* At Louveciennes, troop trains rumbled north across the Seine. Bearded poilus stood in the open doorways smoking their pipes—impassive-looking men, veterans. The troops no longer waved and cheered from the trains as they had done during the first year of the war. But then no one was doing much cheering these days.

The house looked good to him, a place of his own, the deed signed, sealed, and delivered. Rilke Manor.

Seven rooms and a kitchen. The trees in the garden were barren and stalky, but they would burst into greenery in the spring. The windows were tightly shuttered, and a pale wisp of smoke rose from one of the chimneys.

"What the—" He stood transfixed on the path and wondered if he should hurry down to the inn for help. But that seemed stupid. A housebreaker wouldn't light a fire. "Jacob," he muttered to himself. And when he unlocked the door, there he was, standing in the hall looking sheepish.

"Now how in hell did you get in?"

"Penknife. Slipped it under a shutter."

"That's nice to know," Martin said irritably. "Why didn't you come by the office? I would have given you a key."

"Didn't have the time, old sport. Two beefy *flics* were right on my heels."

"Detectives?"

Jacob nodded. His face was haggard and there were dark rings under his eyes.

"Sûreté Nationale. I came a cropper, Martin. Only two issues of the paper, and every gendarme in Paris came pouring into the print shop, busting heads with truncheons. I dove through a window without a sou in my pockets and legged it out."

"It was bound to happen sooner or later."

"One of the writers betrayed us." He ran his hands through his hair and smiled bitterly. "God Almighty, never get mixed up with strident anti-war types. Not one damn thing you do pleases even one-quarter of them. My particular Judas was an elderly anarchist who was furious with me for not devoting the first issue to a primer on how to assassinate politicians and generals. Not that I'm particularly against that sort of thing, you understand, but I thought it a bit thick for the first issue. Anyway, cutting a long story short, I'm on the run from a charge of sedition, and this seemed the best place to hide."

"Stay as long as you like."

"I'll borrow some cash from you and try to get into Spain . . . or even go back to Blighty. At least they don't shoot you there for having a difference of opinion."

Jacob moped around the house for two days, debating with himself whether to go to Madrid and put out another paper, which might be smuggled into France, or return to England and take his chances as a conscientious objector. His depression was palpable, like a dark cloud following him from room to room. It was on the morning of the third day that Danny, the copy boy and general errand runner, arrived from Paris on his battered motorcycle. Along with a few letters and some articles for proofing, he carried a bulky package in his canvas knapsack.

"A limey officer dropped this off at the office, Mr. Rilke. Said he was doing a favor for a Colonel Wood-Lacy and that it was to be given to you personal."

"Thanks, Danny. Anything new on the wires?"

"U-boats sank another American ship. . . . Congress looks ripe for voting for war in a few weeks . . . and McGraw predicts the Giants will take the pennant this year."

"Good for McGraw. At least there's some sanity left in the world."

There was a letter attached to the brown paper parcel.

Dear Martin:

Enclosed is a copy of the transcript, which I managed to get hold of. After reading it, I think you will understand why I sent it to you. Charles's agonized reflections on the war deserve something more meaningful than a filing cabinet in Whitehall. Just what you can do with it in light of the times I do not know, but I want you to have the ms. nonetheless.

The proceedings went just the way I said they

would go. Charles spoke for two hours or more in front of three impassive men from the Judge Advocate's office. Their findings were foregone—no court-martial justified and Charles to remain at the hospital until the doctors see fit to discharge him. I have sent this across with a friend so as to avoid censors or other curious types pawing over the contents.

Best,
Fenton

"What is it?" Jacob asked, glancing over Martin's shoulder as he sat reading the typed document. "Copy of a lawsuit?"

"More of an indictment, Jacob. But of course, you wouldn't have heard about it. Charles Greville shot his brother in the leg in January while home on leave."

"Good God! Why?"

Martin touched the loose pages he had already read. "You can discover that reason for yourself."

Jacob drew a chair up to Martin's desk. He barely glanced at the first two pages, merely noticing the stilted language of the panel judge explaining the purpose of the hearing, but the first paragraph of Charles's statement held his attention as nothing had ever done before:

I entered this war with the highest of ideals and the firmest of faith in the rightness and justness of my patriotism . . ."

They read through the document several times, Martin lying on the sofa, Jacob slowly pacing the room.

"It took guts for old Fenton to get this hearing for Charles," Jacob said. "I can see why the War Office was content to just let things lie. A pretty damning statement."

"Only if people read it," Martin said quietly.

"I gather that's what Fenton would like to see happen."

"I couldn't get this published, you know that. It's too critical of the high command's handling of the Somme attacks—too outraged at the battle being turned into nothing more than bloody attrition, huge losses being justified because the Germans were suffering on the same scale. A British Verdun. The censors would turn it down flat. And even if I took it back to the States in my pocket, I doubt if I could find a paper that would touch it. They've got war fever over there now. No editor wants to print a cold shower."

Jacob began to stalk the room in agitation, puffing on a cigarette and letting the ashes scatter across the rug.

"Christ, it isn't propaganda . . . it isn't even that critical of the war. It just damns the conduct of it, the senselessness of pushing men against machine guns and barbed wire over and over again. The whole thing is one long cry of despair for men caught in a trap. Every Tommy knows what the Somme was like, but the civilians turn a deaf ear to their stories. Hell, they just like to read the papers and see 'Great Gains' printed on the banner, and study the war maps—the enlarged portions that make every advance look impressive unless you realize the scale is in yards, not miles."

"That's all well and good, Jacob, but the hard fact remains—"

"That the wire services or the newspapers wouldn't touch it? Fine. Sod the bastards! Let's print it ourselves—a thousand copies or more, well printed and bound. . . . Send copies to every member of Parliament . . . every churchman . . . every intelligent human being we can think of."

"Have you been at the brandy?"

"No. I'm drunk with purpose all of a sudden. I feel like flashing a bright light into dark corners. I'd like to see some MP with guts stand up in the House with this statement in his hand and cry out, 'What in the name of God is going on over there? Let's find some generals who aren't dead from the neck up!' " He slumped into a chair, a smoldering cigarette butt pasted to his lower lip. "All right. I'm sober now. That was just Jacob Golden being carried away by his own rhetoric, as usual. You're quite right, Martin. No one wants to read something that might make them question their faith in the war leaders or the holy purity of their cause. To die in battle is such a noble death, isn't it? The wisest thing you can do with Charles Greville's cry to the heavens is put it neatly away in a drawer."

Martin chewed an unlit cigar and stared at the ceiling.

"*Could* we print it?"

"Are you serious?"

"Yes."

Jacob leaned forward and flipped his cigarette butt into the fireplace.

"Not here, unless you care to see the inside of a French prison. Could be done in Switzerland, but getting copies over the border would be very difficult. The French are horribly suspicious of printed matter. Could be done easily enough in London, of course."

"Why 'of course'?"

"My mother's brother, my Uncle Ben, prints foreign books. . . . Russian, Ukrainian, Yiddish. Has a fine letterpress in Whitechapel. Used to work there sometimes as a kid before I got hauled away to prep school and Eton. I can still smell the ink he used."

Martin scowled at his cigar and bit off the tip. "Wouldn't be much point in printing this in Ukrainian."

"Ben? He has fonts of half the world's languages . . . even English. The man collects typefaces the way some men collect old wines. Type and socialism, Ben's twin passions."

"You'd be running a risk going back to England, wouldn't you, Jacob?"

"Well, I'm running a risk staying here, aren't I? All that can happen to me in England is that they give me a choice—go back into the army or get tucked away in a CO camp and spend the rest of the war tilling the soil.

Not the worst fate I can think of. It's a risk I'm willing to run. You face a bigger one, Martin. This transcript is definitely critical of the war and would be an embarrassment to the War Office and the General Staff. They could label you an unfriendly journalist and take away your press passes. The French war ministry works hand in glove with ours, so you might just be twice damned. I can't see how much use you'd be to the Associated Press if you weren't allowed within a hundred miles of the war zone."

"I wouldn't be the first AP correspondent ever kicked out of a war zone because he rubbed brass the wrong way."

"And then there's Fenton. Wonder how much will come down on his head? If he hadn't pushed for a hearing . . ."

Martin swung his legs off the sofa with a groan and then bent toward the table, where the transcript lay scattered. He sorted the pages together with firm purpose.

"He never would have sent this to me if he were afraid of repercussions. This was his cast of the die. Come on, Jacob, if we hurry we can catch the night train to Le Havre."

London, March 25, 1917

Observations and Reflections. There is a great sense of satisfaction in setting type. For me, it is a return to print shop—10 point Baskerville, cranking out the Lincoln High School yearbook on the platen press. A copy of the slim paperbound book that we have worked so hard on lies before me. Far better printed than the old Lincoln High thing, although the method of producing it was essentially the same. Jacob's Uncle Ben designed it, chose the typeface, helped Jacob and me compose the type, and picked out the paper. A master printer's job. Title page reads:

AFTER THE SOMME

An inquiry into the advisability of
court-martial of Major The Rt. Hon. Charles
Greville, 2nd Royal Windsor Fusiliers,
conducted at Llandinam War Hospital

WITH AN INTRODUCTION BY
Martin Rilke, Associated Press

God willing, I will have grandchildren one day,
and they will wish to know why the old man stuck
his neck out a country mile and put his name on
the document. The fact is, I had not thought of
doing it, but Uncle Ben, who looks more like one
of the prophets than anyone's uncle, argued that
the book needed a touch of authenticating, England being the land of the literary hoax and
Charles Greville himself not being available for in-
terview. And so I sat in a corner of Uncle Ben's
shop and wrote an introduction, explaining who I
was and what I had seen of this war to date and
who Major Greville was to me. My cousin's story,
I said, and perhaps your son's story, or your brother's or father's story. "Be cool but passionate,"
Uncle Ben advised. Uncle Ben is a man who
speaks in contradictions. Above his desk there are
two framed, signed photographs. One is of the anarchist Kropotkin, the other of King Edward VII.
The two men appear to be winking at each other
and smiling down on Uncle Ben at the same time.
"Confusion is not always disorder," Uncle Ben
murmurs from time to time. "A poor tool will often blame the workman."

March 28. Hyde Park.
Managed to spend one night with Ivy, Jacob
discreetly leaving the flat to us and taking a hotel
room. She has been curious about my stay in London and I told her the truth. She read the little

book, sitting up in bed with my robe around her shoulders, not saying anything until she had turned the final page. It is nothing new to her—the self-inflicted wounds, the intense gratitude that once-strong men feel when they are carried out of the line with a crushed leg or a shattered hand or arm. Blighty wound. "Better to be a cripple than a corpse, mate." She knows I may get into trouble when this thing is sent around. May even lose my English visa and my French *permis de séjour*. Everyone very touchy at the moment. British battle casualties well over the seven-hundred-thousand mark, the French a great deal more, a major battle about to begin as Nivelle completes his final plans for ending the war before summer. Rumors everywhere among the press corps in London that Nivelle is in for a terrible surprise if he tries to take the chemin des Dames by frontal assault. America trembling on the brink of jumping into this war with both feet and closed eyes. Lousy timing for an indictment of Western Front generalship and the callousness of slaughter. But my Ivy does not try to dissuade me. She is blunt about it. "I have my job and you have yours. Do what you feel is right." Solid Norfolk speech. She may go back to the hospital trains soon—Calais to Poperinghe—so I give her the key to Rilke Manor just in case AP ships me to Timbuktu until the dust, if any, settles. She can use the house when she gets short leaves, give it the woman's touch. Go over the finances with her like an old married couple working out the budget. She is stunned by the balance in the Banque de Rothmann. "You should put it to work for you, Martin." Sounds just like Uncle Paul.

"Hope I'm not breaking your chain of thought."

Martin closed his notebook as Jacob sat down with a weary grunt on the bench beside him.

"No, I was just bringing things up to date."

"Must read that voluminous journal of yours one day, Martin. Give me something to do in my old age."

"All sent out?"

"Well, enough to start things going. Frightening the number of copies Ben ran off. He got quite carried away."

They sat in silence and watched ducks glide across the ruffled waters of the Serpentine. Anti-aircraft guns and searchlights could be seen near the Dell, the slender cannon tubes pointed at the sky, waiting for clear nights and the Gothas or Zeps. There were more guns across the park near the statue of Peter Pan. Guns all across Europe, from Hyde Park to the Swiss border—a thick dark blanket of guns and wire and men.

"It's a very *small* book, isn't it, Jacob?" Martin said softly.

The Honorable Arthur Felchurch, MP, member from Twickenhurst, began the book at breakfast and finished it at the Commons before debate began on the railroad expansion bill. He found it quite curious.

"Odd," he remarked to a fellow Conservative, "this fellow appears to feel quite justified in shooting his own brother in the kneecap."

"What on earth did he do that for, Arthur?"

"Damned if I know."

The Honorable Harold Davidson, Liberal member from Coventry, read his copy as he was driven to Parliament from his flat in Russell Square. He skimmed through most of it because he was a very busy man, but he read enough to add more fuel to his already burning distrust of General Sir Douglas Haig. He knew that the House disliked its members to openly discuss war policies, but after the first debate on the railway bill had been concluded to no one's satisfaction, he asked for the floor and launched into a tirade about Haig's misman- agement of the Somme offensives.

"I 'ave in my 'and a book. . . ." he shouted, beginning a thirty-five-minute speech. But hardly anyone remained in his seat to listen to him, not even members of his own party.

The Honorable David Langham left his usual afternoon meeting with the Prime Minister at number 10 Downing Street and told his driver to take him to Bristol Mews. Only two guests were there: the young Countess of Ashland—without her husband, as usual—and a tall, robust Australian captain who had been a professional Rugby player before the war. The captain and the countess were surreptitiously touching hands as they sat on one of the divans. Lydia Foxe Greville fixed Langham a gin and French vermouth cocktail and then followed him into an adjoining study and closed the door.

"I suppose you've come to bring me a copy of poor Charles's book."

"Yes," he said. "I have one in my briefcase. Care to read it?"

"Not if I can avoid it—but people have been ringing me up all day to tell me about it. The Greville family solicitor telephoned this morning, too. Charles is seeking a divorce. Of course, I shall be happy to give him one. I feel just awful, but Charles did bring all this trouble on himself, didn't he?"

"I suppose you could say that." He reached out and touched her lightly on the face. "You look very drawn and beautiful and tired. I leave for Paris on Monday to have some things out with Ribot and Painlevé . . . also to have a private chat with Georges Clemenceau. Why don't we meet at the Crillon . . . say, Thursday next?"

"That might be nice," she said. "London is so tiresome."

Lieutenant General Sir Julian Wood-Lacy stalked the tiny office in Whitehall, slapping his booted leg with a leather swagger stick. Through the narrow window he could see Big Ben etched against the sky.

"I can't tell you how painful this is, Fenton."

"I'm sure it must be, sir."

"For the life of me, I can't fathom your obstinacy in requesting a court-martial." He looked away from the window and slapped at his leg with the stick. "*A court-martial!* Damnedest thing I ever heard of! Well, what's done is done, as the chap said. Sir Wully was fit to be tied. He's thin-skinned as it is where Haig is concerned, and he found that little pamphlet, or whatever the hell it is, downright libelous, sir. How did that newspaper wallah get hold of the transcript?"

"I gave it to him."

The old general nodded, almost sadly. "Always said I'd thrash you if you ever lied to your uncle. Well, dash it, sir, the truth hurts."

"What happens now? A court of inquiry, I suppose."

"Great Scott, no! The less done about this matter from now on the better. But it means a decided setback in your career, Fenton. No possibility of your becoming permanent commander of a line brigade. You'll be fortunate to find yourself sanitation officer in a Liverpool training barracks!"

"One other thing you used to say, sir. One takes what comes in the army."

The general turned his back, clearing his throat loudly.

"Quite so, my boy . . . quite so."

The telephone call was expected. Martin had already been on the phone for half an hour with the London bureau chief. His bag was packed and he sat by the telephone, waiting. When it rang he picked it up immediately.

"Martin Rilke?"

"Speaking."

"Ah, yes, Davengarth here, Ministry of Information. You caused a bit of a flap here. Do wish you'd taken the trouble to clear the document with the press censor's office. Ah, well, the impetuosity of the fourth es-

tate, what? Well, look here, Rilke, no point in your
coming in here now. Your Mr. Bradshaw phoned us
and said you were being reassigned . . . going back to
America, I take it."

"That's right. New York."

"Well, bon voyage . . . and we hope to have you
back here again one day. Perhaps after the war."

"Yes," Martin said, hanging up. "After the war."

Lord Crewe turned the book every which way, then
thumbed slowly through it, feeling the paper, tracing the
clean imprint of type, sniffing the ink. A Benjamin De
Haan printing job if ever he saw one. He laid it carefully, almost reverently, on his table while Ranscome,
the feature editor, watched him expectantly.

"Damn fine little book," the editor said. "Wish we
could give it a play. No chance of it, of course."

"That's correct," Lord Crewe replied. "No chance of
it. A bad wind for that type of sail." He folded his large
hands across his middle and leaned back in his chair.
"Did we get that piece from Logan yet?"

"Just came over the wire . . . having it typed up
now. He says the spirit of the troops at Arras is first
rate . . . buoyantly optimistic, as he puts it."

"Good. That's what people want to read about,
Ranscome—the buoyant spirit of their lads."

Jacob Golden carried the paper carton through the
streets of Whitechapel until he spotted a bus heading for
Charing Cross. He sat on the open top deck, savoring
the sunshine and the wind, the heavy carton resting on
the seat beside him. Traffic was heavy along the Strand,
the huge War Savings rally in Trafalgar Square spilling
over into the adjacent streets. He got off the bus and
pushed his way slowly through the crowd, moving toward the throbbing drums and shrilling fifes of the London Rifle Brigade band. A man clutched at his arm and
tapped the side of the carton.

"Sellin' ices, chum?"

Jacob balanced the carton on his hip, opened the top flaps, pulled out a book, and pressed it into the man's hands.

The man stared at it in surprise. "What's your game? London Bible Mission?"

"Something like that," Jacob said, moving on into the crowd.

The Rifle Brigade band marched slowly with firm step round and round the broad stone platform at the base of Nelson's column, the sun glinting off fifes and the drum major's baton, the strains of "The British Grenadiers" stirring the crowd to cheers. Tiny Union Jacks in a thousand hands were being waved in time to the music. Ranged wheel to wheel in a square below the platform were artillery pieces of pristine newness, the proud gunners who stood before them having polished them like gems: 6-inch howitzers, 8-inch howitzers, a battery of field guns, and two monster 15-inch crushers that nearly dwarfed the lions that sat hunched far below the admiral's distant figure. And attached to each gun was a small neat sign, giving its price to the taxpayer in pounds, shillings, and pence.

"INVEST IN WAR SAVINGS!" a voice appealed over a loudspeaker, the words forming a rhythm contrapuntal to the martial music. "HELP THE BOYS DO THE JOB! YOUR KING AND YOUR COUNTRY NEED . . . YOU!"

Jacob stood by one giant olive-painted iron wheel, the barrel of the howitzer looming above him, angled toward the upper story of Admiralty House, which could be seen beyond Cockspur Street. Raising the carton above his head, he placed it on an iron flanged tread at the top of the wheel and then quickly climbed up the spokes and straddled the breech.

" 'Ere, now!" a sergeant gunner called out. "Get off there."

He reached down for the carton, picked it up, and held it in front of him. The gunner made a grab at him, but he propelled himself forward, thighs gripping the sun-warmed barrel, up and up and out over the crowd. He heard laughter now and shouts of encouragement from below.

"Pop down the spout, mate!"

He smiled at them. He saw an ocean of white faces below and fluttering squares of red, white, and blue.

"KAISER BILL SAYS KEEP YOUR HANDS IN YOUR POCKETS. . . . BRITTANIA SAYS . . . BUY THESE GUNS."

He was on the lip of the barrel now, the carton before him. Reaching in, he picked up book after book and sent them flying off into the crowd—whirling flutters of paper, grabbed for by eager hands. Half a dozen constables shouldered their way through the crowd, hard-faced and implacable. When the final book was gone, he lay contentedly back along the great steel barrel and waited for the bobbies to climb up and get him.

He asked the taxi driver to wait for him and then hurried into All Souls. The hospital had never seemed so huge, or so crowded, and he felt a momentary panic that he wouldn't be able to find her, but the clerks at the reception desk located her without any trouble, and he was soon walking quickly down a long corridor toward the multiple-amputee ward, where she was on duty. She was his wife and he wanted her with him, but he knew the impossibility of that, couldn't even ask her as he held her hands tightly in an aisle between rows of beds, the mutilated men watching them with drugged eyes. He held her hands and kissed her on the cheek, and then a matron called for her impatiently from the far end of the ward.

He could still feel the softness of her skin against his lips as he sat in the back of the taxi. The driver sped down Gower and through a maze of streets toward Charing Cross Station, but crowds streaming away from Trafalgar Square suddenly blocked their progress like a wall.

"Sorry, guv'nor," the driver said. "Can't be 'elped, but you won't miss your train."

He didn't really care if he missed it or not. "Going home," the AP man had told him. A wry joke. He felt that he was home now and on his way to a strange and alien place. He sat stiffly on the seat, not seeing the crowds or the line of big guns being hauled slowly out of the square and into Whitehall. The great iron wheels churned up paper, the wind taking the scraps and blowing them like pale leaves across the pavement and into the street.

BOOK FOUR

November 11, 1920

Shall they return to beatings of great bells
In wild trainloads?
A few, a few, too few for drums and yells,
May creep back, silent, to still village wells
Up half-known roads.
　　　　　—WILFRED OWEN (1893–1918)

XX

Hotel Gaillard, Hazebrouck

Observations and Reflections. Heaven knows there has been enough soul searching about it, but now it has been done and the rightness of it must wait for the verdict of history. Benteen of the *Journal-American* felt it would do more harm than good, would reopen the wounds now so delicately healed, but I argued against that, as did Fletcher and Wilde and the other AP men, as well as Warrington of UP. It seems, somehow, right to have waited for the second anniversary. Last year was too soon, the armies barely demobilized, the shock of the war still too numbing for any quiet reflection on it to be possible. But we have turned a corner now, stepped into not merely a new decade but what would appear to be another age. The promised return to "normalcy" made Warren Gamaliel Harding president-elect last week. Perhaps it is now "normalcy" to express grief in one final public outpouring and then permit the dead to rest forever in peace, forgotten except in our own memories. Anyway, the deed has been done. Two days ago, just up the road from here in Flanders, plain wood coffins containing the remains of six nameless Tommies—chosen at random from the forest of graves marked "Unknown" that stretch from Ypres to the Marne—were placed in a hut. A British officer was blindfolded and led inside. The coffin that he touched at random was carried out and

taken to Boulogne. There it was placed in a giant
casket of oak, the lid bound with iron straps, and
where the straps crossed there was attached a great
seal which is inscribed:

A British Warrior
Who fell in the Great War
1914–1918
For King and Country

A soldier unknown, a warrior familiar only to
God. Today that poor flesh will be taken through
the streets of London for burial in Westminster
Abbey on Armistice Day. The gun carriage will be
trailed by admirals and field marshals and the
dead man's king.

Fletcher had suggested that I go to London, but
half the world's press will be covering the story,
and I preferred to stay on this side of the channel
with Ivy and gather notes for my own elegy, starting in Paris and driving to Hazebrouck and Ypres
in the Citroën.

Brief impressions. Convoys of trucks on the
road to Albert, filled with bricks, bags of sand and
lime. No more *camions* packed with troops inching
toward the front. The monstrosity of a basilica at
Albert, so badly shelled in 1916 and again during
the German breakthrough in 1918, is being rebuilt, complete with new golden virgin high atop
the tower. Beyond Albert there is nothing but a
wasteland of dead ground, a moonscape of craters
and tumbled-in trenches. Salvage crews still work,
cutting and baling the miles of wire, and demoli-
tion men find and explode or defuse shells. Mametz and Trones and Delville and High Wood
have been cleared of splintered trees and new ones
planted. In time there will be glades and leafy
paths on those scarred hills, and in time there will
be cottages on the patches of brick dust where the

villages had been. The view from Bazentin toward High Wood and Flers is something of a heartbreaker. How short the distances seem now, how vast they were then—paths of eternity. Such a small wedge of ground to have changed so many lives.

Colonel Sir Terrance L. De Gough and his second-in-command, Major Fenton Wood-Lacy, rode in the back of the Vauxhall, the driver keeping as close as possible to the armored car racing ahead of them on the twisting road between Ballingarry and Limerick.

"Dash it, Fenton," the colonel said, "the whole idea of having a ceremony here is most foolish. There are bound to be demonstrations. The garrison stands for two bloody minutes in silence and the blasted Sinn Feiners will take advantage of it. You mark my words."

"We won't all be standing silent," Fenton said. "The cars will be out . . . and the constabulary."

"They'll still manage to blow up something. When Paddy has a will, he'll bloody well find a way. You're fortunate to be leaving. When do you take off?"

"Tonight."

"I hope to God Hackway can do the job. I shall miss you, Fenton."

"Hackway's quite competent, sir."

"Perhaps, but he's not *you*." The elderly colonel toyed absently with the revolver resting on the seat between them, his eyes on the armored car, with its revolving turret and Vickers gun menacing the hedgerows on both sides of the road. "They expect you to chuck it in, Fenton, I suppose you know that."

"Yes, I know it."

"Sending you to Mespot—"

"Iraq now."

"Same bloody difference. If the Arabs or Kurds don't get you, the climate will."

"It's not all one-sided."

"Because they kick you up to lieutenant colonel

again and give you a battalion? Don't be foolish, my
boy. They have a mark by your name. Every job you
get will be a damn tough bullet to chew. The promotion
is just a sop to keep your esteemed father-in-law from
writing angry letters to the War Office. They'll be most
happy to accept your resignation and put you in civvy
street with your honor and colonelcy intact. You should
jump at the opportunity, Fenton."

He should, by all that was logical, do just that. God
knows, it would make Winnie happy. He could become
a country gentleman and manage one of the marquess's
estates. Or learn some sort of trade. It was a bit late for
the law. Business perhaps—import and export. Twelve
years he had been a soldier. It was the only trade he
knew. The regiment was drawn up on the square of
Limerick barracks, the band turning into it now, playing
"The Bonnie English Rose" on drums and fifes. Corporal Harris, the best trumpeter in the band, stood at attention by the flagpole, facing the chaplain. It was fifteen minutes before eleven on the morning of the
eleventh day of the eleventh month. A mild day, with
great fleecy clouds blowing in from the Shannon. He
glanced upward, and there was the flag whipping in the
wind, the colors bright and crisp against the sky. Oh,
damn, he thought. Right or wrong, it was what he did
and it was too late to leave it now.

> Take 'old o' the wings o' the mornin',
>   An' flop round the earth till you're dead;
> But you won't get away from the tune that they
>   play
>   To the bloomin' old rag over'ead.

"You're not packing, surely," Lady Margaret asked
as she came into the room. The twins hung on to her
hands, dragging their feet and shrieking with the fun of
trying to pull their grandmother's arms out of their
sockets. "He hasn't written you yet. He may give up his
commission, you know."

"He's your son," Winifred said as she sorted through a pile of the twins' dresses. "You should know better than that."

"Baghdad," Lady Margaret whispered. "I can't bear the thought of it."

"It wouldn't be Baghdad, Mother—he wouldn't allow us to live there. No, we shall go to Egypt and rent a beautiful cool house in Gezirah. Jennifer and Victoria will adore it and so will you."

"*Me?* You shall never drag me out of Suffolk, my girl."

Winifred smiled, watching the twins tug and pull. "You're being dragged already. Anyway, it would only be for a year or two at most and Fenton will get ample leave. We could hire a houseboat and go up the Nile. It will be very . . . pleasant."

Lady Margaret detached herself from the girls, who raced off like puppies, and sat on the edge of the bed.

"Oh, dear . . . You're not suited to be an army wife. Why in heaven's name don't you tell him so?"

Winifred sighed and touched her mother-in-law lightly on the shoulder. "Because if I told him that, he'd give it up and it has to be his decision, not mine. I'm Fenton's wife and that's all I really care about. That he happens to be in the army is just something I've learned to live with and will go on living with, I suppose."

"Well, they say Egypt is delightful in the winter, and we can purchase two tiny donkeys for the children to ride."

Winifred bent down and kissed her on the cheek. "*We,* is it? Good, but the twins are a bit young for donkeys."

"Oh, are they?" Lady Margaret said ruefully. "A couple of Amazons! I always imagined girls would be gentle lambs, but they're almost Fenton's equal at that age, although I must say that Roger was—" She stopped abruptly and looked down at her folded hands in her lap. "*That* day again. Two minutes to remember in silence. I don't need one day a year to think of him."

Winifred turned back to the piles of clothes and continued her sorting.

"I feel the same way about Andrew and Timothy. And if the bullet that hit Bramwell had been a tenth of an inch further to the left, I would have another brother to remember as well."

"Armistice Day is for the same sort of person who only goes to church one Sunday out of fifty-two."

"I suppose it is," Winifred said quietly. "And yet when they ring the bells . . ."

They looked at each other and then held hands, very tightly, waiting for the first doleful peal of eleven.

It had been an exhilarating drive back from Biarritz with Prince Michael.

The prince had escaped the bullets which had felled many of his kinsmen—not to mention his cousin, the tsar—by having been an aide to the Russian military attaché in Paris from 1915 until events in Holy Russia had made such a post less than superfluous. He had also been fortunate in having had the foresight to transfer a million rubles in gold from his bank in Petrograd to the Banque de France. This money had not only allowed the thirty-five-year-old prince to indulge himself in his primary passion—the quest for speed—but had given him something that few of his émigré countrymen of noble blood could boast of—independence. He had not been reduced, as had so many dukes, grand dukes, and princes of the Romanov swarm, to selling his name to one of the daughters of the new "war rich" who were beginning to flock to Paris from such places as Birmingham, Bradford, Liverpool, and even Gary, Indiana, USA, in search of titles on the cheap. No. He was Prince Michael and he was beyond being bought. The Isotta-Fraschini that he drove, the Breguet biplane that he flew, had been paid for out of his own pocket. It was for this reason, if for no other, that Lydia Foxe Greville sat beside him. She did not like men with price tags on their family crests.

Yes, it was exhilarating. The trees flashing past, the dust whipping back from the tires in long, flat streamers of the palest yellow. The wind in her face as it whirled over the glass screen in front of her. Paris rising in the dawn, spires and towers glinting above the haze. Montparnasse. The Faubourg. The squeal of rubber as the prince braked in front of the Deux Magots. The sleepy kitchen staff opening up the place to serve them coffee and brioches. When at last he parked in front of her house on the edge of the Bois, she felt totally satisfied. It was fifteen minutes before eleven.

"Shall I come in?"

"Shall?" She laughed. "Or *may* I come in?"

He shrugged. "How can I tell your mood, Lydia?"

"My mood is vaguely reflective at the moment. And, besides, we have had quite enough of each other in the past week to last us some time. Drive to the aerodrome and fly your little machine someplace exotic."

He held her hands and kissed them. "*Au revoir.* I will go to Tangiers. Do not entangle yourself *too* deeply with someone else before I return or I shall crash-land my machine on your roof."

"*Galant*" was the word that described him. But then he was a prince, and the right phrases and gestures came naturally. If she married him, she would become a princess with a five-hundred-year-old name. The idea did not intrigue her. They were equals now. "Money," David Langham had once said, "is the only important aristocracy." And then had added with a wink: "But power is the votes of the poor."

Langham crossed her mind as she walked slowly up the staircase, a maid scurrying ahead of her to open her bedroom door. She thought of him because he was so opposite in every way to the tall, athletic prince. It was Langham who had induced her to buy this house so that he could have a quiet retreat during the interminable months of stormy conferences at Versailles. He had solved the complex problem of dividing Hungary after a particularly satyric weekend in this very room, on the very bed that she now stretched out upon as her maid drew the bath. Her closeness to Langham had not gone unnoticed. It had given her an entree into the new society that money alone could never have bought. Money was desirable in this postwar world, but influence was everything.

The bells of St. Jean Baptiste in Neuilly began to ring. It was not Sunday, surely? Thursday morning—it was Thursday, the eleventh of November. The bells had the same soft, melodic sound as the church bells of Abingdon, and memory came in a rush, a flood of images that stunned her with their clarity. She felt that she had but to reach out with her hands and grasp Fenton's, and they would be up—up—up the scaffolding to the tall brick chimneys, with Charles far, far below calling out, "Lydia . . . Lydia . . . Don't fall . . . don't fall!"

The Earl and Countess of Stanmore and their son, the Right Honorable William Greville, were warmly greeted by the Reverend Mr. Toomey, Vicar of Llandinam, as they stepped from their Daimler. The earl remained behind the wheel for a few moments to double-check his parking procedure—gears in reverse, hand brake pulled up, wheels turned at a sharp angle—for he was a meticulous driver of motorcars. The Reverend Mr. Toomey then ushered them into the vicarage for a cup of strong tea to offset the morning's chill. The tea was served, appropriately enough, in a Georgian silver service donated by the Grevilles. Their generosity over the past three years had been extreme, and their company, as always, was genuinely welcomed by the young clergyman and his wife.

"So tell me, William," the vicar said, "how is Cambridge treating you this term?"

"A bit better than I'm treating Cambridge," William said with a laugh. "I don't think I'm quite suited for Classics."

"He's thinking of leaving King's and studying for the bar," Hanna said.

"I couldn't be happier," the earl remarked, drinking his tea with relish. "We could use a lawyer in the family, what with all these new laws and taxes the government, in its arrogance, sees fit to impose upon us."

William laughed again. "Now, Father, let's not get embroiled in politics on Armistice Day."

"Quite so," the earl muttered. He finished his tea and held out his cup for more. "Well, John, what sort of service can we expect this morning?"

"Simple, as usual," the vicar said as his wife poured the tea. "When I was a padre with the South Wales Borderers, the men would become restive if my sermon was too high-flown. Simplicity of language and directness of thought—that's my firm belief. And the choosing of the more popular hymns, the ones the chaps can sing without looking in their hymnals."

"I have always been most fond of 'Oh, for a Thousand Tongues to Sing,' " Hanna said.

"Ah, yes," the vicar agreed. "Very lovely indeed. But 'Onward, Christian Soldiers' is still the one the chaps like best. They always give full lung power to that one."

William stepped over to one of the windows and looked up at the hill behind the house.

"Is he up there, Vicar?"

"Oh, yes. Every morning, rain or shine."

"I'll go fetch him."

"Shall I come with you?" the earl asked.

"I'd rather go alone this morning, if you don't mind, sir."

Hanna watched William leave, could see him through the window as he went up the path. Walking so much better, she reflected, after the surgery in New York in August. A stiffness remained, but there was no marked limp, even going up a hill. The stiffness made it very difficult for him to drive a car, but that was a minor enough restriction on his activities. How tall and strong he was. Powerful shoulders and arms. A young, handsome man and so—very much alive.

*　　*　　*

William walked slowly up the steep sandy path to the top of the hill. A number of wood benches were placed among oak and chestnut trees, and Charles was seated on one of the benches, leaning forward, hands on his knees, gazing out across a valley at the distant slopes and crags of Moel Sych. William sat down beside his brother and took a silver cigarette case from the inside pocket of his jacket.

"Care for a smoke?"

"I don't think so," Charles said, leaning back and folding his arms. "Odd how the shadows race in and out of the ravines and gullies."

"Cloud shadows. A very peaceful sight."

"Quite lulling, as a matter of fact. I often find myself falling asleep watching them."

"It's peaceful, all right."

"Quite. I walk up there sometimes, but one can only appreciate the chiaroscuro effect from a distance."

"I imagine so."

"The shadows race over you, terribly quickly, sweep on by, you see. One hasn't time to notice the clean definition of light and shade."

"I understand."

"But seated here—or even further along, near the old wall—it's quite a different matter. Do you come here often?"

William lit his cigarette with a windproof lighter he had bought in New York.

"As often as I can."

"I rather had the feeling that we had talked before. Perhaps not here exactly . . . but . . . somewhere."

"Oh, we've talked together many times. Last time I was here we talked about Derbyshire."

"Did we?"

"Buxton . . . the Peak District. It's a very lovely spot. Masses of hills and crags. We've owned a house there for years. A smallish place, but comfortable. There's a hill beyond the house, and from the terrace one can watch the patterns of light. A great many clouds sweep over and the shadow patches change constantly all during the day. Quite an interesting sight."

"Ah, yes, I'm sure it must be."

"Would you care to see it one day? Perhaps even stay there?"

Charles frowned and looked back at the hill, at the shadows of the wind-driven clouds as they dipped in and out of the hollows and raced across the slopes.

"I'm not sure I could. I really don't know about that. I must watch this hill, you see . . . watch it . . . in case the men come back."

Observations and Reflections. There were touring buses parked beside the road near Beaumont-Hamel, the occupants—almost all of them with cameras slung over their shoulders—being led by a guide to see the old trenches. Quite a new industry. More touring buses north of the Somme at Arras. Middle-aged people for the most part, tramping gingerly over new duckboards laid down by the tour companies to keep their clients from being too discomfited. Near Cambrai, a few rusted tanks remain partially entombed in mud. Along Vimy Ridge the wire has turned orange with rust. At Messines, great flocks of ravens along the skyline wheeling above the stumps of bombarded trees.

Odd, how peaceful it is. No major stories to be gathered here. The storms have shifted. The Riffs cutting up French and Spanish legionnaires in Morocco. Turks and Greeks fighting to the death at Adrianople. The British pouring troops into Iraq, into Ireland, into northern India. And Russia—at war with the Poles, at war with itself. White Russians, Red Russians, Denikin, Semenov, Trotsky, the Czech legion. No lack of work for me among those whirlwinds. Jacob, too, in those winds, somewhere between here and Siberia. A special observer for an agency of the League of Nations, keeping an eye on political developments in the new nations carved from the old empires. "Watching the new hatreds grow," as Jacob put it so sardonically when we sat in the Hotel Adlon in Berlin last year. New hatreds breeding to replace the old on this second anniversary of the end of the war-to-end-all-wars. I wonder if Wilson, lying half paralyzed in the White House, sees the joke in that, as he listens to the cheers for Harding and his "normalcy"?

All of us scattered. The beginning of the rootless age? Or is it just a new restlessness, the old horizons no longer as safe and comforting as they once were? Back and forth we go, like so many migrating birds—Petrograd, Berlin, Paris, London, New York. Back and forth. Trains to Milan, Belgrade, Warsaw. Back and forth across the oceans without giving travel a thought anymore.

Strange to think of Alexandra living in Canada and working in a clinic for war wounded with a doctor who may or may not be her husband. She seemed so much a part of the ambience of Abingdon Pryory and Park Lane. The belle of all the balls. An English society girl to her finger tips. All is changed. She wrote to Hanna that even Toronto is not far enough away. She and her doctor plan to keep moving west once the reservoir of the maimed is lowered, to get as far away as possible from where I now sit, Hazebrouck, the edge of the great Salient.

It's a good, new road from Hazebrouck over the Messines Ridge to Kemmel and Ypres, but the earth is sour on both sides of it. Mustard gas and lyddite permeating the soil. Still, grass is beginning to grow, inching over the lips of the shell holes, sprouting rawly along old parapets and amid sandbagged bunkers. Sandbags to Sandburg. Yes, Carl, the grass does cover all.

There is no one Golgotha for the British Army, but Ypres will do and it is the closest battleground

to the coast. It is here—near the waste of stones
that had once been a lace-making town—that the
six unknown Tommies had lain side by side in a
hut, waiting for one of them to be chosen for im-
mortality, to symbolize the apotheosis of all the
million dead. Those who remain here are not forgotten. The Commonwealth War Graves Commission has spared no expense to lay out cemeteries.
Low walls surround them, and trees and shrubbery
soften the lines of stone. At Poperinghe the cemeteries are like English gardens and the caretakers
dedicated and efficient men. It takes only minutes
for them to locate any grave for visitors among the
neat rows of white crosses, each with a name on it.
On one of them, the name Ivy Thaxton Rilke.
Beneath the name are the initials of the military
nursing service and a date: 9 October, 1917.

There are at least a hundred thousand other
graves from Passchendaele, not that that's any
comfort. She lies in a special plot beside twenty of
her patients who died with her when the shell hit.
Alexandra saw to that. An earl's daughter getting
her way.

A grave in Flanders. Far from the places she
had hoped to see. Chicago, Illinois, on Lake Michigan. Railroads and stockyards.

No. I couldn't face going to London and wit-
nessing the pomp at the Abbey, not with her on
this side of the channel. A quiet spot. Just the
wind and a blackbird swaying on a cypress tree,
and then, at eleven, the distant tolling of a bell.

Dell Bestsellers

At your local bookstore or use this handy coupon for ordering:

Dell | **DELL BOOKS**
P.O. BOX 1000, PINEBROOK, N.J. 07058

Please send me the books I have checked above. I am enclosing $_____
(please add 75¢ per copy to cover postage and handling). Send check or money
order—no cash or C.O.D.'s. Please allow up to 8 weeks for shipment.

Mr/Mrs/Miss _____

Address _____

City _____ State/Zip _____